THE BAD LIFE

ALSO BY TONY MASERO

Belle Slaughter: The Complete Series

Rogue Indiscretions: Western Tales of Sins, Misdeeds, and Gross Misconduct Across A Wild Frontier

Western Disorder: Western Tales Of Murder, Romance, And Revenge

Misty Blue: The Complete Series

Stageline: The Complete Series

Hellion Heroines: The Complete Series

Tears of Apache Stone: The Complete Series

The Watch Man : The Complete Series

Dust Was the Day: A Western Duo

Tony Masero Collection 1

Tony Masero Collection 2

Tony Masero Collection 3

Tony Masero Collection 4

Tony Masero Collection 5

Tony Masero Collection 6

Tony Masero Collection 7

Tony Masero Collection 8

Tony Masero Collection 9

Tony Masero Collection 10

Tony Masero Collection 11

Tony Masero Collection Volume 12

ALSO BY T[illegible]Y MAS[illegible]

[illegible]

THE BAD LIFE

TONY MASERO

The Bad Life
Paperback Edition

Wolfpack Publishing
1707 E. Diana Street
Tampa, FL 33610

www.wolfpackpublishing.com

Paperback ISBN 979-8-89567-819-0
Ebook ISBN 979-8-89567-304-1

THE BAD LIFE

PROLOGUE

Drochshaol* in Gaelic meaning: *The Bad Life / Hard Times

It was raining.

A thin, weak, and miserable driving flail of light weather that turned the stone walls of the orphanage darker and leeched all color from the sky.

Alva knew none of that troubled the tough resilience of stern Sister Bridget, the bitter old Mother Superior of the holy order of nuns. Her tiny bent body had survived much harder penances than this veil of tears.

The Mother Superior's black veil was perfectly placed, the coif and wimple framing her features were the pristine white of fresh meringue, and the whole of her black pleated habit was neatly pressed with a shining crucifix on her breast and rosary beads swinging from her waist like so many glinting eyes. But the face that peered out at Alva was ancient, lined, and withered, a yellowish brown in color like the shrunken head of a monkey or the skin of decaying fruit. The same venom that Alva had withstood for twelve years seeped out from that decrepit creature in the keen sharpness of her eye that missed nothing and the tightness of her cracked lips that were lined with inherent meanness.

"*Eedjet—A phleidhce!*" She breathed the curse in Gaelic, leaning forward so that Alva could experience the full force of the withered breath in her Donegal accent. "You're an *eedjet,* Alva North, and I'll tell you that I'm to be glad to see the back of you. God will forgive me for saying it, but there it is, never have I known such a witless, ungrateful child."

Standing her ground, Alva looked over the Mother Superior's shoulder at the four other girls waiting in the gig with the old gardener Pádraig seated in the driving seat. They were ready, and like them, Alva could not wait to get going. To be finally leaving the Holy Arbors Orphanage was like a release from prison, and her heart sang with the prospect.

Since she had arrived at five years of age after her ma and da had both died thanks to the lingering effects of *an Gorta Mór—The Great Hunger*, the terrible famine that had swept the country some twenty years before with its skeletal finger of rot destroying the staple potato crop, only then had the years seemed endless and not improved any by the presence of this Mother Superior, surely the harshest and most vindictive of the convent body that oversaw the orphanage.

"You will hear me now, *eedjet,*" Mother Superior went on in the same spiteful tone. "You will behave yourself on this journey. Mr. McCorkinell is a gracious Catholic man as well as owner of the shipping line, and it is only by his beneficent act of charity that he gives a wretched girl like you the opportunity to emigrate across to the Americas." She leaned forward and barked, "Not many get this chance, you should know that, Alva the *eedjet*!"

The *eedjet* kept her gaze fixed steadily on the ancient nun. From past experience, Alva was confident that she had only to suffer a short while, and then she would be free of this particular brand of malevolence. She also knew full well that the nuns would only be too glad to be rid of her, her wild and profligate ways did not agree with the moral rectitude of an ordered religious life, and the repression she had constantly struggled to break out of had caused much uproar in the cloistered corridors of the orphanage.

Besides, the word was out amongst the girls that the wealthy Mr. McCorkinell was in no way as charitable as he pretended, but merely seeking redemption from the archbishop after being so sinfully discovered having a lady friend besides his wife, and that this free passage was surely to be atonement for his act of adultery.

Alva North was not a particularly tall young woman, yet still she towered over the aged nun, and her seventeen-year-old eyes that were normally a sea crest of clearest blue at this moment held all the frosty rigidity of rock crystal. Her skin was pale, so white it had the smooth clarity of milk and was enhanced by the full raven-wing black of her shoulder-length hair that she kept center-parted and framing her rather long yet pretty face. There was an austerity about her, an aura that gave her the appearance of more years than those she owned. It was a dangerous civility that kept her above the other girls and brought with it some quality of leadership, a sorry fact that often got her into trouble, even though innocent. It was her authority that was blamed when others went astray.

Alva smiled at the nun's words. A smug smile, a slight uplifting of the corners of her mouth and an arching of the drawn line of dark eyebrows penciled across her brow.

"Listen to me, *eedjet!*" barked the Mother Superior, angry at the sight of the mocking smile. "You have gotten away with far too much here with us. That is because we are good and kindly Christian souls and know the meaning of service, but once you are over there in that wild country, things will be very different, believe me. Perhaps there you will learn to behave with humility and grace, qualities we have unfortunately been unable to instill into your untamed nature."

"They're waiting," said Alva, with a nod towards the gig.

"So they are," agreed Mother Superior brusquely. "Get going and be off with you then."

Alva quickly glanced around, nobody was watching from the dark walls of the orphanage. All the other nuns had scurried back inside to shelter from the inclement weather.

Alva leaned forward and puckered her lips as if to give the ancient a farewell kiss. With a surprised look of expectancy, the aged bearded chin was tilted and the eyes half lidded as Sister Bridget prepared, in all vanity, to accept the parting kiss of an errant yet grateful orphan upon her seamed cheek.

But not so—Alva hawked throatily and spat a rich gob full of spit straight in her eye.

"That's for you, ye wily auld witch," cursed Alva.

Mother Superior wailed, and both bony hands

clutched at her blinded eye as a laughing Alva skipped away and ran for the gig to urge Pádraig on.

"Get going, Paddy, you bloody spalpeen!" she shouted as she hauled herself aboard. "For Londonderry at top speed before that miserable old bitch fetches the constable."

CHAPTER ONE

At seventeen years of age, Alva North arrived on the cobblestones of New York Harbor dressed in hand-me-down clothes in a gray January in 1874. She was traveling with the four other girls from the Holy Arbor Convent and Orphanage in County Galway. Two of them, Irene and Saoirse, were as young as she, the survivors of starved families cast out indifferently by tenant landlords on British-held properties. The other two, Aoife and Niamh, were dressed in the gray robes of novitiates and intended for holy orders. The whole group, both orphans and novitiates were to be sent across America to serve in various Catholic dioceses in different states.

For, as well as regarding the orphans, it had proved for the more enterprising to be a grand way of getting young girls away when everywhere was still recovering from the effects of the famine that had crippled the country. The trouble was that too many hungry parents had had the same notion, and Holy Arbors was at a loss. Mother Superior could barely feed her own nuns, let alone a group of young and lively teenagers whose parents swore that the girls had been moved by the holy word to take orders and join the nunnery.

As soon as Mr. McCorkinell's illicit affair had become common knowledge, the archbishop had found a solution for the overcrowding, and soon the eager youngsters had been packed in steerage and sent by McCorkinell on his three-masted barque *Charybdis* as cheaply as possible across the Atlantic to land on American shores and thereby relieve pressure on the convent.

And here they were, newly arrived and surrounded by a vigorous new world in the form of the busy bustle of New York dockland. Immigrants poured from ships in great babbling queues and headed for the receiving station at Castle Garden, carrying their lives in wicker baskets and travelling trunks. The harbor skyline was shrouded by hundreds of berthed masts swaying in the sloping tide as if trees in a forest with their rigging dangling like a hanging vine. Smoke from steamers and factories painted the sky in pillars of black, and the terrible noise of it all deafened ears.

Carriages and freight wagons with steel-rimmed wheels and drawn by heavy horses clattered over cobbles whilst shouting workers rolled hefty barrels, and overhead gantries swung great loads from ship to shore and shore to ship. Coffee houses, bars, and warehouses surrounded by noisy crowds of working men, sailors, officials, and businessmen all babbling as loudly as they could against the row.

And in the middle of it all, a great group of curious listeners was gathered around a bearded preacher, as he held forth loudly from halfway up a ship's gangplank. His manic sermon was of a critical nature and condemned the dangers of immigration and its detrimental effects on the nation. The target of his vitriol was the queues of foreigners bound for the Castle Garden immigration center as they trooped past him without giving a second glance or understanding a single word of what he said.

All was dazzling activity and confusion for the Irish girls. It was indeed a great curiosity to them, having come from the monastic seclusion and peaceful tranquility of their rural existence, and suddenly cast into the turbulence of this trade-driven dockland. They marveled at it all for three hours before they began to wonder. Nobody had come to meet them, and they were promised on arrival that they would be guided to lodgings before they started their various journeys westward.

It fell to Alva to take things in hand.

"What shall we do?" begged a troubled Niamh. She was a lush young woman, somewhat overweight and filling her novitiate gown to bursting. Her round-cheeked, pale skin was smooth, and she had unfortunate bullfrog eyes that bulged and always seemed to be about to burst into tears. "I'm not sure I like it here."

"You'll keep your head about you," advised Alva coolly. "There's plenty going on here, but we'll find a way."

"How then?" asked Irene, a thin but hard-nosed and independent red-headed girl whose fiery nature Alva approved of and kept close as she saw some use in the girl's fierce attitude.

"Look, here's what to do," said Alva. "One of you girls dressed in holy orders, you go along to that young, pretty sailor boy standing over by the gangway on our old ship the *Charybdis* back there. You ask him where the owner is to be found?"

"What?" said the other novitiate, Aoife, turning up

her nose proudly. She was a rather serious girl, sweet-faced and very pretty yet intent on making her way inside the religious orders and always sure to do things in a very proper manner. "Ask that fellow?" she snorted haughtily. "I cannot go alone to a strange man and ask for anything in such a manner."

"Of course you can," snapped Alva. "He'll look at your habit and being a good Catholic man out of the old country will do all he can for a sisterly looking nun. Now get over there and ask!"

Aoife pulled a stoic face and turned away, assuring Alva she would do nothing of the sort. It was the chubby Niamh who stepped up. "Oh, for heaven's sakes, I'll do it."

There was in Niamh an emotional nature that would often express itself in tears or good humor, but she was also at heart an adventurous girl restricted only by the belief that, given her size, she would never be popular.

Smiling whimsically, she bustled over and began a conversation with the sailor, who promptly pulled off his cap whilst talking to her.

"There, I told you," said a smug Alva at the sailor's show of respect. "I'm telling you, you can go a long way in them nun's outfits."

Both Irene and Saoirse, the homely fourth girl of the group and also Irene's close companion, chuckled at Aoife's discomfort.

"Will you look at you, Aoife," said Irene with a snort. "Going pink around the gills, are you?"

"Will you watch your manners, Irene," said Aoife sharply. "I'll take no grief from the likes of you."

"You'll not, will you? Watch your tongue or I'll break your bloody nose for you, ye holy gobshite," growled the aggressive Irene, giving Aoife a hard, meaningful stare.

This disturbance went no further as it was then that Niamh rolled back to them. "A nice young fella, indeed he is." She smiled, casting a bashful glance over her shoulder at the sailor. "He says that there is no owner here but only an agent, and they have the name James Taylor and Company. They've offices over there." She waved a pudgy finger in a vague direction. "Not but a minute's walk, so the gentleman says."

"Right then," said Alva, striding off full of purpose. "Let's go and see about this."

The others followed, hiking their small bundles and carpetbags with them.

THE OFFICE DOOR to James Taylor and Company was a glass-paneled one set in a row of brick-built offices of a similar nature, and when Alva pushed the door open, or more properly slammed it open, the little bell above the door flew off its catch and the glass panes rattled with the force of her savage assault. The bell landed with a ringing crash on the counter, and the diligent clerks all seated at their desks behind the counter jumped up in shocked surprise.

"Wh—what—are you doing?" asked one sprightly gent. A long-legged man in a slim drape jacket and striped pants with greased-down black hair parted to one side and shining like polished boot black on his head.

"What are you playing at?" Alva barked back at him, thinking that attack is the best resource when dealing with any office-bound clerks with attitude.

"You—you can't come in here, like that," burst out the man with eyes rolling in offence.

"Are you James Taylor?" asked Alva, taking a warlike stance with her hands on her hips before the counter. The man was about to answer when the four other girls pushed their way in, struggling with all their baggage as they came.

"Wh—wh—" bleated the man, opening the flap on the counter and bursting into the foyer. "I don't believe this."

"Are you Mr. Taylor?" repeated Alva.

"N—no. No, he's not here. I'm Cecil Longworth, his head clerk. But what's the meaning of this?"

"We've been stood out there for three hours," said Alva. "Interesting as watching sweating stevedores may be, even so, three hours is long enough."

"Who the devil are you?" asked Longworth, beginning to shift from shock to anger.

"Well, would you like introductions? No, I didn't think so," ranted Alva. "We should have been met."

"Who—who—what do you want?" said the flustered Longworth.

"Whooo—whoooo, what are you? A foghorn tug? Look, Logwort, we've come a long way on your damned ship, and we're tired and hungry and in need of some assistance."

"It's Longworth," the clerk corrected. "Now am I to understand," he continued, taking a grip and forcing himself to speak in a more restrained tone. "You have been passengers on *Charybdis,* being the craft most recently docked, and now have complaint. Because I can assure you that we take every—"

"For heaven's sake, man," cut in Alva. "Just tell us where we're to go."

Longworth looked at her, dumbfounded. "I've no idea what you are talking about, madam."

"*Madam*!" spat Alva. "What the devil, kind of *madam* am I? You're stepping over yourself here, are you not?"

Longworth was helpless. "Just tell me why you are here?"

"Are you going to give us help or just stand there bleating?"

A frowning Alva cast a sidelong glance at Irene, and that look was to prove a pivotal moment in their relationship and also with the rest of the girls. Silent understanding flashed between the two, and Irene lowered her forehead and a tight smile crossed her lips. This was not a smile of amusement.

Irene raised an eyebrow at Saoirse, and with no spoken word between them, they both leapt forward and grasped hold of the tall, angular man by the arms. Longworth wailed pitifully, torn between defending himself and his more natural gentlemanly aversion to strong-arming the feminine kind.

Brought to his knees before Alva, she loomed over the whimpering Longworth. "Will you assist us now?"

"Yes, yes, whatever you want."

"We need lodgings and a meal."

"Of course, of course, it can be arranged."

"An advance, too." The sudden mercenary thought occurred to Alva. "We need some running around cash money."

"What? No, I cannot—"

He gave a short squeal as Irene twisted his arm.

"Terence O'Donohue," Longworth called to a young clerk. "Fetch a dollar from the expenses and take these ladies around to the Millborough Hotel. Tell them I have sent them and they are to supply rooms and supper at the company's expense."

"Yes, sir," said the boy, who couldn't have been no

more than twelve or thirteen years old and was grinning secretly at his employer's discomfort.

WITH THE BOY in the lead, the girls followed him out into the whirl of the docks again.

"How are you called again?" asked Alva.

"Terry O'Donohue, the same it is."

His face was impish, and he wore a battered flat-topped hat at an angle on his head of unkempt sandy colored hair.

"And you work for that fool in there, do you?"

"It is of a temporary kind of position," admitted Terry. "More your fetch and carry sort of thing."

There was a trace of Irish in his voice, but it was obvious he had been in the country long enough to lose most of the accent.

They had not gone more than three blocks and were in the wagon roads supplying the docks when Terry stopped suddenly and the others cluttered up behind him. "Now listen, ladies," said Terry, turning on them in a serious manner. "I must give you all a warning."

"Why's that?" asked Alva.

"Because right now, Mr. Longworth will be contacting the harbor police. He'll hope to catch you at your meal in the hotel and have you up for assault on his person and theft of a dollar from his accounting."

"How d'you know that?" asked Alva.

"I have worked for the man for a six-month and I know how he is."

"You're a bit of a lad, are you not?' grinned Irene.

Terry looked at her evenly. "I know me way around."

"Then what should we do?" asked Alva.

"Who were you supposed to meet here?"

"We've no idea, they told us in Ireland somebody would be here on the dock for us."

Terry nodded knowledgeably. "Is that right?"

Alva met his suspicious gaze. "You don't think it is so?"

"You're orphans, are you not? With no parents to cause a fuss, they'll not be bothering about you too much. Probably hoping you end up in prison or on the street and are no longer their problem."

"The pox on them!" cursed Irene. "The wee wretched shites."

"Do you want advice?" asked Terry.

"We do," echoed Alva and Irene.

"Then here it is. You have spirit, I've seen that, and the only way you make your way in this town is with a helping hand, for no one will lift a finger outside of charity."

"What have you in mind?" asked Alva suspiciously.

"The Bucket Boys."

"The Bucket Boys!" A curious Niamh frowned. "What are they?'

Terry drew a breath and, sighing, leaned back against the dark brick wall behind him as he explained, "This town is run by gangs, there are plenty of them, and if you want to make your way as strangers, it's best to associate with one of them."

"Gangs?" asked Alva. "You mean criminals?"

Terry shrugged. "If you like."

"If they are so hot, how come you are working in an office and not with one of them?"

Terry gave her a raised eyebrow and a slow smile. "Who says I'm not?"

Alva was studying him with a calculating eye. "You

are there at the docks watching what comes and where it goes. You see the value of the cargo and what warehouse it ends up in. My! You are a lot more than a wee skit of a clerk, are you not?"

Terry clicked his tongue. "You have it there, lady. You are a smart one all right."

"So what are you suggesting for us?"

"The Bucket Boys. They hang out in The Four Corners, and they'll be the ones for you. Their place is in Manhattan, and it's where these four streets meet up, Anthony, Cross, Orange, and Little Water to make up the four corners, and they are right smack bang in the center of it all."

"How did they get that name, the Bucket Boys?"

Terry set off again and explained as they walked, "It was like this when they started out. They worked mainly the street markets, dipping and taking what they fancied—"

"Dipping?"

"Pickpockets. Well, once they had whatever they wanted, a watch, a wallet, a ring, or your favorite auntie's silver brooch, they would throw it into a bucket attached to a long rope. One of the others would haul it up high right quick, maybe to the tenement roof or some relative's window, so if anybody came after the fellow, he would have nothing on him with the goods long gone, and he'd be as innocent as a newborn. Anyway, that was how they did it in the past, and now they do many more things than that, but that's how they started."

"And you know them?"

"I do, Benny McGuire is the boss right now and I can take you there. It will be a lot safer for you than the Millborough Hotel, I'm telling you."

CHAPTER TWO

BENNY MCGUIRE SAT IN A LARGE, run-down room off Mulberry Street. It was a slum area, and the building was condemned and showed it with large cracks across the ceiling and plaster falling in chunks to expose the lathe beneath. At some time in the past, it had been a prime property with molded colonial cornices and decorative fittings where chandeliers had once hung. But now there was only the scent of decay in the air, with speckled mold and damp marking the lower reaches of the peeling corners.

Candles lit the room, and they glimmered and fluttered in melting groups, sending shadows spinning and looming over the dilapidated walls. There were about twenty people in the large room that had all the attributes of a high-ceilinged dining room, they were mostly men seated at tables or slouched on cushions, with a few women and young girls milling about in the background. The men were all dressed reasonably well in suits and hats and generally occupied in card playing or conversation. Tobacco smoke filled the air from their clay pipes, and the scent of strong liquor and beer indicated that the glasses before them were not full of black tea or coffee.

McGuire was a clean-shaven, broad-faced man with a wide forehead and implacable features. Of sturdy build, tending towards plump, he lounged in a high-backed chair and viewed the entrance of the young women in lordly fashion without expression. Beside him and to one side stood a monumental Negro, a powerful-looking man, muscular and dark skinned with a gold earring in his ear. His large hands hung from thumbs hooked into a tartan waistcoat that spread tightly across his impressive torso.

"What have we here?" asked McGuire in a low guttural voice. "What have you brought me, Terry boy?"

"Some new faces, your honor," said Terry, whose demeanor had immediately altered from cocky young lad into one of a more subservient posture. No longer the cheeky chap, he was now broadcasting a more serious demeanor. "No one will have seen them before," he said. "They are fresh off the boat."

"Is that a fact?" McGuire said, pouting a lower lip and canting his head doubtfully to one side. "And what about our more pressing concern? That's all I'm interested in right now."

"The ship is provisioning now, sir. They won't be moving any of the cargo from the warehouse until Friday or Saturday. So there are two whole nights before they move it."

Aoife gave a sudden rasping cough and McGuire looked at her suspiciously. "What's wrong with her? It's not the consumption, is it? I'll not have the diseased in here, saw enough of that in the army, by God! Killed off more than the Rebels it did."

"His honor served boldly with the 151st New York

Infantry in the recent affray not seven years since," Terry explained with due deference. "He was there and saw Lee surrender, that he did."

"No, it's no sickness," said Alva. "We've been stood out in the cold on the docks for hours, she'll have caught a chill, that's all it is."

"Nobody came to get them," Terry went on in explanation. "I think maybe they are forgotten."

"Looks like a bloody nun," muttered McGuire, viewing Aoife askance. "Are yous all nuns?"

Alva shook her head. "They're novitiates in training, the rest of us are orphans."

"Well, I'll have no offence against the church in here, y'hear that?" McGuire warned, crossing himself religiously. "There's already enough sins on my plate as it is."

"The warehouse," Terry reminded him gently.

McGuire raised a forefinger and the big Negro leaned forward. "Balthazar, see to it, will you? I reckon you'll need three carts and a team for each, maybe twelve men in all. If there's any trouble from the night watch, then throw them in the river, but no killing, you have that? Puir wee bleeders are only doing their duty, and the Bucket Boys will not have a name for bloody murder."

Balthazar nodded understanding and turned away to whisper with one of the seated groups.

"Now," McGuire said, turning to Alva and the others. "What makes you think these will do for us, Terry boy?"

"They have the brass, your honor," said Terry, eager to please. "I saw 'em take down the chief clerk Longworth." He giggled. "It was a thing to see, they had him down on his knees, they surely did, believe me, I saw it with me own eyes."

McGuire rubbed his jaw and sniffed. "And you, have

you yourself finished now with Taylor and Company? It's been a while, has it not?"

"It has, sir. I think I've done all I might, and they will be a touch too suspicious after the warehouse job."

"What about these colleens here then, they're a skinny bunch except for that fat one, she's pretty enough, a spot of *hooring* do you think?"

At that, Irene started forward with clenched fists. "If that's what you think of us, you gombeen, I'll have you kissing the floor in a trice."

"Oho!" A surprised McGuire barked a laugh. "You cheeky little wretch! You should know I could have your scrawny throat sliced I give the word."

"You could try," sneered Irene. Alva laid a hand on her arm to still her and she could feel Irene's anger vibrating through the skin.

"No, sir," cut in Terry. "Not *hoors,* I reckon they will be grand at the *clouting* and maybe some maid work as well."

McGuire rubbed a stubby finger across his lower lip thoughtfully. "Clouting—that's not a bad thought, Terry. As you say, no one will know them, indeed they won't. See to it then, will you? Get them billeted and new clothes, and some of the immigrant dirt washed off them. Ma Tallow will see to their makings."

"Aye, your honor," answered Terry.

"Then get it done."

As they trooped out of the building and followed Terry, Aoife bowed over and gave another hacking cough.

"What's the matter with you?" asked Irene.

"Leave her be," said Alva, but a worried frown creased her brow as she looked at Aoife.

Niamh swanned past them, secretly smiling to

herself, her fat cheeks glowing, and there was a bounce to her step. "He thought I was pretty," she muttered.

"What's this *clouting* you have us down for?" Alva asked.

"Here's how it works," Terry said, hurrying them along and leading the way over damp paving stones and through a maze of gloomy alleyways. "You'll dress up fine, good-looking in the best of clothes, and then you'll go into some of the finest stores in the city like customers." He carried on briefing them over his shoulder as he marched briskly ahead. "The shop girls will take to you right away, as you'll look rich and of the proper class. Then, when their heads turned, you'll thieve what you can, necklaces, jewelry, hatpins, and handbags. You'll carry it away out under your clothes, your *clouts*. You get it? The salesgirls will not look twice, nor will they challenge, as you are of the elite, fine folk high above them in status."

"And you think we can carry this off?"

"You just have to act bold, girl. Behave like you own the world, believe me, they'll fall over themselves aiming to please."

"I don't know if I can do that," mumbled Saoirse, her shy looks crumpling in on themselves.

"Then you can do the maid work," said Terry cheerfully, not to be defeated.

"And how does that work?"

"You'll look for adverts in the newspaper. We'll be giving you references, they'll be forged but of the finest. When you get the job, you will record what they have in the house and where it is, and we will come one night when suitable and clear the place out."

"You mean you will steal everything?"

"Aye, but they'll be rich folk, no? It means you'll make

a pretty penny for yourself when it's fenced through the Bucket Boys."

"Oh, I see," said Saoirse doubtfully.

Aoife gave a racking cough again and covered her mouth with her hand. "'Tis all sinful," she complained. "We cannot do this for fear of mortal sin."

"Just you watch me," Irene said with a grin, her tiny teeth white in the shadows.

TERRY FOUND them rooms that night, although they were more like barracks quarters than any hotel, with straw for bedding and thin blankets on the pallets. Yet the girls were used to the harsh conditions of the convent, so it was little hardship for them. Alva, though, held a secret concern for Aoife as she continued to cough throughout the night. Alva feared that McGuire might have been right and the novitiate was actually showing all the symptoms of consumption.

She stretched her blanket over Aoife to allow her extra warmth, and she found the novitiate laid on her back and sweating with her rosary in hand and eyes pressed shut as she mumbled her Hail Marys.

"How are you doing, girl?" whispered Alva.

"I've a terrible pain in my chest," Aoife said as she wheezed. "D'you think I'm dying, Alva?"

"Dear God, no! Don't be thinking that. You lie there and throw of this chill, we'll take care of you."

"But it's sinful what you'll be doing, our souls will have to pay for it, you know that, don't you?"

"Hush now, none of the sins are yours, so rest easy."

For some reason, Alva found she was becoming sympathetic to a girl she had previously found to be suffocatingly moral and stiffly religious. There was a concern entering her heart, and she supposed it was there because now they were all together and alone on this foreign shore. For some reason she could not quite explain, she was beginning to feel an empathetic responsibility for this group of females. There was no doubt they had already turned to her for leadership, a position she found untenable as she had been a loner all her life, and yet here and now, obligation was being thrust upon her. It was an invisible bond that was forming, and as she returned to her straw bed, she gave objective thought to the girls under her wing and their abilities.

Red-headed Irene, thin as a rake, hard as nails, and always ready for a fight, she would be most suitable to stand at her shoulder, Alva decided.

Plain-looking Saoirse, Irene's best friend, small but equally tough and a loyal soldier, not much brain, but where Irene led, she would follow.

Fat, good-humored Niamh, round of body and nature, and her goodwill was a leveler for them all.

And then poor religious Aoife, sickly now and reliant on them all.

What could she do with them, Alva considered. Well, first they must learn the ways of survival in this city and perhaps make themselves enough money to choose their life away from Benny McGuire and his like. That would be her aim, she thought, if they have to steal to live, then they'll make it so a portion goes to McGuire, but the rest would be salted away for themselves. That way, they will have a secret reserve that will give them some flexibility when it comes time to make their move.

MA TALLOW PROVED to be an ancient crone dressed in black with a widow's bonnet on her white head of bobbed hair. The face reminded Alva of the Mother Superior back at the orphanage, it had the same sly look to it amongst the creases and folds of age. But she knew her business.

"Your ambition, me darlings," she creaked. "Is to look demure and natural, like regular folk and not like half-starved Irish beggars straight off the boat. We'll be wanting pale skin and not tanned and freckled from the open air, that looks too common. So lemon juice, with cream and powders that I have here of me own creation, to lighten your looks. We want rosy lips and cheeks and bright eyes. We'll darken your eyebrows and lashes with ash and put some berry juice on your lips. You'll see, sweethearts, it's like everything else in this life, it's not the content, it's how you package it."

In her long black skirts and small steps, Ma Tallow moved across the floor as if on wheels as she led the way to an array of hanging garments. Dresses of all shapes and sizes, some colored or dull, but more variety than the girls had ever seen in their entire lives.

This was Ma Tallow's domain, and she stored all manner of clothing for the many subversive tasks that McGuire and his crew took on. It was an extensive command that McGuire had evolved, and the Bucket Boys had become a recognized gang under his tutelage. Everything the gang stole went through a regular fence, another older woman who maintained a regular business as cover for the more illicit activities she handled.

Ma Tallow chose the dresses suitable for the *clouters,* and Irene, Saoirse, and Alva were picked to fulfill those roles, being the bolder of them, whilst the more gentile Aoife and tubby Niamh would act as serving girls.

"Will you look at us," squeaked Niamh as she squeezed herself into long skirts and a puffed sleeve blouse with necktie and bow and a straw hat perched on her head, none of which disguised the bloom of her bountiful breasts or the broadness of her beam. "Don't we look the business?"

Even Irene whirled around in front of a full-length mirror, admiring herself dressed in a more matronly bustled skirt with a coquettish hat and feathers and a key chain about her neck. "Do I look a lady?" she mumbled in amazement. "My God! If my poor departed ma could see me now she would swallow her tongue, I swear she would."

"If they could see us back at Holy Arbors." Saoirse chuckled, twirling a parasol and pleased with the corset that gave her an even tighter hand-width waist. "They'd be green as grass, it would bring tears of envy to their eyes."

"Look here," Ma Tallow interrupted their girlish appraisal with sudden sharpness. "This is your work clothes, you understand? Don't be going all *prima donna* on me now. You'll need eyes as sharp as needles when you go into a store, seek out your mark—kid gloves, ostrich fans, fancy shawls, and the like. Anything that will fetch cash money on the sly, because that's your task, and if you don't come back with the goods, then McGuire's leash dog, that big black beast of a man Balthazar, will come pay you a visit, and believe me, you won't like that. You hear me?"

BUT IT WAS Alva who impressed upon them the real mission in the privacy of their barracks room.

"Money, girls," she said. "That's the key to us getting out of here and finding our own way. So, each of you hear me out, we want a percentage for them and a percentage for us. Now don't be greedy, don't let them get suspicious, but each time they send us on the prowl we'll stash a little aside for ourselves."

"Why?" Saoirse frowned. "What have you in mind?"

"There's a lot out there," said Alva, spreading her arms wide and a knowing smile filling her face. "This is one big country, so Terry tells me. It's huge, girls, much bigger than you can imagine after where we came from. We are born country girls, each one of us, and we can thrive and make our mark better out in the country than we ever can here in the city."

"So you think to go roving, is that it?" asked Irene. "Why should we do that?"

"To make something for ourselves, that's why."

"Like what? Ah! You're a dreamer, Alva, to be sure. Scheming and planning. Does this not seem like fair enough already?"

"With money in our purse, we can make a start wherever we want," promised Alva.

Irene shrugged and pulled a face. "Doesn't matter a damn to me, but if that's what you reckon, Alva, then it's good enough."

Saoirse shook her head then nodded, leaving it unclear what she was thinking exactly.

"I like the idea." Beamed Niamh. "I just hope I can do well enough as a serving girl, I've never been really good at waiting tables."

Aoife said nothing but hawked and spat into a handkerchief. Alva noted how pale she was and the dark rings that had formed about her eyes.

"We need to get a doctor for Aoife," Alva said.

"We do?" asked an indifferent Irene.

"Yes, she cannot work, and we must cover for her. McGuire must not find out, or he will throw her out."

Irene pulled a dismissive face and Alva caught the gesture. "You'd best see to it like I say, Irene," she said. "One of us goes down, then we are all the weaker by one. We need to stand together and for each other, never more than now in this place."

Irene shrugged and curled her lip in disdain. "So you say, I can do just fine on my own. When it comes down to it, I don't need any of youse."

"You think so, Irene. Who got you into the agent's office? That wasn't you."

"No, but it was me and Saoirse brought the foolish clerk to his knees."

"So you did, but don't you see we did it together, you, me, and Saoirse?"

Aoife was sitting slumped with her hands in her lap and her head hanging down. Her chest was heaving and her breath coming fast and ragged. Alva noted that the cloth in her hand was bloodstained.

"We'll get Terry to fetch a doctor for her," said Alva.

"Can we trust him not to tell McGuire?" asked Saoirse.

"We have to, he knows his way around here, but if he does us wrong, then I shall be sure he will pay."

Irene cocked her head to one side and laughed. "You'll make him pay, will you? Oh, you'd be taking on a parcel there, you'll know what it means, don't you now?"

"Listen," Alva hissed angrily. "We are not convent girls, are we? No, we must be as tough and hard as any gang here. So you had better decide what that means, might just be a knock on the noodle for some poor soul, or maybe perhaps a cut throat if need be. So be sure you shape up, or I tell you, you'll be all alone as I'll not carry you."

Irene rocked back on her heels, folded her arms, and glowered at Alva. She did not say a word, but Alva knew that the irascible Irene had received the message, and she was content that the redhead would play along. Irene would always buck against the harness, fighting for her independence and individuality, but Alva knew that she never had enough prescient consideration to reach beyond her present state. She would always fall short, and the sad thing for Irene was that she would secretly know this but never own up to it.

CHAPTER THREE

THE IMPOSING department stores in Union Square and along Broadway and 6th Avenue were frighteningly impressive. Tiffany and Co., Bergdorf Goodman, Henri Bendel, Siegel-Cooper, Lord and Taylor, and Macy's all vied for prime position. They stood in an awesome array of gray majesty rising in towering stories of architectural splendor, stabbed by a multitude of windows that shone with inviting allure. Blinds ran out across the sidewalk and shaded the steady flow of window shoppers and hurrying public amidst the hectic traffic of tramcars, carriages, and delivery vans that filled the roads below. There was something implied by the substantial imposition of the fine buildings towering above the multitudes, it was as if they represented more than a storeroom for fine things but also the coming of a new age of merchandising.

As well as department stores, other suppliers lined the streets, some selling dry goods, there were tailors, boot makers, barbers, fabric and trimming businesses, all kinds of costume and textile manufacturers. It was into this treasure trove that Alva and her friends sallied. They found it was as true as they had been told. The tentative counter personnel were only too ready to fold obsequiously to their wishes, and the girls soon fell into the pretense of their position. Fingertips fluttered as they sent counter staff scurrying off on fanciful missions whilst they raised their skirts and hid the stolen goods lifted from nearby displays before flouncing from the store with innocence written over their bogus nobility and borrowed clothing.

"I feel like a damned dowager kitted out like this," groaned Irene. She wore a large and wide flowered hat, a long, high-necked dress with puffed, filigreed lace sleeves, and an ivory-handled parasol. Her waist was nipped in by a corset that squeezed her already slender body and left her standing tall and breathless, but gave her the classic lines of a wealthy woman of New York society.

They had both been seated on soft banquettes whilst the serving girl attended them. They had already seen to it that a collection of decorative jewelry lay scattered in trays on the counter.

"Here you are, ma'am," said the young serving girl, hurrying back with a courteous smile on her face and two trays of selected rings. "Perhaps there is something here to please."

Alva did her best to look disinterested as she expected a woman of class to behave. "Oh, yes." She sighed with a bored expression. "Let us have a look."

She too was dressed in a fine peach-colored dress with a wide lace-fringed hat and her hair tied up high and off her neck. The serving girl, in contrast, stood in simple black with a white celluloid collar and cuffs and held a fixed smile on her face, showing an attempt at interest, although by now she was thoroughly bored by the two women.

"What do you think, dearest?" asked Alva, turning to Irene.

Irene leaned over and peered at the collection. "Hrmph!" she grunted, not knowing quite what to say.

"It's for my niece, you see," explained Alva to the server. "A debutante, so a small coming-of-age gift. We are visiting here and would like some gift to take back for her."

The serving girl nodded. "Of course, ma'am."

"These are genuine gold, are they?"

"They are indeed, ma'am. Fourteen to eighteen karat and the finest quality you can be assured."

"How about silver? Do you have something in silver?"

"We do, ma'am. Some very fine brooches and pins."

"Then can you run along and fetch them, as I would like to see?"

"Of course." The unsuspecting girl scurried off.

"Grab a handful," hissed Alva.

Both of them delved into the trays and swept the rings and jewelry into their reticules.

"Let's go."

"Poor kid, she's going to pay for that," observed Irene. "Leaving us alone with all this merchandise."

They were making for the busy double glass doors of the store, where there was constant movement coming and going.

"This place employs hundreds of them girls straight off the street," said Alva, looking around at the bustling crowds gathered around the special deal counter where tins of olives were stacked like serried mountains in row after row. "At two dollars a week, them girls don't reckon they've ever had it so good."

"Should try digging peat for a living," grumbled Irene.

"Excuse me, madam!" they heard a loud male voice cry out.

"Uh-oh!" muttered Irene.

"Madam! Oh, madam!" called a tall mustachioed fellow in long black tails and striped pants, waving a raised hand and hurrying after them. "Forgive me, madam, but I think you may have inadvertently picked up an item from our jewelry counter."

Irene tensed, ready to run, and Alva locked fingers on her arm. "Are you talking to me, young man?" Alva asked as imperiously as she could manage.

"I am, I am," the overheated man gushed. "You will forgive me, I'm sure. It's a mistake—the girl at the counter—" His voice dropped to a whisper. "The girl says some rings are missing."

Alva pulled herself up to her full height in apparent shock. "I am not quite sure what you are saying."

By now, the clerk was looking about himself in embarrassment. "It's just that she says—"

A frown crossed Alva's brow. "Are you implying something, young fellow? Good heavens, I have never—you do know I have been coming into this store on many previous occasions, don't you? I am a frequent customer."

"Well, well, yes, of course, madam. We would never want to imply that any loyal customer should—or could—" the flushed store man babbled. "It must be an error, the girl will have made a mistake, I am sure."

Sliding into the background, Irene worked her way through the passing crowd of shoppers that were by now beginning to take an interest. She arrived at the forefront of the gathered women buying special offer tins of imported olives at the deal counter. Lost amongst the press and with a dexterous underarm push with the parasol, Irene undermined one of the displays of stacked tins. The mountain swayed, it gave way and tumbled, and in doing so clattered against the next stack. As there were four carefully arranged piles on the counter, they went down one after the other with a rattle and bang and a shocked chorus of feminine squeals and rushing bodies hurrying out of the way.

In the confusion, Irene swept up Alva by the elbow and dashed for the doors. The store man was spun around in a crush of panicked shoppers, and turning this way and that, he lost Alva and Irene in the crowd as they slipped from the store and into the street.

In the large and almost empty barrack room with pallet beds divided into curtain-hung sections for privacy, they found Niamh lying on her bed in her rumpled maid's outfit and smiling at them distantly. Alva looked around the room, but they were alone, and she wondered why Niamh was lying there with her skirt rucked up and collar awry.

"How is Aoife?" asked Alva.

The smiling Niamh shrugged vaguely and waved a fistful of coiled paper at them. She rolled her round body provocatively over the bed and onto her ample belly and bit her bottom lip coyly.

"What the divil are you playing at?" snarled Irene. "Feeling a mite skittish, are you?"

"Look," said Niamh, fluttering her eyelashes. "Look what I made."

Alva walked over and snatched the roll from her fingers. "My God! Niamh, these are dollar bills. What have you got here, one, two—it's three dollars. Where did you get it?"

"We don't have to tell McGuire," said a smug Niamh. "I got it from my employer, a regular gentleman he is."

"What did you have to do for that?" Irene asked suspiciously.

"Don't matter, I enjoyed it."

"Oh, Niamh!" sighed Alva. "You'll not be giving him sexual pleasure, will you?"

Niamh raised an arched eyebrow and maintained her smile. "He certainly gave me some of that along with the cash. I told him, if I did it, he'd have to pay me something for the rumpty, I'll not be doing it for nothing."

Alva shook her head in dismay, but Irene interrupted her concern. "Hey, we'd best sort out this gold first. Set our take apart before McGuire comes calling for his cut."

That was not to be, for at that moment, McGuire burst into the room with Balthazar at his heels. The black man was holding up by one arm the sagging figure of Aoife.

"What are you skits playing at?" McGuire roared.

Alva and Irene glowered at him whilst Niamh sat up on the edge of her bed and watched them nervously.

"Look at her," shouted McGuire. "She's too sick to stand, and you send her around to play at maid. I told you, nobody sick gets in here. The damned girl fainted the minute she arrived at the door."

"Set her down gently," Alva ordered coldly, and Balthazar obeyed, letting pale Aoife settle herself on a chair. The girl had dark rings under her eyes, sweat upon her brow, and she sagged weakly on the chair, almost sliding from the seat until Niamh crossed over and enclosed her in her arms.

"You'll get your things, the lot of you, and get the hell out of here," said McGuire with a snarl. "I'll not be playing with the likes of you."

"You'll not be wanting your cut of today's take then?" snapped Alva.

"What?" McGuire frowned. "What are you talking about?"

"This!" said Irene, emptying her reticule onto a nearby bed and leaving a glittering heap on the unmade sheets.

"And this." Alva also emptied her addition, and the light of gold gleamed in McGuire's eyes.

"You did this today?" McGuire asked in a slightly awed voice. "That's a good haul. Not much we get in the way of gold."

"Our first run," Irene said proudly.

"Not bad at all," said McGuire, his chunky fingers raking through the heap of rings.

"Still want us out of here?" pressed Alva.

An overly dressed Saoirse walked in the door. She was about to say something and then froze as she saw them all. "What's going on?"

Tongue in cheek, Alva was watching McGuire as he went through his mental machinations. "She'll need a doctor."

McGuire looked over at the sickly Aoife and then at Balthazar. "See to it," he ordered. Turning to Alva, he said, "If you're to keep her around, it's your problem, you got it?"

"It always was," Alva answered.

THE DOCTOR PROVED to be a pragmatic younger man more used to modern techniques than some of his older peers. He was a slight man of average build with the same carefully managed expression that many medical people will wear. The same look that could range from a façade of deep concern to one of absolute indifference, all of which indubitably worked for such people as a natural human defense against the vicissitudes of any over-sympathizing. Even so, he was their best bet, and Alva listened to him attentively.

Dr. Seckle was smart and speedy, and after leaving Aoife in her bed, he took Alva to one side and gave her advice in his best bedside manner.

"Yes, your young friend is in a bad way. Now I can recommend various types of medication for her condition. I would suggest copper sulphate and morphine pills, you may also find that inhaling turpentine vapors will help, but by far the best recognized treatment is still found in plain old bed rest and good diet."

"Is that all we can do?"

"Here in New York, yes, I believe so. The ideal would be elsewhere in a sanatorium with fresh mountain air and bright sunlight."

"There is such a place?"

"In Appalachia, I believe there is a sanatorium solely for consumptive sufferers."

"Appalachia?"

"Yes, North Carolina, it is a backward place," Dr. Seckle went on. "Rather unholy intermarriage of simple folk that results in some deformities." He leaned forward confidentially. "I'm told there are places there where the local population are born with six fingers."

"Well now!" breathed Alva in dutiful awe.

"The upside is the brisk mountain air fresh with a

chill in it, so I'm told. Ideal for chest complaints and highly recommended."

"And Aoife would prosper with such treatment you think, Doctor?"

"There or somewhere dry and warm." Seckle cocked his head and stared into her eyes, his shrug was the slightest movement of his shoulders. "It can do her no harm. No harm at all."

WHEN HE WAS GONE, Alva stood with arms folded and considered the options. She leaned against the doorjamb to the room and gazed around abstractedly at her fellow inmates.

Irene and Saoirse were pushing their pallets together to make one large bed. There was nothing unusual in this, many youngsters back home shared a family bed, cousins and sisters sleeping together in cramped conditions, and nobody thought anything of it. However, Alva viewed it with some other consideration, she had seen how Irene and Saoirse behaved in each other's company and thought there was more than friendly companionship in the arrangement. But to Alva, it was of little interest as it was their own concern, and she saw nothing other than that the two girls were content.

Chubby Niamh was changing with each day. Alva could see it plainly. She lay now on her bed with scarcely any clothing on and her large breasts and thighs plainly in sight, spilling across the sheets in fleshy abandon as she studied herself in a small hand mirror. Her voyage of discovery towards any assuredness, Alva believed, was a sexual one. The rejections perceived because of her size were being swept away by her new experiences, yet Alva hoped that her profligate ways would not lead her into dismay.

Aoife, hoarse and breathing wheezily, was Alva's main concern. The pretty Aoife, now wan and pale with the sickness leaching her youthful beauty away. She looked to Alva even more nun-like now, with the stillness of pallid skin giving her the quality of some kind of plaster saint set up on a church wall. Alva was determined she would not die. The desire burned strongly in her breast, and the resolve that not one of these girls would be lost to her. They had become her kin now and as close as family. The umbilical cord with the old country had been severed, and all that remained of that life was here in each other's company. Alva knew she was alone in understanding this, and that is what made it her responsibility that they survived, and she intended to see it was so.

She was sure now that to remove Aoife from the city was the only course that would benefit her health, and perhaps a trip to dryer climes or somewhere equally suitable was necessary. Perhaps it was foolish to risk all their lives for the sake of Aoife, but then Alva firmly believed that if one was lost to them, they would disintegrate as a group, and all too soon, all the others would fade away. It was imperative that they stay together. They were lone young women without guardians or kin to protect them in this foreign land, all they had was each other.

But how to achieve their removal from the city? Alva had no knowledge of what lay beyond the few streets she knew in New York, the country was enormous, and she had no idea of where to go or how to get there. They would need money of course, and they were busy making a reserve of that, but it was specific knowledge they needed right now, worldly and geographic information, and of that, they had none.

Yet, although she did not know it just then, a part of the solution would come with their next raiding party amongst the department stores downtown.

CHAPTER FOUR

Alva was stealing silk and satin scarves in the Wurtz Brothers store when he approached her.

Working alone usually made Alva more attentive and sharp, so it was surprising that she missed him. After she had seen the shop girl off for more fashionable wraps, Alva steadily took the better and more expensive quality headbands and veils left on the counter and hooked them over the garter under her skirts.

"Fine work," he said in a soft drawl as he came up unheard behind her.

Alva spun around and saw a tall, slender man dressed in surprisingly light tan colored clothes, when the rest of the city-wear around her was usually black or dark brown. He was not a pretty man, his face was lozenge-shaped with large jug-handle ears, a drooping mustache, and wide, loose lips that seemed made of some kind of rubber. Additionally, he wore a wide-brimmed thirty-dollar Stetson *Boss of the Plains* hat with a Carlsbad crease on his short-cut head of hair. With the high hat and his heeled boots, he had extra height and seemed to tower over her.

"What did you say?" Alva burst out in haughty fashion.

"That there." He grinned, and his voice belied his poor appearance as it was deep and mellow with a soft southern accent. "Sweetest pair of limbs I seen in a long while."

"What are you doing? How could you spy on a lady when she is adjusting her private garments?"

"Yeah, sure thing, ma'am. Tucking all them fine dooh-dahs in there. Will you be paying for them, I wonder?"

"Of course, of course," said a flustered Alva.

"See, I seen you in the reflection of them mirrors over there. Now I don't reckon you has spotted that, has you? Lady, in all truth, I think you been doing a little bit of light-fingered larceny here."

Defeated, Alva dropped her shoulders. "What are you, some kind of store security?"

"No, ma'am," he said, tipping his hat. "My name is Ernest Fairweather Grant and I'd surely like to take you out for a coffee or lemonade or any damn thing you please."

"You would?" A suspicious Alva frowned. "And what might you have in mind?"

"Why the pleasure of your company, ma'am. You are surely the prettiest gal I seen since I got here in New York City."

"Is that so," said Alva, tilting her head curiously. "It's for sure you are not from around here."

"No, ma'am. Now, you mind if I ask you your name? I'm sure it'll be as sweet as you are."

"My name's Alva North."

"Then I'm pleased to meet you, Miss Alva."

Just then, the serving girl returned with another selection of long Tule scarves. "Oh, good day, sir. If you will be kind enough, I'll just see to this lady and be with you directly."

"Quite all right," said Ernest. "I do believe Miss Alva has concluded her shopping now, and I reckon we have another engagement." With that, he took Alva's elbow and lifted her from her seat. "Shall we mosey along now, darlin'?"

He was slick, Alva had to give him that, and she wondered at his swift assessment of the scene and ability to handle things with such consummate ease.

THEY FOUND a tearoom and Ernest took off his hat and set it on an empty chair as he ordered a coffee for himself and a China tea for Alva. It was an elegant, gentile place with well-to-do and finely dressed women taking a break from their shopping and filling the room with chatter. Plants grew in shining copper vases, and the tables and chairs were set tastefully apart with high windows giving the marble floor a gleam that shed light throughout the room.

"You do that regular?" he asked as the serving girl went to fetch their order.

"You mean pick and choose as you saw?" Alva smiled.

"I do. You don't look like a lady who needs to do that kind of thing, you being so well dressed and fine looking."

"Looks can be deceptive."

"They sure can, I reckon I'll never get used to this city life."

"Where exactly are you from, Mr. Grant?"

"I come from Texas, ma'am. Place called Avagar Rhodes, sweet little town full of cows and flies."

Alva arched an eyebrow. "That doesn't sound all that pleasant."

"Oh, no, ma'am. It sure is a swell place, it ain't at all as bad as it sounds."

"And what do you do amongst all these cows and flies?"

Ernest set back in his chair, which was an elegant artistic creation cast in iron, and it squeaked under his long form. "Me, I'm a Texas Ranger some of the time, rest of the time I'm a bit like you. I tend to step around the law on occasion."

"Really." She chuckled. "Is that a fact?" Alva found she liked his rather lackadaisical attitude and was surprised by his honesty. "And how, exactly, does that work?"

"Why"—he smiled—"the very reason I am up here just now. Needed to take me a short respite from things down south. Certain parties weren't too keen on my behavior."

"A Texas Ranger and at the same time a lawbreaker, how do you manage?"

"A Texas Ranger is indeed a lawman, a peacekeeper of sorts, down in Texas." He shrugged. "Just sometimes the borderline between law and disorder gets a mite blurred, that's all."

"If you can make it so, I guess," she said with sly understanding.

He laughed. "Exactly."

The girl arrived with their order and set the cups down, and Ernest smiled his thanks.

"I'm on holiday," he confessed when the girl had gone. "Like to take me some time and rest easy for a short while until things have cooled down back in Avagar

Rhodes. I'd sure be obliged to spend some time with a soul that understands my predicament. What do you say to that, Miss Alva?"

Alva demurred, she had to admit she quite liked the idea of spending time with Ernest, but wondered how that might work out. "Just what did you have in mind?" she asked.

"Oh, I thought some roller-skating, strolling Central Park, maybe visit the menagerie, and perhaps a show or two. You know, the regular things folks do."

Alva pouted. "Might that be a tad boring?"

Ernest shook his head. "No, ma'am, I intend to make every moment the most interesting you've acquired during your entire time on this planet."

"Holy Mary!" She laughed aloud, and the women at the other tables turned to look. "Ernest, you do say the dandiest things."

He gave her a broad smile then said in a whisper, "Alva, come along of me, I would surely like to show you the splendid view from my hotel room. It's a dandy, you can see the whole danged city without moving from your chair."

Alva sat back and eyed him steadily. She knew very well what he intended and had to admit to herself that, to a certain degree, the idea appealed. It caught her unawares, and yet it brought a mellow feeling into her chest. She was a seventeen-year-old virgin girl imbued with the strictures of an Irish Catholic dependence born on guilt and forgiveness, and she felt it was time to shuck ofoff those chains. Ernest was not a handsome man in the accepted sense, but he had a charm that she enjoyed, and she believed that there was within his personality a gentlemanly strain that meant her no harm.

"I hope this view is worth the effort," she teased.

Ernest slid back his chair and got to his feet. "Lady, we all roll the dice and see how it turns out. That's the chance you take."

As she waited whilst Ernest fetched a Hansom cab, Alva considered Niamh and the casual way she slept with her admirers. She hoped this would not be the same with Ernest, for she saw things differently than her friend. Niamh sought fond company and admiration, a thing lacking from much of her developing years because of her size. The profligate life gave Niamh some sense of worth, although an illusionary one, Alva was sure. And it was tied to a gift of money, cheapened by the stigma of prostitution. Still, that was how Niamh wanted it and the means by which she found not only pleasure but also received recognition despite what the world might think of her.

As Ernest sat beside her in the confines of the cab, Alva felt the warmth of his thigh pressing against her. She found that something was stirring within her, and tentatively she placed her hand under his elbow and through his arm. Ernest smiled down at her, and she saw a sparkle in his eye and read the crinkles there and the white crow's feet from a skin tanned in the sun.

"Is it dry in Texas?" she asked.

"Sure, it can be dry." He shrugged. "Depends on where you are. It's a mighty big place is Texas."

"I have a friend who suffers from the consumption, you think it would be good for her?"

"I reckon so. A lot of folks with the chest complaint come down there to get out of the damp. Plenty of good air, open space, it's a right nice place, Alva."

He was staying at The Centennial Grand, an established, large, and fine hotel, and it took Ernest a discreet payment for Alva to be secretly ushered up to his room. A grand suite awaited her with tall windows that certainly gave a fine view across the rise of ten-story city buildings around City Hall Park. Alva felt diminished as she stood by the window and looked down at the busy street below.

Then Ernest was behind her and enfolded her in his arms. "Sure is a fine view, ain't it?"

"Have to tell you, Ernest," a shy Alva confessed. "I'm not what you'd call practiced at this."

"Y'all just relax, sweet thing. Nothing bad will happen." He nuzzled his lips into her neck. "By God, woman, you smell fine. Like fresh dew on green grass when a warm wind comes down the valley from the plain."

Alva turned in his arms and they kissed. There was a soft touch in her mind and a grateful feel of his fingers brushing her cheek. Alva sighed and pressed herself up towards the tall figure, and despite this gift of surrender, she was only too well aware of the tension that ran through her as he pulled her close.

The first time was not how she imagined it would be, and she feared that her clumsiness had blunted Ernest's desire. Yet he seemed content enough as they lay together afterwards. The bed was large with soft plush coverlets and deep pillows of crisp white linen, and their distraction played on Alva's mind as she realized that some people lived with this kind of comfort all their lives.

She thought of Aoife, her sad eyes staring back vaguely at Alva as she lay in her bed back at the barracks. Weak, pale, and unkempt, with her natural beauty leaking away across the sweat-soaked sheets of her illness. Alva wondered if, in fact, a movement to a drier country would improve her condition and give her back some strength.

But her concern for Aoife and the others was swept away as Ernest did as he promised and kept her pleasantly diverted. Over the next few days, he wined and dined her and carried her to one entertainment or another. Before she knew it, a week had passed, and to Alva it all felt like a guilty but enjoyable holiday. For seven days, she had thought about nothing else except herself and Ernest, and each night beside him in bed had been full of the same warm pleasure. She luxuriated in the hotel facilities, a hairdresser and masseuse, room service, and a cleaning and mending service. Alva felt totally spoiled, and it was only with some remorse that she finally admitted to Ernest that she must return and see the others.

They parted ways over coffee in the hotel lounge.

"I, too, am bound home," Ernest allowed.

"It is safe for you now?"

"I had me a telegraph from my sister-in-law down there, and it appears so."

Alva reached across the table and laid her hand over his. "I shall miss you," she admitted.

"That's a given." He smiled. "As I shall you. Maybe you'll head down to Texas one day and we can meet up again."

"Maybe," she said with a brief assertive jerk of the head.

"It's easy," he went on. "Head down south and leave

off Oklahoma at the Red River, then make on until you come to Debonne County in Texas. You keep going south across there, but at the Slick Grass River, turn left. It has a few oxbows, but never give that no mind, as the country round about is real pretty to see, so taking your time ain't no hardship. Follow that river until you hit the range of mountains called The Stairway, easy to tell as they is all rocks shaped liked steps, then go on along that range and right at the tip, with pines on one side and water on the other, that there is Avagar Rhodes."

Alva grinned. "That's the sweetest map I ever heard described."

"You get there and you'll find that it's the sweetest town as well."

"Just one that's full of cows, flies, and Texas Rangers."

"Aw, it ain't so bad," he said shyly, wishing now that he had not described his home in such an offhand manner when he had first met her. "Maybe I exaggerated a mite."

Alva got to her feet and, taking her farewell, held out a hand to him. Rather gallantly, he leaned over and kissed the fingers. "You are one hell of a fine lady, Miss Alva North, and I shall not forget you."

CHAPTER FIVE

WHEN SHE ARRIVED BACK, Alva found that things were not as she had left them.

"Where you been?" hissed Irene. "It's all gone to hell in a terrible way since you left."

Alva looked around the room at them, and they all watched her with a fixed gaze as she unpinned her hat, eased the gloves from her fingers, and laid them with her reticule carefully on the top blanket of her bed. Irene and Saiorse sat together on the edge of their wide bed, both of them leaning forward tensely, their narrow frames looking like feral dogs about to leap forward and attack. A hollow-eyed Aoife lay weak in her bed and looked up from her pillow at an overheated Niamh, who lounged red-faced and dressed in a fancy dress with skirts raised up and showing the garters on her great thighs.

"So, why don't you tell me?" asked Alva.

"Go on, Niamh," urged Irene. "You saw it, you tell it."

"It is this," Niamh began. "McGuire is dead."

That made Alva take a step back. "*McGuire dead*, there's a thing. What happened?"

Niamh made herself comfortable, drew a deep sigh, and folded one massive thigh over the other. "It was like this. My friend took me out for dinner—"

"Her friend," cut in Irene spitefully. "Is that rat-like gambling snake Joe Jagger, him that runs the rag trade on the East Side and the roulette wheel in the Bridge Café."

"He pays his way," Niamh complained pompously. "Certainly sees me very well. Why are you always putting me down, Irene?"

"You lay your plump derriere on the line too often, that's why, sweetheart."

Niamh rode back on her seat and sneered pointedly. "What's it to you. Is it that the only friend you can manage is another of the female kind?"

"Why you, pork stuffing!" snarled Irene, starting forward with fists clenched.

"Hold it!" barked Alva. "Will you two cut it out, for heaven's sake. Now tell me, Niamh, this could change everything for us if McGuire is gone."

"Oh, he's gone alright," Niamh went on.

"Then tell it," Alva ordered.

"As I was saying," said Niamh, glowering at Irene. "My friend is taking me for a bite in The Leather Jug."

"That's a Bucket Boys place, isn't it?" asked Alva.

"It was," Niamh agreed solemnly. "McGuire is at the bar with his big Negro bodyguard, Balthazar. Then in walks Ryan O'Bannion and a few of his boys. There's only ill feeling between the two. It's been festering for a while, so Joe tells me. O'Bannion runs The Terrible Delayed Gang, maybe you heard of them. Anyway, there's a fair old crush in The Leather Jug this night, so it looks like O'Bannion is about the shake McGuire's hand in friendly fashion. He steps up nice as can be and they shake.

"Thing is, O'Bannion is holding on tight and won't let go. McGuire turns to Balthazar, but that black-hearted knave turns his head away. He's sold out to O'Bannion, that's as plain as day. Now, Curtis Mulvenny, O'Bannion's right-hand man, is alongside, and he has a six-shot pistol in his hand. Mulvenny pushes the barrel about where McGuire's heart should be and pulls the trigger. Benny McGuire keels over and hits the deck like a herring on the fish market hard."

Alva blew air and allowed her breath to escape slowly. "So, d'you know what this O'Bannion hopes to do?"

"I came as soon as I could," Niamh said, fluttering fanning fingers in front of her glowing cheeks. "Joe thinks O'Bannion will be taking over everything, and that means us as well. I believe we had best prepare for it."

"What will he do?" asked Saoirse, turning to Irene for reassurance. "Surely we're as good a business for him as we were for McGuire."

"That's as maybe, we'll have to wait and see," speculated Irenc.

THEY DID NOT HAVE long to wait until Ryan O'Bannion made his presence felt.

A day later, Balthazar eased the door open to their room and O'Bannion stepped inside with Mulvenny and two of his Terrible Delayed gang members alongside.

"Good day to you, ladies," greeted O'Bannion.

He was a broad-shouldered man of average height, his face was as bland, white, and broad as a peeled potato. Short, thinning curls of fair hair topped his round head, and around his eyes and forehead were drawn areas of wrinkled skin like the cooling milk on hot coffee. O'Bannion liked to show them, they were battle scars remaining from the days he spent street fighting for pennies in his early days.

He had a presence evident with his arrival in the room, a silent pressure that was physically intangible yet manifested as if a drop in temperature or a change in pressure had entered. The beaten eyes were half closed, not from the beatings they received in the past but rather from the cool dispassion with which he scanned the cautious young women watching him without any interest or concern.

"You will have heard of the sad demise of your late employer," O'Bannion went on, easing his way into the room and standing spread-legged with both hands deep in his jacket pockets. "You'll be pleased to hear that it seems that me and my fellows are to be taking over all aspects of the Bucket Boys business from now on."

Alva stepped forward boldly and gave Balthazar a disdainful look. "Then that black traitor there will no doubt have told you that we have done well enough at the *clouting* for McGuire in days past."

"I heard, I heard," said O'Bannion in a dismissive fashion. "But I have little interest in that, lady. I'm thinking that you could all be turning your hands to a better form of money-making for us."

The two of O'Bannion's men sniggered quietly in the background. They were cocky, thuggish young fellows with hats set askance on their heads and arrogant poses that spoke of a brutal confidence in the company of their boss.

"And what exact form do you have in mind?" asked Alva.

"*Mr. O'Bannion,*" hissed Mulvenny. "You'll address the man as Mr. O'Bannion, if you will."

O'Bannion's shadow and killing machine was a tall, slender fellow, stooped and gaunt with sunken cheeks and slick, night-dark glossy hair, and a broad Irish accent. Mulvenny's black eyes were as dark as the universe and unmoving, with no glimmer of life appearing to glow in them. They were dead objects, and if they were any symptom of the life behind them, they spoke volumes about Mulvenny's chilly emptiness and his meager capacity for charity. It was plain to see a stone lived where his heart should be.

Irene looked him up and down and could not resist. "What manner of man are you, you hold his hat and coat, do you?"

"If it's called for," answered Mulvenny evenly, he stared impassively at Irene and smiled thinly as he glanced across at Saoirse. "How about you, sister. What is it that you hold close and dear to you?"

Alva stepped up before matters got out of hand. "What is it exactly you have planned for us?"

Aoife gave a raw and deep chesty cough, and the sound distracted O'Bannion, who glanced over at her lying on the bed. "What's wrong with her? She sickening for something?"

Balthazar sidled over and whispered in O'Bannion's ear.

"Bah!" spat O'Bannion in distaste as he stared down at Aoife. "Then you can get out of here, girly. I've no place for the likes of you, pack your things and get out."

"You can't do that!" burst out Alva.

O'Bannion ignored her and continued, "The rest of

you can get your stuff together and move over to Molly Turnover's place within the week. You'll all serve me better on your backs, and I'll want to be seeing fourteen dollars a week from each of you. Balthazar will be watching over you, so you will behave." He swung around and turned to point directly at Niamh. "And *you!* I know all about you. No more freelancing from now on, you understand? You work for me now, and if you want to keep the nose on your face, you'll do as I say."

Abruptly, he turned his back on them and lumbered from the room with Mulvenny and the others following close behind, only Balthazar stayed. He folded his arms and glowered at them from the doorway.

"Who is Molly Turnover?" asked Alva.

"She runs The Terrible Delayed's whorehouse for O'Bannion," supplied Niamh. "He's wanting us all to turn tricks for him now."

Aoife was sitting up in bed, her sheets clutched to the breast of her nightgown. "What shall I do, Alva. I don't know where I'll go?"

"You'll go nowhere, Aoife. Do not worry now, I will sort this out."

"And how will you do that, Alva?" burst out Irene, pointing an accusing finger at the silent Balthazar. "They have us held fast, and that black dog guards the gate."

"Come here will you, and settle down, speak quiet, we'll not want him to hear anything. Niamh, use your charms. Smile and keep the black devil content."

Only too pleased to have her allure recognized, Niamh bustled over with the tip of her tongue teasing between her teeth and a beguiling eye for Balthazar.

"We are gone," breathed Alva. "This is it, no messing now, we must be out of here soonest. There's not one of us, I'll be bound, that wants to service O'Bannion and his cronies."

"Except maybe for Niamh," said Irene, glancing wryly over her shoulder at the two engaged in conversation over by the door. "Could be she'd quite enjoy this new source of employment."

"I think not," said Alva. "She likes to go her own way and please herself with her associations. Now we must make our move to escape, and we'll take Aoife with us as we cannot leave her here."

"And where shall we go?" asked Saoirse. "O'Bannion will have this town tied up."

"We'll need to arm ourselves first and also carry as little as possible when we go. There's two main routes we can take to get out of New York, either a steam packet or by locomotive."

"Sounds like you've been thinking about this for a while," observed Irene archly.

"Been giving it some thought recently," answered Alva blithely.

"You never said where you were these last few days," said Aoife in a reprimanding tone. "I hope you have not been involved in anything sinful, Alva."

"God! I swear," burst out Irene. "You sound more like Mother Superior each and every day."

"I'll take that as a compliment," huffed Aoife, before breaking into another hacking cough.

"I've met someone," Alva confessed. "He is a fine man, and he has told me of a place."

"Well, good for you, Alva," came praise from the normally reserved Saoirse. "I am glad to hear that, about time you found some company."

"The climate will be good for you, Aoife," Alva went on, disregarding Saoirse's kind words. "Dry and clean, and it is far enough away from here to keep O'Bannion only as a memory."

"Where is this paradise?" asked Irene.

"It's in a place called Texas."

"Wherever that is."

"South of here. I think a locomotive would be best to get us there, might take two or three weeks, but it's more comfortable than swaying on the ocean. Remember how it was coming across here on the *Charybdis*?"

"Aye, I've never been so sick in all me life," agreed Saoirse.

"Why will we need weapons?" asked Irene. "Not that I'm against it, but are we meaning to make a fight of it?"

"If we have to," said Alva. "We'll get Terry O'Donohue to fetch us some guns, he was fond enough of McGuire to do the deed.

"Good," said Irene, spitting on her palms and rubbing them together. "I'll be wanting to put a nail in that black boy Balthazar's brain first off. I had no love for McGuire, but a two-faced traitor selling out is far worse in my book."

"Hold off, Irene," said Alva. "I think we'll have a quieter way if Niamh is okay with it."

"You think she'll seduce the poor fellow. Is that the plan?"

"Will you look at them now." Alva nodded towards the couple at the door. "Thick as thieves they are, but if Niamh will not come across and play the part, then indeed we will have to take Balthazar to task."

"Oh dear, I see you are all planning cold-blooded murder," wailed Aoife. "You cannot, it is a grievous mortal sin."

"You can always stay here and die on the street," answered Irene roughly. "If that's your fancy, Aoife, know this, girl, that is what O'Bannion has in store for you."

"It's true enough," Alva agreed. "There is no mercy there. If we stay here, we'll all be dead from whoring or worse within a six-month. You want that, Aoife?"

"Oh, forgive us, sweet Jesus," moaned a mortified Aoife, clasping her hands before her in silent prayer. "Let this cup pass from us, I pray."

Alva ignored her. "We only have a few days to organize this, so let's get to it. Now we'll be needing money, so somebody must slip out with what we have in our store and get the fence to trade it off for cash."

"Saoirse and I can do that," said Irene.

"Good enough," agreed Alva. "I'll see Terry and arrange our railroad tickets and the weapons."

"I love it, I surely do, this is the real craic." Irene grinned, full of eagerness and keen with the prospect of action. "To be poking a finger in O'Bannion's eye and shaking the dust of this place from our feet will be a grand thing, will it not?"

In a quiet moment later, Alva took Niamh to one side and, speaking quietly, told her of their plans.

"What will you do, Niamh. You know you can come with us if you wish?"

"Ah!" Niamh smiled. "Bless you, dear Alva, but I like it here. It is a joy for me to be wanted as I am. I don't think I will be leaving with you, but you know I wish you all well, even that sorry creature Irene."

"What about O'Bannion, once we are gone? You will be on your own."

"Ach! He's just another crooked soul, and New York

is a mighty big place to get lost in. I have many friends now, Alva. More than I ever had in the old country, there I was just a fat cow in the byre ready for milking, and here I feel that I belong, no matter how I look. Don't worry, I'm truly sure I can make a go of it in the city, there's plenty here that will pay my way for me."

"Be sorry to leave you, that I will."

"We part as friends, Alva."

"We do indeed, Niamh."

TERRY CAME with a sack full of supplies. There were bread rolls wrapped in cloth, butter, eggs, cheese, and a side of bacon, but underneath and hidden from Balthazar's eye were weapons. Irene's eyes lit up at the sight of the hardware, and Alva was hard put not to allow her to take everything in the sack, as it was she armed herself with a knife, pistol, and brass knuckleduster. The rest of them hid a weapon of their choice inside their beds, except that is for Aoife, who maintained her religious reservation and would play no part in the proceedings, much to the disgust of Irene.

Alva thanked Terry and asked him how O'Bannion was making out as the new boss.

"He is taking over every ward where he can and using force to do it. There's three bosses I know of already that have ended up in the East River with their throats cut. The man's waging a war, he wants to own the city, and Mulvenny is waving a flag right alongside him and enjoying every bloody moment."

"And you, are you safe, Terry?" asked Saoirse.

Terry slid a sidelong glance over at Balthazar, where he was busily engaged in conversation with Niamh. The black man had a distant look in his eye and smiled self-consciously as Niamh pressed her ample form up against him. Balthazar was a simple man short of everything except muscle, and by now, Niamh had him around her little finger.

"As much as anybody is alright now," said Terry. "I keep my head down and hope he never finds out about these goods I've given you."

"He'll not hear it from us," promised Alva.

"Well, look, I have come with a message from the man himself," said Terry with an apologetic shake of the head. "It seems tomorrow is O'Bannion's birthday, so it will be a celebration time for him and all his boys. There will be a party in The Leather Jug with all kinds invited, he'll have politicians and businessmen, fancy socialites, even the police commissioner and mayor, all the powerful bigwigs in New York who'll be wanting to shake his hand and kiss the ring."

"That's grand news, Terry." Alva smiled. "It could be ideal for us as they will all be distracted. Might be a good time for us to make a move."

"I think not," said Terry sadly. "You see, he wants you all there looking your best. O'Bannion told me to tell you girls to be there, he thinks you will offer diversion for his guests."

"I do not like the sound of that," said Alva.

"Best you don't," agreed Terry. "He'll be serving you up as a dessert when the liquor's done its work, I've no doubt of that."

"Then we must make our play, party or not."

"A divil of a time to do it," said Saoirse.

"Not if we plan this right," said Alva. "But we must do it like we mean it, there'll be no surrender and no coming back. There might be blood, ladies, you had best believe it, and I'll ask you now, can you do it?"

"Of course we can," said Irene hoarsely. "Are we not Irish girls and full of pluck?"

"Very well," said Alva. "Our first task will be to rid ourselves of Balthazar, he cannot be allowed to get word back to O'Bannion. Then we'll need to make the midnight train out of here heading for Chicago. I have the tickets, four hundred fifty dollars worth, second class and sleeper, enough for us four. I have to tell you, Niamh chooses to stay here."

"That's too bad." Saoirse frowned with a quick glance at Irene.

"Don't you be looking at me," said Irene callously. "If that fat geebag wants to stay here with these gowls, then who am I to say nay?"

"She'll distract Balthazar," cut in Alva.

"And who will bring that black beast down?" whispered Irene.

"That's for me to do," answered Alva coldly.

"Can you do it?"

"I will."

CHAPTER SIX

THE LEATHER JUG was a Manhattan dive bar on Water and Dover Street, not far from the East River docks. One-Armed Charley Morell ran the place, and it collected some of the hardest and meanest souls on the waterfront, and this night, it was full to overflowing with them. The scabrous street gang members with black eyes and rolled cigarettes lingered uncertainly whilst they rubbed shoulders with the finer elements of city society, slumming and keeping a careful hand on their wallets.

On this night of celebration, the drink flowed freely, and many were already rolling, some of them sailors who would be missing their pay come morning, along with their throbbing heads. Waiters dressed in long jackets and aprons and hired for the night swayed dexterously through the throng with large trays swimming with pots of beer held above their heads. Suave-looking gents in top hats and derbies sat at tables with smart ladies dressed in extravagant, flowered hats, downing half glasses of German lager and eating soft crab sandwiches whilst laughing loudly with their mouths half full.

Upon a raised stage, a noisy Irish band played traditional numbers with the wail of Union pipes, a beating bodhirán drum, a fiddle and fife, and a raw-voiced singer giving it his all. The music was loud and wild enough to compete with the general uproar from the crowded room.

Tobacco smoke hung low, and the air steamed with the overheated crowd of people pressed cheek by jowl in the small barroom.

O'Bannion beamed drunkenly, sitting snugly on a chair surrounded by his most able lieutenants. His smiling face was red with heat and greasy with sweat, yet his veiled eyes spoke a different story as they viewed all about him with indifferent coolness and calculation. The men joked and milled about O'Bannion, laughing raucously and passing full glasses of beer and lit cigars. Whilst to one side and watching with shrewd attentiveness was the dark and unsmiling figure of Mulvenny.

With an imperious wave, O'Bannion brought young Terry O'Donohue over to his side.

"Tell them," he whispered loudly. "I want them girls here now, you hear me? Two-bit chippie's should be earning their porridge, go get 'em, Terry."

"Right away, boss," said Terry, turning to go.

"I have a mind for the fat one," O'Bannion said, leering. "So see she comes prepared for a dip in me trouser pocket." He gave a loud, dirty laugh, and those around him joined in, not really knowing what amused him so.

But despite his interest in her—Niamh was otherwise engaged.

Alva twitched back a gap in the curtain around Niamh's bed.

Niamh caught her eye, smiled, and gave her a wink. She was kneeling on the bed and resting on her elbows, her rumpled skirts were up to her waist, and her broad bare rump shone like a white moon in the black hands of Balthazar. He was transported, his eyes lidded so that only the whites showed. All his efforts were concentrated on the job in hand, and he worked solidly at his task, groaning with pleasure as he did so.

Despite Balthazar's energetic assault, Niamh gave an impish grin and raised one hand to show a roll of dollar bills tightly enclosed in her pudgy grip. Notwithstanding their carnal liaison, a mercenary Niamh was seeing that Balthazar was paying his way.

All the other girls in the dormitory watched Alva tensely, and the room was taut with an electric air of expectation.

Alva stepped back and let the curtain fall in place. She brought the hammer back on the Colt revolver held down by her side to full cock. She stepped to her right and swept back the end of the curtain, then swiftly placed the Colt next to the side of Balthazar's unsuspecting head, just above the ear with a gold earring, and she pulled the trigger.

The blast was loud and sudden, and half of Balthazar's head was splashed over the opposite side of the flapping bed curtains in a dark spray of blood and bone. Without making a sound, the big Negro's body flopped sideways and tumbled to the floor in a tangle of limbs. Even before he had completed his collapse, Niamh was on her feet, her skirts lowered and her hands searching for her stockings. A stunned Alva watched her in amazement as she threw on a shawl, laced her boots, and dragged a travelling case out from under the bed.

Niamh finally looked up at Alva. "I have to be on my way right quick, and I suggest you all do the same."

Alva found that her insides were shaking, whilst outside her features were frozen, and she showed no evidence that she had just killed a man. She fought to take a tight grip of herself and started to pay attention to the others in the room who were all watching her in a state of some kind of silent awe.

"What have you done?" wailed Aoife, her voice rising in horror as she clapped her hands across her mouth. "Oh, dear Lord, you have killed a man." She started to rock backwards and forwards in dismay.

"Had to be," said Irene through gritted teeth. "That two-faced blackie got what was coming."

"Come on now," said Alva, swallowing her guilt and suddenly in charge of herself and the others. "Get your things, we have to move."

"So long, girls, I'm away," called Niamh from the door, but she collided with Terry as the breathless boy came running into the room. "Oh, damn, get out of my way, boy!"

"What do you want here, laddie?" called Irene. "It's not a good time."

"Himself wants you there right now," said Terry, looking in annoyance over his shoulder at Niamh as she brushed past him and hurried down the stairs, her boots clacking intemperately on the wood. "What is her problem?"

"O'Bannion wants us this minute?" asked Saoirse. "Already?"

"He does," pressed Terry. "And he's mighty impatient." Terry paused a moment and sniffed the air. "What's that I smell, is it gun smoke. You ain't—"

He rushed over to the blood-splattered curtains around Niamh's bed and threw them back. For a frozen moment, Terry stood stock still as he looked down at Balthazar's body.

"Oh, dear God!" he breathed. "Did the fat girl do it?"

"No, it was me," confessed Alva.

"Well, be quick, best you roll him up in something and hide him away and then get the hell away from here. I thought you were just running, not going in for a killing as well. Oh, there will be merry hell to pay when O'Bannion finds out you've killed his blackamoor."

"Come on, girls," pleaded Alva, her eyes widening as she realized that Terry was right. If they hid the body, it might give them some extra minutes to make good their escape. "Let's roll him in the bedding," said Alva, ripping down the bloodied curtain and pulling sheets from the bed.

Irene and Saoirse ran forward to help, but Aoife sat on her bed, coughing and weakly clutching her blanket about her.

"I'd best get back," said Terry, turning to leave. "Tell O'Bannion you're on your way."

"Very well, Terry. Goodbye and thanks for all you've done."

"Just move," said Terry, his voice full of urgency. "Get out of here, I don't much fancy my chances as it is with you running off. If he finds out that I've given you them pistols that shot down Balthazar, then I'll be getting a swim in the river for sure."

"Get out of here," growled Irene. "Go and save your own arse and we'll save ours."

When Terry was gone, they struggled with moving the corpse, but it was no easy matter. Balthazar had been a large and muscled man and was heavy enough before death.

"Dear God!" puffed Saoirse as they attempted to roll the dead man over in the combined space beside the bed. "Can we not just cover him up and put the bed on top? I reckon that's lighter than he is."

"She has a point," said Irene, exchanging a glance with Alva across Balthazar's broad shoulder.

"Let's do it," Alva agreed.

They achieved the task with Aoife sobbing woefully in the background.

"Give up your greeting, will you?" roared Irene. "You've more whining in you than a kitchen cat."

"Now we must move," said Alva. "We have less than half of one hour to get to Grand Central Depot. The New York Central leaves from there at midnight, so we must make it by then. Will you get your things and let's get going?"

"Is it a long way once we're on the train?" asked a querulous Aoife.

"It is indeed," agreed Alva. "From here we go to Albany and Buffalo, and from there across Ohio and Indiana to Chicago. Then we'll change again and head down through Illinois to St. Louis and from there along to Texas. Going to be quite an adventure."

"My! That sounds like a whale of a journey."

"It is that, so it's best not to miss that locomotive, or we'll be stuck here."

"Will there be wild savages down there?"

"I think not, no, we bypass the Indian Territory. You'll be safe enough."

"The only wild savages you'll be meeting, darling

Aoife," sneered Irene, lowering the lid on her suitcase, "are the hard-headed jackanapes that are running loose around here."

TERRY HAD FORCED his way through the birthday crowd at The Leather Jug, who were now well into their cups, and already a number of fights had broken out in the raucous tavern.

O'Bannion sat seething and the worse for drink. He leered at Terry as the boy approached. "Let him through here," he bellowed, and at his shout, Mulvenny moved in to shove the intervening drunks aside and allow the boy to approach.

"Come here, you wee snaif!" ordered O'Bannion, and Terry nervously approached him. "What have you to say?" spat O'Bannion. "Where are my whores?"

"They're coming, boss, for certain they are on their way."

O'Bannion stared at him, his red face beaded with sweat and his eyes like hard, glowering marble stones that missed nothing. "You're lying," he hissed, peering into Terry's face. "You little weasel, you're lying."

As if sensing an impending outrage, a sudden silence fell over the crowd around O'Bannion.

"You're lying, why are you lying, Terry boy?" wheedled O'Bannion. "I see it, don't think I don't. I have the skill, y'see, I can see right through a man, have done so for many a long year—*Is that not so*?" he bellowed drunkenly and was echoed by a chorus of agreement.

Terry shrugged. "No, no, sir, they are just nervous, that is all. A little afraid, they are, after all, no more than convent girls and poor lost orphan children."

But the gang leader was not listening. "So these damned girls are up to something, are they?" asked the now suspicious O'Bannion. "What about my black boy Balthazar? Why is he not here telling me all this? I don't like it, no, I do not." He leaned forward in his chair like an ancient king on his throne and kept a terrified Terry frozen under his gaze. "What d'you know, Terry, me lad? Are you not sure what it is you have for me, then—Mulvenny," he called. "Will you help our wee boy to remember what he has to tell me?"

The dour Mulvenny moved forward and grasped Terry by his tousled hair and jerked his head back. With his stone-dead eyes fixed on Terry's, Mulvenny began to drag the boy backwards. "So we'll have a few words now, Terry."

"No, no," cried a desperate Terry. "I don't know anything. The girls don't want to come here, I do know that, they just don't want to come."

"What's happened to Balthazar? Why's he not here?"

Terry gulped and swallowed air, he was frightened now and desperately searching for a way out. "I believe they may have put him out. I think they must have, yes, I think so."

"Put him out, what's that mean? They knocked him down? They knocked down that great big pug-ugly black giant? I don't believe you."

Mulvenny now had Terry on his knees, dragged down by his hair, and as he held him, he pulled a long, curving blade from the scabbard at the back of his belt and held it to the boy's neck. The blade was shaped in a strange *S*-shaped curve and honed to an eighteen-inch-long razor-edged sliver of sharpness.

"No!" screamed Terry as the ice-cold, sharp steel closed with his flesh. "They shot him, they did. I tell you, they've shot him dead, I don't know how they did it," he confessed rapidly. "They have guns and forced me to say nothing. It's terrible, I would have said something, but I was a-feared. They're screaming mad, I'm telling you, those girls have gone crazy."

"Don't gabble, boy," said Mulvenny, looking past him and up at O'Bannion with humor in his dead eyes. "It does you no good."

"Look, Mr. O'Bannion," pleaded Terry, both hands clasped together before him, as if in prayer. "I swear to you on me mother's life, I knew nothing of all this. You know me, I wouldn't do you wrong. I couldn't do that, you know that, sir, I'm begging you."

"Show some friggin' dignity," snarled Mulvenny. "You're just a wee whelp dog and you're not worth the leash you're kept on."

O'Bannion glanced at Mulvenny and gave a swift jerk of the head, and Mulvenny dug in and dragged the blade across the resisting flesh in a single slash.

"No, no! Spare me, I beg," squealed Terry, but already blood was pumping.

O'Bannion ignored the squirming body of Terry as he leaned forward in his seat and over the dying boy, his face inches from Mulvenny, and spoke with quiet venom, "You will take Séamus and Finbar and bring me them girls. I'll not be bested by ragtail skirts, y'hear me? They get away with this and there's not one female in Five Corners will abide me."

Without hesitation, Mulvenny turned to the two men named and indicated they should follow him. Séamus and Finbar were not the sharpest knives in the drawer, but they were big and intimidating men and took direction without question. Their blind obedience had brought them from poverty in Dublin across the sea to serve at the feet of O'Bannion with a grateful devotion unworthy of the thuggish gang leader. So now they padded dutifully behind Mulvenny as he ran through the darkened streets and headed for the girls' dormitory rooms.

Mist was seeping in off the river and turning the roughly cast street stones wet underfoot and covered with a sheen that shone eerily in the sparse lantern glow. There was little enough light amongst the gloomy houses lining the street, and shadows blossomed darkly as the men hurried on through the narrow alleys and walkways. Their boots clattered on the stones and echoed from the enclosing walls of brick like the repetitious clack of a watchman's warning rattle.

Séamus and Finbar had both indulged in free drink at the party and were struggling to clear their fuddled brains as they followed Mulvenny. Séamus was the shorter of the two, a copper-headed man with a rough beard that reached his chest. Finbar stood taller, dark-haired with heavy black eyebrows, long sideburns, and pink cheeks. They blinked with determination to keep up with the fast-moving figure of Mulvenny, for each had no doubt that if they fell behind, then word would reach O'Bannion of their failings and neither wanted that.

Mulvenny burst into the dormitory, eyes glaring and knife in hand. The place was empty, curtains were pushed back, and bedding lay scrambled over empty beds. Odd items were scattered across the floor in the rush to quit the place. A hairbrush, hair clips, and a few handkerchiefs lay amongst the remains of a broken hand mirror. Unwanted dresses and shawls too large to pack and carry were piled untidily in corners.

"Damn!" cursed Mulvenny. "They're already gone."

"Where to, boss?" asked Finbar.

"How the hell should I know? They have fled, that is all there is for sure."

"There's something here," advised a curious Séamus, looking at the unevenly angled bed set over a rumpled roll of bedding.

"More of their rubbish," growled Mulvenny.

"No, boss, there's blood here, will you take a look at this?"

Finbar crossed over and helped his partner unravel the untidy rolls of bedding before stepping back suddenly. "Jasus, Mary and Joseph!" he cried. "It's the Black fella, he has his head half blowed off."

Mulvenny viewed the corpse with an air of ice-cold venom. "The wee bitches, I never believed them capable. O'Bannion will want their heads now."

"He liked this black fella then, did he?" asked Finbar.

"Of course not, you lummox, O'Bannion likes nobody. The thing is that Balthazar was *his*. His personal possession, think on it like that, and to have his pet killed like some stray doggie will set the boss on a bloody murder path."

"So what do we do now?" asked Séamus.

"We go and bloody find them, that's what. They won't have gone far. It will either be to the docks or the station. Get out and start knocking on doors, someone hereabouts will have seen their direction. We have cabbies on our payroll, I'll fetch one, and when we know where they're headed, we'll get there double quick."

THE GIRLS WERE GOING AS FAST as they could with bags bumping against their legs and struggling with their long skirts. Irene and Saoirse pressed on ahead easily, but Alva felt obliged to help the weaker Aoife, whose short breath rasped in her throat and was fading fast as she lagged behind.

They headed north in single file through the empty streets of the city, but Alva was only too aware that the time for the locomotive's departure was drawing close, and she was worried that they would not make it in time.

The encroaching dampness did not help Aoife either, and she would break down and pause as coughs racked her body. Alva encouraged her to keep going and took the weight of her suitcase to help, but still, the breath sobbed in her body, and her pleading eyes told Alva she was fighting hard to keep up.

Whilst they waited on a corner for Aoife to recover, Alva noted a solitary cab taking a cross street and called out. But the driver did not hear or already had a fare and drove on, ignoring them.

The houses they past were all darkened, no window showed a light, and the streets were lit only by the brightness of the moon and the occasional pool of a streetlamp.

Odd stray figures loomed out of the night, drunks finding their staggering way home or whores arm in arm with a trick as they made for their crib. The only movement was from these night creatures that inhabited the city streets at this late hour, and they flitted vaguely from shadow to shadow as if they were a part of the obscure shades themselves.

"I can't," Aoife said, panting. "I can't go on."

"For Christ's sake, Aoife," complained Irene. "You're dragging us all down."

"You go on," said Aoife, leaning weakly against a brick wall. "I'm done for, I can't take another step. I'm sorry."

"Come on," urged Alva. "Just a little further, will you try some more?"

"Can we carry her?" asked Saoirse.

Alva pondered the suggestion a moment. "We might if we shed the suitcases."

"Come on," growled Irene. "This is all we have that is ours now."

"Well then," said Alva. "Keep only what you really need and throw the rest out. One can carry the bags, and the other two help Aoife. We must keep going, that train won't wait for us."

They all set down their bags and began to rifle through the contents, and then Alva jerked upright as she heard the clop of horse hoofs on the road.

"A cab!" she cried, running out into the center of the street. "Quick, call him down."

Irene and Saoirse joined her, waving their arms and shouting as the Hansom drew nearer, its black shape looming out of the darkness. The cabbie began to draw on his reins as he pulled to a halt, and Alva breathed a sigh of relief as she realized that now they could at last all make it in time to catch their train.

The Hansom's folding front doors opened and three men burst out into the street.

Identifying the occupants took the flash of a second. "It's them!" snarled Irene.

"There y'are, girls." An unnaturally jovial Mulvenny smiled. "Thought to leave us, did you? Well, Mr. O'Bannion has some ideas about that."

"Let us go our way, Mulvenny," said Alva. "We'll not be worth it."

"Mr. O'Bannion thinks y'are. Now, are you coming along sweetly, or is it to be otherwise?"

They stood facing each other in the street, Mulvenny's two heavyset Irishmen standing solid and expectant with their bunched fists hanging down by their sides. Behind them, the cabby's horse fretted as if it sensed the unpleasantness in the air. It took a hard pull by the driver to still the animal.

"I'll be leaving you then," said the nervous cab driver, hauling on the reins. "It seems I must be getting on."

"You'll wait right there," said Mulvenny in a voice not to be argued with. "You're at our pleasure, remember that, mister."

There was a shining flash that seared the night as Mulvenny drew the curved dagger from his belt.

"The devil take the lot of you!" shouted Irene as she leapt boldly forward and, without forethought, drove at the bearded Séamus who stood before her. The man was taken completely by surprise despite the fact that the lightweight Irene bounced off his burly frame and dropped into the road.

Not to be outdone, Saoirse joined her friend and, with a scream, ran at Finbar with curled fingers ready to claw at his face. She leapt into the air, giving her height enough to rake her nails down the big man's cheek. Finbar howled as she drew blood, then with a backward swipe of his bunched fist, Finbar swung back and sent a stinging blow into Saoirse's shoulder, knocking her flying away from him.

"Why, you cheeky little bitch," Finbar growled, rubbing his jaw with his fingers and then looking at the dark stain of blood on the fingertips. "I'll have you for that."

Alva turned to look over her shoulder and see that Aoife was safely to one side and hovering in the shadows, then she drew the pistol from her skirt pocket. She turned back to see Mulvenny backing away towards the carriage horse with the others struggling before him.

Even in her long skirts, Irene had dropped to all fours in the wet street, and the heavyset Séamus was attempting to grapple with her as she nimbly snaked her body around him. As she wove about, she laughed in derision at each of his clumsy attempts to grasp her, and Séamus was so enraged by the teasing that he did not see that Irene had slipped the knuckleduster over her fingers. It was a savage device, not only covering the knuckles in loops of brass, but each loop was embedded with a sharply pointed pyramid of metal. Irene was not one to hold back, and when she drove her fist into Séamus's jaw, it was with all the power her angry nature could muster.

The smack was harsh and sounded bright in the night. Séamus swung his head away in a slow loop, blood streaming from his broken lips and smashed teeth. He cowered, bent over and spitting blood into the street, but Irene had him now, and she came in low, delivering a merciless blow to the side of the head. That hit took the senses from Séamus and he went down fast, spreading flat out in the road.

Saoirse, meanwhile, was recovering herself from Finbar's blow, and she pushed Alva aside as she ran lightly forward to attack the man again. Irene and Séamus momentarily distracted Finbar's attention, but as Saoirse came at him, Mulvenny pushed out from the shadows around the cab and swung the curved blade.

In a streaming arc, like the rippling wave of an electric flash on a stormy night, the blade coursed through the air with a soft hum. It ripped across Saoirse as she was in mid-flight, her own volition adding to the already vicious blow from Mulvenny. So severe was the combined effort of speed and thrust that the head of Saoirse swung back, almost detached from her slight frame. She flipped in the air and her body tumbled to the ground with an unpleasant-sounding smack.

Without thought, Alva fired. Mulvenny was right there in front of her, his head to one side and attention turned on his victim. Her pistol, a loud bang in the deserted street, sent out a bloom of exploded gases, blasting the .45 caliber bullet straight into Mulvenny's face. The spinning lead entered his cheek, destroying his tongue and back teeth as it exited through the opposite side of his mouth. Mulvenny was thrown back against the carriage horse, which bucked nervously at the fall of his body and the loud noise of the gun.

In disbelieving awe, Alva stared down at the unmoving body of Saoirse, and then her gaze swung up as Irene also saw her friend and uttered a great and terrible cry, so awful that it sounded almost animal in its bitter cry full of raw grief. Finbar backed away at the sight of the almost decapitated Irish girl, but he did not move far before a vengeful Irene fell on him. She was bereft of reason now and assaulted the bigger man with all the fury and maddened rage of a berserker warrior. Blinded by vengeful bloodlust, a screeching Irene attacked Finbar and, try as he might to ward her off, the terrible knuckledusters did their work and smashed at the bonework of his face over and over again.

Behind them, Mulvenny was choking and gagging as blood ran from his torn face. His eyes were wild as he swung his head from side to side in an attempt to clear his breath. Mercilessly, Alva approached. She felt nothing now and raised the hot pistol to close in on Mulvenny. He crouched, raising the knife, but was already stunned and short of breath. Mulvenny begged with his eyes and raised his hands defensively, but Alva was without pity. She fired again at point-blank range, a cloud of smoke and fire bursting from her pistol. Twice and then again, she shot directly into the quivering body of Mulvenny, so close that his jacket caught fire and smoldered. He stood a moment, swaying and gasping for air as his gaze circled wildly, and then he crumpled, slipping sideways and rolling down to the street.

The cabbie tried to turn the horse away, but Alva stood and pointed her Colt pistol long armed at him.

"You will stand there," she roared. "Do not move, we have need of you. Take off and I'll kill you."

"Alright, alright, lady," said the driver nervously, already he was calculating the cost of his lost fare. "I ain't going nowhere. By Heavens! I never thought of this when I left the depot tonight."

Alva turned to Irene, who was standing over Saoirse, her eyes wide and staring and her whole body shivering.

"Come, come on," said Alva, putting her arm around Irene's quivering shoulders. "We must go, come on, girl, get yourself together."

"But—Saoirse—" whimpered Irene sadly, her thin body racked with a loss she did not yet fully understand.

"She's gone, Irene. Come now, we must get going."

"Look at her," rambled Irene, arms down by her side with the bloody knuckledusters still hanging from her fingers. "Oh, God!" she sobbed, placing one hand over her mouth. "Will you just look at her?"

Alva took stock of the men lying on the ground around Saoirse. Red-headed Séamus was not moving, Mulvenny was certainly dead, and Finbar was trying to crawl away, the blood on his skull from Irene's fevered blows blinding him.

It was then, surprisingly, that Aoife took the initiative. She grasped Irene by the arm and hustled her over to the cab, whispering to her gently as she pushed her inside.

"That's it, Irene, come along with you. So sorry for the loss. Saoirse was a brave girl. Think of her only with kindness, she gave her life for us. There is no greater gift, and I will pray for her."

Alva watched in amazement at Aoife's transformation for a moment and then rushed to gather their baggage and thrust it inside the cab. The three of them scrambled to squeeze inside.

"To the Grand Central and Harlem Railroad Depot, driver, quick as you can, we have to make the midnight special."

"Then you're too late," grumbled the driver. "It is ten past the hour already."

"Don't argue, just get us there."

"What about my fare? There's three of them lying stricken there that owes me and you three sitting inside, that's three dollars fifty right there."

"You'll have it," cried Alva. "And a dollar more if you're quick about it."

With only a grumbled muttering, the driver slapped up the horse and urged it on to a speedy jog. "I seen it all," he rumbled with a shaking head. "Not like tonight though, three little girls taking on brawny men. Never seen the like. Bless me, I don't know what this world is coming to when women no longer know their place."

THEY WERE LUCKY, a porter took their baggage at the station entrance and told them with a knowing smile, "You're indeed fortunate, ladies. The midnight train's been delayed by thirty minutes, seems the engineer forgot his bifocals and can't see the signals without them. He's off to his lodgings to get them and will be here directly."

Gratefully, the three climbed aboard and barely had they settled themselves in the carriage when a whistle sounded, steam hissed, and with a jerk and steady chug, the locomotive set off.

AMONGST THE BATTERED remnants of celebration inside The Leather Jug, O'Bannion fumed sullenly and studied the battered and bandaged heap of Finbar sitting slumped in a chair across from him, and then he turned to one of the men.

"Damon, now tell me, will you. Did not Mulvenny have kin back in Ireland?"

"He did, sir. Three brothers, I believe, and a fair number of cousins."

"I think they would like to know of their man's unfortunate end at the hands of four little girls. Four wee stripling chickadees not yet past their majority. Will they not feel a brazen insult like that against their family honor? Will it not be as painful as a red-hot branding iron? I'm sure they will, indeed they will. Dear Lord! Mulvenny of all people, can you believe it? Tell them I'll pay their passage if they've a mind to come over."

"I'll do it, Mr. O'Bannion."

"You will indeed, and whilst you're about it, find for me that fat one of them girls, it seems she is still in town according to Finbar there."

O'Bannion cast an eye over the unfortunate Finbar and wrinkled his nose. His eyes flicked across to Damon and with a crooked finger brought him down so he could whisper in his ear, "Finbar there, God bless him, is of little use to us now, he can see nothing past the end of his nose. I believe it is time he was allowed respite from these worldly woes, so take him down to the East River and see if the waters will soothe him, will you?"

CHAPTER SEVEN

EXHAUSTED AND SHAKEN by their flight, the early part of the journey was a haze for the three young women. They barely noticed the passing scenery and hardly saw the banks of Lake Erie as they rattled past and only began to recover when changing at Buffalo and moving onto the Michigan Southern R&R to travel on to Toledo and then Chicago. It was a long and arduous journey, and the names of towns they passed through meant nothing. Each railroad had a different title, and it was left to Alva to decipher the changeover and confer with the various conductors and ticket officials. The Chicago and Alton R&R took them down to St. Louis, where they climbed aboard the St. Louis Iron Mountain R&R and went on to a town called Marshall, where the railroad conductor assured them that they were finally over the border and into Texas.

The two-week journey had taken them across the state of New York, then to brush against Pennsylvania, Ohio, and Indiana, and through Illinois, Missouri, and

Arkansas until they were on the Texas and Pacific R&R riding into northern Texas. It was a map too large to encompass from their meager experience coming from a small island across the Atlantic, and after an initial awe at the many geographic and urban changes flying past their carriage window, they settled down enough to reconsider the recent past.

It was Irene who took it most hard. Her loss of Saoirse hit the normally hard-assed young woman with a poignancy that was difficult to determine. Aoife drew her close and comforted her whilst Alva saw to their more practical needs, their food in the dining cars and the sleeping quarters, the correct train to take, and stations of transfer.

In her mind, Alva retained the fanciful map that Ernest had drawn for her, and it took on an almost mystical quality of promise. It was to be a future where they could all prosper. Aoife would recover and shed the effects of her illness, Irene would grow strong again in a hardy rural environment, and she perhaps would find Ernest Fairweather Grant again and maybe some of the tenderness she had enjoyed in the city with him.

Alva hardly noticed the changes that had taken place in herself, she had been so busy handling their travel arrangements. But some things had altered for her, not least of all that her own natural determination and instinct for survival had made her a killer of men. Two of them had died by her hand, and she knew she should be feeling something like remorse for their passing, no matter that they had both been characters who meant her and her friends harm. So her pragmatic mind told her it had been necessary, and as such, it had given her Catholic upbringing barely a passing murmur of guilt. If she had not done as she did, the men would certainly have done the same to her.

"She is free." Alva heard Aoife telling Irene as the two sat side by side in the carriage as it bucked over the points. "Does not her name Saoirse in the English mean *freedom,* and that is what she is now. A free spirit, and she lives with you, Irene. She always will."

"I miss her," Irene croaked in a broken voice and hung her head in sadness. It was the first time Alva had ever seen her show some sign of emotion. "And spirits don't do it for me."

"Her memory is strong in you, is it not?"

"Of course."

"Then hold that close, keep it in your heart."

Irene turned away, unhappy with Aoife's hopeful resolution, sighing disconsolately, she stared out of the carriage window. She saw a lone wagon out there wending its slow way across a hot, dusty landscape of endless plain. A young boy was driving, and he stood up on the driving seat, took off his hat, and waved enthusiastically at the passing train. Irene half raised her hand to give an answering wave, but they were already past and the wagon was lost in the black smoke pouring out of the engine smokestack and staining the blue sky behind them.

"He never even saw me," Irene muttered to herself.

"LISTEN UP," said Alva. "We are nearly at our destination. The station is at a depot called Hole Springs, and that's where we're getting off."

"Thank the Blessed Virgin!" groaned Irene. "I believe

I am done with railroads, my bony arse is sore from sitting for so long."

"There will be a wee bit more," said Alva. "According to Ernest, we must take a stagecoach ride."

Irene cocked an eyebrow. "Ernest! Your lover boy, is it?"

Alva gave her an expressionless look. "He is the one who told me about this place."

"What's it called again?" asked Aoife.

"Avagar Rhodes."

"A strange name indeed."

"It is, I don't know how they came by it. Might be the name of a person, the one who started the town. They have a liking for that sort of thing here, I believe."

The train was slowing, clanging its bell, and giving off hoots from the steam whistle as it pulled into the station. At sight of the station signage, Irene raised her eyebrows. "Well, I'd really like to be meeting Mr. Hole Springs, if he's a regular around here then."

It was the first time Irene had made a humorous aside on the trip, no matter how cynical, and Alva was pleased to hear it.

THEIR WAIT WAS A LONG ONE, and they spent it on the lone platform with their luggage. Not much happened at Hole Springs, which was obvious as the place was near deserted and the ticket clerk closed his office as soon as the train had left and then took a buckboard ride to God knew where.

Alva called after him, "Where you going. This place shut down?"

"There ain't no train 'til tomorrow," he called back from the buckboard. "Station be open again then."

"What about the stagecoach? We're hoping to get to Avagar Rhodes by tonight."

"Avagar Rhodes?" the clerk said and shook his head doubtfully. "By nightfall?"

"Is the coach coming?"

The clerk looked at the horizon and then up at the sky as if gauging time and distance, or asking for heavenly guidance, neither was a sure thing. "Overland be along directly," he said decidedly.

Then he was gone, leaving a thick cloud of yellow dust hovering in his wake.

THE CLIMATE WAS WARM, and Aoife fretted against the heat by waving the end of her novitiate veil before her face to get some air. Irene slumped in a daze on the hardwood bench against the ticket office wall, and Alva walked impatiently up and down the boardwalk platform.

The scenery was bleak without a single tree or shrub and only a sea of dust and rock that stretched away to an infinite horizon. A lowering thunderstorm rumbled in the far distance and a steady wind blew from the south, keeping the storm at bay.

After three hours, it was Alva who first spotted their ride.

"Here it comes," she said, and both the others rotated their heads to see the Overland Stage with a six-horse team bowling over the dunes and heading their way. The great coach bounced and slewed to a dusty halt alongside the station.

The driver, a slender, older man with a grizzled chin and wide-brimmed hat pinned up at the front, drew on the reins and kicked the brake handle. "Hole Springs, people! If you got to relieve yourself, do it now out there in the desert, if you will." He wrapped his reins around the brake and climbed athletically down from the driving seat. His partner, the guard, a pie-faced man with pouting lips and narrowed eyes, stayed unmoving and only hoisted the stock of the shotgun up to rest on his thigh in a lordly fashion as if he were monarch of all he surveyed.

"Howdy, ladies," said the driver, tipping his hat with a gloved forefinger. "Name's Gilbert Penny, this here sorry-faced soul is my guard and partner, Ezekiel. Now, are you traveling with us today?"

"We are that," said Alva, stepping forward, waving the long chain of paper tickets. "Paid our way through to Avagar Rhodes."

"Very well, ma'am," said Penny, taking no notice of the tickets. "Load your possibles in the rear boot and find yourself a place inside. We'll be stopping for supper along the way as it's getting kinda late now."

"Does that mean we will not get to Avagar Rhodes before night?"

"No, no, dearie. Won't be making it until tomorrow afternoon with a couple of team changes along the way."

"So long? I thought it was nearer."

"Well, we gotta make it along the river up to the mountains, through the pass, and head on along the range until the end. A fair way, I'd say."

"Yes," said Alva doubtfully. "The Slick Grass River and The Stairway Mountains."

"Yeah, that's it. You been here before?"

"No, sir. I've just heard about it. Avagar Rhodes, is it a nice place?"

"*A nice place*?" he asked incredulously. "I never heard it called that."

"Come on, Gil!" called out the guard Ezekiel. "We're wasting daylight. Cut the jawing and let's move."

"Okay. Sure," said Penny, hustling them. "Come on, ladies, inside. We have to go."

They all eased their way into the coach to find two other passengers already inside. Both of them men, one tall with an indifferent look to his face and the other smaller and pot-bellied.

"Good day," said the smaller man, lifting the brim of his derby hat whilst his companion looked out of the window in a bored fashion and stretched his long legs out before him and crossed his feet at the ankles. He wore a dark drape jacket, a black fedora, and creased pants with shiny boots, in all a neat-looking man, but so tall that his feet reached under the seats opposite.

"Hello to you," said Alva as the three of them seated themselves opposite.

"Supposed to get nine of us in here," said the tubby fellow, easing his collar with a finger and twisting his head to ease his double chin. "But it's a squeeze, however many there are. I'm Mr. Jonas Rhett Baldwin, cattle buyer, pleased to meet you all."

Alva did the introductions, but the tall fellow paid no heed and said nothing until Irene nudged him. "And who are you, big fella?"

The tall man turned to look at her coolly. "I'm Gar Seleen, if you need to know."

"Hold tight!" called Gil Penny from the driving seat as he cracked up the team and sent the stagecoach rolling. The lurching ride began as they crossed over the railroad tracks and bounced down the gradient on leather springs. Penny whistled and hollered and the team picked up the pace as they hit level ground.

"You have business in Avagar Rhodes?" Alva asked Baldwin.

"Surely do, ma'am. Buying cattle for my company Armour and Co., hope to get eleven hundred head at least."

"That's a lot of cows, do you guide them yourself?"

"Well hardly, I just buy them and see they are on their way up to the railhead at Abilene."

"Must be hard work."

"I presume so." Baldwin smiled. "I don't do that myself, of course. They have drovers to do that kind of thing."

Seleen huffed a gentle laugh of derision and Irene looked at him with a cocked eye. "You don't approve?" she asked. It was apparent that, for whatever reason, she did not like Seleen, and her natural aggression was already showing.

"Ain't my call, ma'am," he said and then added pointedly. "I just mind my own affairs."

They jounced along, the coach swaying from side to side with the occasional lurch as they hit a dip in the road. The passengers were hard put to keep their seats with the violent passage, and the women shifted from side to side as they bounced along.

Dust ploughed up by the team filtered into the cabin, and soon Aoife had to hold her veil across the lower part of her face so she might breathe easier.

"Mighty awful, isn't it?" sympathized Baldwin with a frown. "Perhaps we might pull down the leather blinds and cut off the noxious supply."

He turned to Seleen, who was on the window side of the coach. "Would you mind, Mr. Seleen?"

Seleen looked at him without expression and did not move.

"For the ladies," Baldwin pressed. "The dust is irritating them."

"Sit still and keep quiet," growled Seleen. "They got a problem, then they can settle it."

"Well, dear me, aren't you the gent," said Irene.

"And ain't you the mouth," snapped back Seleen.

"More than you might know, mister," said Irene, in a voice cold as ice.

Alva, who knew of Irene's loss and the anger it raised in her, could see she was not prepared to hold back, yet she herself felt instinctively that Seleen was a very dangerous man. There was something to him that breathed its way into the air, and she could see no braggart before them but only a terrible caution that Seleen carried about him like a cloak.

"I'm sure it's fine," she said, blunting the mood of disagreement between the two. "We'll survive, will we not, Aoife?"

"Y—Yes," murmured Aoife, not wishing to be any cause of distress.

Suddenly, Irene leaned forward and snapped the binding knot that tied the rolled leather blind, letting it unravel and block the window. She stared at Seleen, daring him to come back at her, but he only shrugged and lowered his gaze.

They all bucked as the stagecoach continued on its way, and there was the sound of Penny and Ezekiel carrying on an indistinct conversation outside. The countryside rolled by unchanging until they could see through the remaining open windows the curve of a distant river, its gleam a snake that rippled and shone in the sunlight as they angled around it.

"Must be the Slick Grass River you spoke of," observed Aoife to Alva.

"It is indeed," agreed the amenable Mr. Baldwin. "Tell me, ma'am, are you a lady of the church? I mean, your garb implies to me you are a sister of sorts."

"I am a novitiate in the order," Aoife agreed coyly.

"Why, a fine thing," said Baldwin. "So little concern for religion amongst the young these days. Well, you may be assured that there is a great degree of faith amongst the Mexican people in the area to which we travel. I am not of the Catholic persuasion myself, nonetheless, I enjoy the fondly held principles amongst the more dusky brethren down here."

"And what principles are they?" asked a bland Seleen, suddenly jolted from his vacant daze. A simple question, but it seemed he could offer nothing without an acid taint to it.

"Why, their churches and chapels and attention to services on Sundays and holy days. I have enjoyed the many celebrations and parades, so colorful and joyous."

A half smile quirked at the corner of Seleen's mouth. "You ain't never seen them Mex bandits raiding through the border country then."

"Admittedly, I'm sorry to say, I suppose not all are lawful in the following of their religious guidance."

"Danged right there, cattle buyer. I'll be betting that half the cows you aim to buy have been rustled across the Rio Grande by those sleepy-eyed *hombres* you favor so."

"I sincerely hope not." A slightly appalled Baldwin frowned.

"You been here before, bucko?"

"No, sir, I do admit that this is my first visit this far south."

"Then you don't know squat about the Mex, that's for sure."

"You do, I suppose," cut in Irene with a sharp gleam in her eye.

"Sure I do, girl."

"How exactly might that be, riding a stool in the local saloon?" smirked Irene.

Seleen gave her a broad smile, peeling back his lips to show an even row of pearly whites. "I think I like you, sister. You got some brass, I'll give you that."

"Go stick your head in a bucket," snarled Irene, and Seleen barked a laugh in reply.

"Shit!" He chuckled. "What's your problem, woman? You sure do have it in for me."

His remark lit Irene's short fuse. "Strikes me you got more cheek than your skinny ass allows, mister. I seen goats with smaller horns and bigger balls than you got, you long streak of water."

"Hey!" barked Alva. "Cut it out, Irene. There's no need for that."

"Well, he irritates me."

Seleen was slapping his knee and roaring with laughter. "By God! Don't that beat all."

He rode back in his seat as they hit a rut, and his coat fell back to reveal a black leather holster and the glint of a silver-framed ivory-handled revolver. Silence followed the exhibition of the firearm, and a mollified Seleen, although still smiling, carefully dragged his coattail over to cover the gun.

"Expecting trouble?" asked Irene.

Seleen shook his head. "Not from you, little darlin'."

"Ben Jolly's way station ahead," Penny hollered down

from above. "Git yourselves some grits and a sleepover here."

The stagecoach slowed and drew to a halt over shingle-lined gravel that crunched under the wheels.

Everybody inside the coach breathed a sigh of relief and stretched themselves to shake off the physical tension incurred during the bumpy ride. Stiffly, they eased themselves out of the stagecoach to see a large adobe-walled building with a veranda and striped awning against the fading light from a setting sun. The sky was turning a sallow yellow, and falling dust churned from the stagecoach shone as a ball of orange light in its glow.

"You go ahead on inside, Ben Jolly will see to you," said Penny from the driving seat. "We got to get the coach over to the teamster."

BEN JOLLY LIVED up to his name, he was fat, red-cheeked, and with the general air of disposition that allowed nothing to faze him. He looked up at his visitors over the rim of a pair of wire-frame spectacles with the same amount of excitement as he might have greeted a war party of rampaging Cheyenne, that is to say, with complete indifference.

"There." He indicated the benches and table with a long ladle and a broad smile.

The metal pot he leaned over and stirred once the directorial advice was over was a large, good-smelling container of beef stew. Ben Jolly's apron was proof that he had been working on it in readiness for their arrival.

"Come on up then, ladies and gents. Get yo'self a

bowl and spoon," he called. "We got bread on the table and coffee on the brew. So set yo'selves and git stuck in."

Penny and Ezekiel arrived, slapping dust from their pants and coats.

"Howdy there, Gil, yo' boys ready for supper?" asked Jolly.

"You bet," said Penny, grabbing a bowl from the pile and letting Jolly serve him.

They all arranged themselves at the long table, with Seleen moving quickly to the shadowed far end and taking a place with a clear view of the doorway. The others ranged themselves along each side, and the basket of bread chunks passed rapidly along the length, with each helping themselves. Everyone was hungry, which proved to be so as bowls were scraped clean within minutes. A smiling Jolly strolled the table, doling out seconds to all who wanted them. Whether he was pleased at the success of his stew or just content to feed them is hard to say, but he certainly had an empty pot at the end of it.

Coffee followed, and Baldwin lit himself a cigar whilst Gil Penny took out a pipe and began to stuff tobacco in the bowl.

"You got anything a mite stronger, mister?" called Seleen.

Jolly took a quick sidelong glance at Penny, who obliged with a sharp and quick nod of agreement.

"I reckon we can find a glass," said Jolly. "'Course that ain't paid for by the company, you got to buy that yo'self."

"What you asking his permission for?" said Seleen. "He your mother or something?"

Heads rotated along the length of the table at the challenging remark, but Jolly handled it like he handled the many customers that traveled through the way station. "Yo' want some liquor or not?"

"Put it here," said Seleen, jabbing the tabletop with a forefinger.

"See, mister," said Penny, leaning forward and pointedly staring down the table at Seleen, who was seated opposite at the far end. "We get all kinds on this line. We get big mouths with high ideas of themselves, we get tight-mouthed, reserved folk without no soul or hope, and we get mean-spirited punks who would shoot down a body without no consideration. So, Mr. Jolly, who ain't been traveling with y'all, has no recourse but to refer to me before he cracks open a bottle of drink, as that tends to make the thankless even more aggressive. And, no, I ain't his nor nobody else's mother, that answer your question, sir?"

Seleen, who was covered in a veil of cold calm, pushed his chair back from the table and kept his eyes fixed on Penny. "You'd best just keep your attention on driving that four-wheeled box, whipman."

At his words, Penny's guard, Ezekiel, who was seated next to him, lifted his shotgun from the floor and, without any overt display of aggression, kept it placed across his lap.

In that moment, Alva could see that Gil Penny and his partner were not afraid of Seleen and recognized that she had entered a whole different world in this part of the country. Here, men lived on their individual pride and were prepared not to suffer any affront without a response, no matter what its source.

It was Jolly who broke the moment as he bustled around with a bottle and glass in his hand and, without a word, stationed them in front of Seleen.

"We got bunks out back if you ladies would like to

retire," Jolly said on his way back to the kitchen. "There's facilities over by the corral if you have need."

"Obliged to you," a cynical Seleen called after him a little too loudly. "Mighty grateful."

Alva got to her feet and the other two girls followed suit. "Thank you, Mr. Jolly," said Alva. "A fine meal indeed."

"Despite the company," muttered Irene.

"Night, ladies," called Penny. "We start sharp tomorrow, right after breakfast."

CHAPTER EIGHT

ALVA FOUND it hard to suffer the heat, these were not temperatures her pale skin was used to. She went to bed hot and woke up with early sunlight streaming between the planks in the shed where they had struggled to sleep fully clothed on hard bunks. It was stiflingly hot and close with the dense air in the room, and along with sunbeams came the hum of intrusive flies.

Alva awoke groggy after her restless night and she slid from her bed and saw that the others were still sleeping. She made her way to the dining room and the open door to the yard outside and some kind of fresh air. Morning daylight streamed through the open doorway with a bright golden glow, and it momentarily dazzled her.

There was the scrape of a chair and she looked around. At the end of the dining table, still seated in the far shadows, sat Gar Seleen as dark as the gloom around him. Alva could see his eyes glinting as his gaze followed her across the room, but she ignored him and walked through and out of the door.

Early sun beat on her, but at least it was free of the stale pressure of the air inside. She made her way across to the pump-trough and worked the lever until water flowed and she could cup a handful to splash on her overheated brow.

She did not hear the man. Suddenly, he was behind her and his arm was around her throat. Alva gagged as he jerked her backwards and she saw the shining blade of a machete swing around before her eyes.

"*Silencio, senora,*" he breathed in her ear, his breath sour and strong with the scent of chili peppers.

She could feel his unshaven chin and smell him as he held her close, a rank odor arose from the man that was an unpleasant mix of unwashed sweat, leather, and alkali dust.

The man hissed, and from the corner of her eye, Alva saw three more men move towards the station door. Each wore floppy sombreros and worn clothes colored brown by dirt and dust. They carried rifles and wore gun belts with holstered pistols and long knives in silver Concho scabbards. Fanning out, they approached the door cautiously with a silent tread.

Seleen stepped out into the daylight and all the Mexicans froze.

"Hey, howdy boys," said a casual Seleen, his coattails were brushed back and thumbs hooked in his belt. "You're up early."

"Do not move, *senor,*" said the man at Alva's back. "You will please stay quite still."

"We're about to have breakfast here," said Seleen as if nothing unusual was happening. "You're welcome to join us."

Seleen's face was expressionless, but a quick glance

locked on Alva and the man at her throat. "You okay, Miss Alva?" he asked her quietly.

"I've been better," she replied.

"Just you hold still, ma'am. I'm sure these fellows are real friendly, ain't that right, boys?"

"Drop the weapon, mister," ordered her capturer.

Then she saw a thing that dazzled her memory for many a day afterwards. Seleen held his hands before him as if ready to oblige, but then he dipped into a rapid crouch and swept back the tail of his coat to clear the holster. His gun hand moved with unbelievable speed, and before she could take in the blurred movement, the shining pistol was in his hand. A tattoo of shots ripped the quiet morning air, three, four of them. Wide-eyed Alva watched as Seleen's gun spat fire and smoke, and the three men before him were plucked away as if drawn by invisible wires.

One spun around, his arm flung out, and his rifle flying through the air as he stumbled away, almost falling over his own feet. Another gagged and grasped at his throat with both hands as he dropped to his knees, and the third curled over backwards in an impossible position before he hit the ground in a cloud of dust.

Seleen turned his gun on the man holding Alva. "Best let her go, *cabrón*. Or you're dead in an instant."

"We shall see," cried the man at her back, and he swung up the machete above Alva's head.

Seleen's gun barked and he fanned the hammer, sending his last bullets at the raised hand holding the blade. The Mexican screamed as his wrist was split open and he dropped the machete, whilst shredded pieces of bloody flesh fell on Alva's shoulders. Clutching his shattered forearm, the Mexican released Alva and stumbled away backwards sobbing in pain as he went.

Two of his companions were down and in all probability dead, the other survivor painfully wounded in the arm, the same as he was, and both of them were cursing loudly in Spanish. Seleen did not stop. His Colt was empty, and he slipped it into his holster before bending down and picking up one of the dropped rifles.

Moving towards the two Mexicans, he levered a shell under the hammer of the Winchester. Alva watched in awe, and she saw the cold rigidity in Seleen's face as he walked forward and fired from the hip. Both Mexicans catapulted from their feet and dropped to the ground as Seleen blasted them, cranking the lever repeatedly and firing shot after shot from the Winchester.

Just then, others ran out from the station door, Penny and his partner in the forefront. "What the hell—" he gasped, standing with his six-shooter in his hand.

Seleen stood over the fallen bodies, and when quite sure they were dead, he tossed the Winchester aside.

Seeing her standing quite still and shaking, Penny called across, "You all right, Miss Alva?"

"I am," she said, hardly noticing the quiver in her voice.

"Who are these fellows?"

"I don't know, but I believe they meant us harm. Mr. Seleen was—well, he was proper amazing."

Irene and Aoife ran out and over to Alva. "Did they try to hurt you?" asked Irene. "Look at you, you have blood all over your shoulder."

"It's not mine, one of them threatened me, and Mr. Seleen shot him and saved me. He was so fast, I cannot believe it."

"Who are you, mister?" asked Penny. "You know these Mexicans? They some kind of renegades?"

A wide-eyed Baldwin tottered out in his shirttails

and stood open-mouthed and staring at the crumpled bodies where they lay blood-soaked and ragged under a sifting cloud of thin dust.

"See there," said Seleen, fixing his eye on Baldwin. "There's some of your God-loving Mexican *banditos,* don't look so holy now, do they?"

He turned to Penny and flipped over the lapel of his drape jacket to reveal a shield badge with a star stamped in the center.

"A US Marshal!" breathed Penny.

"You carrying anything valuable?" asked Seleen.

"Not much unless you count five hundred in gold for the bank in Avagar Rhodes."

"Then that's what they were after."

"I guess," agreed Penny, scratching his head. "Then I'm obliged to you, Marshal. Must be you saved us a real mess. Lord knows what they would have done to these ladies."

Seleen looked across at them, a slow smile spreading on his face. "Oh, I don't know if I'd want to tangle with any of them, 'specially not that skinny one with red hair."

Even Irene smiled at that.

Breakfast was a lighter affair, everybody seemed more relaxed now that Seleen had proved himself to be a competent agent of the law and their savior.

"If I may, what are you doing in this part of the country, Marshal?" Penny asked around a mouthful of bread and beans.

"Picking up a prisoner in Avagar Rhodes."

"He coming in from Yuma prison?"

"That's so, due for trial up in Alamoso."

"Is he a bad one?" asked the curious Baldwin, somewhat careful in his speech with Seleen now he had seen what the man was capable of.

"Bad enough," came the curt response.

"Do you know any of the Texas Rangers, Mr. Seleen?" asked Alva.

"Some," answered Seleen. "I served with them a while."

"Then perhaps you know, Mr. Ernest Fairweather Grant, a Ranger I befriended whilst he was visiting New York. He is from Avagar Rhodes, and I hope we shall meet up again soon."

Seleen gave her a crooked grin. "Ernie Grant! Sure, I know him, we served together in Company C under Captain Wheatsheaf. *Ole Jug Ears* been up in the big city, has he? What's he been up to now? Must have been something wild to drive him so far afield."

"I really couldn't say," said Alva, a little taken aback by Seleen's response. "He was a perfect gentleman at our meeting."

"You don't say," said Seleen, barely suppressing a knowing chuckle. "That ain't the Ernie Grant I recall."

"What do you mean?"

"He was a damnable horny goat in the old days. A regular charmer, even if he did look like a rubber fence post with handles."

"I really don't know about that," mumbled an embarrassed Alva.

Irene was looking at Alva over her breakfast dish with an expression of dismay and surprise.

"I really don't." Alva hurried to explain to her. "He was a gentleman to be sure."

"Sounds like a fellow I should meet," said Irene with a tight smile.

Aoife chided her, "Now Irene, do not be so bold in your chatter. You can see you offend our friend."

Penny pushed away his empty dish and got to his feet. "Well, folks, we got to be making time. We're on a schedule here, so if you'll take your places, we'll be on our way." He turned to Jolly. "Your boy got the team rigged, Mr. Jolly?"

"Ready and waiting, Mr. Penny."

"Then, obliged for your breakfast, and we'll be heading out."

"May I ask?" a tentative Aoife interrupted. "What about those poor souls outside? Shouldn't we be saying some final words over them?"

"You mean them dead Mexicans, ma'am?" asked Penny.

"Yes, if you wish, I can lead the prayers."

Penny paused then, with all diplomacy. "Well, that's mighty thoughtful of you, sister, you being a church lady and all, but I reckon Mr. Jolly and his boy will do all the praying that's necessary. Ain't that right, Jolly?"

Jolly smiled beneficently. "We'll get them under with all propriety, don't you doubt it."

With a disdainful look, Seleen pushed back his chair and, shaking his head, made for the door.

"*That man*!" said Alva as the Marshal left. She was still smarting after his description of Ernest and decrying him in such a manner. "That's not the manners I approve of."

"Oh, get off, Alva," said Irene, baring her teeth in a faintly evil grin. "Maybe you don't have yourself such a perfect beau after all."

"And now you approve of Marshal Seleen, do you?"

"I do think he has a certain something."

"Yes, the ability to slaughter four men in double quick time."

"May God forgive him," breathed Aoife in a hushed and saintly tone.

"Come on," said Irene, elbowing Alva and still smiling. "Let's go, princess, your fairy carriage awaits you."

THE JOUNCING RIDE started off with a hoarse hollered shout from Penny, and the bucking stagecoach soon shook them up enough to remind the girls of the previous day's assault on their aching bodies. Seleen settled in his corner as expressionless as usual, whilst the tubby Baldwin puffed and wheezed as he struggled to adjust his waistcoat and set his Derby firmly in position.

Aoife sat patiently with her hands gathered on her lap, with Irene squeezed between her and Alva, and all three abstractedly watched the countryside rush past.

Baldwin, who was sitting facing the front of the cab, leaned forward. "I see the mountains up ahead, ladies. Mr. Penny advises that we are approaching a strip of land that is Indian country. I do hope that we do not encounter any of the savages."

"Indians, huh!" exclaimed Irene, stretching her neck to see out of the window.

"There, you see," said Alva, pointing. "They really are like steps, The Staircase Mountains. We seem to be travelling towards a gap there at the base of one of the steps."

"That will be a pass," advised Baldwin. "Our way of getting through the mountains."

"That's Ambush Pass," grunted Seleen.

"You know the place?" asked Alva.

"Sure do," Seleen said with a sniff. "Lot of people died in that pass."

"You don't say," breathed Baldwin.

"Didn't I just say it?" Seleen frowned.

"Yes, yes," Baldwin said hastily, obviously not wishing to upset the often irritable Marshal. "I just meant you must have experience of the place."

"Certain do. Back in '64 was a whole wagon train of sodbusters massacred in there."

"Was it Indians?"

"It was—me and the rest of the Ranger company found them. Weren't pretty."

"Really!" breathed Baldwin.

"Ain't I just telling you so?" growled Seleen.

"No, I meant—oh, please, go on. I do like to hear these tales of the olden frontier days."

"Well, it ain't that long ago. Anyway, it was maybe Comanche done the deed. Cut up the bodies real fine, they like to do that so the dead 'uns won't be intact enough to follow them into the afterlife. Rest of them they toyed with, the usual burning and thorn sticking, cutting off body parts, that kind of thing. Women was assaulted before their throats cut, some kids taken, but we never did find them."

"Good Lord!" breathed Baldwin. "It sounds awful."

Suddenly, Aoife spoke up. "It does seem there is no religion here."

Seleen huffed a laugh. "General Sheridan said it a whole lot better, if he owned Hell and Texas, he'd rent out Texas and live in Hell."

Irene barked a laugh and Alva snorted in amusement, but Aoife was serious. "It seems that maybe that is why I am sent here."

"Little girl," said Seleen. "A whole lot of other

missionaries have tried that already. Most of them ended up with their head stuck on a pole."

"No matter," said Aoife, her eyes alive with a sudden light of excitement. "I see a way."

Irene looked across and raised her eyebrows. "You know you don't have to take this Holy Orders thing too much to heart, Aoife. Not any more now, we're away from the convent folk."

Aoife turned on her. *"But I do,"* she stressed. "I see it as a purpose I never saw before, maybe that is why I am brought to this dry foreign land so far from green Erin."

"You'll do what you think best," advised Alva sagely.

"Here we go!" interrupted Baldwin. "We are entering the pass."

SURE ENOUGH, on each side of them were sheer walls of rock rising up so high that they blotted out the sun and sections of sky. The stagecoach was dwarfed by the huge vertical walls of aged stone fashioned by mighty movements of the earth eons before and then sanded and weathered by time. Suddenly, the sound of the coach and team was echoed back by the brittle slabs, each rattling hoof beat was repeated and echoed over and over so that they traveled through a clattering sound that was carried backwards and forwards across the pass in a chaos of noise.

"Hi-yo!" called out Penny, and he received back the call a thousand times. "Hi—i—i—yo—o—o." Soon, both he and Ezekiel were having fun laughing and shouting at the walls of stone as they steered the stagecoach on through.

"Damn fools," snorted Seleen.

Eventually, the pass widened out and they rode along a raised and level shelf of rock with a drop to one side that sloped to the bed of a dusty hollow. It was a gloomy place marked by shadow and the ghostly remains of stone and wooden markers awkwardly leaning and angled by age.

"Is that where it happened?" asked Irene.

"That's it," said Seleen. "Fifty-four dead down there, them Indians sure made it a killing field."

"Certainly makes one shudder," whispered Baldwin. "Those poor souls."

"Amen," added Aoife. "I shall say a rosary in memento."

"The whole place," Alva observed. 'Is like a great big tomb."

Passing out of the echoing valley, the pass widened out and the walls around them began to break into jagged heaps of stone like giant fingers. All was quiet in the stagecoach as they peered out at the passing majesty of the huge natural display.

"Soon be at Jude Station," Penny called down. "Won't stay long, fifteen minutes only, time enough to change the team."

Hardly had they heard the words when the stagecoach began to slow and they heard Penny calling to the team to stop.

"Hold on, folks," Penny called again, this time with an edge to his voice. "We got a couple of Indians ahead."

"Oh, heavens!" wailed Baldwin. "Are we about to be massacred?"

All the passengers leaned over and peered out the windows.

Two Indians on horseback stood across their path, blocking the route. They sat impassive and still, both dressed in white shirts and pants stuffed into knee-high moccasin boots. Their long black hair under wide headbands was ruffled by the slight breeze and blew in threads about their heads.

Penny was climbing down from the driving seat and they heard the click of Ezekiel's shotgun as he cocked the hammers. Inside, Seleen drew out his silver Colt and rolled the barrel along his thigh, checking the load.

"Are we about to fight?" asked Irene.

"Looks like they want to parley," said Seleen, getting up from his seat and levering open the stagecoach door.

"Best stay inside," advised Ezekiel from above. "Don't know how many of them."

Seleen ignored him and stepped down into the dust of the pass and stood beside the stagecoach with the door left open and the pistol held by his side.

Penny had walked forward and raised a hand in greeting before speaking with the Indians.

"He talk the lingo?" asked Seleen.

"If they're Apache, he can," Ezekiel answered.

"What the devil do the blasted feckers want?" asked Irene.

After a few words pastpassed between Penny and the Indians, he turned and walked slowly back to the stagecoach.

"What is it?" asked Seleen.

"It's you they want," answered a grinning Penny. "Seems you done them a great favor."

"The hell you say," grunted Seleen.

"Them Mexicans you put down, appears they worked some evil deed afore they came on to us. Rode in and killed a family of Apache, mother, father, and two kids, shot and scalped them. These here are their kin, so they're obliged to you. They got something for you."

Seleen tsked a laugh. "And what might that be?"

"Go on up there and collect, Marshal. Best you do as we don't want to upset these boys."

"They don't owe me nothing."

"They think they do, now get along. Won't take but a minute, then we'll be on our way."

"You sure this ain't some ruse. We ain't going to get mown down here, are we?"

"Just walk proud, Marshal. They don't mean you no harm. Honest, they is real grateful to you."

"If you're bullshitting me, Penny—"

"Get it done," said Penny, climbing up into the driving seat.

Slowly, Seleen turned away, slid the revolver back in his holster, and walked towards the Indians.

"This'll be fun," those inside heard Ezekiel mutter to Penny.

"He won't know what to do," agreed Penny.

Alva leaned out of the window. "What is it, Mr. Penny. What do they have to gift him?"

Penny leaned over and said quietly, "They got a whole danged mule deer to give him, hunted it themselves special."

"Oh!" said Alva. "A deer, what will he do with that?"

"Suppose he'll eat it," said Irene.

"Probably raw," sniggered Baldwin quietly.

Ahead of the stagecoach, Seleen was standing before the Indians, one of whom slid the carcass from his saddle and dropped it to the ground, shouting something to the Marshal as he did so. Then both Indians turned their horses and rode off, leaving the perplexed Marshal staring down at the dead animal.

Seleen turned to the stagecoach and raised both hands in query.

"Come on," a chuckling Penny said to Ezekiel. "Best we get up there and load that beast on top. For sure, The Avagar Eating House will have deer steaks on the menu tonight."

WITH THE BODY of the dead deer tied on top and covered by an oilskin against the dust and flies, they rode on into Jude Station. As promised, the station manager had the team ready, and the speedy changeover was completed within fifteen minutes and they were on their way again.

Baldwin was mopping his brow and complaining, "I don't think I can wear much more of this. We are hardly at our destination and we have already been confronted by savages and in bloody battle with road agents. I dread to think what awaits us at Avagar Rhodes."

"I don't think you were quite the one involved in the confrontation, Mr. Baldwin," said Alva. "That would be Mr. Penny and Mr. Seleen."

"I know, I know, dear lady, and bless them both for their bold courage, but still I feel as if I have been at the center of the whole process myself. It is most exhausting."

"Have no fear, Mr. Baldwin," said Alva. "Once we're to where we're going, I'm sure there will be a touch of civilization."

"I surely hope so, Miss Alva, I really do."

THE MOUNTAIN RANGE was now on their right-hand side as they traveled south, and the weaving pathway led between and around fallen boulders that lay strewn across their path like the cast-offs from some giant hand. All the passengers were tired with aching bodies after having been tossed about by the rough stagecoach ride. Tempers were shortening, and Alva knew she would be glad when the journey was finally over. Only the drivers and Seleen seemed to manage the same level of indifference to their travel.

"Tell me, Mr. Seleen," asked Baldwin. "Will your prisoner be awaiting you at Avagar Rhodes?"

Seleen shrugged. "Maybe, maybe not."

"So you may well have some free time."

Seleen looked at him curiously. "Why you asking?"

"I've a thought that it might be I will need an able hand when I am dealing with the cattle folk. I shall be carrying some cash, and it might be wise to have protection. The company will be quite willing to pay for your time, I'm sure."

Seleen rubbed his jaw and, after a few moments of thought, nodded affirmation. "That's a fair thought. If my man is still on his way up from Yuma, it could be I'll have nothing but time on my hands."

"Then you'll do it?"

"It's possible if I'm free."

"Very well, twenty dollars a week, is that agreeable?" Baldwin smiled, holding out his hand. "Let us shake on it."

"Got yourself a bodyguard, mister," said Seleen, taking the hand.

A gratified Baldwin turned to the Irish girls. "And where will you fair ladies be going when we arrive?"

"The hotel, I guess," said Alva.

"So shall we all, no doubt."

Irene leaned into the conversation with a cheeky tilt

of the eye. "I do believe Mr. Seleen here has already laid on supper for us all."

Seleen huffed a soft laugh. "A dead deer for four Mexicans, not a bad deal, I'd say."

They descended into a sloping plain and great areas of forest became visible with a cooler taste of air away from the dusty heat they had become used to.

"Be at Avagar Rhodes within the hour," called Penny, and an air of anticipation rather than irritation overtook the passengers.

Alva looked at her two companions to see if they fared the same. Irene sat back, arms folded across her flat chest with a grim expression and half-lidded eyes. Aoife held herself sitting upright with hands folded neatly in her lap, with the only movement being the fingers as they played the beads of her rosary and she prayed in silence. Alva wondered how Niamh was faring alone in New York without their company and hoped she was doing well.

"There it is," said Baldwin, lifting his head as he spotted the town ahead.

Avagar Rhodes sprawled along the slopes of a long hillside, with its lower reaches surrounded by the greenery of trees and the still waters of a broad lake visible between the pines. Above the town, the last of The Stairway Mountain Range claimed some majesty as they hovered over the skyline in a distant mauve haze. The houses that ranged over the hillside seemed to present themselves in no particular arrangement but sprawled randomly with only a central roadway running along the spine of the slope. Wooden structures mostly, some of them neat and maintained, with others roughly made with yards full of detritus. Towards the lake end of the town stood a few Indian tipis that looked as if they were just outside the town boundaries.

As they neared the outskirts, the sound of chopping wood came to them, and the roads were occupied by great haulage wagons loaded with long pine logs. Parties of men in wagons and on foot moved along the tracks heading towards the forest, many of them with double-headed axes over their shoulders. The industrial noise of a steam whistle and clank of hefty chains came to them along with the smell of hot oil and smoky fires. Above it all came the sound of a chapel bell ringing, and Aoife perked up at the sound, looking around for the spire, but she could see no sign of a cross set high.

As they neared, large pine log corrals became visible. They were empty now, but it was obvious that, come the time, they would be filled with cattle, and it was here that Baldwin would be occupied with some trade.

The stagecoach rumbled onto a hard-packed road, and Penny slowed as they picked their way through the busy Main Street. Riders on saddle horses and buggies passed them along with freight and supply wagons. The boardwalks were busy with noisy pedestrians walking about their business, and stores with plenty of signage marked the road as being the main area of trade.

Penny pulled up the stagecoach outside The Columbine Hotel and shouted out, "This is it, people. Get you down and get your baggage."

Baldwin bustled out first, suddenly businesslike and a figure of keen activity. Seleen stepped down and Penny caught his attention as he made to move off. "Here, Marshal, you aim to take your prize with you?"

Seleen looked up at him. "I'm heading along to the sheriff's office, you can do what you like with that damned deer."

"Then you want me to give it to the restaurant?"

"Sure," answered Seleen before turning away abruptly and walking off quickly to be lost in the crowded walkway.

Alva and the two girls climbed down and stared about curiously. The wide porch of the white painted hotel was before them, surrounded by a delicate frame railing, and inside the open veranda were chairs and tables set aside for clients, where a few men sat reading newspapers and puffing on cigars. Louvre shutters open to show the interior allowed a view of the lobby with banquette seating and tall plants in great pots with tasseled drapes tied off to hang beside the windows. The inviting double doors stood wide open with pretty sand-blasted glass panels sporting intricate designs, and the general impression was that the hotel was a clean and acceptable place of residence.

Ezekiel was handing their few cases out from the baggage boot. "You want these inside the hotel?" he asked.

"If you will, that would be most kind," said Alva, stepping up onto the boardwalk and standing a moment looking into the hotel lobby. She turned and saw Penny balanced on his seat and tying off his reins with the long whip in one hand. "Thank you for your time, Mr. Penny," she called.

He turned, surprised by the show of gratitude. "My pleasure, ma'am. You ladies have a pleasant stay."

"May the road rise up to meet you and the wind be always at your back," called Irene with a traditional parting wish.

"The same for you." Penny grinned.

BALDWIN WAS AHEAD of them at the lobby and busily signing his name in the register.

"There, it's done," he said, swinging back the register and turning to the three girls. "A pleasant time, ladies." Then, doffing his derby, he hurried off to find his room.

"Ladies, how may I help?" said the clerk.

"I wonder," said Aoife gently. "I heard a chapel bell, is there a church nearby?"

The clerk was a stoop-backed fellow in a striped shirt and tie with a white celluloid collar. He wore steel-rimmed spectacles that he kept long down a beak of a nose, and he stared at her over the top of them. "You are a lady of the church I see. Well, there is a chapel and a house run by some nuns. I am afraid you should know it is not in the best part of town and run by Mexican women."

"Where is that?" asked Aoife.

"Over yonder." The clerk waved vaguely. "Not many streets away, I don't know your particular creed, but you should know these are Roman Catholic people."

"That's fine," said Aoife. "Thank you."

"You have rooms for us?" asked Alva.

"Will the three of you be sharing?" he asked.

"Is that possible?"

"We have a suite available that would suit, I believe."

"Then we'll take it."

"Very well, I should say, ladies, that we run a respectable establishment here and that no gentlemen are to be invited up to the rooms. Dinner is served here in our dining room, or there are other restaurants in the town if you so wish. I will have your baggage carried up to your room for you if you will just sign in, please."

Alva took the pen and asked, "Tell me, do you know of a Mr. Ernest Fairweather Grant from hereabouts?"

The clerk looked skywards a moment, the light shining from the circles of his spectacles. "I do indeed. Ernie Grant. He has a ranch outside of town. You know the gentleman?"

"I do, yes."

"I see," he said with an overlong and enigmatic pause. Then he quickly turned and collected their room key. "Have a pleasant stay at The Columbine. If you need anything, my name is Mr. Grenville. Please call on me."

Their travels had been long and arduous, and once in their room, the three exhausted girls washed ofoff the heat and trail dust of days and were soon in their comfortable beds and asleep. It was not until the following day that they could at last explore Avagar Rhodes and all that it had to offer.

CHAPTER NINE

Aoife was intent on finding the local chapel, and the next morning, she set out with determination, unconcerned whether the others were with her or not. Without a look behind, she ambled off, still clothed in her novitiate habit, and soon vanished into the crowded street.

Irene watched her go and sat outside the hotel under the porch-covered veranda with a cup of coffee before her and idly viewing the throng in Main Street with no particular purpose.

Alva, though, had other thoughts in mind, possibly to visit her friend Ernest Grant, but first she intended to corner the hotel clerk and question him further about his rather ambiguous earlier response.

He sat behind his desk, engrossed in a ledger.

"Mr. Grenville, I would question you if you don't mind?"

He looked up from his account book and peered at her over his spectacles. "Ma'am?"

"Yesterday, when I asked of Mr. Ernest Grant, I noted a certain reluctance to talk of him. May I ask why?"

"Well, Miss—um"—he reminded himself of her name in the register—"Miss Alva, it is of course not really my affair."

"I dare say, sir, but you have posed me with a problem by your reticence."

"How so, may I ask?"

"I had thought Mr. Grant a dear friend, although we are not that well acquainted, but you seem to know a great deal more of him than I do."

Grenville drew a deep breath. "Might I say that Ernie has a certain reputation around here."

"A reputation for what exactly?"

Grenville held a momentary look of surprise on his face, and his voice dropped to a whisper, "Why, of murder, Miss Alva."

"*Murder*!"

"Indeed, Ernie is of an independent frame of mind concerning his ranch, and any approach is deemed an invasion. I certainly would not recommend you visiting without company, Miss Alva."

"But how is this concerned with any act of murder?"

Grenville sighed again and peered skywards as he gathered his thoughts. "There was a woman—"

"A woman, he has a wife?"

"*Had*—being the operative word here. And three little ones."

Alva's jaw dropped in amazement. "Are you saying he was married with three children?"

Grenville, who had now taken on the guise of a secretive gossip, this being an obvious aspect of his personality. "Why, yes. It is said, now pray don't quote me on this,

Miss Alva, but they say that she had an affair with a beau."

"A lover, you say?"

"The same, and it was he that Ernie strung up over the gateway to his ranch."

"Strung up—as in *hung*?"

Grenville circled his neck with one hand and twitched his head in a playact of lynching.

"Oh, my God!" gasped Alva.

"You will know he is a Ranger, of course?"

Alva nodded affirmation.

"Amongst other things," Grenville went on. "There was talk of doubtfully acquired cattle and various other acts of a suspicious nature. Not unusual, I hasten to add, in today's behavior amongst the Rangers who are quite often called upon to cross the lines of legality in pursuance of their duty. We are almighty glad of it sometimes, I must say. Or we would be overrun by renegades and bandits from across the border, but nonetheless, you will understand that their behavior is of necessity often questionable."

"One does what one must to get things done sometimes."

"Exactly."

"Still, murder is rather extreme."

Grenville huffed a soft laugh. "Not down here, miss, this is Texas, and I fear that life here is a lot cheaper than in the Yankee cities up north."

Remembering her own recent experiences in New York with Ryan O'Bannion and the others, Alva was doubtful of that, but she said nothing.

"Is it possible to hire a carriage here?" she asked.

"Indeed, the Crozier Corral just down the road a-piece will have buggies for hire."

"Thank you, Mr. Grenville."

"I am here to serve." He gave her a tight smile in a rather obsequious manner before returning to his ledger and the accounts.

Alva took her leave and passed Irene, who was dreamily watching the parade outside. "It seems," she said. "That my Mr. Grant is something of an enigma."

"Do tell," said Irene, demonstrating her lack of interest with a yawn.

"I'll leave you to it then."

"I believe so," breathed Irene.

"I'm off to get a horse and carriage, do you want to accompany me?"

"Ach! You're a gobdaw about this wee fella, Alva." Meaning she was a gullible soul when it came to Ernest Grant. "It will be a waste of your time."

Alva twisted her lip in irritation and strode off to find the Crozier Corral.

As sheAlva moved away, Irene was surprised to see GarsonGar Seleen approaching along the crowded boardwalk.

"Good day to you, Mr. Seleen."

"And to you," he said, stepping up onto the veranda. "I'm here to see that Baldwin fellow."

"Take a pew, will you?" said Irene, offering him a chair. "I've not seen him yet awhile."

Seleen drew up the chair and seated himself heavily with a defeated puff of air.

"What bothers you, Marshal?" asked Irene. "You look a mite out of salts."

"Ach!" he spat in disgust. "The fool sheriff from Yuma has lost my prisoner."

"You don't say." Irene smiled, for some reason, it amused her to see Seleen in a grumpy mood, even though it was a common enough condition with the man. "What happened?"

Seleen looked at her for a steely minute, then decided to elaborate, "He brought the man from Yuma prison on a mule, a mule for God's sake. The lawman wouldn't pay out to hire a horse, so the prisoner, a knucklehead called Lyle Jakes, kept falling off."

"How so?"

"The sheriff had him chained, hand and foot, that's no way to ride a mule. Anyway, the fool had to unchain his leg irons from under the mule, and that did it. Jakes, who is a mean enough customer, beat him about the head with his manacles, knocked him down, stole his weapon, and then his horse, and is now in the wind."

"And you must catch him?"

"Indeed, I must, so I'm here to tell Baldwin the facts."

"You'll not be riding guard for him then?"

Seleen shook his head. "No, I won't."

Over his shoulder and across the road, Irene noticed a neatly dressed, fair-headed, and slender young woman in a print dress outside a dry goods store. She was attempting to move a heavy roll of baling wire and haul it into the back of a high-sided buckboard. A slight creature, willowy and not sufficiently strong enough for the task, and despite that, four men stood and watched the young woman and ignored her struggles.

"Will you excuse me," said Irene, getting up from her seat.

"Yes indeed," said Seleen, embroiled in his own worries and ignoring Irene as she hurried out into the road. Ducking around passing riders and narrowly missing the wagons rolling by, Irene made it over to the other side.

Turning on the four men watching, who all wore the rough clothes of lumberjacking men, she snapped, "What's the matter with you gobshites, will you no help this lady?"

"Mind your business, woman," growled one of the men.

"And watch your tongue," said another. "If you want to keep it in your head."

"You have enough lip for the pair of us, you dandy dancer," spat Irene.

The men all laughed at her impudence.

"Here," she said to the struggling young woman. "Let me help you."

"Why, thank you," gasped the woman.

Together they heaved the heavy roll of wire into the flat bed of the buckboard.

She was a pretty lady, Irene noted, with hair the color of wheat and freckles across her nose. Her eyes were periwinkle blue, and she wore a pale blue dot-patterned frock that was too light for any manual labor.

Irene was stricken.

"I think maybe you are a blessing," said the woman with a smile. "I am Thora Beeding, schoolteacher here in Avagar Rhodes."

"Well, hello to you, Thora. My name's Irene, and I just arrived here, but tell me, what will you be doing with all this wire?"

"There is a small tract of land outside of town beside the schoolhouse, and I am thinking of making a wire fence and pen to keep some livestock in for the children."

"Will that be hogs and the like?"

"More probably puppies, chickens, or goats perhaps. I haven't decided yet."

"Are you done now, you skinny redhead?" called out one of the workers. "Sure you don't want us to help you out some more. Looks like you could use a real man."

Irene turned on him. "If your brain was as big as your mouth, I might give your words credence, you oaf."

"I'll smack you," warned the man.

"Gentlemen, please," cried Thora. "I beg of you, will you desist in this unpleasantness?"

"Be quiet, teacher. You know what, boys," growled their leader. "I think we should take these two around back and give them a lesson or two of our own."

"You can try," snarled Irene.

"I think we might do just that," said the brutish man, starting across the boardwalk and moving towards them

"Oh, no," squeaked Thora. "Please don't."

"Get aboard the buckboard, Thora," said Irene. "I'll handle this."

She turned to face the oncoming man with hands held balled into fists by her side.

"I'll teach you a lesson, you little bitch," snarled the fellow.

"Will you now?" boomed a calm voice, and the man looked up to see Gar Seleen leaning both arms on the wall of the buckboard. "How are things, Miss Irene. This fellow troubling you?"

"Ah, now hold on, Seleen," said the lumberjack, a fearful tenor rising in his voice. "I didn't know you knew these two."

"Am I talking to you, dog breath?" growled a cold Seleen before turning politely to Irene. "Can I help you aboard, Miss Irene?" He held out his hand to Irene and helped her climb into the driving seat.

"Obliged, Marshal," said Irene with a slow smile of thanks.

"You dimwits got any more to say?" Seleen asked the men, who were suddenly mute. "Then get along and stop troubling young ladies."

The men slunk off and then, without a word but only a tip of his hat to the two women, Seleen turned away and crossed over, heading back to the hotel.

"You know Gar Seleen?" Thora asked in awe. "Surely he is a fearsome man."

"Not so you'd notice," said Irene blandly. "Now drive on, Thora, I think you might be needing my help to unload this baling wire."

"Why yes, of course," Thora said brightly. "I shall make us some tea. Do you like tea, Irene?"

"Just love it," admitted Irene.

With a flutter of eyelids and a blush to her cheek, Thora took the reins and geed up the horse.

ALVA FOUND the Crozier Corral easy enough and hired herself a buggy for the day, and then mounted on the four-wheeled open carriage, she set off for Ernest Grant's ranch. The directions given to her by the corral owner led her out of town for some nine miles before finding the cutoff to the ranch. It was a bare track she followed at first, leading through stands of oak and then into more open country that rolled over dry grassland. The track dipped and weaved until an entrance way made of pine poles straddled the road. It was here, Alva surmised, that the errant adulterer had been hung, and she eyed the overhanging poles with some apprehension as she drove underneath.

Over the brow of a hill, a valley opened up on the other side with a house standing alone in the lowland at the bottom. A fine enough wood-built property on three floors with a surrounding veranda and front porch under a gabled roof. Just beyond the house, a narrow creek ran crooked through the valley with a flurry of mesquite bordering the slopes.

There were fat brown and white cattle roaming on the far hillside where the grass grew thickly, thanks to the creek water. Cresting the far hill were clumps of buckthorn and some flowering dogwood.

The whole effect was quite a picture and lived up to Alva's expectations after Ernest's description.

She drove on down to the house and pulled at the empty hitching rail outside.

Alva wondered how Ernest would find her now that she was in his part of the country. She also wondered about the woman who was claimed to be his partner and the children they had produced. She was soon to find out as a tall woman opened the door and stepped out onto the veranda, wearing a curious frown on her face.

"Good day to you," the woman said with her gaze quickly checking the hillside behind Alva. "Can I help you?"

Tall and slender, she wore a long white apron over her dress that was a high-necked black mourning ensemble, and her hands were white with flour. A dark-haired woman in her late thirties with gentle, worn features, not unpretty but with the cautious times telling in her evaluating face.

"How do you do indeed. My name is Alva North, and I am looking for Mr. Ernest Grant."

The woman cocked her head to one side and studied

Alva. "He's not here, Miss Alva. I am Grace Grant. Will you step inside for a minute and take a cool glass of lemonade? It is almighty hot today."

"That is kind of you," said Alva, climbing down from her seat. "I believe I will take your hospitality. Is it alright if my buggy stays here?"

"Of course." Grace jerked her head in invitation. "Come on in."

She held the door open for Alva, who appreciated the sudden cool inside the hallway after the heat.

"I'm busy at the bread making," said Grace, leading the way down a corridor sided by a stairway to the upper floors. "I hope you will not object to joining me in the kitchen as I have the dough on the make."

"Not at all, I hope I am not intruding."

"No, my dear, you come on through. If you can bide with me while I am working, then it will be fine."

It was a large open-plan kitchen with a sizable heavy wooden table in the center, with a large ball of floured dough standing on it. Grace sided the table and went to a glass jug with slices of lemon floating in the water. Pouring a glass, she handed it to Alva.

"With the oven going for the bread, it gets a mite hot in here," Grace advised. "If you'll forgive me, I'll go on with the kneading. Will you tell me why you wish to see Ernest?"

Alva sipped the cool drink and said, "We met up in New York, and he spoke of this place with such fervor that I thought I might see it as I was here."

Alva found herself being evasive without knowing the standing of the woman and how things were with Ernest.

"May I ask why you were in New York?"

"My friends and I had just arrived from Ireland, and we were finding our way about. Ernest was most helpful."

"Ah, he is that," said Grace as she pummeled the dough. "Always helpful."

Alva was not sure if she detected some note of criticism or praise in Grace's voice.

"It seems he was in a little trouble down here at the time," Alva went on. "I do hope that is over now."

Grace paused and glanced up. "He is settled now," she said. "You do not know then?"

Alva shook her head. "No."

"There was a man here." Grace sighed. "A man who gave me and the children some trouble. Ernest was rather direct with him."

Alva arched an eyebrow. "I heard in town that he lynched the fellow."

Grace chuckled and shook her head. "The stories they tell, no, it's true, Ernest certainly did lift him at the waist and raise him off the ground and left him hanging by his belt strap after he had given him some rough treatment. But it was merely to shame the man for the advances he made. He lives still but is a vengeful soul, and we must tread with some care."

"They say he was your lover."

Grace burst out laughing. "*They do not*!" she cried in amazement. "Surely not."

"They do, I swear."

"By heaven, what people will say."

"It is mere gossip then."

"It is indeed, Miss Alva. No truth in it at all. Ernest is my brother-in-law, and since my husband's death, he has been caring for the children and me. The fellow is a neighbor who misguidedly believed he had some claim on me and annoyingly pressed his suit. It took strong words and actions by Ernest for him to see the error of his ways."

Alva breathed an internal sigh of relief to hear her words. It proved that her Ernest was indeed the fine person she had believed him to be and no murdering philanderer.

"When do you think Ernest will return?"

"He has been called away on a temporary Ranger posse, so I'm not sure."

"I wonder if you would mind telling him of my visit when he is back."

Grace gave her a gentle smile. "Of course I shall. He has not spoken of you, but I'm sure he will be happy that you are here in Avagar Rhodes." She rolled the dough abstractedly for a moment. "Dear Ernest is a lonely man, and a friend would do him the world of good."

"He is not married then?"

Grace shook her head. "No longer, his wife passed some years ago. It was an unhappy affair as she was with child and they were both lost to him."

"That is a sad thing indeed."

Grace gave her that same gentle smile marked with a question. "Forgive me for saying, but I feel you may hold some affection for Ernest yourself."

Alva returned the smile but did not answer, instead, she asked, "Where are your children now?"

Grace brightened. "They attend school with Miss Beeding, but I believe school is over for today, so they are probably roaming somewhere along the creek."

"Will they be safe out there?"

"Safe enough, children will be children, and I do not

believe in restraining them. The eldest boy is twelve, then eight, and seven, so they are old enough. Perhaps I am remiss in believing it so, but my own childhood was one of freedom, and I think that children learn more in the countryside than from a blackboard, although pray do not tell Thora Beeding I said so."

Alva watched her hands work strongly with the dough, kneading and rolling. "It sounds as if you have things well worked out."

"As good as this bread." Grace laughed, wiping a wrist across her brow. "And now I'll let it rise."

"Then I will be away," said Alva. "Thank you for your time, Mrs. Grant."

"Grace, please, and I hope you will call again."

On her return to the hotel, Alva found Aoife sitting patiently awaiting her in the lobby.

"How are you, dear girl?" asked Alva.

"I am truly fine," breathed Aoife. "I have been to the chapel and met the sisters there. Oh, Alva, it is wonderful and all I wished for. They are gracious people, and there is so much to do."

Alva could see she was flushed with joy and pleased that her consumptive illness seemed to be under control, even in her excitement. "Then tell me all."

"They are a working order of eight nuns serving the Sisters of Holy Redemption, and their chapel, the *Iglesia de Santa Margarita,* is for the poor folk and lost children. It seems many are bereft of parents after the deprivations caused by Indian attack, and the sisters will take them in." Aoife gushed on, "Also, they move amongst the barrios, the poorer places, helping the sick and lonely. It is all I have dreamt of, Alva, to serve Our Lord Jesus in such a worthwhile manner."

"Is it easy to speak to them without the Spanish?"

"It is, we use Latin sometimes and do rather well, some of the sisters have a few words of English. They have taken to calling me Sister Belleza, as my Irish name Aoife meaning beauty. I take the name with joy and am truly grateful for their welcoming kindness. They come from all over South America as well as Mexico, from the Empire of Brazil, from Venezuela and Colombia—all over. They are kindly and devout folk, Alva."

"You sound like you have found a true home then." Alva smiled.

"Truly, I believe so. I hope that you and Irene will forgive me for deserting you, but I must go and be with them."

"Will they have you?"

"Yes, yes, they need all the help they can get. It is an awesome task they confront."

"As long as it's nothing like Holy Arbors back home."

"No, it could not be further removed. The nuns are sweet ladies and all committed to the life."

"Then go with our blessing, Aoife, dear girl."

They were interrupted as the clerk Grenville called across from his desk, "Miss Alva, a letter for you."

Alva was irritated by all the false information the gossiping clerk had given her about Ernest, and glowering at him, she snatched the letter with abrupt thanks.

"Did you find the Grant Ranch?" he asked with a simpering smile.

"I did, and found it to be not at all like you said. There was no lynching, sir, and the lady is no wife to Ernest Grant, she is his sister-in-law and under his protection."

"Oh, really," Grenville said with a sigh, disappointed by the rather tamer truth than the story he was spreading. "Well, it's what I was told."

"Then I hope you will correct that tale," snapped Alva. "It does little good to spread such calumnies."

Angrily and standing in the lobby next to Aoife, she hurriedly ripped the envelope open and found it to be a note from Niamh in far-off New York.

Dear Friends, it began.

I miss you so, indeed I do. But now this is a letter of warning that I must bring to you. O'Bannion is livid at the death of his man Curtis and the blackamoor, so he has brought over the three Mulvenny brothers from Ireland to avenge him. Will you take care, my friends, even though as yet O'Bannion does not know where you have gone.

I do well and have found myself a wealthy friend, who sets me up in a fine apartment with servants and my own carriage. He is a grand fellow who owns a clothier and hat factory, and not so you be misled by any such tailoring commerce, I have to tell you he has more gelt in his pocket thatthan we shall see in a lifetime, so here I intend to quite happily stay.

Your dearest friend, Niamh.

Alva passed the letter to Aoife, who scanned it rapidly. "That is troubling. We must let Irene know to be sure."

"We will, but as Niamh says, O'Bannion does not know our whereabouts, so we are quite safe for now."

"But for how long do you think?"

"Let us make our lives here, Aoife. Your health is better already, and you have found a great incentive with your newly found sisters at the chapel. I shall talk with

Irene, but for now, we are finding our feet in Avagar Rhodes and cannot let it be undermined by any doubtful fancies. It may well be that we shall continue our lives quite freely and never see these Mulvennys."

"Pray God it is so."

CHAPTER TEN

NIAMH WAS INDEED BLISSFULLY HAPPY. She lived in brownstone comfort in Madison Park and alongside other leading families of the times, far away from the stews of the Lower East Side. She is a kept woman, and her rich factory owner keeps her in a certain style with an allowance that suits her needs. Her lover is a portly soul himself, and her size only increases his desire whilst his wafer-thin wife spends most of her time engaged in prim dinner parties and other equally dull social events. His demands are not too testing for Niamh as he is a man into his prime and seeks only a comfortable companion with whom to indulge in moments of clandestine sexual distraction.

None of this worries Niamh, who is at last accepted by a society that, despite the whispers, values her appearance due to the display of designer gowns and extravagant jewelry. Outside her window is a walled front garden with maintained flowerbeds and iron railings, beyond that a broad tree-lined avenue with a wide stone pavement. It is a tranquil stretch with little traffic apart from the occasional delivery vehicle or neighbor's carriage. There are even armories nearby in the unlikely event of any civil uprising by the local marginalized and poorer population. A quiet and peaceful place for Niamh to play out her courtesan role and enjoy a contented existence as a well-heeled mistress.

But not today.

Niamh was busy in her parlor deciding on what to feed her male friend for supper that night when the maid arrived to tell her she had callers.

"Excuse me, ma'am," said the maid, a curly-haired young woman of eighteen years and dressed in servant style with a white cap and apron over her black skirt. "There is a Mrs. Carpenter and Mrs. Wittenmyer to see you. They are from the Women's Christian Temperance Union and are calling on certain ladies of standing in the neighborhood."

Niamh looked up from her menu. She had heard of these do-gooders praying their way through saloons and drinking houses and had little time for them, but she considered that they would be making calls along the street, and maybe it would be wiser to see them rather than demonstrating for the more austere neighbors a show of rejection. "Let them in will you, Dorothy."

The two women bustled in, big women overloaded in black dresses and basque jackets with bonnets perched on piled hair. One clutched a sheaf of leaflets. As a mark of their cause, each of them wore a large white ribbon tied to the upper arm.

"How do, dear sister," said the bolder of the two, a flushed red-faced woman whose skin tone Niamh noted with some uncertainty demonstrated little use of any alcoholic temperance. "We come to lead you into the way of abstinence, purity, and fellowship in a most Christian manner."

"That we do, sister," said the other one, a narrow-faced, mealy-mouthed creature with sly eyes. "We are speaking to a lady of Irish descent, are we not, then you will know 'tis a land of demon drink over here, is it not?"

Niamh was suspicious, and she scanned the two women who seemed to fill the whole parlor, they were that large. These two did not appear to have any relationship with the Christian Methodist Union, and there was something vaguely familiar about them.

"Dorothy," said Niamh. "Perhaps the ladies would like some tea."

"No need," said the one called Mrs. Carpenter, wrinkling her nose in a tight smile. "Now pray don't you bother on our behalf."

"I know you!" said Niamh, getting to her feet as recognition flooded in, and in her anger, the broad Irish accent coming to the fore. "You're not Temperance at all. Jane the Grabber and Red Light Lizzie, I've seen you in that wretched Gopher Gang dive. You're nothing but a petty thief and a hooker. What the devil do you want with me?"

"We come for you." Jane Grabber called Carpenter grinned evilly.

"Oh, dear!" gasped the maid Dorothy nervously. "Shall I fetch the constables, ma'am?"

Lizzie/Wittenmyer spun around, her features made of stone, and in a quick swing, the silver flash of an open razor ran in a slash across the girl's throat. A glugging Dorothy fell to the floor, both hands at her neck where blood poured in a dark stream, and with wide, begging eyes she stared up at Niamh.

"God's Teeth!" cursed Niamh. "There was no need for that! She was but a child."

"You'll be coming with us now, whore," growled Jane. "And with no trouble or you get the same."

Lizzie was wiping her knife on the maid's apron as the girl juddered into death. "Get your hat and coat, missy," she said. "Don't want you catching a cold, do we?"

Niamh's face was set in grim fury. "You'd better know what you're doing, you gobshites, I have powerful friends."

"Sure you do, you fat cow, but ours are more powerful and twice as deadly, now get going."

"Where are you taking me?"

"To see an old friend, now get out the door, we have a carriage waiting."

THE CARRIAGE TOOK them south into Manhattan and to a decaying warehouse at a slip on the riverside. An empty building, crumbling and with stinking slurry floating in the still waters of the nearby dockside. It was a dank, deserted place, forgotten and overgrown with tall weeds. Rubbish lay strewn about, and the tired remains of a broken rowboat lay at the water's edge. Inside the place was all darkness and heavy with the stench of damp rot, with fallen ceilings and warped boards that creaked underfoot.

Niamh was hustled into the ancient warehouse where four men stood waiting in the gloomy interior.

"Here y'are," said O'Bannion with false levity. "Well, you're looking fine, are you not, Mistress Niamh?"

"What do you want of me, O'Bannion?" spat Niamh.

"Set her down, girls," said O'Bannion. "Have you no manners?"

The two women pushed Niamh into a rickety chair where she sat uncomfortably and taut with fear as her hands were lashed at the wrists and tied to the chair back.

"Now get along," O'Bannion said to the two women. "We'll take it from here."

"What about our service fee?" wheedled Lizzie.

"Your service fee!" snorted O'Bannion. "You wee skit, get your skinny ass out of here before I take me hand to you."

"Now hold on," pressed Jane. "We done our part and we need paying."

"For foul bloody murder!" burst out Niamh. "Killing that child Dorothy was a mean thing to do. She meant no harm."

"She was getting in the way and saw our faces," complained Lizzie with a callous shrug. "Had to go."

"Get out of here," said O'Bannion. "You'll get your money, I'll see to it later."

Mollified, the two women bustled out, complaining softly to themselves.

"Now then," said O'Bannion, turning to Niamh. "I have three friends here who are keen to meet you."

The three men standing in the shadows moved forward into the evening light coming through the broken windows so that Niamh could see them. The oldest was a man hunched and with broad shoulders and a dark, full beard to his chest, gaunt-featured and grim-looking, he peered closely at Niamh.

"I have come a long way to see you, girl," he growled in a rasping voice. "My name is Dermot Mulvenny. I believe you knew me my brother Curtis. Well, we've come to talk with you about him, me and my brothers. This here is Edmond." He indicated the tallest of the three who stepped forward and glared at Niamh. 'He don't say much,' said Dermot. 'But he's hell in action on the Hurling field, are you not, boy? Now the little fella there," Dermot went on, jerking a thumb at the smallest. "Is Wee Finley, he used to be a bold figure in the fisticuffs world of bare knuckle fighting. Look at him, ain't he a picture."

The little man who was no more than five feet tall stepped forward, he was muscular and bow-legged, with hairy arms and a hunched body looking more ape than human but with a bald head laced with scars over a puffy forehead and battered ears.

"Fought many times in the Traveller Horse Fairs, did you not, Wee Finley?"

O'Bannion, meanwhile, stepped quietly to one side, rubbing his own scars as he remembered his past days as a fighter and saying nothing but watching closely. Outside, the setting sun was descending quickly, and it cast an orange glow as it settled over the city.

"Now we have a question for you, girl," Dermot went on. "See, we hear that one of your friends was the one to bring our brother Curtis down in wanton murder. Now we want to see those young things and have a word or two with them, so we need you to tell us where they are to be found."

Niamh watched him from under lowered eyebrows. "I have no idea where they are. They left, that's all I know."

"I think not," said Dermot, looming over her threateningly. "Now you will tell us eventually, you know that, don't you?"

"They went off and left me. I don't know where they went."

There was silence in the great empty hall of the warehouse, the only sound the steady drip of water and the soft whistle of wind blowing through the broken glass of the windows.

"You're making it very hard for us," rasped Dermot. "See here, Edmond's brought his Hurley stick with him. D'you know the game? It is a mite tough at some times, but they hit the wee ball between some posts with mighty blows, mighty blows indeed. Will you show her, brother?"

Edmond grinned, showing his bad teeth as he waggled the bat before her. It was made from sturdy long-handled ash wood with a flattened hockey stick end. Edmond swung it a few times in the air, passing it before Niamh, before taking a wide swing and bringing it down with a savage smack across her shoulder. The crack echoed around the dark room, and a trembling Niamh jumped and screamed in pain.

"There, there," said Dermot. "Why you're shaking like a jelly."

"A big fat jelly," sniggered Wee Finley.

Niamh sobbed, bent over, favoring her shoulder and swaying on the chair.

"Aye," agreed Dermot. "Shall we see what she is made of? Why don't you do the honors, Wee Finley? Get her stripped."

"No!" cried Niamh as Wee Finley moved towards her with an unhealthy-looking leer. "Don't, I beg of you."

"Ach, don't be so shy, little girl," snarled Dermot. "Have you not lain with many already, so I am told. Surely plenty of men will have been gawping at you in y'er sweet natural way."

Wee Finley leapt forward and, in demonic fashion, began to rip at Niamh's clothing, tearing and snapping buttons. He was breathing heavily and his eyes rolling in a fiendish manner as he tore the cloth from Niamh's body. She was screaming piteously and begging him to stop with tears streaming from her eyes, but Wee Finley paid her no heed and only continued with his grotesque assault.

When she sat quivering and almost naked with the ripped clothing hanging from her body in ribbons, Niamh tugged at her bound wrists, but they held her tight. Her round cheeks were stained with tears and her eyes red-rimmed with the crying.

Edmond stepped forward before her and took up a two-handed batter's pose with the stick swinging menacingly over his shoulder.

"You'll not be walking away from this, you know that, don't you?" warned Dermot in a quiet voice dark with gloomy promise. "Best you speak up now and put the pain behind you. Because, I swear by God, it will be the most awful."

Niamh trembled, her body cold and hollow with a tense coil of fear rising up her spine, and yet she thought of the safety of Alva and the others and tried to hold herself apart from the terror for their sake. In her heart, she knew she could not hold out for long. She was weak-willed, and she knew it. Her character was still undermined by the childish anxiety that had kept her always as an overweight outsider, shunned and vilified by most of those around her. But she determined she would try and hold out as long as she could.

"Money!" she cried. "I can get you money. A fortune to line your pockets, I have a rich man at my beck and call, and he will send it if I ask. As much as you want, you can have it and receive it anywhere."

Then Edmond delivered the first blow, and a shivering stream of agony ran through Niamh.

"Leave her face," Dermot warned. "We need to keep her talking, but hit her wherever else you fancy."

"Except her thighs," leered Wee Finley with a rusty chuckle. "I'll see to them meself later."

Dermot turned to the figure of O'Bannion standing in the shadows. "Will you be wanting a piece of this for yourself later?"

The smacks and shrieks continued unabated in the background as O'Bannion stepped out of the shadow. He studied Niamh's shuddering body, now covered in bright red bruises and lacerations.

"I think not, this is your affair. I called you boys over out of respect for your brother. Now, if you need anything else, money or a place to stay I'll see you right, but other than that, this is your business and not mine."

"Then you'd best run along, O'Bannion, and leave us to our work."

With a last hasty look over his shoulder at the large wailing woman pinned to the chair, O'Bannion strode from the warehouse out into a thin, dank mist writhing up from the water. He stood a moment watching the last vanishing moments of sunset and the navigation lights flickering on the sluggish waves as the black outline of a ponderous river barge moved by, then with a dismissive shake of the head, he moved off.

THE TALL FIGURE of Ernest was standing waiting in the hotel lobby.

Alva was pleased to see him, and an uncanny flood of relief flowed through her. He wore the same Plains hat as he had before but other than that he was clothed in dusty leather chaps and boots with spurs. A short Mexican jacket barely covered the ammunition belt with a long holster and pistol at his side and a colorful bandana of Spanish silk hung over his chest.

Ernest tugged at his mustache and allowed a grin to part his lips as he saw her.

"I came soon as I heard you were here," he said.

"It is good to see you, Ernest," said a breathless Alva, biting her lower lip with girlish pleasure.

"You surprised me," he allowed. "I had never thought to see you again."

"Well, here I am."

"And is Avagar Rhodes all you expected?"

"I hope to find it so."

"Will you come along ofwith me, Alva. I shall buy you a coffee and we can sit and talk."

"Here," she said, indicating the hotel dining rooms. "We can go in here."

The dining room was almost empty, with only a few hotel guests taking breakfast, and they found themselves a table easily enough. A maid was soon by their side and they ordered and sat waiting for the girl to bring them coffee.

"You look fine," said Ernest, his eyes fixed on her face. "Every gentle bit as sweet as I remember."

Alva said nothing but lowered her head to hide the glow of gratitude that he might still think of her so.

"You have been out on a posse, so Mrs. Grant told me."

"Yes." He nodded. "She it was who told me you were

here—made my day, I have to say. How did you find dear Grace?"

"Nice as pie, she was very kind. But did you catch your bad man or whoever you were after?"

"No, we did not, just a parcel of border rats who were troubling some settlers but we did run into a friend of yours while we were out there, Gar Seleen. Been a while since I seen him, but he says he met you and some other girls on the stagecoach."

"So he did, and what was he up to?"

"Looking for some fellow called Lyle Jakes, appears he's a runaway due for trial."

"Mr. Seleen is a strange man indeed, a moody character that some might call abrupt and certainly not a gentleman to be fooled with."

"Despite his cranky ways, he is a hell of a lawman for all that."

Alva could not contain herself any longer. "Oh, Ernest, it is *so* good to see you."

Ernest arched an eyebrow. "Been thinking of me?" he teased and then relented. "As I sure have of you."

Alva drew a deep breath, and beneath the table, she pushed clasped hands into her lap as their coffee arrived. Her thrill was one of youth and the romantic flush that ran through her so that, despite his big ears and slip of a smile, she thought Ernest the handsomest man she had ever met.

"Would you like anything else?" asked the serving girl.

Ernest shook his head and gave Alva a sidelong glance. "Obliged to you, missy, but I reckon we have all we need here."

He toyed with his mug before asking, "How are your friends making out?"

"They are well, I believe," said Alva, brightening at thought of the others. "Aoife has found a place with some sisters here. She is of a religious frame of mind so it suits her well. And Irene seems to have found a friend in the local schoolteacher and has taken to working on the woman's farm."

"And you—nothing troubles your horizon?"

"No, not really. There is some news from our friend in New York that is unwelcome but little to realistically trouble us I think."

"There were five of you, were there not. What happened to the others?"

"Aye, one is left behind in New York, one is dead, sadly murdered, and the others are with me here."

"It was difficult for you to leave?"

"Yes, something of a mess, I fear. In taking our leave, it was necessary to leave in haste. We had to flee a street gang that wanted us for no good purpose. There was a fight, and two of them were left dead in the road."

"Don't that beat all." Ernest chuckled. "You don't give up, do you, Alva North?"

She gazed at him attentively with a flicker of romantic adoration and said nothing.

Ernest rested back in his chair and stretched out his long legs so that the spurs jingled. "But you have left it all behind you now?"

"So I believe."

"Then there is no reason that we cannot spend some time together."

"Indeed not, I hope it will be so."

"Well, look, Alva. Why do you stay here in town, come out to the ranch, your friends seem all settled, so why not be my guest? If you find Grace a good party and will like her children, I would surely enjoy your company there."

"Oh, Ernest, do you think so? Surely Grace will take offence at such an imposition and I would not like to upset her."

"No, no." He waved off her complaint. "She has already told me in confidence what a fine girl you are, and believe me, that is praise indeed coming from my sister-in-law, she is not one to give out such plaudits freely."

"Well—yes—I guess so," said Alva flustered by the notion. "It would be pleasant."

"Then you must collect your things and come out right away. There is much here I want to show you, Alva."

"Your house is such a fine place with the little stream and everything."

Ernest frowned slightly at the mention of the creek. "There is a spot of bother there, I will admit, one of the reasons I thought best to take a turn in New York. Anyway, I hope it is done with now."

Alva noted his concern. "What is it?"

Ernest stroked his mustache between finger and thumb, easing the hair along each side of his broad mouth. "Concerns a neighbor of mine, a scratchy fellow called Jud Brown who made claim on the water and tried to dam it off from my land, then with no water coming through, my cows were left dry and that could not be."

"So you went to see him about it, surely."

"I did so, but Jud was a mite obstreperous and thought to argue. It ended in a bad way. His son Billy took his side and tried to make a fight of it."

"What happened?"

She waited for him to go on, but could see the matter troubled him, so did not push it.

"A boy of fifteen," said Ernest eventually. "A kid, and believe me, I did not want it so, but he came on at me whilst we were arguing over the dam on the creek. Billy was a fool, and I believe his father saw it as such, but still the kid raised a shotgun against me."

"Oh," gasped Alva.

"There was little I could do. His father called at him to lower the gun, but he would go on and left me little choice, so I had to plug him in the legs. Now he is laid up and unable to walk, which is a crying shame for one so young."

"That is terrible. Now this wouldn't be the same difficult neighbor that Grace spoke of, would it, the man who was troubling her?"

Ernest's eyes widened. "She told you of that! Yes, it was he, and I took him to task over that earlier foolishness. My guess is that is why he dammed the creek out of some kind of pettiness and to pay me back for shaming him. There was a local uproar about the whole affair, and I thought it best to go away until things calmed down. There is nothing worse than upsetting a neighbor, indeed there isn't."

"I have heard some of the lies going about, there is indeed some nasty gossip concerning the matter here in town."

"Well, I hope Jud has seen the error of his ways, and while I feel sorry for his son, he brought it on himself to be sure."

Tentatively, she reached her fingers across the table and laid them over his hand. The skin felt strong and warm, and she savored the feel of it under her touch. "I'm sure there was no fault."

Ernest raised eyebrows. "I fear I have a name around here by being a Ranger and not adverse to a little trouble. Best you know that, Alva, for I'm afraid it hangs over me and with the shooting of this kid I reckon it will be thought I am a rough egg and only trouble."

"No matter," she said quickly. "I will get my things and settle up here, and if you will take me, I shall come with you to the ranch."

He grinned broadly at her words. "You got a deal, lady."

"I will say farewell to my friends first and tell them where I shall be."

"We'll get it done on the way."

THEY FOUND Aoife working in the vegetable patch outside the church, which was a small and whitewashed adobe building with a bell tower and barely enough room inside for a small congregation.

Aoife was working with three other nuns, with sleeves rolled up and her pale beauty shaded by the wide brim of a straw bonnet tied down by a scarf under her chin. She was smiling at their arrival, and Alva could not help but notice the new sparkle in her eyes. She was happy, Alva decided, even though she was raking hard ground with a hoe.

Introductions made, Alva informed her that her home would now be at Ernest's ranch.

"Why that is wonderful," said Aoife, her eyes dancing over Ernest's tall figure. "Will you both be very happy I trust."

"You certainly seem so yourself," said Alva, casting a

glance over the group of nuns, all of whom smiled greeting at her.

"I am at home," said Aoife, resting on the long handle of the hoe. "It is hard work," she said, taking a deep sigh. "But I find it is where I should be."

"Nice to meet you, sister," said Ernest as he helped Alva up into the hired buggy.

"And you too—pray take good care of my friend."

"Of that you can be sure, ma'am," promised Ernest with a finger tipping the brim of his hat.

THEY FOUND the schoolteacher's property easy enough outside of town, and Alva knocked to be greeted by the slight figure of Thora Beeding.

"Forgive me," said Alva. "My name is Alva North. I am a friend of Irene and believe she stays with you. Is it possible I might see her?"

Thora's eyes lit up. "Ah! So you are Alva, what a pleasure to meet you. Irene has told me so much about you."

"She has?" asked Alva curiously.

"Indeed, but won't you come in?"

"I'd love to, but we are on our way, and I hoped to take a minute with Irene before we left."

"I fear she is out," Thora said with a frown. "Hunting for a rabbit supper, I think, she really is a marvel, takes up a shotgun, and off she strides. Just like that." There was a moment of appreciative respect in her voice. "I cannot believe how hard she works, and no problem is too great. You see, there outside, she already has a pen built for the animals. I really wouldn't know where to begin, but she does it without a moment's thought."

Alva noted the gleam in Thora's eye when she spoke of Irene and guessed that her friend had found herself a new companion.

"Will you tell her I am at the ranch of Ernest Grant if she needs me?"

"I shall, of course, but please, Alva, when you have more time, you must come and visit."

"I shall, I promise."

THEY RODE on with Ernest taking the reins and with his saddle pony tied off at the rear. Alva, sitting beside him, slipped her arm through his once they were beyond the town limits. She beamed with contentment and gave Ernest pleasurable sidelong glances, feeling the joy that rose in her like a spring.

It was when they reached the cutoff amongst the oak trees that he pulled on the reins and drew the buggy to a stop. Under the shade of the trees and in the brush and scrub beside the track, he took Alva in his arms and kissed her. She answered with intensity and clasped him tight, feeling all the weeks of separation, their stressful escape, and her continued concern for the other girls falling away in Ernest's embrace. They stayed that way a long time until Alva, dizzy with desire and his kisses, drew back to take a breath.

She sighed and stared into his eyes then whispered his name, "Ernest."

"I am lost," he rasped, the breath dry as rust in his throat. "Each time I look at you, I cannot breath or know where I am. You have undone me, girl."

She pulled him close, her fingers digging into his

shoulders, and stared blindly over his shoulder. "I am with you," she whispered in his ear. "You shall never feel lost with me. Never, you hear me? And—"

Something stopped her in mid-sentence. A distant, small figure was running towards them along the track, a young boy. Hatless and his shirttails flapping, he looked desperate, and the slight figure appeared to be about twelve years of age. The boy was calling out to them, his keening voice over the distance barely discernible.

"Ernest," she said, pulling back. "A lad is coming, I think he is distressed."

Ernest spun around from her and then was quickly down from the driving seat and over the side of the carriage. "It's my nephew. Caleb boy, come here, I am here," he called out as the boy neared.

Ernest reached out with his arms and Caleb fell into them, exhausted. Sweat beaded his brow, and his breath came fast as he panted.

"Uncle Ernest! Uncle Ernest!" the boy gasped, tears filling his eyes.

"What is it, boy?" asked Ernest.

Trying the recover himself, Caleb sucked air and looked desperately up at his uncle. "Ma—he has Ma!"

"Who has?" Ernest frowned.

"The—the man. He has taken Ma, Chrissy, and Levan. He holds them. Uncle Ernest, I didn't know what to do. I was fishing in the creek and saw it as I came home. They did not see me, so I ran."

"It's all right," said Ernest, kneeling to take the small vibrating frame in his arms. "Take your time. Breathe easy."

A worried Alva climbed down to join them. "This man, he has Grace and the other children?"

Caleb stared at her and nodded confirmation.

"What the hell?" breathed Ernest.

"I didn't see him arrive," said Caleb. "I guess Ma asked him if he would like some water and he went in."

"He is inside the house?"

"Yes, yes, maybe this is about Billy. Do you think so, Uncle Ernest?"

"Billy Brown?" mused Ernest. "Then it's Jud Brown, the boy's father, could it be so?"

Caleb sagged in Ernest's arms. "No, it isn't him. I don't know this man. He is ugly, Uncle Ernest, and he has a gun."

"Oh, dear Lord!" said Ernest, slowly rising to his feet.

"You must go," said Alva. "He has them captive, whoever he is."

"Yes, of course," said Ernest thoughtfully. "But it would do no good to rush in, we don't know his intent."

"It is wrong whatever it is," said Alva. "But it does seem that Jud Brown has most claim against you."

Caleb gripped his uncle's sleeve and jerked it hard. "I think it is *you* this man wants, Uncle Ernest."

"Hmm," growled Ernest thoughtfully. "Who can it be, I wonder, if it is not Jud Brown?"

"Then perhaps somebody hired by Brown," suggested Alva.

Ernest agreed. "More than likely, but even so, we will not know who we are up against. What kind of man this is, is he a killer or just some no-account hired thug? It will make a difference."

"What will you do, Uncle Ernest?" asked Caleb.

"We will save your ma, have no fear. No one will harm my family as long as I breathe."

Ernest had his Colt pistol out and on half-cock now, he spun the chamber and checked the load. Alva watched as he stood stooped over the weapon and she read the signs that told her of the man. He was taking on a different mode now, something was changing in his demeanor. A grim hardness was like a cloak on his shoulders, a coldness that she did not recognize.

"Hot damn! I will kill this mother, I promise he will not see out the day," he muttered to himself, and then he turned to Alva. "You will stay here and mind the boy. I will take the horse and ride on in."

Alva held her hand up and placed it on his chest. "You cannot go straight in, Ernest. He will be waiting for you."

"I must," said Ernest, his eyes already glazing over as he prepared to fight.

"No, no, listen, I have a better plan. Let me ride in on the carriage with Caleb, it will be a diversion. I shall say I met Caleb on the road whilst on my way to visit with Grace and am bringing him home. You will come around, unseen whilst this fellow is distracted."

Ernest listened to her, his eyes flicking from side to side and tongue playing over his lips as he thought it through.

"Can you do that, do you think?" he asked doubtfully. "Maybe this is a madman. Did he seem crazy, Caleb, wild and out of his mind?"

"He looked crazy alright," agreed Caleb. "But not insane."

Ernest rubbed his jaw and stroked his mustache. Finally he pouted and fixed Alva with a hard stare. "Can you do it?"

"I can," she assured him.

Ernest turned to Caleb. "Boy, it is time for you to become a man. Alva here is a fine woman and my friend, will you go with her back to the ranch? If not, say so, we can hide you in the brush until this is over."

Caleb, who was obviously a boy of spirit, raised an annoyed eyebrow. "Of course I can, Uncle. Never doubt it. My ma is in danger, but she will know that I ran for you."

Ernest smiled despite his set jaw. "Well said, Caleb."

"Come along," said Alva, holding out her hand to the boy.

Obediently, Caleb followed her as she climbed up onto the carriage seat and Ernest untied his mount from the rear.

"Take no chances, Alva," said Ernest with his boot in the stirrup. "I will be there, and if there is gunplay, you will all be on the floor as quick as you can. You hear me, Caleb?"

"Yes, sir."

"Good, give me a half hour, I must ride around and come in on the blind side."

Alva took the reins and chided the horse into a slow walk and they rode on down the track as Ernest went off in another direction and was soon lost amongst the trees.

She remembered the road and was silent until they passed under the pine pole archway, then, thinking she should be keeping the boy focused, she said, "So tell me about your brothers."

Caleb looked up at the pine poles and then at her. "Brother and sister," he corrected. "Chrissy is a girl, she is eight, and Levan, the little one, he is only seven."

"So you are the oldest of the bunch. Do you like your brother and sister?"

"They are all right," he replied with a shrug. "How about you, Miss Alva, do you have brothers and sisters?"

Alva mused a moment. "No, but I have four good friends who are all like sisters to me."

"You speak funny, I never heard talk like that, where are you from?"

"I am from a place called Ireland."

"That in Canada?"

"No, from across the sea, a long way away."

Caleb did not take his eyes from her, and with all the abruptness of youth, he asked, "Why did you come here?"

"Well"—she paused—"they threw me out, but I didn't like it much there anyway."

Caleb frowned. "Are you going to be my aunty? Appears my uncle kind of likes you."

Alva smiled. "Well, that will depend on your uncle, I believe."

"You like him then?"

"I like him just fine."

THEY BROACHED THE RISE, and there, appearing before them in the valley, lay the ranch house. Alva searched the countryside around but could see no sign of Ernest, and she hoped he was close enough by now.

"Look," cried Caleb. "There's my ma."

On one end of the high veranda that rose some four feet off the ground, Alva made out the seated figure of Grace with a child cradled on her lap and beside her a small girl who stood hanging onto her skirts.

"I can't see the man anywhere," said Alva.

"He'll be around somewhere," promised Caleb. "Maybe in the house."

As she moved the carriage forward down the hill, Alva could see that the front door stood wide open, and only shadowy darkness was evident from the hallway inside.

"That's where he'll be, I bet," murmured Alva. "Inside the doorway."

"He'll be waiting on Uncle."

"That's right, now look, Caleb, we pretend we know nothing about what's going on, okay? I'm just here on a visit and found you on your way back."

"That's fine," said Caleb a little abruptly, and it was apparent he was beginning to feel some tension now with the moment at hand.

They were arriving level with the veranda, and Alva was pulling on the reins to bring the carriage to a stop.

"Hello there, Grace," she called with an air of gaiety she did not feel. "Just come to pay a visit and met Caleb on the road."

Grace stared back at her with eyes hard as glass, and she clutched the small child tight in her arms whilst the little girl at her side cringed closer.

"Perhaps you should come another day, Miss Alva," said Grace.

Playing the part, Alva said airily, "What on earth for? I'm here now, and I have Caleb with me."

"Yes, I see that. Maybe it is best you keep him with you in town—"

A gravelly low voice came from the doorway, and a man holding a Winchester rifle stepped out. "You stay right where you are, Missy."

He was a squat figure, tending to fat with a flabby double chin that was covered with a three- or four-day growth of black hair. The beat-up hat on his head was a dusty sweat-stained brown, and the chewed brim rose up at the front. A loose bandana hung over a checked wool shirt under a stained waistcoat, and the pistol he carried stuck in his belt hung from his middle.

"What?" gasped Alva in feigned surprise. "Who are you?"

"Name's Lyle Jakes, and I want you to get down. Boy!" he called to Caleb. "You get over with your ma."

Carefully, Alva descended from the carriage, watching Jakes and, at the same time, cautiously trying to see if Ernest was nearby.

"What does he want here?" Alva asked Grace.

"He's after Ernest," replied Grace, watching Alva to see if there was some sign of help implied by her presence. "He is paid to kill him."

Alva spun to face Jakes, who stood at the top of the veranda steps and kept her under the rifle. "How dare you!" she cried. "A paid hireling and killer to boot, who is it that wants this done?"

"You just get up here and sit with the lady," said Jakes, and surprisingly, he spoke quite gently. "Behave yourself, and you'll come off fine. Give me trouble, and I'll blow you away like dust."

"Oh, dear me," snapped Alva, giving him a defiant eye. "Fine words for a tuppenny-ha'penny deadbeat, I'll bet you think with your feet as well."

"What?" Jakes frowned. "What the hell are you talking about?"

Alva was at the top of the steps, an irate figure leaning in with her fists on her hips and her face close to Jakes's. "Who was it sent you on this dirty deed, mister? Who could do such a felonious thing?"

Jakes was a little unnerved by her aggression. "That Jud Brown fella, he's paying good money to see this Grant put down. I'm just doing a job, lady. I been on the run for weeks now and I need the cash."

"I'll give you money if you let this lady and her children go."

Jakes snorted a laugh. "Get you gone, girl. You ain't got the kind of money I need, now get over there with the other one and sit tight. All we got to do is wait a while until his highness shows up, and then it'll all be over."

As Alva moved over to join Grace, she saw movement below the high edge of the veranda and guessed Ernest was creeping along down there.

"It's alright, Grace," she whispered. "Help is at hand."

Grace drew a deep breath as their eyes met, and she read the meaning and a smile quirked the edges of her lips.

"This your youngest?" asked Alva.

"Indeed, this is Levan, and here clinging onto me with all her might is my daughter Christine."

"Hello to you both, children. You know you're not to worry now, everything is fine, is it not, Caleb?"

"It is," promised Caleb, placing his arm protectively around Chrissy's shoulder, and she shook it off with girlish irritably as it was obviously not a normal show of affection from her brother.

Grace leaned forward conspiratorially and whispered, "You know there is more than one of them, don't you?"

"*What?*" gasped Alva, looking around wildly. "Where the devil is the other one?"

"He's lying out around back somewhere," advised Grace.

Dismayed at the unknown other, Alva was halfway to her feet when they all heard a thump and the heavy fall of a body in the dust.

"*Yay*! *I got him*," cried a voice from below the veranda

wall, and a man stood up to his full height and grinned at Jakes. "Damn it! You were right, Lyle. You said he would come creeping up rather than ride in."

"Yeah, we have him now," said a smiling Jakes, licking his lips in pleasure. "That's good work, Tad, you done real well."

Tad, a tall man, thin as a rake and with loose fair hair like a bundle of straw sticking out from under his sombrero, stepped over the prone figure of Ernest. "So what do we do with him now. You want we should plug him?"

"Brown wants him hung up first, a rope put around him and set up swinging."

"Like a lynching?"

"Brown says no, he just wants him shamed like he was, but I reckon why bother, let's do him and be done with it, that way he ain't ever coming after us."

"Good thinking," agreed Tad with a slow, leering grin. "Let's do just that. What after then, we going to make the most of one of these fine ladies here?"

Jakes's eyes slid sideways to encompass the women and children. "Why not, might as well make it a clean sweep. Best you hog-tie that Grant fella first and get a noose on his neck, I'll keep an eye on these females as you do."

Tad tossed the loose end of the lariat up over a veranda roof beam, and when the noose was tight around the semi-conscious Ernest's neck, he began to pull on the rope.

"*No*!" screamed Alva. "You can't do that."

The children were all whimpering now, and Grace had begun to scream denial as well.

"Shut up!" roared James. "This is going to happen

whether you like it or not. So just shut it and keep quiet, or I'll put one in the whole bunch of you."

"Ha!" grunted Tad as he began heaving on the rope and Ernest began to rise off the planks of the veranda.

Ernest was beginning to come around, his eyelids flickering as the noose began to cut off his air supply.

"Don't, don't," pleaded Alva. "Please don't do this."

"He's going to swing, girl," Jakes said with a grin. "Just you watch, he's going to swing."

CHAPTER ELEVEN

The noose was not well placed, and rather than break Ernest's neck, it was slowly strangling him. Gagging, he was lifted until his feet were off the plank floor and he swung, twisting on the rope and kicking out in an endeavor to get free. Ernest's eyes were popping, and his face was slowly turning pale when, in desperation, Alva lunged forward, attempting to hold his legs and take his weight. Jakes stepped forward as she ran in and, with one swoop of his rifle, slammed her with the stock. Alva flew back at the blow and tumbled onto the veranda floor.

Tad, grunting with effort, lashed the loose end of the lariat around a support post and tied it off. "There he goes," he said, staring up at the dangling Ernest with smug satisfaction.

The two men stood back admiring their work as Ernest spun at the rope's end, the life slowly being choked out of him.

"Ain't seen a sight like this since Yuma prison," observed Jakes. "Might take a good half hour."

"We got time." Tad chuckled. "Geez! I like to see 'em dance like they do, kicking and jumping better than a hoe-down."

Tad stood a moment, his eyes fixed on Ernest, then strangely, he wobbled a moment, unbalanced on his feet, and staring curiously over at Jakes, he slipped sideways and tumbled to the floor.

"Wh—" began Jakes, and then he turned as he heard the loud sound of the rifle shot echoing around the valley. He was about to dive for cover when a long sluice of blood spun away from his head, and at the sound of the second shot, he fell away to clatter down beside his companion on the board floor.

For a brief second, all was silence and amazement, and then Alva was on her feet. She dashed across and slipped Ernest's knife from its scabbard and slashed at the taut rope. It gave way instantly and sprang back as Ernest fell heavily. Alva was quickly on him, dragging at the noose and freeing it from Ernest's neck.

There was the sound of fast hoof beats approaching, and Gar Seleen rode up, his rifle held high in one hand.

"He all right?" he asked, sliding his horse to a standstill and leaping down from the saddle.

Alva looked up at him, cradling the dazed head of Ernest in her arms. "I think so," she said with a gasp. "Oh, thank the Lord you came."

Seleen was quickly up the steps and peering over the two fallen outlaws to make sure they would make no further move, but both men were quite dead. Satisfied, he turned his attention to Grace and the children. "Are you all right, ma'am?"

"All the better for seeing you, sir," said Grace. "You saved us all, you surely did."

Seleen knelt beside Ernest and patted his cheeks

none to gently. "Come on, old boy, that ain't nothing but a little necktie. You'll be just fine in a minute or two."

Alva was working with the knife and cutting through the bonds that bound Ernest's wrists.

"What brought you here, Mr. Seleen?" she asked.

"I been chasing this ass a while," he replied, jerking his chin at Jakes. "Didn't know he'd partnered up with the other one though. Thought I'd drop by to see if he had come this way and almost didn't believe my eyes when I saw him here."

Ernest was sitting up, rubbing his neck and clearing his throat. "Obliged to you, Seleen, saved my bacon for sure. I never knew the dog had some help with him, sucker came up behind me and nailed me good."

"Got to help a fellow Ranger, don't I?" said Seleen. "Mind you, I lost out on taking Jakes to trial, had some cash money coming my way for that, still, we'll put it down to resisting arrest."

"There'll be a reward."

"I reckon, if there ain't, I'll want to know why."

Ernest dragged himself up onto his feet and stood a moment with one hand on the veranda support, steadying himself. "Where's my gun?"

"It's here," said Alva, fetching the pistol that had been cast aside when Ernest was being bound.

"Good," said Ernest as he slipped the Colt into his holster. "I'm going to need this."

"Why?" asked Alva. "What do you intend?"

Ernest drew himself up and took a deep breath. "Gotta go see Jud Brown, we got things to settle."

"What are you going to do?" asked Alva with a troubled frown.

"He don't come here sending men to threaten my family, bringing his pissant notion of retaliation on women and children, that is one sure thing," said Ernest, his voice rising angrily.

Alva could see Ernest was furious with the same cold blanket veiling him that she had seen before. It seemed to her in that moment that nothing would distract him from the icy state of his ferocious intent.

Seleen was watching him with the same chilly understanding. "Best get it done, brother."

"Right, stay with my people, will you?"

"Be my pleasure. Sure you don't need help?"

"Nope, I can manage."

"Well, go to it then."

Alva watched as Ernest stepped down from the veranda and strode off to find his horse. She turned to Grace. "What will he do?" she asked.

"I don't know," said Grace. "But when he is like this, there is no telling. Now, I'm going to get these children inside and see them fed. Best you leave it, Alva. Ernest is his own man and will do what he has to. Now, Mr. Seleen, you ready for something to eat? Be happy for you to join us at the table."

"Yes, ma'am," answered Seleen as Grace ushered the children inside. "You want me to clear away these two dead people?"

"There's no rush, they ain't going nowhere," Grace said indifferently. "Leave it until after we've eaten."

Alva stood for a minute alone on the veranda except for the bodies of the outlaws, both of them rigid in death and seeping blood over the boards. She stared down at the corpses and then off to where Ernest had ridden off. She was breathing hard, and her mind fixed in a moment of indecision. Then she quickly ran down the veranda steps and over to the waiting carriage.

It was quite beyond Alva how this man who had been

so gentle with her could suddenly change to become such a solid rock of character impervious to any show of charity or compassion. There was something almost mechanical in it. She had seen the same thing in Seleen but was still surprised to see it in Ernest, and it troubled her deeply. Her thoughts of Ernest until now had been only ones of love and affection, and to find that there was this other side to him was confusing, and she felt she had to know what his intentions were with Jud Brown. With that in mind, she set the carriage off to follow Ernest as he struck out for the Brown ranch.

Ernest rode on fast ahead without looking behind, he seemed fixed on his task, and there would be little that would distract or interrupt him. Alva managed to keep him in sight in the early stages, but the track they were on soon entered high hillsides peopled with pines, and keeping sight of him was difficult in the bends and twists. The single dirt track was simple, and the only route through it was rough and uneven, but she stayed with it. The deep banks of a creek ran alongside the track, and the sound of running water filled the silence between the enclosing hillsides.

She came to a tall corner of rock, and a waterfall played down from above and entered a deep hole of dark water. Around the side were scattered logs and signs of stacked earth and rocks, and Alva decided this had been the site of the dam that had been the initial cause of all the trouble.

She drew up the carriage as she saw Ernest's horse standing at the base of a steep grassy climb. Above on a plateau was a wide single-story building, a long, pleasant-looking wooden structure with an angled roof and a deeply covered veranda walled off at each end with railings.

Jumping down, Alva began to climb up the sloping rise but stopped when she saw Ernest standing on the veranda with his gun arm outstretched and his pistol pointing at an unarmed Jud Brown. Behind them both, sitting in a wheelchair, was the fifteen-year-old Billy with a blanket on his lap covering his damaged legs.

"You come sending your men to threaten my family and kill me," Ernest was shouting. "You damn lame-ass jackal! Why in God's name you think you can do that?"

"You can come shame me and cripple my boy without a comeback, is that how you see it?" Jud replied angrily. "It's one law for you and a different one for the rest of us. That how you reckon it?"

Alva could see that Ernest was quivering with rage. "You called it off, Jud. You dammed my water and made eyes at Grace and bothered her when she was mourning my brother, your boy there pulled a gun on me and got the result. What did you expect, huh? That I would roll over and take it all lying down."

"Grace led me on," Jud spat spitefully. "She wanted me, I know she did."

"You are one hell of a fool, Jud, but you stepped too far out of line this time."

Then Alva saw something she thought she would never see. As she watched, it seemed as if a steel curtain descended over Ernest. At least it appeared so. His features stiffened, and his eyes narrowed to a lifeless gaze that bored into the man opposite.

Jud snorted a dismissive laugh. "And I'll do it again."

Alva jumped as Ernest fired. He was no more than three feet away from Jud with his pistol centered on the man's forehead. The Colt blazed fire and smoke and a haze of red droplets burst around Jud's head like a cloud. He was carried off his feet by the impact of the .45

caliber bullet and rose up, spreading his arms wide as he flew through the air to land heavily like a heap of wet cloth on his back on the veranda deck.

As he slapped down, Alva heard Billy cry out and sweep away the blanket to reveal a cut-down shotgun. The barrels had been sawn short, and the stock shaped into a grip handle, but Billy hardly had time to lift the weapon before Ernest, with his arm still extended, shifted his aim slightly and blasted Billy with a bullet in the chest. The boy slammed back in the wheelchair and the shotgun slid from his lap as his chair started to roll backwards across the wide veranda. Ernest fired again, his gun arm kicking up with the recoil, and Billy's body jumped under the impact as the wheelchair was sent rolling faster across the open space until it came to a battered halt against the low wall at the far end.

White smoke drifted slowly across the porch in a mist as Ernest lowered the Colt. He turned and for the first time, saw Alva halfway up the slope staring at him. She watched as the transition took place. There had been no recognizing the earlier Ernest in his terrible killing mode, but here, changing before her eyes, was the man she had come to know and admire.

Alva's hands rose to cover her mouth in awe and horror, the shock of the conversion sending waves of confused terror through her.

Ernest's eyes widened at the sight of her and his features softened, a smile began and then he opened his mouth to call to her, but Alva turned away quickly and fled. She raced down the hill and leapt into the waiting carriage before whipping up the horse and driving recklessly away. The track was bumpy and rugged, and the carriage leapt and bounced on the stony path, but Alva did not care. Her mind was empty except for the vision of the transfigured Ernest standing cold as ice and killing without hesitation or remorse.

Alva did not look behind herself to see if Ernest was following, she just drove wildly with no idea where she was going. In a daze, she pounded the track with an empty feeling that in some way she had been deceived. Tears streamed from her eyes, not from the wind of passage but from the anguish and confusion she felt inside.

Ernest had taken on the role of a perfect man for Alva. He had shone in New York, and it was her true desire to see him again that had drawn her to Texas. She knew it now that, in truth, her friends had been in second place with her wish to reconnect with Ernest as he had taken on an unrealistic character that would become all the things she had lost and missed from her sad upbringing. It was he who would fill the great ache left in her heart by the demise of her parents and the terrible life under the nuns in the orphanage.

In actuality, she had now seen that he was none of those things, and the reality had cut through her. Ernest was an angry man to whom violence and vengeance were second nature. It was a side she had witnessed in the schizoid version he had displayed in the house on the hillside. To murder the unarmed Jud and kill his crippled boy with such callousness was a heartless act of insensitivity in Alva's eyes. She wondered now what she had seen in Ernest and how he had meant so much to her.

She had killed, she knew that and did not underestimate herself for it, but that had been a matter of survival. Shooting down Jud and his son Billy had been purely a display of contempt for human life.

ALVA DID NOT STOP until she brought the sweating horse to a standstill outside The Columbine Hotel in Avagar Rhodes and tiredly dismounted. She was sore in mind and strangely sick in body, and she still ached from where Lyle Jakes had struck her with his rifle.

The Main Street was as busy as usual, and as she stepped up onto the boardwalk, it was in her mind that she had her baggage in the carriage and there was the possibility that Grenville might still hold her room. As she made her way to the entrance, she saw that Aoife was waiting for her. Dressed in her gray habit and sitting as still as a painting under the porch entrance, her pale hands were neatly folded in her lap, and the young novitiate seemed withdrawn and tense. Alva knew that something must be wrong for Aoife to come here like this.

"What is it?" Alva asked.

"It's Irene," said Aoife, glancing wide-eyed at Alva. "She's missing."

"How do you know?"

"That woman she has befriended, Thora—the schoolteacher, she came looking for Irene. Said she had gone out hunting but had not returned."

Alva shrugged. "Perhaps she will be away for a while, it is normal on a hunting trip."

"I think you should see the schoolteacher. She is convinced something is wrong."

Alva sighed, she was tired and upset and did not really feel like more problems. "I have to see about my room, then we'll go and see her."

"Is everything all right with you?" Aoife frowned, seeing the troubled look in Alva's face.

"Not really," Alva allowed. "I have a problem with Ernest."

Aoife lowered her gaze. "Do you need to talk about it?"

Alva shook her head. "No, look, let me sort out my room, then we'll go and see the schoolteacher."

Inside the lobby, she found that Grenville was amenable, and although the regular room was not available, he had a smaller alternative for her. She was about to return to collect her things, and as she stepped out onto the veranda, a worried and hollow-eyed Ernest confronted her.

"Alva," he said. "What's wrong? Why did you go off like that?"

Alva did not want to go into it all in such a public place. Aoife was sitting patiently, but many of the hotel's occupants were walking in and out of the hotel entrance and passing them by.

"Not now, Ernest," she said. "I really don't want to talk about it now."

"I came as fast as I could," he said in a disturbed tone. "You know I had to do what I did, surely you don't think ill of me for that."

"*Not now, Ernest,*" she repeated loudly. "Irene is missing and we have to go find her."

Ernest dithered for a moment, unsure of himself and the sudden change in Alva. "Would you like me to come with you?"

"No, we will sort it out."

"Then when will I see you? Are you coming out to the ranch?"

"Not just now, I believe I will stay here at the hotel. I'll see you later."

Turning away abruptly, she took Aoife's hand and pulled her from her seat and strode out to the carriage.

Unmoving, Ernest watched her go with a deep frown furrowing his brow.

Alva and Aoife climbed aboard and they quickly drove out into Main Street, leaving Ernest watching them go with a stunned expression on his face.

"He seems very troubled," said Aoife as they drove out of town.

"So am I," Alva replied bitterly.

"But you seemed so happy. What went wrong?"

"I saw him commit bloody murder. He killed a man and a boy. They had no chance, Aoife."

Aoife shook her head. "Why would he do that?"

"This neighbor sent hired killers to his house, they threatened his family, Grace and the children."

"*Killers*!" gasped Aoife.

"Yes," said Alva, a thread of doubt beginning to charge through her mind. "They tried to string him up. I suffered a blow, and I think we may have faced rape from those men after the deed was done."

"It does seem he had some call for animosity then."

"He did, he did," stressed Alva, concentrating on the reins. "But it was the way he exacted his revenge. Without any thought, it seemed. I have never seen that in him. It was as if Ernest were a changed man."

"I dare say he was changed," Aoife offered off-handedly. "I think I might have suffered some alteration in such a predicament."

Alva looked across at her. "But you're a nun, for heaven's sake. Are you saying that Ernest was justified in what he did?"

"No, I'm not saying that. I'm saying that I understand how he must have felt."

Alva was silent, musing over what Aoife had said, and

she was still lost in thought as they pulled into Thora Beeding's front yard.

She was at the door before they had even pulled to a standstill. "Any news?" she cried. "You have found Irene?"

"No, no," said Alva as she climbed down from the carriage. "Not yet."

"Thank God you came," groaned an obviously stressed Thora. "I've been so worried. I don't know what to think anymore."

"Do you want to tell us what happened?"

"There was a man," said Thora. "That's what scared me the most."

"A man?"

"Yes, a man came here asking for Irene. He was an unpleasant sort and set me wondering where she was."

"What kind of man?" Alva said with a frown.

"An Irishman, going by his accent, he said he knew a friend of Irene's, Nee—am, something like that, I think that was her name."

"It's Niamh," said Aoife in a low voice. "Oh, dear me, I fear we are going to need heaven's help now."

"What did he say had happened to Niamh?" asked Alva.

"He did not say, just that he knew her and had come to find Irene. I told him she was out after game and he left. That was all. But now Irene is not here, she has not returned, and I hope all is well, I really do. Oh, I am so worried."

"Tell me," said Alva in a thin voice. "What did he look like?"

"He was a big-shouldered man, kind of hunched over, and he wore a dark beard. Not a very pleasant person, I think."

"Mulvenny!" spat Alva. "It has to be."

"Oh, they are come as Niamh warned us in her letter," breathed Aoife. "God help us all."

"He was alone, Thora?" pressed Alva.

"Yes, he was."

"I wonder how many of them there are," mused Alva.

"Who are these people?" asked a concerned Thora. "They obviously mean you harm."

"They do indeed," answered Alva. "It is from our time in New York, some kin to a fellow that came off badly and we thought that we had left that behind us. How the devil they found us, I don't know."

"It must be Niamh," said Aoife, and her voice quivered. "She's the only one who knew where we were."

Alva's hand flew to her mouth at the thought. "Sweet Jesus! I hope nothing has happened to her."

"Do you think these same men have taken Irene?" asked Thora.

"That may be. We shall have to find out."

"Oh, Alva," said Aoife. "They are come for us all, it has to be. They are here in Avagar Rhodes and come all the way from New York. It is us they want."

"They want you—why?" asked Thora.

"To kill us," said Alva in a thin and brittle voice. "They are a family, and it is revenge they want."

Thora hunched her back, put her head in her hands, and began to cry, and Aoife moved to comfort her.

"Don't worry, Thora. It is not you they want, they will not come here again."

"It is not me," she said as she sobbed. "It is poor Irene I am concerned about."

"I'll find them," said a determined Alva. "I'll find them and try to reason with them. If it's anybody they'll want to settle with, it will be me."

CHAPTER TWELVE

THE THREE MULVENNY brothers had arrived with their cousins Liam and Gerald, and the five had settled in a rented shack outside of town. It was a large, unkempt single room with bunk beds and a drafty kitchen area that was not the cleanest. The plank walls were warped and spaced by the weather, and mud filled the gaps. The whole place had seen better days. This did not worry the Mulvennys overly, as they had existed in far worse places back in their homeland.

The two cousins, however, were pleased with the adventure. Both were thirty-year-olds, and a visit to the United States was a magical experience and they were wonderstruck at all they had witnessed so far on their travels. The size of the country staggered them, the building and modernity amazed them after the sodden heaps of their own homes. They were eager too to avenge their kinsman, which allowed them something of a bumptious attitude, and in this they were overconfident, unlike their cousins the Mulvennys.

Liam and Gerald swaggered, laughing and joking

whilst the dourer Mulvennys watched their play through other, more sober eyes.

"Will we be getting us a drink soon, Dermot?" asked the curly-haired and ruby-cheeked Gerald, who wore heavy dark eyebrows that barred his brow over a pair of surprisingly bright twinkling blue eyes. "For I sure have a thirst on me."

"There'll be drink enough when this business is done," grunted Dermot.

"So what must we do?" asked Liam eagerly. A chunky fellow with battered slab-like features and the signs of hard labor in his large hands and brutish character. "Give us the word, Dermot, and we'll get it done."

"You'll be patient," warned Dermot, looking at them both from under his furrowed brow. "We are in a strange land here they call Texas and do not know the way of things. It's best to tread wary, you understand? We come here to exact a due for our brother Curtis, God rest his soul. So we have right on our side, by heaven we do. Thing is, these wee girls are hereabouts, and we shall find them and make them pay the price."

"Indeed, we will," echoed Gerald. "But they are no more than colleens, are they not. The one in New York was but a wanton whore, so you said, and that was easy enough, was it not?"

"Did they not slay Curtis, these little girls?" warned tall Edmond. "It was no easy matter to kill our brother, you will be sure of that."

"Agreed," grunted Dermot, raking fingers through his dark beard. "Do not underestimate them."

"Ach!" spat Liam. "I fear you boys are giving them more credit than is due."

"Hold your tongue," said the ape-like Wee Finley belligerently. "You bring nothing and know less. You are here at our behest, so do our bidding and bide your words."

"Well, 'tis a bore to be hanging here and doing nothing," complained Gerald.

"Then get out there, cousin," railed Dermot. "Go on then, get out there. Go find this skinny redhead, Irene. We know she is alone on the hunt. Go find her and bring her to me."

"We shall, God love us," cried Gerald. "Come, Liam, let us go find this hussy for them."

"To be sure they'll not do it sitting here on their bums," agreed Liam with a laugh.

"Is this wise, Dermot?" asked the solemn Edmond.

"Ach! Let them go if they are so bold. I'll not be bothered with it."

The three brothers watched the jaunty cousins leave, and when they were gone, Dermot turned to the others. "Let them make their mark, we have more serious business. There is the nun, the one they call Aoife."

"What of her?" asked Wee Finley. "Easy meat to be sure."

"She is the church-going one," Dermot went on. "To be found in the chapel here, but like I have said to the cousins, we go softly and not upset the believers around here. But if we take her, she will be our way to the one we really want—Alva North."

"Should we be so a-feared?" asked Edmond. "Like in the city, I've seen no sign of any Peelers here."

"No, nor I," concurred Dermot. "But I have heard of something called the Rangers, and it seems they exact the law."

"Aye and the sheriffs and marshals, wherever they may be," agreed Wee Finley.

"Well then, will you boys stay here and prepare us

some supper while I go and search out this chapel?" asked Dermot.

"You are the eldest, Dermot. We do as you say."

"Aye," agreed Wee Finley. "I've not eaten so well since we came here. Not like at home, here they have meat and eat it every day, even on Friday."

"Very well, I'll be on my way then."

Edmond was his normally sober self. "I just pray those eedjet cousins do not go astray."

"Ach! Damn them for fools," grunted Dermot. "I'm beginning to wish we had never brought them over."

"We'll use them, brother," said Edmond. "Let them walk the danger path and clear the way for us."

"Indeed," agreed Wee Finley. "I just want to get my hands on those little girls and make them pay in every way I can think of."

"Ah! You're a horny little devil indeed you are, Wee Finley," snorted Edmond.

FROM FORCE OF HABIT, Dermot dipped his finger in the font and crossed himself. He genuflected and took a pew at the rear of the chapel. It was a colorful place inside, unlike the churches he knew in his own country. Local artisans had created and painted in brash colors the simple naïve statues and stations of the cross that hung from the adobe walls. He sat for a moment, smelling the lingering scent of incense and wondering at the brightness of light inside the small place. In truth, the only mode of religion that existed in Dermot was one of habit and superstition. He was no believer, and the church only occupied a part of the past that he had grown up with, like an old coat he might disregard yet still keep in the wardrobe.

He was not a racist, unlike many in this country, and had no interest in either the Negro or Mexican other than a rather indifferent sense of superiority over them. The only people he truly hated were the British, who had ruled his country and misused it for many years.

As a young man, Dermot had been born into the Irish Republican Brotherhood and had taken the oath of allegiance as a matter of course and not from any genuine patriotism. He had followed their orders and obeyed their demands as if he were a member of a club, but with no desire to forge any new partition to his country. Rather, for him, it was a matter of custom and convenience. Dermot was concerned only with his nearest and dearest, and despite his lack of fervor in this church, he offered a silent prayer of memory for his brother, the deceased Curtis.

At the age of twenty and forced to feed his brothers, he had joined the British Army to earn enough for them all to survive. At that time, the United Kingdom had sent him and twenty-six thousand other Redcoats to join the French Army in confronting the Russia military in the Crimea.

The war had given him some things that he had approved of in later life. The harsh discipline he had witnessed had forged an army that had become paramount in the age. He had learnt the value of strict command and control that maneuvered thousands of men on the battlefield. He had learnt how to handle a Martini-Henry rifle and to kill with the bayonet. Lying under the Russian guns on the slopes of Alma and watching his companions pulverized, he had discovered the terrible horror that war brought, and it had created in him the iron will and indifference to death that was still his fashion all these years later.

A man alone without any ambivalence, his only ambition was the welfare of his brothers and to seek full payment against any man or woman who assaulted his family. It was a matter of course that Alva North and the other girls should pay that price. A morality he held so strongly that it had brought him across the thousands of miles to this place.

The Brotherhood had asked him on his return from service in the Crimea to become the *center rank of a circle,* as they called the colonel of a regiment, and continue to make war against their invaders. But he had avoided the issue, taking himself and his brothers into the more lucrative world of criminality, mainly theft and assassination. It was Dermot who had initially sent Curtis across to America to discover whether it was worth their while to emigrate and find richer pickings on the American continent. In part, Dermot experienced some guilt over this, as if it were he, in a way, who was responsible for sending his brother to his death.

Dermot felt movement in the empty chapel, and a nun brushed past him, heading down the aisle. She carried a bunch of flowers to set upon the altar, and their scent was strong in his nose as Dermot raised a hand in query.

"Tell me, sister," he said in a low voice full of polite respect. "Do you minister this fine church?"

She smiled at him benignly. "We do indeed, sir. I tell by your accent you are a visitor here. I hope we shall see you at service, there is a Mass every morning at seven o'clock and a rosary in the evening."

"That will be fine, sister. Do all you nuns attend the Mass?"

"We do indeed, there are so few men to offer altar service that I fear we sisters must play the part."

"Bless you," said Dermot. "I will be sure to come along."

She gave him a broad smile and hurried off to her duties with the arrangement of altar flowers.

Discovering all he wanted to know, Dermot rose from his seat, took one cool look at the white clad nun at the altar then turned and left the church.

THE COUSINS WERE ENJOYING their moment of freedom as they strolled along Main Street, dazzled by the display in storefront windows. Haberdashers with modish dresses, hats, and ribbons. Hardware and a sprawl of tools and equipment across the sidewalk, a butcher's shop with great haunches of meat, the likes of which the cousins had never seen before.

"Sweet Jesus!" Gerald said, gaping. "What have we come to in this place?"

"Indeed," agreed Liam. "It's a rare Paradise compared to Moore Street Market in Dublin town."

"Certainly more life here than at Goldenbridge." They both roared with laughter at that one, as he spoke of a cemetery.

Moving through the throng that populated the street, it was Gerald who first lifted his head and sniffed the air. "Have you got that, Liam?" he asked.

Liam paused, and he too raised his nose with his head tilted to one side. "Begod, I do! That's liquor I smell."

"Look there, a drinking house," said Gerald, pointing at the swing doors of the Number Thirteen Saloon.

"Grrr! Come now, Liam, I could do with a drink, could you not?"

"I can indeed, but how much money do we have?"

"Well, Dermot gave us one of these silver things, a bit like a shilling piece, but I've no idea what it's worth. He said it was at least a day's pay over here, whatever that may be."

"At least we'll get a pint with it, let's have a go."

Together, they mounted the sidewalk and pushed open the swing doors to take in the saloon's interior. Card players sat at the side tables, whilst facing them across the floor, other men leaned against a long wooden bar with an array of bottles and glasses behind the bartender. Moderately occupied at this hour, the air was still heavy with low chatter, pipe and cigar smoke. As they stood, a waiter crossed their path dressed in a long apron and carrying a tray with foaming schooners of beer.

"Good day, gentlemen," he said. "Will you take a table or head for the bar?"

They followed the direction of the man's nod and took it that he meant the counter where fellows dressed in city suits and working clothes leaned shoulder to shoulder.

"What can I get you?" asked the barman, a large, well-built fellow with slicked hair and a handsome mustache.

"How much will this get us?" asked Liam, boldly slapping the coin down on the counter.

The barman looked from the coin up to their faces. "You're new in town, ain't you?"

Both cousins nodded affirmation.

"Well, look here," explained the barman. "That there is a US silver dollar and it's worth a hundred cents. Couple of them silver dollars will buy you a grand bottle of brandy, but if you're aiming a bit lower, then two bits buys you a bottle of whiskey."

Both of their eyes lit up at the mention of whiskey. "And what exactly are two bits?" asked Liam.

"Twenty-five cents."

Both calculated, and that took a few moments. "So with this silver dollar here, we can get us four bottles of whiskey, is that right?"

"You can, it's not the best, but it's the cheapest."

"Oh, dear Lord!" breathed Gerald. "I've died and gone to heaven."

BY THE TIME two hours had passed, both men were well into their cups. Gerald, who had a strong voice, was singing loud traditional songs from where he stood and stamped out rhythm on a tabletop. Liam drunkenly lumbered around, demonstrating a clumsy step-dancing jig. The last bottle of the four was being passed from one to the other as they carried on their routines, oblivious to all others in the saloon. At first, this was seen as an amusing display by the locals gathered at the bar, and drunkenness in the saloon was not an unusual sight, but the two cousins were putting on something of a noisy show that, after time, became tiresome. Until finally, one man at the bar, who was trying to discuss a business deal with his companion, turned to them in annoyance.

"Will you boys lay off a while?" he hollered. "I'm trying to talk to my buddy here."

"You what?" slurred Gerald, stepping down awkwardly from the table.

"Keep it down, will you?" pleaded the man with a

spread of the hands. "I'm trying to have a discussion here."

"And so we should be hearing what you have to say?" argued Gerald, swaying towards the man. "Is that it?"

Liam, wavering under the effects of the rotgut whiskey, lumbered towards them, his eyes lighting up at the prospect of a fight. "Will you be putting up your fists with me, you pokey weasel?"

The man stared back at him. "I'm asking for some quiet."

"You are, are you?" snarled Gerald as he clumsily drew a short-bladed knife from his pocket and waved it threateningly. "Let's go to it then, Yankee Doodle, and see who's the better man."

The man opened the wings of his coat. "I have no weapon."

"No matter," growled Gerald. "I'll gut you anyway."

He was about to lunge forward with the blade when a boot caught him firmly in the rear end and shunted him forward, already unsteady on his feet, Gerald tumbled into his opponent, and both fell in a tangle to the floor.

"*Goddamn*!" roared Gar Seleen. "Will you two shut your racket? I'm trying to play cards here!"

"Hold on now!" blundered up Liam, taking Seleen by the shirtsleeve.

Without a thought, Seleen's gun was in his hand and he brought the grip down hard on Liam's head. The legs went from under the Irishman and he collapsed straight to the floor.

"What the hell are you bog-trotters doing here?" snarled Seleen, looking down at the cousins, both on their backs on the floor.

"You have something against the Irish?" snapped

Gerald, angry despite his predicament but ready to take offence at any slur.

"Nothing at all," said Seleen. "Except for your yap."

Liam was sitting up and rubbing his head. "We're just looking for some Irish women supposed to be around here, you know any?"

That clicked in Seleen's brain, his having met Alva and her friends, but he answered evasively. "We're all looking for some women," he said off-handedly. "What are these ones to you?"

"There's money in it if you know them," said Liam, floundering as he tried to get to his feet.

"Did I say you could get up?" snapped Seleen. "You stay there where you belong."

"Hey!" cried Gerald. "We're just saying, if you know of any Irish girls, let us know." He turned to the watching crowd. "Any of you. We'll pay for good information."

"You want girls, try Madame Pompadour's down the road."

"They're common but not that kind."

"Looks to me like you spent your prize money already anyway," said Seleen, jerking his chin at the three empty whiskey bottles on the counter. "Where you going to get this cash from?"

"Oh, we can get it," promised Gerald. "Just give us good word and there'll be a reward."

"Why you want these girls?" asked Seleen.

Liam, who was beginning to feel slightly uneasy at the information he was giving out and with Seleen's show of curiosity, mumbled a facile reason, "Their families back home wish to know how they fare, that's all."

Seleen was dismissive. "Well then, you'd best get of your ass and get looking."

"Who are you to tell us what to do?" blurted Liam, the

residue of drink making him belligerent. "Huh? Where do you come off treating us this way?"

Seleen looked down at him and flipped the lapel back from his badge. "US Marshal, dummy. Now get up and get out. I got a hand of cards waiting on me and I had enough of you two bums."

Thoughtfully, Seleen took his place at the card table again and watched the backs of the cousins as they barged out of the saloon doors. Then he turned his attention back to the table and the cards he had waiting and promptly forgot about the two Irishmen. "Well, gentlemen," he said to the other players. "I apologize for the interruption, but I do believe that I'll just have to raise that last bet."

CHAPTER THIRTEEN

It was Thora who brought Alva the news.

"She is safe," Thora told her. Her eyes were bright, and she was short of breath from excitement and her speed at coming, mostly though it was her beating heart under the dress that pulsed with relief.

"Thank the Lord," breathed Alva. "What happened to her?"

They sat on the busy hotel veranda and Alva sagged with relief at the news. It was late afternoon, and the usually busy township was settling down as folk made their way home for supper or settled in the saloon for a drink before their evening meal.

"Oh, my!" said Thora, her hands fanning her over-heated cheeks. "I am quite overcome with it all. The poor girl is completely exhausted," gushed Thora. "Foolishly, she went off alone into the forest high up along the mountain slopes. I cannot believe she would do such a thing. Everybody knows one does not do that without an accompanying partner, it is *much too* dangerous. What a reckless woman she is. Apparently, she thought to get a deer or elk there, but unfortunately, she only found a mountain lion."

"Dear me." Alva frowned, noting that although Thora's tone was critical, there was an element of pride in her voice as well. "Is she all right?"

"The lion treed her, so she had to climb up to escape the beast. She was up there two days and a night without food or drink, as it kept snuffling around and circling the tree. When she finally risked getting down, she was exhausted and set off to make her way home."

"Quite an adventure," said Alva.

"She fell, slipped on some scree coming out of the mountains, and took a nasty tumble. I guess she was too tired to pay proper attention but had to hobble the last few miles back on a twisted ankle."

"Does she need a doctor?" asked a worried Alva.

"Well, there is a nasty graze, some bruises and scratches, but I have cleansed and bandaged her. I think she will be all right. I just thank the heavens she is back, and well, I thought I'd lose my mind with the worry. I left her sleeping and thought I had better come and let you know."

Alva saw that the schoolteacher was too highly strung, a kindly soul yet prone to nerves and quite the opposite of tough-minded Irene, and yet Thora genuinely appeared to care about her. Alva was glad that her friend had found a kindly soul mate.

"I must tell Aoife," said Alva. "She'll be worried enough with the Mulvennys being here. I think we had better get together now Irene is back and discuss what we should do."

"Will you come to my place?"

"Yes, I'll fetch Aoife and bring her over."

After Thora left to watch over Irene, Alva hurried to

the chapel to let Aoife hear the good news. Her mind was only half on the relief at Irene's safe return as her thoughts were still occupied with Ernest and her feelings about him. She now found that her earlier anger and dismay over Ernest had receded a little after the scare with Irene and the advent of the Mulvennys, somehow it had jolted her into a more objective and rational frame of mind.

She decided she must meet with Ernest and talk things through. It had not been fair how she had turned away from him without a word, and she felt bad about it now. Although secretly and though she would not admit it openly, she missed him, and his warm presence played in the back of her mind like a happy memory. It was strange how she could eradicate the dark image she had created after the killing of the Browns but now she recalled their time together in New York and what a gentle man he had been then.

The dichotomy confused her. On the one hand, the able killer, and on the other, the same man who had taught her so many soft lessons in their bed together. Was she being fair, and had she acted precipitously? She had no resolution, and it was a matter that troubled her sorely.

Alva put all the scrambled thoughts to the back of her mind for the present and went to hire a buggy at the corral.

SHE DROVE to the chapel and picked Aoife up in the hired rig, and they rode together out to Thora's place.

"What was she thinking?" asked Aoife as they drove

there. "Climbing around mountains with a gun like some hunter."

"That's just her reckless inclinations," said Alva, giving the horse a little more rein and slowing the pace. "Irene likes to test herself."

Aoife bit her lip and half turned on the seat so she peeped at Alva around the edge of her veil. "Have you seen any sign of them?"

"You mean the Mulvennys, no, nothing. If they're here, there's been no sign except the one of them who visited Thora."

"How is she taking it all?"

"Thora?" Alva asked and then shrugged. "I don't know, she is the fretful type though, and I believe she will worry about anything if she sets her mind to it."

"But aren't we bringing that *worry* to her?"

Alva nodded. "True enough, but she can always walk away."

"She cares for Irene."

Alva looked across at her and saw the implied meaning behind Aoife's lowered head. "I thought the Church was against that kind of thing."

Aoife was coy and faintly embarrassed by her reply. "Well, yes, that's right, it is so. I just happen to feel I am glad that Irene is comforted and happy."

Alva smiled. "And that's all you need to feel."

THEY FOUND Irene inside the house with her bandaged leg resting on a chair and Thora fussing over her.

"Good night to you," said Alva in greeting. "So you plan on becoming lion feed now, is that it?"

Irene grinned. "Have to admit I thought my time was up and I didn't even catch anything."

"Just a wounded leg by the look of it," added Aoife.

"Well, dear sister, you spend so much time on your knees," Irene came back archly. "It's a wonder you're not on crutches yourself."

"Now, now," shushed Thora. "Don't go getting yourself in a tizz, will you?"

"You see how she looks after me," said Irene with an ironical smile. "Brings me tea—I'd much rather coffee. Brings me soup—when I'd rather a steak. Who can fault such a woman?"

"You're certainly well looked after," said Alva.

"Enough of this banter," said Thora, playing the host. "Will you all sit down, and what would you like to drink?" She paused, recalling what Irene had just said. "Tea or coffee?"

There was general laughter from the girls at the quizzical look on Thora's face.

"They'll take what you bring them, dear," Irene said, chuckling. "And be glad of it."

"Very well," said the flustered Thora as she hurried red-faced off to fetch water from the pump.

"Now then," said Alva, taking a serious tone. "We must make some decisions."

"Agreed," said Irene. "The damned Mulvennys are amongst us, and we must prepare. There are three of the rascals, so Niamh said in her letter, and it is best we are ready."

"How?" Aoife asked with a shrug. "What shall we do?"

Alva leaned forward with both hands clasped on the table. "First off, we had better arm ourselves, gun or knife, axe or hammer."

"I have the shotgun," said Irene.

"So you have, how about you, Aoife, can you manage this?"

Aoife frowned, her pretty face twisting in concern. "I fear not, bloody warfare is not to my liking, and against my calling I fear."

"Come now," said Irene. "This is your life we are speaking of, you must defend yourself at least."

"If it is God's will, then I will follow His calling. We must try for peace," said Aoife, her voice trailing off.

"Listen to me, Aoife," said Alva in a forceful tone. "They came here knowing where we were to be found. The only place they could get that information was from Niamh, and I don't believe she would give us up for anything. Do you understand?"

"No, what do you mean?"

Alva looked at Irene at a loss, and not knowing how to tell the gentle-natured Aoife.

"She is dead, Aoife," said Irene bluntly. "They will have mistreated and killed her to get knowledge of our whereabouts and to be sure that she did not forewarn us. But they were too late on that score."

"Oh, no!" gasped Aoife, her hands flying to her mouth. "Dear Lord, not Niamh."

"It will be so," said Irene darkly.

"Ah, God help us," said Aoife, lowering her eyes and clasping her hands in prayer. "May we bless the soul of our sister, I pray, oh, I pray it is not so."

"There is no other way. Niamh gave us warning, and then these creatures show up here all the way from New York. We had our trail pretty well covered, and it must have happened so. How else could they have found us?"

"I don't know, I don't know," wavered Aoife. "Perhaps somebody else told them."

"There is nobody else," Irene said with finality.

A worried Thora came in with a tray and set it on the table. "There is tea and coffee, I didn't know which you wanted."

Irene rested a hand on her elbow. "That is just fine, Thora. Just fine."

"Oh, good," Thora said with a sigh.

"I don't think we should be apart," cut in Alva. "We should stick together now."

"Well, you can stay here," said Thora. "And welcome."

They all muttered their thanks, and then Aoife said, "I must just attend Mass tomorrow, the sisters expect me, but I can return after that."

"Even if you play no part, Aoife, and stay here, I think it will be best," said Alva.

"Very well, I shall be guided by you. Although I should like a Mass said for the repose of the soul of dear Niamh, if you will agree."

Both Irene and Alva nodded approval before Alva turned to Thora. "Do you have any other weapons here?"

"I have a Henry rifle, it was my father's when he was in the Confederate forces during the war, and he left a revolver too. Daddy prized that rifle, he said he could load it on Sunday and it would fire all week."

"Is there ammunition?"

"I believe so, it is a while since I have seen them. They are put away since my father died."

"Would you mind getting it out for us?"

"Of course," said Thora, hurrying off again.

"If one of us carries the revolver and another the rifle and you keep the shotgun, Irene, we should be well equipped, I think," said Alva.

"I don't think I can do that," said Aoife with a look of disdain on her face. "Not handle a gun."

"Well, all right," said Alva. "Then Irene and I will carry the guns."

"Here they are," said Thora, coming back in with a canvas sack. "I'm sorry, it's a little dusty."

She opened the sack and pulled out a rifle with its brass receiver cover and an Army Colt revolver with a belt, an old holster, and a CSA belt buckle.

Alva pouted and picked up the rifle. "I know nothing about these things, do you, Thora?"

"Oh, yes, Daddy was very sure I learnt how. See here, you unlatch at the top of the barrel and slide the bullets in there. The rifle holds fifteen rounds, so it has a lot of firepower, but there is no safety, so you must be careful not to knock it."

"Why's that?"

"Because if you jar it, then it might go off and hurt somebody, of course."

"And the pistol?"

"Look," said Thora, falling easily into her role as teacher. "There are percussion caps and bullets in the pouch."

"Perhaps we could experiment with these?"

"Certainly, we can go to the yard outside. I'm sure you'll soon get the hang of it."

Thora was quite cheerful about the whole process, and this surprised Alva, but then she realized that Thora had grown up surrounded by firearms all her life and was quite confident around the weapons.

"I think I had better get back," said Aoife. "It is time for evensong, and the nuns count on me for the choir."

"As you will," said Alva a little doubtfully. "I will drive you."

"Are you sure?" asked Aoife.

"Indeed I am. It will be safer."

"As you wish."

IT WAS on her return to Thora's after leaving Aoife at the chapel that Alva thought of Ernest and that perhaps this was a quiet moment to enable her to call on him and talk. With such a thought in mind, she turned off the road and made her way through the cutoff heading for the Grant Ranch.

It was a moonlit night, and the silver circle sat shining in a black sky. Once out of the trees, the countryside was an array of light and shadow with little definition other than the highlighted crests of the rolling hills.

It was a strange sensation for Alva driving through the silence, and as a lone traveler with only the buggy for company, she felt suddenly alone. Something stirred in her breast though, and she realized it was the prospect of seeing Ernest again, and that surprised her.

At the overlook to the ranch, she could see the house lighted by lamps and looking inviting as it sat surrounded by darkness.

She rode on down, and as she neared, she saw a tall figure waiting on the veranda silhouetted against the lamp glow from inside.

"Heard you coming," said Ernest as she pulled up before the house. "I hoped it would be you."

"I think we should talk," said Alva, laying aside the reins and climbing down.

"Anything you like, Alva. Come up here and we can sit a while. Grace is inside putting the kids to bed."

"Thank you."

She followed him to the far end of the veranda,

where there were chairs and a small table. A glass and bottle of whiskey stood on the table, along with gun oil and rags beside the pistol he had been cleaning.

"Can I get you something? I was just enjoying a glass myself."

"No, I'm fine."

Strangely, Alva found herself at a loss. She had tried to prepare for how the meeting would go, but now all preconceptions seemed to evaporate as she looked at his face outlined by the lamplight.

He sat with one hand rubbing his jaw and fingering his mustache thoughtfully, and looked at her but said nothing. In the darkness, his shadowed eyes showed her nothing, but she could see pinpoints of light reflected from deep inside.

"I just wanted—" Alva began.

"I'm glad to see you," he cut in.

"Look, Ernest, I know that—"

"You look good, Alva. Real good."

"I—I—"

"You know, this cannot be."

"Damn you, Ernest, will you stop interrupting me!"

"Oh," he said quietly. "I'm sorry, just that I was a-feared I wouldn't see you again, and now you're here, it's a real delight."

"How can you be like this?" said Alva, leaning forward intently. "One minute you are as mellow as a berry and the next a bloody killer, I just don't get it, I really don't."

He settled back in his chair and it creaked as he eased himself. "Well," he said with a sigh, "that makes two of us then, as I can't see how you do not understand."

"How so?"

"Are you so far removed from killing that you will judge me?"

Alva moved back on her seat. "You mean the gang in New York?"

"Just how many were there, Alva?"

Alva drew a steadying breath. "Curtis Mulvenny is the main concern."

"Is he. And is he the reason you are down here?"

"Yes, they thought to stop us, and I killed him as he had just cut off the head from my friend's shoulders. It was an act of necessity, Ernest. Those men stood in the way of our freedom, mine and the others. They were defensive acts, not assassinations."

Ernest spread his hands. "I too fled to avoid carnage, did I not? That is why I was in New York."

"But it was so disconnected, so detached, Ernest, the way you shot the Browns was like a different person. As judge and jury all in one, and permitted to carry out the act as a lone executioner. I did not think you were capable of such a thing."

"Of protecting mine, is that so hard to understand?"

"It was not the protecting but the cold-blooded murder."

"That was justice you saw," said Ernest. "You didn't like it, but that man had it coming. He came bringing damnation on my house, and that does not happen without me taking exception."

Alva knew he was absolute in his feelings, and she felt as if she were facing a brick wall, he was so obdurate.

"And the boy," she said. "The boy in his wheelchair, a helpless young man, was that also necessary?"

"He had a shotgun, Alva, and he would have used it unless I stopped him."

"I don't understand it at all," said a perplexed Alva.

Ernest spoke quietly and calmly as if time stood still and all he had for her was long and careful patience. "Perhaps you have known things differently, Alva. For a long time here we have had to be prepared to defend ourselves. There is a history of raiders, of renegades, outlaws and warring Indians—it's in our blood to stand ready before such invasions against our lives and values. There was no one else to turn to. That's why I joined the Rangers, to try and bring some element of order into what is a wild and dangerous country for ordinary folk."

"Can men be so worse here than anywhere else? Sure, we too have trying times and terrible ways back home ourselves," said Alva. "But is it necessary to destroy these unfortunates in such a callous fashion?"

Ernest nodded and continued, "These kinds of men think little of what may have been built with effort and care. Something is missing in their makeup, and they will destroy, rape, and kill without any thought at all for their victims. I know I've seen it many times, and maybe the life you led back home was free of such things, but unless you stamp it out, it will rise up and run you off."

"You think that is what would have happened with Jud Brown?"

"Yes, that is what he would have aimed at eventually. His wife had gone, his boy legless, and there was a big hole where his heart should be. It don't matter the reasons for his problem, maybe they were fair enough, I don't know that, but I do know he came at me to solve his difficulty and in that he met his match."

There was a pride in what Ernest said. It was not arrogance but only a tall man with assurance in the rightness of his actions. As Alva looked at his silhouette outlined in the shadows, she could not help but admire his singular attitude. He was a law to himself, but it was a kind of rough law based on the morality of necessity with no arbitrary causality, and that left her bemused.

"I don't know, Ernest, I just don't know, maybe it isn't for me."

"I have a suggestion for you," said Ernest. "Let's lay that aside for the moment. I've feelings for you, Alva, and I don't want to see you go. This is a good thing, and I'm holding out for you here."

Despite herself, Alva reached across blindly and laid her hand on his, where it rested on the chair arm. She did not know how it happened, but once she felt the firm and smooth skin, it was a comfort to her.

"It was good in New York, wasn't it?" she asked.

"The best I ever knew."

Suddenly, they were standing, and he held her in his arms and was kissing her. Alva closed her eyes and felt the warmth wash over her. She gasped in pleasure and threw her arms around his neck and pulled him close, and they kissed for a long time.

In the shadows and soft lamplight, Alva knew, despite everything, he was the one for her, and however he was made, she could not let him go.

"Now will you come live with me?" he asked, his breath soft in her ear and as if he sensed the shift in her attitude.

Alva smiled. "I cannot just now, I must stay with the girls at Thora's."

"Why is that? I thought she had company enough there with your friend Irene?"

"It's not that." She lowered her arms and turned to look out from the veranda at the moonlight lighting the pale track leading down to the ranch. "There are some people here from New York."

"Is it trouble?" he asked, a serious tone entering his voice.

"It might be."

"Seleen told me about some Irish fellows he met in town. Couple of drunken roustabouts full of fuss and bother, he said they were looking for some Irish girls and wondered if they might mean you."

"Sounds about right, but we are ready. They'll not come near us without finding out we are more than they can handle."

"Oho!" He laughed softly. "You sound pretty sure of yourself. Are you that confident?"

"We can take care of ourselves."

"I reckon you can, but remember I am here if you need me."

"I'd best get back, Irene will be worried."

She held his hand and let her fingers slide through his as she crossed to the veranda steps. "Say hello to Grace for me."

"Dammit, girl! She's probably listening at the keyhole right now." He turned to the house and called out, "Ain't you, Grace?"

"I ain't hearing nothing," came Grace's voice from inside. "I'm putting my children to bed."

"See," said Ernest, turning back to Alva with a grin. "I told you so."

Smiling, Alva puckered her lips and blew him a kiss. "I'll see you soon, big man."

"I sure hope so, sweet lady."

NEXT MORNING, out in the yard, Alva and Irene practiced gunplay under Thora's tuition. She showed them how to half cock the Henry rifle before levering it open, then how to load the .44 caliber cartridges. After that, the Army Colt with its black powder load and ball, before pressing it down and carefully placing the percussion cap of fulminate of mercury, which fired off the powder when the hammer was dropped. It was a long-winded procedure, and the more modern brass cartridges were easier to use, but for now, this was all they had.

Shooting was the difficult part, not so much squeezing the trigger as hitting anything after that. Both guns were heavy, and Alva found that the weighty Henry rifle barrel tended to float all over the place as she tried to hold it steady on the target.

They shot at old bottles and china cups set on a rail in the pet enclosure Irene was building.

But it was Irene who brought an end to their rather halfhearted practice when she came out with her shotgun and blew the entire target range to pieces with one blast of her double barrels.

"*Jesus*!" she cursed as she hauled off with the shotgun. "I'm sick of this. If the Mulvennys come running, I'll blow the beggars away with this blaster."

"Well," snapped Thora in her best schoolmistress accent as she looked at the shredded posts and coils of broken wire. "It looks like I'll have to buy some more baling wire now."

"Oh, I'm sorry," said the cowed Irene. "Don't worry, I'll build it up again."

"You have a temper on you, Irene. If you were one of my pupils, you would be standing in the corner with a dunce's cap on your head."

"You're beginning to remind me of the nuns back home," returned a cynical Irene. "Would you prefer smacking my bare arse just like them?"

"I dare say you would rather enjoy that," was Thora's acid response.

"Hey! Hey!" Alva laughed. "Cut it out, you two. Look, I guess we have the principals now, we know how to load and how to shoot, just pray that if it comes to it, we might actually hit something."

"Yes," agreed Thora. "We had better get those guns inside and cleaned before Aoife gets here."

Alva paused thoughtfully. "Aoife, where is she?"

Irene looked up at the sun's position in the sky. "What time is it? Surely the Mass is over by now."

"She should be here."

"Perhaps you'd best go fetch her," suggested Thora.

"Maybe I should. I don't like that she's late."

"Take the buckboard," said Thora.

"And the pistol," added Irene. "Just in case."

Alva was moving over towards the corral and ready to harness the horse when they all heard the sound of approaching hoof beats.

"Here she comes!" called Irene. "Late as ever."

But the man who rode into the yard bore no resemblance to their friend the nun.

"Now look here," he called, holding his hands over his head. "I come in peace, there's no need for them firearms."

Irene paid him no mind and raised the shotgun. "Who the hell are you?"

"What do you want here?" called Alva suspiciously.

"My name is Gerald, but you can call me Jerry if you've a mind, cousin to the Mulvennys." He sat back in the saddle and smiled, spreading his apple-red cheeks in a ready grin. "I've come with a message from Dermot Mulvenny."

"The devil you have," spat Irene.

"Indeed, I have. You see, he holds your friend, the little nun."

Alva gasped, and Irene stiffened and the blood drained from her face. "What have you done with Aoife?"

"Not to worry, she is quite safe—for now. Dermot wants a word," said Gerald. "He wants to talk with you two concerning his brother's death. Would like to know the details, you know, that kind of thing. After all, wouldn't any relative want to know the last moments of a loved one?"

"He didn't say much at all as I recall," snapped Alva, remembering Curtis' sad begging eyes looking at her.

"Not as much as that dear fat friend of yours," leered Gerald. "So I'm told."

"*Niamh*!" croaked Irene. "You hurt Niamh? What did you do to her?"

"What do you know of that?" asked Alva.

"Only what I hear," said Gerald, raising the bar of his dark eyebrows in casual indifference. "I was not there myself, but heard she had a smacking time of it, so the brothers say. She told them everything, where you were and how to get here, quite the mouthpiece in fact, a regular source of travel information."

"I ought to blow your fecking head off!" spat Irene.

"Now that would not be advisable." Gerald chuckled, eminently sure of himself. "Harm me and they'll barbecue that nun of yours on a grill fire."

"Wouldn't help *you* though, would it?" threatened Irene.

"Calm down," ordered Gerald derisively. "You'll not get anywhere like that."

"Oh, the hell you know," snarled Irene. "It'd give me a world of satisfaction to lift your head from your shoulders."

"Where's it to be?" cut in Alva.

"He wants you two there," said Gerald. "You're to come to the sawmill when they are shut down for the night."

"And will Aoife be there?"

Gerald shrugged. "That I don't know."

"Well, she had better be there or we will not."

"You'll be there," snorted Gerald, turning his horse away.

"I'll be looking for you, you red-faced bastard," promised Irene.

"Pray you do." He grinned over his shoulder as he rode away. "I could do with a little back home wrapped around me legs."

The three women stood watching him depart, and after a long moment, Thora spoke, "How terrible."

"Had to come," said grim-faced Alva. "They did not follow us from New York to have a pleasant conversation."

"I'm glad of it," said Irene. "Beats waiting around for them to make a play."

"You don't have to go," urged Thora.

"Of course we do. They made sure of that by taking Aoife."

"Are you convinced they have her?" asked Thora.

Alva nodded. "They have her alright. Do you know this sawmill, Thora? Can you tell us anything about it?"

Thora considered for a moment. "Well, you know it is the biggest industry around here with all the forest. Actually, I took the children to see the place last year. Mr. Larenstone, that's the owner, was quite kind and gave us a complete tour."

"Well, that is useful, Thora. Can you tell us what you know?"

"I certainly can, the forest is huge, about forty thousand acres, and the camp has quite a few men working there as lumberjacks, and they have a purpose-built tram railway to take them deep into the forest to cut the trees. The children really enjoyed that, I can tell you."

"Yes, but what about the mill?"

"Right, that is alongside the upper banks of the lake, and they have two large sheds for cutting, one of them is a little old now, and that holds what is called the gang saw with several parallel blades, and the other with a circular saw, a huge thing for cutting great timbers into planks. It is quite fascinating."

"There are other buildings?"

"Oh, yes, quite a few, there's a cook's shanty, barracks for the men, and at the back, a big stabling area for the horses that chain-haul the logs. Then there is also a steam engine that powers it all, and great banked piles of logs ready to be sawn up. Mr. Larenstone says that they can process between a thousand and eighty thousand feet of lumber a day. It is quite an enterprise, I can tell you."

"What about guards? Do you know if they have any?"

"I don't think they bother too much. There is an old fellow they call a Lobby-Hog, who is just a caretaker and keeps the barracks fires going. Sweet old man, really, full of jokes and tall tales."

"But no patrols?"

Thora shook her head. "There is not much worth stealing except for pine logs, so I doubt it."

"Fine," said Alva, biting her lip as she thought it through.

"You can't trust them, you know that, don't you?" said Irene. "They surely intend to murder us."

"I know it," agreed Alva. "But we still have to get Aoife back safely."

"So we have to go."

"Yes, we do. We have no choice, and after what he said about Niamh, I feel a great urge to face up to these Mulvenny dogs."

"Aye, me too," agreed Irene. "But how many do you think there are?"

"There will be the three brothers, and we've seen one of the cousins. Seleen mentioned two of them, so it'll be five altogether."

"You can't," cried Thora. "Not two of you, you can't confront five men on your own."

"Don't worry," said Irene grimly. "They have never come across two like us before."

"We were raised in a hard school," Alva told Thora. "And we have faced their sort before, have we not, Irene?"

"We have, and left the scum lying in the street as well."

"What can I do?" asked Thora. "I don't know how I can help."

Alva looked at Irene, and both knew that the gentle Thora would be little help in the fight to come.

"Perhaps you might drive us there in the buckboard?" said Alva as a kindly means of appeasement.

"Oh, yes, I can do that."

"If we can free Aoife, we shall guide her to you, and you must ride away at full speed with her. Will you do that?"

Thora nodded a nervous affirmation.

"Then it's best we prepare."

CHAPTER FOURTEEN

THEY WAITED UNTIL SUNSET.

Then, with Thora at the reins and the two others on each side of her on the driving seat, they drove into town. Their road led through Main Street, where halfway along a broad opening between the houses branched off and a wide wagon road led down a long incline to the lake and the sawmill below.

There were gas streetlights along the Main Street, but only a few of them and widely spaced so that between them were areas of deep shadow. Lamps were lit in some of the houses and shone with a yellow glow behind blinds and in windows. The three looked around warily as they passed along the quiet street, with the only sound coming from the Number Thirteen Saloon, where the noise of laughter and loud conversation against a jangling piano in the background broke the night.

"Keep your eyes peeled," warned Alva. "There's no telling where they might be."

"D'you think they'd try it on in Main Street?" asked Irene, her head rotating warily from side to side.

"No telling with these yelps, you watch that side and I'll watch this."

A few figures hurried along the boardwalks, their forms and features indistinct in the darkness, but as they drew level with the saloon, one figure stood out. He leaned casually against the porch support with a beer glass in one hand and watched them come close.

"Evening, ladies. About time you got here, the mill's been closed for hours."

"Who's that?" called Alva, leveling the Henry rifle. "State your name before I blast you."

"Steady on," said Gar Seleen, stepping down from the saloon porch. "And stop waving that rifle around."

"Mr. Seleen, what are you doing here?"

"Well now, we couldn't let you take on these assholes by yourselves, could we?"

A horseback rider moved out from the shadows on the other side of the road and came closer, and as he moved into a pool of light from the streetlamp, Alva gasped. "Ernest!"

"Yes, it is," he said, drawing up alongside.

"What—why are you here?"

"Gar got the word earlier this evening," Ernest supplied. "Those cousins cannot hold their liquor, and before long, they were blabbing about how things would change around here soon enough."

"Bragging little toadies, it seems they have some almighty plans for you ladies," Seleen went on. "I thought Ernie ought to know."

"But they have Aoife," said Alva. "They're holding her against our arrival at the mill."

"Yes, indeed," said Ernest. "I've been past just now, and they are waiting. But it will be hard for they are spread out on the site, it's best you let me and Seleen deal with this."

"But no, you cannot risk yourselves on our behalf," cried Alva. "This is our problem alone."

"Surely not," said Ernest, and Alva saw his grin shine against the shadows that encompassed his face under the hat brim. "We are the law, and these fellows seek to break it."

"These peckerwoods piss me off," grunted Seleen. "Far better this than playing minder for that cattle buyer Baldwin."

"Well—I don't know what to say," breathed Alva. "You both take my breath away."

"We'll just say God bless you and God speed," burst out Irene. "Glad of your company, boys."

"Then listen," said Ernest in a serious tone. "You must bide by what we say, both Seleen and I have experience in this, and if you are insistent on coming, then you will do as we say, agreed?"

"Of course," said Alva without delay.

"Just let's get on with it," urged Irene. "I have a mind to burn some errant Paddy boys."

"We go on foot," stressed Ernest. "We must know where they hold your friend the nun prisoner, if it is here or elsewhere. Like I say, they are spread around the camp and will hold plumb positions with good cover, so we must spread out and approach cautiously from different directions. My intention is that we move in on them in a roundabout, stealthy manner."

"You must become like ghosts or creeping Indians, you understand?" said Seleen. "Don't go tripping over your toes in the dark."

"We understand," said Alva. "Thora will be waiting

here with the buckboard in case we have to leave in haste."

"Hell! Against this crew?" Seleen chuckled. "You'll be lucky if we can leave at all."

"Indeed," agreed Ernest. "Don't go thinking this will be an easy thing."

"More than likely we'll all end up dead anyway," quipped Seleen.

"*Jasus*!" spat Irene. "Will you cut that out, gawping like an auld women. We will ream these bastards, sure we will."

"Hah!" Seleen laughed. "There she goes. By God! This gal has more balls than most men I know."

Alva and Irene climbed down and Thora began to turn the buckboard as they stepped into the wide opening of the wagon road. With a comforting hand gently placed on her arm, Irene parted company with a fearful Thora.

"What are you carrying there?" asked Ernest.

"I have this Henry rifle," said Alva. "And Irene has a shotgun and a Colt pistol."

"Well, look," whispered Ernest. "Stay close to me if you can."

Thc four spread across the road and began the slow walk downhill into the blackness below.

"I will tell you how it is," said Ernest as they began their descent. "The farthest point beyond the lake is the forest, and then there is the lumberjack camp. Nearest is the sawmill, with the camp boss's administration shack on the left of us, next to the horse corral and wagon park. The two sheds at the center are the sawmill pits, on the left the gang saw, and on the right the circular with long beds for the logs." He waved a hand directly in front at the extended rectangular sheds, dark and indistinct in the poor light as the gas streetlights on Main Street hardly reached this far. "Over on the right is the mill workers' bunkhouse and the cookhouse. Maybe you can see there's outhouses on the slope behind and some piles of timber stacked ready for sawing."

"We'll take the right," said Seleen. "You ready, girl?" he asked Irene.

"I am," she answered, and Alva could hear the tense excitement in her voice.

"Any of the workers wandering around?" asked Seleen.

"I reckon most are up in the saloon, but maybe a few staying home in the bunkhouse," said Ernest. "Probably playing cards and darning socks, they'll stay there once it kicks off."

"So how many we looking at?"

"There will be five," said Alva. "The three brothers and two cousins."

"Can't wait to run into those two particular cretins again," growled Seleen.

"Okay," said Ernest. "Alva and I will head left, making for that wagon park. Between us, we'll circle around each side and meet up at the far end where the lake edge lies beyond the sawpits. There's the steam engine house up there to power the saws, you can tell it by the chimneys. Now, are you all ready?"

Without giving any answer, the four reached the base of the incline and silently separated. Seleen and Irene sloping off towards the cookhouse, and Ernest and Alva making their way over the wagon road with its deep and uneven ruts towards the outlines of long, high-sided wagons looming in the shadows.

Ernest had his Colt in hand, and he glanced across at

Alva, indicating with the pistol that she should spread away and leave space between them.

It was quiet, and only the distant sound of the forest came rippling across the flat, calm waters of the lake. There was no moon, so the darkness was complete, and all the buildings rose indistinct and black against the star shine. Alva smelled the crisp scent of cut pine, of sap and wood chippings laid against the oppressive stench of oil and grease and hot metal cooling after a day of work.

They were in amongst the wagons and Alva lost sight of Ernest as he moved into the shadows. There were pools of water here where some of the wagon wheels had been washed free of mud, and their glaze reflected the starlight in sudden sheets. Stepping carefully, Alva moved forward, hunched over her rifle and attentive to every sound, no matter how faint.

She heard the clink of chains and wondered where it came from, somewhere ahead, she guessed.

The flash when it came surprised her into immediate stillness, she froze even as the bang of the firearm echoed around the empty work site. Something hit the side of the wagon near her and an explosive spray of splinters powdered her cheek. It was then she moved, ducking back as the first shot was met by an answering volley from Ernest somewhere off to the wagons on her left.

Peering around the edge of the wagon, Alva raised the rifle and fired blindly in the direction of the gun flash.

"So you came, didn't you now?" the voice of Dermot called out. "And brought a few friends with you I see."

"Where is Aoife?" Alva cried out.

Dermot laughed loudly. "Come on, come get her if ye can, ye wee bitch."

Ernest fired again and the bullet must have hit the iron-bound wheel of a wagon as it spat sparks and then whined away into the night. It was followed by the sound of running feet heading over gravel as a body ducked its way towards the horse corral beyond.

The horses, big dray animals and strong for the chain hauling, were skittishly running around the fenced stable yard and nervously whickering in dismay at the loud gunshots.

"Come on," said Ernest, his voice closer than Alva imagined. "He's moved off now."

There were heaped logs piled in a great pyramid in front, and they lay between the wagons and the corral. To avoid them and keep to some cover, Alva worked her way along the wall of the administration building that rose out of the darkness on her right-hand side. Before her, she could make out a narrow alley between the building and a store shed that lay just beyond.

Firing now was coming from the corral and somewhere in the darkness beyond the store shed. Alva made out the different sounds that a pistol and rifle made. She could no longer see Ernest, but knew he was firing as his shots came steadily from her left.

Then she heard it.

A soft bumping and crashing coming from inside the administration building. There was a faint mewling sound and she thought she made out the words, *Help me*!

Startled, Alva recognized the sound of Aoife's voice. She wanted to call out to Ernest, but now the sound of shooting was coming from the far side of the site, way over beyond the saw pits, and she knew that Seleen and Irene were in the fight also.

Edging carefully over to the alley, she clung to the shadows and slid into the gap between the buildings.

Then she heard Dermot again. "That's it, Edmond, give 'em good measure and blast the blood."

"I'm with you, brother," yelled Edmond in reply, a wild-sounding laughter in his voice. "We'll kill them all for Curtis's sake."

Firing raged through the night in great ragged flashes as the two brothers blazed away and Ernest gave them good reply from his hiding place amongst the stacked logs.

Alva saw her chance, and whilst they were engaged, she ran along the narrow alleyway to the front of the office building. There was a raised platform and a porch over a doorway and two dirt-rimmed windows impossible to see through. No light, but she could hear the struggles from inside more clearly now. Clambering up onto the raised entrance, she stood alongside the door and called out as loud as she dared, "Aoife, is that you?"

"Alva! Alva, are you there?" Aoife cried. "Thank God you came! Can you get me out of here?"

Alva tried the door, but it was locked. In frustration, she kicked the woodwork, the cacophony of the various gun battles across the yard hid the sound and she took to using the stock of the rifle against the door handle. With repeated blows, it finally gave way, and the whole lock piece fell out and the door flew open.

Aoife was inside, lashed to a chair. There was little light, so Alva found it hard to see her clearly. The veil was gone from Aoife's head, and her habit ripped open, exposing her upper body. There were bruises and blood streaking her face, but the relief was obvious in her eyes.

"Oh, Alva," she gasped. "They were awful, I think they would kill me."

"Never mind now," said Alva, going behind and looking at the binding. "Let's get you out of here." As she struggled with the rope, she whispered hurriedly to her friend, "Now listen, Ernest and Seleen are out there with Irene, they are battling the Mulvennys, so I must go and join them. Once you are out of here, you will run up the hill back to Main Street. Thora is waiting up there in a buckboard."

"But will you be coming?" asked Aoife, as one arm came free.

"Later, first we must finish with the Mulvennys."

"Let them go, they are the Devil himself. Rotten creatures and vile, they touched me, Alva," she said, sobbing. "I didn't want them to, but their filthy hands—"

"We'll never be free of them if we let them go."

The last of the ropes gave way and Aoife was able to stand.

"Do like I say," Alva ordered, pushing her towards the door. "Run and don't look back, you understand me?"

"You—I—," she stuttered.

"Go!" said Alva, shoving her outside.

Stumbling and clutching her torn garments around her, Aoife made her weaving way back towards the wagon road. A pale and lonely figure in the darkness as she climbed the sloping hillside.

Alva took one look to make sure she was safely on her way and then turned, and as she did so, the storage shed next to the office suddenly exploded. She was thrown back by the force of the shock wave and landed on her back on the raised platform as a great ball of fire blossomed into a blinding light before her eyes. The shed flew apart, timbers and debris flying in every direction. Flame curled high, licking the darkness and rising into a pillared spark wild, orange fire that spread a glowing light across the whole sawmill site.

By the glare, Alva saw Edmond veer back in shock,

one arm held up against the sudden heat, and as he did so, Ernest stepped forward with his Colt leveled. He fired twice, and Edmond jumped back, his mouth working in a bloody cough as his hands grasped at his throat.

"Edmond!" Dermot cried out plaintively from his position over by the corral. *"Oh, dear God, Edmond!"*

But his brother was not hearing him, he was staggering in broken steps as he struggled to breath with blood pouring in a thin stream from between his lips. Ernest did not hesitate, and Alva saw that same cold blanket descend over him as he coolly aimed and fired again. A killing shot, and Edmond dropped like a canvas sack empty of anything resembling life.

Alva felt stunned and a little giddy, but she figured whatever had been inside that shed had been volatile, and it must have been a stray bullet that set it off. She clambered to her feet and, using the building wall for support, staggered towards the blazing heap. She glimpsed from the corner of her eye a figure moving fast and saw a silhouette going at the run towards the corral fence.

Dermot was still hollering loudly, almost screaming in a terrible, high-pitched voice that seemed inhuman. His cries were curses and wails of pain and anguish, all directed at the assailant who had cut down his brother. The horses inside the corral were panicked now and crazily crashing around against the fence posts, dust was rising and mixing with the smoke from the burning building. Then she saw Ernest outlined against the smoke, but only for a moment until he vanished again in the cloud. She heard gunfire and knew he was after Dermot as he continued to rage madly somewhere beyond the corral.

SELEEN HAD SET out in a wide arc and taken the higher ground above the cook's kitchen shed as Irene moved down along the front side heading towards the barracks. She heard the first shots coming from across the broad yard over on the far side and knew that Alva and Ernest were in the mix. Holding the shotgun across her chest, she slid along in front of the kitchen and could smell the aroma of grease and fried meat that hung heavy in the night air. It was hard to see in the dark, and every shadow seemed alive with some movement waiting to surprise her. The breath came fast in her nostrils, and yet her eyes gleamed as excitement raced through her. Irene vibrated with anticipation. She was determined to bring the Mulvennys down. She knew if she did not, they would be coming for her and the others, and it would be a hard ending for them all.

As she reached the far end of the kitchen building, instinct told her that something was not quite right and she paused. She stood there in the darkness with her back against the wooden planks of the shed and listened intently, trying to make out any sounds above the distant gunfire from beyond the sawpits.

ON THE HILLSIDE behind the kitchen shed and moving at a low crouch, Seleen was coming up on a lurking figure he had separated from the other shadows. The fool had lit a hand-rolled cigarette, and the smell of tobacco was strong in his night air.

They do not think at all, Seleen thought to himself. *They are so damned sure of themselves.*

He watched the glow of the cigarette, which was situated near him on his side of the kitchen, with the owner squatting amongst some brush. Treading carefully, Seleen edged forward, his pistol held at the ready. He had heard the heavy tread of Irene as she made her way up the far side and cursed her for the noise she was making. It was no way to move at night where every sound was amplified.

Snake-like, he came up behind the figure, moving the thorny brush aside carefully before sliding forward. The crouching figure before him sniffed and puffed air. He was bored, Seleen decided. The sounds of distant shooting gave him a false sense of security. Nothing was happening here on this side, and he was safe for a while.

The rifle he held in his right hand was pointed skywards and the cigarette was pinched in the fingers of his left hand. He burped a soft waft of whiskey and released a gentle fart, making a gratified grunt as he did so.

"Hey!" Seleen said.

He was so close that Liam jumped. "What the devil—is that you, Gerald?"

"No, you dumb Mick," said Seleen, as he swung his gun around hard and whipped the barrel across Liam's face. The cigarette flew away in a burst of sparks, and a splash of bright blood sprang from Liam's nose.

The Irishman yelped and tried to leap away, but the coarse brush and thorns pierced his shirt and held him in place. Seleen lunged, rising up and over and hitting him again, this time with the gun butt and hard on top of the head. Liam wobbled where he squatted, he blurted something obscure before Seleen was on him again and striking repeatedly. The hits were solid and made hefty thuds of impact, and Liam slipped down as unconsciousness took him. Seleen continued hitting mercilessly until he was sure that the man would not be any trouble to them anymore, then he lifted his head to listen to the battle going on over on the far side.

"Sounds like Ernest is having a fine old time," he muttered.

Stepping out of the clump of scrub and at a loping run, he began to work his way along the back of the kitchen heading towards the outhouses at the back of the bunkhouse. Outlined against the gray wood of the outhouse was the dark shape of a figure posed to raise a rifle and take aim. Seleen knew he had to be aiming at Irene, who was leaving cover to cross the space between the kitchen and bunkhouse.

With no time for subtlety, he snap-aimed and fired at the same moment the shooter let loose. Both shots coincided, and their aims were disturbed. Seleen's target jumped back as the warped timbers of the outhouse wall behind him exploded and split in dusty eruption.

THE SHOOTER'S rifle bullet flew high, and Irene heard its snap as it passed close by over her head. She dropped flat out to the ground instantly and looked to the side just in time to see Gerald crouch down and duckwalk out of sight behind the outhouse. Quickly, she was on her feet and running, heading for the security of the bunkhouse wall.

She made it and peered around the corner, looking towards the long covered shed of the rotary sawmill. Along the side of the bunkhouse, windows were open, and two curious workers poked their heads out, staring in the direction of the firing opposite. The single door alongside Irene was set high on an entrance of three broad steps. The door swung back and a figure was about to step out.

"*Get back inside*!" Irene screamed.

As she did so, the storage shed opposite exploded with a loud roar, and a searing light flashed across the yard, exposing everything in its lighthouse brightness. Heads quickly ducked back inside the bunkhouse and the glass in the windows imploded with the blast. The noise of shattering glass was met by the sound of the door slamming shut and cries of shock and horror coming from inside.

In that brief moment and exposed by the sudden spread of light, Irene saw an ape-like figure lope quickly out from behind a stack of logs beyond the bunkhouse and make for the sawpit. A low figure bent over, and an ugly stain on the whiteness cast by the explosion. It looked to Irene like some kind of primate, he hugged the ground so close.

She fired both barrels in a single blast and saw an eruption of sparks from some metal stanchions as the figure dived inside the far end of the shed, and Irene was sure she had missed. Dropping the shotgun, she pulled the long-barreled Colt from her belt and set off into the shadows of the long shed.

Inside, Irene found it was a long, open-sided, and flat-roofed building. The flames from the exploded storage shed were sending a confusing array of flickering shadows across the entire interior. A rack and pinion bed ran along the base, ready to take the uncut logs, and at the far end gleamed the big four-foot diameter of the steel circular saw. At rest now, its half-inch-wide, round edge sparkled with a set of angry-looking, sharp teeth that sliced their way with ease through the great pine logs felled in the forest.

Irene saw no sign of her adversary, even though she was sure he was somewhere inside. Cautiously, she worked her way along the bed towards the blade at the far end. The sudden pistol shot was directed from where she was not expecting, the pistol blast came from above. The figure perched up in the dark of a ceiling support sent a bullet that cracked down against the side of Irene's temple before it pierced her shoulder between collarbone and scapula and exited above her left breast. The blow sent her tumbling into the rack and pinion bed, and she lay there running in and out of blurred consciousness.

Wee Finley barked a laugh at his success and swung monkey-like from one roof support to the next. His bald head gleamed in the firelight as he worked his way along the ceiling to peer down at Irene and place a killing shot in her body.

IN THE FLURRY of dust and smoke that had lost Ernest to Alva, she searched desperately, making her way across towards the steam engine at the lake's edge. The horses had escaped the corral and were running loose, and in the confusion, she did not know where Ernest had gone amidst the dust and smoke, but she hoped to find him at the meeting place by the engine shed. Moving past the gang sawmill, she heard the sudden boom of Irene's shotgun and ran towards the sound. The crack of a pistol shot led her to the circular sawmill and she saw Irene's figure lying sprawled on the bed at the base.

Shadows flicked across her path as she stepped

inside, and in a flash of light, she caught a sudden movement in the flat ceiling above. Both parties saw each other at the same time. Alva swung her rifle up, and Wee Finley struggled to bring his revolver around. The upright he was hanging from caught the barrel of the gun as he fired, and the bullet winged over Alva to rattle harmlessly against the metal bed. Alva did not miss, and Wee Finley jerked back as the bullet hit. He lost both his grip and footing, and with a loud cry of dismay, he tumbled down.

Wee Finley hit the edge of the great saw blade, and its sharp edge sheared through the weight of his falling body between armpit and neck. His frame was cut in two as easily as a hot knife through butter, and his cry was cut off as easily. The two body parts fell away, and Alva gagged in revulsion as she saw the dissected pieces slide in gouts of blood and tissue. Turning away with the sickened gorge rising in her throat, she hurried across to where Irene lay.

CHAPTER FIFTEEN

Alva sat with her back to the engine house, her legs were spread wide, and between them, with arms wrapped around, lay an unconscious Irene. A tall figure came out of the darkness and Alva was relieved to see Ernest standing over her.

"He got away."

"Who?" she asked. "Dermot?"

"Yes," he said, nodding. "How is she?"

Ernest crouched down and looked at the blood-soaked wound on Irene's shoulder.

"What do you think?" asked Alva.

"Straight through, pretty good. We'll need to get the bleeding staunched."

He pulled off his bandana, and as he began to bandage Irene's upper chest, she moaned softly.

"Where do you think Dermot went?" Alva asked.

"He lit out towards the forest. I think maybe he caught one of the dray horses and rode off along those tram tracks back there. I couldn't see much in the smoke, but that's my reckoning."

"Are you all right, Ernest?"

He looked up at her and grinned. "Sure, how about you?"

"I'm fine, one of them is dead back there. He shot Irene before I got him."

Ernest nodded approval. "That's good, how about the nun?"

"They were keeping her in the administration building, but she's all right. I got her out and sent her up to Thora. But, Ernest, tell me, what was that explosion? It came from nowhere."

"Must have been stored dynamite they use for blasting out roots, I guess a stray bullet got to it."

Just then, the tall shape of Seleen came out of the darkness, he was dragging a limp form along the ground behind him by means of the shirt collar.

"Who you got there, partner?" asked Ernest.

"This is one of them cousins," Seleen answered, dropping the body heavily, and it groaned as it hit the dirt.

"That will be Liam," supplied Alva.

"Well, the other one's in the wind," said Seleen somberly. "He made it over past the outhouses and hid out in the stacked logs. I reckon he's running into the woods right now."

"That's Gerald then," said Alva with a sigh. "So Dermot and the cousin have both made it away."

"How's this one faring?" asked Seleen, looking closely down at Irene.

"She'll live," said Ernest.

"We have to get her to a doctor," added Alva. "Can we carry her?"

"No, it's okay," said Seleen, his voice suddenly softening. "Poor kid, I'll take her."

Ernest and Alva both looked at him, surprised by the sudden change in his usually indifferent behavior.

"Well!" he snapped, annoyed at their stare. "She can't walk, can she?"

"What about this one?" asked Ernest, pointing at Liam. "Looks like you gave him one heck of a beating."

"Keep him," said Seleen, hoisting Irene into his arms. "He'll tell us where all of them were holding out."

THEY FOUND the rented house empty, of course.

Liam was duly sober after his beating, and through swollen lips, he spoke freely about the brothers and their murder of Niamh and cruel plans for the others. He said he was disappointed in America, he confessed it had not been what he had been expecting.

Seleen was heading back to Alamosa to claim his reward for Lyle Jakes and said he would take Liam along with him, as they had a fine jail in Alamosa, and Liam could work out his feelings of disappointment in there.

The wounded Irene was placed in the caring hands of Thora, who seemed to enjoy the task even though the irritable Irene grumbled at her own enforced inactivity constantly.

Aoife was enfolded into the gentle arms of the sisters and given quiet and solitude to ease away the effects of the assault that the Mulvennys had laid on her.

That left Ernest and Alva to themselves.

"How shall we do?" she asked as he held her in his arms.

They were on the veranda of the ranch. Grace was somewhere inside, busy in the kitchen, and the children were playing noisily along the lower land by the creek.

Ernest smiled thinly. "Barely well, I think."

"Are we done with it all?" she asked.

"You are?" he said, brushing her lips with his.

Alva frowned. "What do you mean?"

He stepped back and held her at arm's length. "They are still out there," Ernest said quietly. "Two of them, the worst one and the weaker of the two, what makes you think they won't be coming after you still?"

"Surely not, they have been beaten."

Ernest raised his head and nodded slightly. "We have killed three of that man's brothers, and if all that is said of him is true, he lives for vengeance."

"You think Gerald will have joined up with him?"

Ernest shrugged. "Who's to say—maybe."

"So what do you intend?"

"I will go after and catch him."

Alva was shocked. "What! No, not alone, you cannot, Ernest."

"Why not? I've done it many times before. He is just another bandit, a killer running wild that has to be caught before he brings back harm to you."

"Me— So it's me you are worried about?"

"Yes, I am. Your safety is paramount, Alva. We could stay here in the ranch and try to forget about Dermot, and then one unexpected day, he would come. Sneaking up on us, killing us while we slept, maybe hurting Grace and the children. I cannot let that be."

"Oh, Ernest," she said, resting against him with her head on his shoulder.

"This is best," said Ernest. "I will track him down, and if he has the other one with him, I'll settle them both."

"I will not let you," said a suddenly determined Alva, standing away with arms folded and her gaze fixed on the hillside above the house.

"What?" He chuckled. "I love you dearly, Alva, and I will marry you if you will allow. Look, you must know I will do certain things at times, and you must not interfere. I hope you understand. You will not let me go—*really?*"

"I did not say that."

"What?"

"I said in answer to your tracking him down that I would not let you."

"I do not understand," said Ernest with a deep frown dividing his brow.

"I will not let you go *alone*."

Ernest shrugged. "You mean take a partner, but I work better alone. Always have, always will."

"Not this time."

Ernest stroked his mustache and tugged at an earlobe. "I'm confused," he confessed. "What are you trying to tell me?"

"That I will go with you."

Ernest reared back. "Oh, no, Alva. This is not for you. I need to know you are safe here with Grace, not out there. It will be a hard ride, Alva."

"I am with you now, Ernest," she said earnestly. "We are together, come what may, and I want to be with you, whatever the circumstances."

He sank his chin to his chest and spoke softly, "This will be a killing ride, dear girl. I mean to track this man down and finish him for good. There must be no qualms, and I cannot be thinking of you whilst I am doing it."

"Don't patronize me," Alva said sharply. "I am not about to sit safely at home while you are risking all. You know I am capable, you have seen it. My friends are all taken care of, so I will come with you. You'd best get that through your stubborn head right now."

"You are determined," he noted doubtfully.

"I am, and don't think you can ride off secretly and leave me. I will not abide that, Ernest. If you love me as you say, then we shall do this together."

He had to laugh at her seriousness. "Girl, you are something, you really are."

"Come," she said, easing her way over to him. "Kiss me and let us agree."

"Now you will use your woman's guile on me," he said with a raised eyebrow. "What a terror you have become."

"I have missed you," said Alva, putting her arms around his waist and pulling him close. "There has been so much else going on we have barely had time to enjoy each other."

"True," he agreed. "I think that Grace is busy elsewhere, perhaps we could sneak away for a minute."

"Longer than one minute, I hope," she said archly.

It was decided, and despite Ernest's misgivings, a pack mule was madc ready with supplies and two saddle ponies with bedding rolls and mackinaws tied to their cantles. Then, with Ernest in the lead and Alva leading the mule, they rode out from the ranch. Grace and the children stood on the veranda and waved them off, although Grace could not hide the concern on her face.

"Go careful, you two," she called after them. "Write to me if you can and let me know all is well."

There was no set aim in their direction other than north, that being the direction Dermot was last seen heading. As they rode through the denseness of the forest, it was already alive with the echoing sound of lumberjacks back at work. The noise of creaking wagons and the rattle of chains, along with the sound of shouting haulers and teams of dray horses pulling their loads, were all around them. But the men stopped and stood suddenly silent, watching as the two riders reached their workings and passed by without a word. The tall pines enclosed them and they wove a zigzagging path as Ernest searched the ground for any spoor sign. They reached the end of the tram track with the horse-drawn carriage that had brought the workers in, and then the couple left it and the lumberjacks far behind as they moved into the untouched part of the woods.

Here was only the diminishing sound of the distant axes at work, and the wind brushing the tops of the tall pines could be heard. It brought with it an eerie feeling for Alva, she had never known forests on such a scale, and the trees stretched away on every side until they were lost in a soft azure haze of distance. The moss and pine needles beneath their horse's hoofs left a carpet they trod on in silence, but their passage raised a fresh scent as they stepped across the bruised surface.

Nothing moved other than the treetops far above, with only the steady breeze-blown movement and a soft susurration like the sound of waves on the seashore as they rode forward. Alva looked up to see brief moments of blue sky amongst the pines and then drew a contented breath of confidence and security as she watched the broad and straight back of Ernest leading on steadily before her.

"Here!" he said, pulling up sharply and peering at the forest floor.

Alva moved up to join him, dragging the mule by the lead rope. "What is it?"

"See there, that disturbance. He was here not long

ago, probably the night he left. That moss is dry now, and that is a shod horse that has made the mark. A big horse, one from the lumberyard corral, no saddle, so he rides bareback."

"Will he be far ahead, do you think?"

Ernest raised his head and looked off into the forest before them. "I would be, if I were him."

"Will he know that we follow?"

Ernest puckered his lips. "He will think as if we are. Playing it safe and get as far away as he can."

"Then we must press on."

Ernest glanced at her and allowed a brief smile, then he said, "There is time."

It was patience he was telling her, and she took it on board and suppressed the flutter in her chest that she recognized was an eagerness to get the matter settled. Dermot Mulvenny was a threat that she must hold in her heart, a threat not only to her and the others but also to Ernest. That realization struck hard as there was no way on earth that she wanted to lose him and what they had together. But the bitter irony was that here they were, risking that very thing.

It was slow going through the forest, fallen trees blocked their path, and the undergrowth was so dense they often had to find another way around. The land dipped and folded, the rough rises hidden by the growth of brush and banks of vine and fallen foliage.

It was at the further reaches of the forest that they stopped for the night, making camp beside the creek that ran down from the mountains to supply the lake at Avagar Rhodes.

The animals were tired, and Alva felt exhausted after having to tug the mule through places it did not want to go. Ernest fed and watered them whilst Alva set up a campfire and prepared them supper.

As they lay back afterwards, side by side with the fire at their feet, Alva looked out towards the forest edge. By the last rays of the dying sunlight, she could see through the trees and what awaited them on the morrow.

"Is it very steep?" she asked.

Ernest followed her gaze out to the black cutout lining the horizon.

"The Staircase?" he said. "Not so bad along this part of the lower range, looks worse than it is. A rough climb, but we can do it with the animals."

"And Dermot will have come this way?"

"Yes," he said, nodding. "I'm pretty sure there's no other route he can take. He has to stick near the creek as he and the big horse will be thirsty, and he has no canteen."

Alva snuggled up close to him and he put his arm around her. "You okay?"

"Sure. Tell me about Grace. What kind of sister-in-law is she?"

Ernest thought a moment. "Smart question," he said. "You're planning on spending your days with her and need to know you won't be trapped in the house with a she-bear. Ain't that so?"

She laughed. "You have me there."

"Grace is good people, have no fear. She married my brother and they had the kids, and it was always fine between them. He was out one night, fetching a runaway steer when the weather kicked up, a real mean storm. Richard, that was his name, he was struck down by a lightning blast that hit a tree, it fell down on him and crushed the life out. Wasn't nothing anybody could do about it, just one of those things, although the meanest accident I ever seen."

Ernest went quiet for a moment as he pondered on the waste and loss.

"I'm so sorry," whispered Alva.

"Well," Ernest said with a sigh. "Broke poor Grace's heart, as you can imagine, and I thought to take her in for the company and to take care of the kids. She sold up her place, Jud Brown bought it, and he took to fancying he had some kind of claim on her along with the house. It was awkward for her with all his unwanted attentions, her being in mourning an' all, but she come out with it and told me eventually, and I had a few words with Jud and—well, you know how that turned out."

"She's had a hard time," said Alva.

"She has, but she come through with good humor, and I always found her to be straightforward and real loving to those kids—though sometimes, I find her a little too loving, if you get my meaning?"

"You mean she spoils them?"

Ernest pulled a face. "Yeah, well, I think I might be a little tougher on them sometimes."

"You ever had any kids, Ernest?"

"No, never did."

"Well, you and I get to make some, then you are not going to do anything but give them real good loving, you hear me?"

Ernest smiled. "Yes, ma'am."

"Glad we got that straight. Now, about that baby making…"

NEXT MORNING EARLY, they started out across the foothills that rolled in waves until they crossed the tree line, then it turned to rock and scree.

It was a gray day with low cloud scudding across the sky, driven by a sharp wind that brought tears to Alva's eyes and blew her hair in dark flurries about her head.

The trail led them higher, and Ernest gave out little cries of exclamation as he picked out some sign of Dermot's passage. But soon they lost track of him as the sign faded and disappeared on the hard surfaces of rock.

"Now we are trusting to luck," said Ernest. "Best guess from now on."

"There's only so many ways he can go," said Alva.

"Let's hope we pick the right one."

By afternoon, the weather had lifted and the sky cleared of cloud, but in its place, the sun beat down in the crystal air and was hot on their backs.

They camped that night on a plateau high up in the range of mountains. It was cooler at this height and Alva took a moment to stand and look back over the spread of the forest below them. The sun was setting in a golden sky and laying a soft, warm glow across the land and lighting up the great spread of trees stretching away far below. Ernest came up behind her and put his arms around her.

"It is very beautiful," she said.

"Indeed it is," he agreed.

In her mind was the sorry notion of the mission they were on and that the dark days ahead could possibly spoil this present joy that the view gave her.

Alva breathed a deep sigh. "I look forward to the time when we enjoy such sights at our leisure."

"Yes," he agreed. "You cannot have had much time since you arrived."

"No." She nodded sadly. "So much has been marked with trouble and loss."

"Was it so bad, what you have left behind in Ireland?"

Alva shook her head and compressed her lips. "No regrets on that score."

"So you think you will like it here?"

She spun in his arms and looked up into his face. "With you, I think I shall."

Ernest smiled and kissed her gently. "I believe I am longing for the day when we can settle."

"It is like a taint, isn't it? This cursed Mulvenny business, oh, how I wish it had been different. It seems that whatever good you do, there is always something out there determined to bring you down. I mean, we came across to America with some high hopes, and now I have already lost two of my friends, and the others have suffered because of the vileness of men both here and in New York."

Ernest drew a long breath. "Nature of the world, I guess. Been that way ever since I can remember."

"Even with this all around us," she said, twisting and looking over her shoulder at the last embers of the setting sun as it moved towards the darkness of night.

"Come, let's set up camp and get something to eat."

Hand in hand, they strolled back to where the animals cropped scrub grass amongst the limestone boulders.

THE NEXT DAY, they climbed higher.

The air was sharper, and a cold wind ran across the treeless mountainside. The way was rough, and yet there was a track of sorts made by the passage of wild animals.

Ernest kept stopping and dismounting as he searched the earth for signs of Dermot's passage, and he grunted with satisfaction as he found horse droppings or some scrape of the large hoof against a loosened rock.

Around them, the spread of cold gray rock grew in a tumble, and Alva was hard put to control her horse and the tug of the recalcitrant mule as they climbed. When they reached the high point, she could see the stepped peaks of The Stairway Mountains reaching away to the far distance in a long ridgeline. A lone eagle flew overhead with its long keening call emphasizing the bleakness of the place inhabited only by the sailing bird and the blast of wind.

"He will be needing feed for that horse," said Ernest. "For he sure ain't carrying any and he's been driving it hard."

"Where will he get that, I wonder?"

"Below, somewhere," said Ernest, pointing down the far side of the mountain that sloped away before them. "If his horse is failing, it might be we shall catch up with him there."

Saying no more, Ernest turned his horse and began the descent. Soon, though, the trail petered out, and they had to lead the animals on foot. Alva found the climb down was as arduous as the climb up. Then Ernest stopped them and took the mule's lead rein and looped it over his saddle horn so that the animals moved one behind the other. In this way and in single file, they continued a wayward passage across the rugged downward slope of the mountain.

By late afternoon, they had reached the lower reaches of the range and below saw a wide dirt road that angled between a wall of gray boulders as high as houses that covered the foothills.

"That'll make going a sight easier," said a relieved Alva.

But Ernest was standing still and peering down into the gullies below. "Something going on there," he said.

Alva joined him and followed his gaze to where a stagecoach stood resting at an angle, perched next to the road with a group of people standing to one side.

"Is that the regular Overland?" asked Alva.

"Appears so," breathed Ernest, half to himself.

"Why are they stopped?"

"Not for any good reason, I reckon," breathed Ernest. "We'll leave the animals here and go take a look."

"Is it a breakdown?" asked Alva, watching Ernest slide his Winchester from its scabbard. "Or trouble?"

"Come on, keep low and we'll get nearer. Take that Henry with you and be ready with one under the hammer."

Mobar Palm was a strange one.

He wore a long, dust-stained black jacket with great puffy white cloth angel's wings sewn on at the shoulders. On his head was a top hat crowned with a ring of turkey feathers, and badges and medals festooned his chest with their weight, dragging down the lapels of his coat. His pants were ragged at the ankle, and he wore sandals that showed his dirty bare feet. At that moment, he was holding forth as was his want when he was in the process of a robbery.

"I want y'all to sit in a circle," he commanded, waving a Schofield pistol in command. "My friends will move amongst you and take collection."

The two other masked men with him obediently

made their way through the seated group of five passengers. There were two women and three men, plus the driver and shotgun guard. By chance, it happened that Gil Penny and his guard Ezekiel had been making their regular run to Avagar Rhodes. When Ezekiel had taken a bullet in the side, they had been forced off the road.

As the watches, wallets, loose change, and jewelry were collected in two flour sacks, Ernest and Alva watched from an overhanging boulder where they spread themselves over a level rock and lay flat, peering over the edge.

"Hey," whispered Alva. "I recognize that man, Mr. Penny, he was the same driver as when we arrived."

"Looks like one of them is wounded," said Ernest, studying the hunched figure holding a bloody wound in his side.

"That's Ezekiel, the shotgun guard."

Mobar Palm was holding forth in preacher-like fashion. "I hope you will see this is not your common highway intervention." He spread his arms wide in beneficent fashion with the long-barreled Schofield hanging from his fingers. "This, my friends, is an opportunity. A chance for y'all to see how others in the world have a perspective a mite different than your own. At this moment in time, you are allowed to share with us the God-given right to add to the bounty of those lesser fortunate than yourselves."

He strutted up and down, barely glancing at the nervous people sitting before him.

"Charity, brothers and sisters, share and share alike. Isn't that how the holy rollers would have it? Well, we ain't no churchgoers, no siree. We're just common folk holding out a hand like beggars at the meetinghouse door. You ever give us a second thought?" he asked, suddenly glaring at them in a sweeping glance. "No, I didn't think so. How we doing, brother Gerald?"

The masked bandit holding the flour sack shook it so that the contents rattled.

A frowning Alva looked across at Ernest. "Do you think that could be our Gerald?"

"Looks like cousin has joined up with some road agents."

"Is the other one Dermot, do you think?"

Ernest shook his head. "No, too short, that's not him." He was scanning the layout below. "Where are their horses?"

"Somewhere amongst the rocks below us, I would think," answered Alva.

"Exactly—do you think you can work your way down to them?"

"I believe so," said Alva, studying the boulders and picking a route.

"When I start shooting," said Ernest. "They will make a run for the horses. That means they will head straight for you. Straight to you," he repeated. There was a hardness in his voice, and his eyes were flat and unfeeling. "You cannot miss, you get me?"

"I understand."

"This is it, Alva," Ernest stressed. "This is what it comes down to. You okay with that?"

"I'll do it," she replied, although in her heart there was a tremor of insecurity.

"Then be off with you, I'll give you some time to get there."

"VERY WELL," Mobar was saying in lordly fashion. "Then that concludes part of the lesson."

"If'n you done with us," perked up Gil Penny. "I'd like to get my passengers on the road and my partner to a doctor."

"Now hold on there, brother," said Mobar. "I said—*part of the lesson.*"

"What else you got in mind?" asked Penny.

"I'd like these two fine ladies to stand up. That's it, you two honeys."

The women, one well dressed and in her fifties, and the other, pretty and not much older than Alva, slowly got to their feet.

"Now I know you gals like to hide valuables about your person. So for the sake of modesty, I'd like you to go behind that stagecoach there, and my associates will check you out in private, see if you been holding out on us. Won't you boys?"

There was an eager and leery agreement from the two bandits as they moved towards the complaining women.

"They do so enjoy their work," said a grinning Mobar. "Come on, gals. Won't take a minute, just a perusal by my trusted fellows."

"You cannot do this," cried the white-haired older woman, her face had gone pale, and she clutched clenched fists to her ample bosom. "Have you no decency?"

"Left that behind when I got me my wings," smarmed Mobar. "That's me, sister, Angel of Mercy is me, sent here to educate the world against all its foibles."

"He's crazy as a box of snakes," whispered Ernest, but it was to himself as Alva was already climbing down as quietly as she could.

ALVA WORKED her way reasonably easily, as there were plenty of foot and handholds on the way down. As she neared the base of the gigantic boulder, she could see that there were alleyways that were almost made into canyons by the other high-sided boulders. She glimpsed a gap and noticed the hindquarters of a horse standing patiently.

AS ALVA DID SO, one of the passengers, an older, well-built fellow in a pressed suit and handsome beard, was joining in the cacophony of complaint. "You cannot do this, you rogue," he cried in an educated voice. "Unhand those ladies this instant! I will have you know I am personal assistant to our senatorial representative here and cannot abide this foul and demeaning behavior. He shall be told of this, I assure you, as I intend to report the matter forthwith."

"You hear that?" growled Gerald, and his accent was clear. "Sounds like he has a fancy for himself, the bloody spalpeen."

"Dexter," Mobar said to the other bandit. "Will you take care of it?"

The shorter man whirled and, without hesitation, clipped off a pistol shot, and the senatorial assistant dropped as if he had been slammed in the head by an invisible bat.

As Dexter fired his killing shot, Alva, hidden from view by the boulders, mistook it and thought that Ernest had started, and she broke into a run, desperate to reach the horses before the bandits.

The women screamed as the passenger was shot, and Penny dashed over to the fallen man. "Hell's Teeth!" cried the driver. "You done killed the fella."

"I'll plug you too, you give me reason," said Dexter, waving the smoking pistol in Penny's direction.

"Enough, boys," said Mobar. "Now will you take those ladies out of sight and do your duty so we might be on our way?"

The two men, Dexter and Gerald, moved over and took the struggling women by the arm and pulled them towards the stagecoach.

"Who the hell *are* you?" cried Penny.

"I am," said Mobar, raising his top hat gallantly, "Mobar Palm, at your service."

His slight bow from the waist saved him, as, at that moment, Ernest's Winchester cracked, and his bullet severed the neck of Mobar's medallion-packed jacket in a flurry of shredded material. He straightened up in shock, and the coat promptly split down the seam at the back and dropped around his arms, carried forward by the weight of the decoration.

"What the—" he gasped, his eyes going round. "My best coat, godammit!"

Dexter wildly pushed past him in panic. "We're under fire! It's the Rangers, they come for us. Run for it!"

He was going at a pace, running in front of Mobar, leaving Ernest with a clear shot, and his .44-40 caliber bullet took Dexter in the chest, lifted him off his feet, and threw him down on his back on the ground. Miraculously, he was so full of fear and tension that he was up on his feet in a moment and ignoring the wound. Wailing desperately, Dexter headed directly for the tethered horses. He was also heading straight for Alva, who had that minute turned the corner and appeared alongside the horses.

Mobar was watching all this in bemusement, and Gerald, following Dexter's lead, pushed past. "Get out the way, ye bloody fool."

"Shoot them!" cried Mobar, searching the skyline and looking for the rifleman. "Stand your ground and hold fast."

"Not here, you dinkum, we have no cover," replied a speeding Gerald.

THE WOUNDED Dexter was lumbering towards what he considered safety, and his wild eyes were alight with the promise of escape when Alva stepped in his path.

"I'm hit," whimpered Dexter sadly as he saw her.

Alva lifted the Henry to her shoulder and fired, sending a second .44 into the bandit. He dropped in an instant, his head wobbling on his shoulders and his eyes rolling to white over the edge of his mask.

Gerald saw Dexter fall and promptly dived to one side and ran in a different direction. Alva watched him go and ran behind the boulder, intending to dash around and catch Gerald at the other side.

MOBAR WAS WAVING his Schofield about without any luck in finding a target, as Ernest was too well hidden on the ledge above. In desperation, he turned and ran over to the huddled passengers, hoping to find safety in their midst. Ernest fired again, but his bullet only cut dust at Mobar's feet, and the bandit with his torn jacket and fallen wings flapping around him ran in amongst the group of terrified passengers.

"You shall be my shield!" he bawled madly. "My protection against the ungodly."

Ernest fired again, and the bizarre top hat spat feathers as it was blown from Mobar's head. In frustration, Mobar ducked down, burrowing in amongst the passengers.

It was then that the elderly lady took a turn. With a grim face drawn into angry lines, she struck Mobar with her reticle, slamming the small bag against his face. Wild-eyed, he stared at her in surprise, but before he could move, the lady was flapping her fists at him.

"You insufferable beast," she screamed. "Take that and that."

An offended Mobar stared at her in affront, then he reached out and grasped her throat in one hand, whilst with the other he brought the Schofield around to point the muzzle in her face.

"You would strike *me*!" he bellowed.

At that moment, Ernest got his range and blew the top of Mobar's head off. The elderly lady was sprayed by the destruction as Mobar flopped forward and entered eternity in a bloody mist of red.

It was Penny's turn to play a part.

Seeing Gerald make a quick diversion and run across the front of the great boulder, he jumped to his feet and took off after him.

Penny was pissed, not only because of the wounding of his good friend Ezekiel but also with the callous shooting of one of his passengers. To add to that, driving him off the road left him furious, and seeing the bandit attempting to escape had fired the elderly coach driver.

He ran at an angle in a line to cut off the fleeing Gerald, and with Alva not yet in sight, it seemed that Penny was the only chance of stopping the man. Above them, the pillars of stone obstructed his view and cut off Ernest's line of sight, but as the two running men vanished from sight, he sprang to his feet and began to make his descent, climbing nimbly down the rock face.

Alva turned the corner of the boulder as Penny came level with Gerald and threw himself at the fleeing bandit. Penny fumbled his tackle, but he struck the running man in the legs and the pair of them tumbled to the ground. Alva came out and raced towards the tangle of legs and arms rolling around in a cloud of dust.

"Get off me, you wee bugger!" shouted Gerald, attempting to bring his pistol into play.

Penny had been hauling on reins and cracking his long whip for many years, and the action had strengthened his arms greater than any normal man his age. His bunched fist connected with Gerald on the side of the jaw and sent his head spinning.

"Damn you," spat Penny, ready to strike again as Gerald crawled away on elbows and heels. His pistol was in his hand and he leveled it at Penny, about to shoot down the length of his body. Gerald was aiming to fire point-blank at the driver when Alva arrived and slammed down the stock of her rifle on the back of his head. There was a clunk like the sound of a heavy door closing, and Gerald keeled over unconscious and lay flat.

Penny looked up at her, sweating yet relieved. "I'm

getting too damned old for all this, you know that?" he complained.

"I fear you are, Mr. Penny," Alva agreed.

"Don't I know you, girl?"

"Indeed, sir, we arrived in the stagecoach with you, me and my friends."

"So you did, I remember now. Irish gals ain't you. Well, Irish, will you help this old man to his feet?"

Just then, Ernest came loping up and helped the driver to stand. "Well done, old timer."

"Maybe old, but I can still cut it," grumbled Penny.

"You sure can," agreed Ernest, looking down at the prone body of Gerald. "Good work, as we need to ask this son-of-a-bitch some questions, we surely do."

PENNY COLLECTED THE PASSENGERS, and with help, he managed to roll the dead man into the boot. Urging them to take their seats, Penny, with great concern, helped Ezekiel into the dead passenger's place inside and then climbed up onto the driving box.

"Any more I can do?" he called down to Ernest. "Can you manage that one?"

Ernest gave the figure of Gerald a rueful look. "We'll take care of him."

"There's a small mining town northwest of here, Solemn Pines. I'll get Ezekiel to a doctor there and tell them to send a party out for the bodies. Then I'll take these people on to Avagar Rhodes."

"They got a jailhouse there?"

"Believe so."

"Okay, good luck to you."

Penny pushed the brim on his hat back and took his

long whip from the holder. "Obliged to you and the lady for the help."

With that, he whipped up the team and pulled the stagecoach out of its rut and back onto the road, then, with a holler, he urged the team forward at a run.

Alva watched him go then she turned to Ernest. "What do you want to do about Gerald?"

"Fetch the horses, we'll take care of them and wait until he comes around."

Alva did not like the look in Ernest's eyes, but she did as he instructed and returned to find that he had tied up Gerald with his own lariat and hobbled one of the bandit's horses and sent the rest off without their saddles.

"Are you hungry?" he asked once their animals were fed and watered.

"Starving, it must be all the excitement."

"Let's eat then."

"And Gerald?"

"He's not with us yet, we'll leave him. You must have hit him real hard."

"Lucky he's still breathing, the ass."

THEY GOT a fire going and made coffee and a pot of ground beef and lima beans. They were settling down to eat when Gerald began making moaning noises and cussing the ache in his head. He was struggling with the bonds and writhing on the ground where they had left him.

"What in damnation did you hit me with, you miserable fecking buggers?"

Ernest glanced across at him. "You set still and keep quiet, or I'll do it again."

"What's your game, mister?" cried Gerald.

"All we want from you," said Alva. "Is word on your cousin Dermot. Where did he go?"

"I don't know," Gerald said with a shrug. He sat up awkwardly and glowered at them from under his dark eyebrows with his cheeks reddening as he became angrier. "He got away, did he? Well, good for him."

Ernest climbed lithely to his feet and strode across to the bound man. He stood over him a long, silent moment, then quickly in an instant, he slapped Gerald hard across his red cheek.

"I ain't got time for you, fella, I'd just as soon finish you like your partners there."

Gerald froze and stared up at Ernest with stony enmity, then he glanced over to where the bodies of Mobar Palm and Dexter lay in bloody pools.

"I just rode with them," said Gerald bitterly. "They don't mean nothing to me."

Alva laid aside her dish and crossed over. "Tell us about Dermot?"

"What's to tell," Gerald said evasively. "If you've crossed him, you had better fear for your lives. Dermot is a mean old fella, that's the truth."

"So where will he go?" pressed Ernest.

"How can I know? As far away as possible, probably, but he'll be back, I can tell you that. Dermot never forgets, oh no, Lord love you, he never forgets. What's happened to his brothers, Edmond and Wee Finley, and my cousin Liam?"

"They're all where they deserve to be," said Alva. "Dead as doorposts, and Liam is on his way to jail."

"Sweet Mary, not Liam in a prison cell."

"You'll have a fine story to tell," said Alva. "If you ever get back home."

Ernest was wry. "This one won't make it past a hanging jury, I'll be bound."

"What do you mean?" asked Gerald.

"You have no idea where Dermot will have gone?"

"No, for heaven's sake, why would I know? He's not telling me anything. If I had the chance, I'd be with him, not robbing coaches with these dumb puppies. Ach! It's always a man's mouth that will break his nose, but even so, I would tell if I knew, for I see in your eyes that you mean me only ill will."

Alva looked at Ernest and shrugged.

"You believe him?" Ernest asked.

"I do, God, forgive me."

Ernest stroked his mustache between finger and thumb. "Seleen said he ran off to the eastern side of the lake, and Dermot took the west. Maybe it's unlikely they would have met in the forest. Too many trees even for a poor fool like this when he's running scared."

"You're right there, sir," said Gerald, pleased to see a way out. "I'm good at finding the bees but not the honey."

Ernest sank his head to his chest and folded his arms. "We'll take you to that mining town and see what the miners make of you."

"Tell me now if you will," asked a dubious Gerald. "Are they the hanging sort?"

"I damn well hope so," said Ernest, turning on his heel and returning to his half-finished supper.

CHAPTER SIXTEEN

Solemn Pines was a busy, dirty place. One of those towns that blossoms like wild weeds when gold is discovered and just as easily disappears along with the gold once it's done. Prospectors rushed in when word got out. Hundreds forged in by foot, horse, or wagon and spread their hasty desire behind them in litter along their passage.

Rubbish lined what once had been a pleasant small town's Main Street, no more than a dusty track now widened and rutted by the passage of wheeled vehicles. Wandering disheveled men trooped around aimlessly, their worn clothing covered with dirt from the diggings. Horse droppings left to ferment in the sun festered along the street and between all the hasty hovels that had spring up. Tents spread out from the few shacks of the original town, and fires burned, throwing up funnels of smoke from tin chimneys. Sanitary provisions were few and far between, and the casual offloading of human waste only added to the general stink. The place was flyblown, and standing downwind was unbearable.

New buildings squeezed their way in between the older ones. Two saloons, a hotbed whorehouse, and a bathhouse fought for position next to the brick-built jailhouse, and it was to there that Ernest and Alva brought cousin Gerald.

The sheriff, a hard-headed-looking man in his forties, stood by the window looking out as they pulled up.

"Good day," he greeted as they entered his office. "Help you folks?"

"Reckon so," said Ernest. "This here is one of the men tried to rob the Overland."

The sheriff nodded. "Ah, yes, I heard. Gil Penny was through earlier with his wounded partner. You the fella that helped save them all?"

"I'm Ernest Grant from Avagar Rhodes, and this is Miss Alva North, and yes, we were able to step in. You'll find two other dead bandits out there if you've a mind to fetch them in."

The sheriff offered his hand and they shook, then he nodded politely to Alva. "Zebedee C. Jones, for my sins, sheriff of this rat hole. Glad to meet you both."

He was a gray-haired man with tanned, rough-cut features and large, work-worn hands. He was soft spoken and welcoming, but the shift of his eyes told of a lean and tougher side to his personality

"This here," said Ernest, pushing his prisoner forward, "is Gerald, one of the Mulvenny cousins. He was running with a miserable cuss named Dermot Mulvenny, wonder if you've seen hair or hide of that one."

Jones rubbed his shaven jaw thoughtfully. "Well, Mr. Grant, we get one hell of a transient population here, so it's hard to know. You say two dead bandits on the mountain road, which ties up with Penny's view. I guess I'll have a wagon sent out to pick them up."

Gerald's blue eyes flashed as Jones laid firm hands on his elbow and pulled him towards the bars of the prison cell. He turned and spat at Alva. "*Maltach Dé ort, bitch!*"

"What's that he's saying?" asked Jones.

"It's bitter Irish," said Alva. "He wishes the curse of God on me."

"Is that right?" said Jones. "Well, your gabble won't get you far before a jury of miners, boy. Gil says you fellas killed a man, and these miners here do enjoy some entertainment, so cussing won't help you on a short walk in their court. Now get in there."

With the barred gate slammed shut, Gerald, still nursing the lump on his head, slumped down on the bare wooden bunk inside. Two other men lay snoring and unmoving on the floor. The reek of whiskey hovered heavy in the air like a miasma over the pair of drunks.

"That's fine company for you now, Gerald," said Alva, a touch spitefully.

Gerald looked up at her from under sunken brows, his face twisted with a look of disdain, but he said nothing.

"So no sign of this Mulvenny?" asked Ernest.

"How'd he get here, on foot or by horse?"

"It was a working horse, and without a saddle, he stole the animal from the logging camp at Avagar Rhodes."

"Then you'd best ask down at the livery, perhaps they can tell you."

Ernest watched the troop of shuffling men through the grimy window as they passed by outside. "You sure get a parcel of folks going through here," he observed.

"The county hired me when they heard there was

gold here," said Jones. "Hell, it's a real heap, them bodies out there work like crazy day and night digging for a streak of shine. The rest of the time, they just drink and whore, it's pitiful but keeps me in work."

"An unenviable task," said Alva.

"I been a lawman for ten years now and seen plenty in my time, been in some rough cow towns all over, but this one is a real peach."

"Okay, Sheriff," said Ernest, preparing to leave. "Obliged for your time, we'll get on down to the livery and ask around."

"You aiming to bring this Mulvenny in?"

Ernest paused a moment. "Something like that."

Jones smiled briefly in understanding. "Well, good luck to you then."

ERNEST AND ALVA worked their way through the files of men on the sidewalk, making for a large corral and storage barn with *JC Stables* painted on the side. Both stood a moment looking over the horses milling around inside thc barred corral, and it was Alva who first spotted what they were searching for.

"He's been here. Look, there I'd swear that was the workhorse."

Ernest followed her pointing finger. "Reckon so, that's the one."

"Help you, people?" said a loud voice at their elbow. Both turned to see a small man with straw in his hair and a stained leather apron. He looked old but was probably younger than he looked, with drawn features and a grizzle of beard.

"Looking at that horse there," said Ernest, pointing.

"Fine animal, a Shire," said the man. "I'm JC, by the way, pleased to meet you."

"So what's the pedigree?"

JC chuckled. "Pedigree, that beast ain't got no pedigree. He's a dray, pull your plow or haul your wagon, he don't need no pedigree for that."

"Looks kinda worn," said Ernest. "He been traveling a while?"

"Fella brought him in said he'd ridden him here." JC scratched his wayward head of hair. "Had no saddle or bridle on him, so Lord knows how he done it bareback. Still, shows what an amenable animal it is, the breed is known for it."

"That guy still around?"

JC tilted his head, stepped back a pace with questions filling his eyes. "What's your game, mister? You ain't here to buy no horse."

Ernest drew himself up and took on an official tone. "Company C, Texas Ranger, sir. We're on the lookout for that fellow. Irishman, kind of mean looking, name of Dermot Mulvenny, that mean anything to you?"

"You ain't got no badge," accused JC. "How'd I know you're a Ranger?"

Ernest reached into the pocket of his jacket and pulled out the Peso-cut star of office. "That do for you?" he asked, showing it to the stable owner.

JC looked from Ernest to Alva, his gaze pausing suspiciously as he looked over the young woman. "Texas Ranger, huh?"

"That's right, you got any word on this fellow because you know he stole that horse."

JC crinkled his lips and sucked in his unshaven cheeks. "Don't know anything about that."

"Maybe you have a bill of sale then?"

JC looked away quickly, his manner becoming defensive. "I guess I have one somewhere. I ain't too good with the paperwork. We're real busy here, mister, as you can see, this town is full to busting with people coming and going all the while."

"Listen," said Ernest. "I don't give a damn about the horse, but I need to know what pony that boy is riding now and where he's gone."

JC reached out a thick-skinned work-worn hand and grasped a pole of the corral, his lower lip working, as he pondered. "I don't want no blow-back on this," he said. "Fella comes in here ready to sell me an animal, it's just trade and nothing more."

"I already told you," said Ernest, leaning over the smaller man. "I don't give a cuss, just tell me what you know, or if you rather, we can go on down to the sheriff's office and have a word with him."

"Okay, okay," said JC, suddenly folding and dropping his attitude. "He left here on an old chestnut nag. I wasn't giving him much in exchange, that thing he came in on is wore out. T'ain't right to use an animal like that as a saddle pony."

"So you give him saddlery too?"

"No way," said JC in surprise. "He's riding out the same way he came in."

"And the chestnut, what kind of animal is it?" asked Alva. "Is it going far?"

JC pulled a wry face and shook his head negatively. "Maybe not."

"Which way?" asked Ernest. "Don't faze me, friend. I don't want to come back here and see you if you're leading me astray."

JC rocked on his heels for a moment. "I guess he was heading back towards the stagecoach road, maybe—" He shrugged. "Maybe going on north. Leastways, he left town in that direction, but I don't know for sure. Check out Favor's Rock, that's a small place north of here, a way station for the Overland. They do a little trading there as well, and maybe he passed by. If they seen him, they can give you better direction than me."

Ernest turned to Alva, then, without a word, they both moved away and back to the hitching rail and their horses.

BY MIDDAY, they were on the coach road, following the dusty trail clearly marked by the passage of many horses and wagons. It angled along below the overhanging crags of The Staircase Mountains and followed rising dips and valleys as it wound its way north.

Although Ernest kept his eye to the ground, there was little to see amongst the confusion of other tracks left along the trail.

They came to a turn in the road heading around a large monolith of sentinel rock rising high and blocking a straight pathway across the plain. Around the bend and off the road towards the rear of a short box canyon lay a log-built house. On three sides, it was enclosed by the rising rock walls and kept in blue shade by their overhang. A large corral was set up to one side, and an old chestnut horse stood alone inside.

Two more ponies were outside the house with blankets over them and paint markings on their flanks.

"That will be it," said Ernest, pulling up. "Favor's Rock."

"And that looks like the horse too," added Alva.

"But whose are those other two? Look like Indian

ponies," said Ernest as he drew his Winchester and held it across his saddle horn.

"The stable man said there were traders that lived here?"

"Hmm!" Ernest nodded thoughtfully. "Best we come in with caution."

They were halfway along the canyon when two Indians tumbled out of the open doorway. Each was loaded down, one with a bulging sack over his shoulder, the other with two bags, one in each hand.

The two were laughing and chattering together until they saw the approaching riders. Then both Indians froze, both unable to do more than stare, as their hands were full.

Ernest raised his rifle to his shoulder. "Hold it right there!" he called, his voice echoing hollowly around the canyon.

Carefully, the Indians laid down their bundles and stood warily watching as Ernest urged his horse forward.

"Keep them covered," he said to Alva, and she raised her rifle.

The two were dressed in shirts with cummerbunds at the waist and loincloths with pants stuffed into moccasin boots. Their long black hair was bound with folded bandanas at the forehead, and strands fluttered about their bronzed faces from the slight breeze. There was something shabby about the men, and they stood with bowed shoulders and the look of hunted animals in their expression.

"What you fellas doing here?" said Ernest as he drew close.

One of the Indians raised his hands and wagged them negatively, his meaning unclear.

"You Apache?" asked Ernest, and the man nodded affirmation.

"You got them covered?" Ernest called to Alva.

"I have," she answered, the Henry rifle at her shoulder with both men in her sights.

"Right," said Ernest as he dismounted. "I'm going to take a look inside, they make a move and you shoot them, got it?"

Leaving his rifle, Ernest pulled his sidearm and stepped past the Indians, first glancing at the heaps at their feet and then crossing over to peer inside the cabin. He paused a moment and then disappeared into the darkness inside.

The Apaches looked from the cabin door to Alva and back again, and she could see by their tension that they were making a decision. Either deciding to stay put or risk a run for their ponies. Alva steadied her aim and called out, "Don't even think it, you heathen men."

"Not us," replied one of the men. "No do."

"Just you stay where you are," said Alva.

Ernest reappeared at the doorway, the Colt held down by his side and a distant look in his eye. "They all dead in here."

"Who are?"

"Man and wife, and a boy, been shot dead."

"These men do it?"

"Don't know but don't think so," said Ernest, turning to the braves. "You want to tell me?"

"Man came," explained the one with a smattering of clumsy English. He was obviously eager to tell all they had seen. "Kill all, take horse."

"You saw this?"

"We see. We watch." He used both hands to show where they were amongst the overlooking rocks.

"What manner of man was he?"

"He white man, much hair on face," the Indian parodied a large man bent over with big shoulders.

"Sounds like Mulvenny all right. Then what?"

"Man go"—he pointed direction—"we come, see no life people. They no want house, we take." His spread hands encompassed the looted goods lying at their feet.

"Dinky pair of thieving little redskins ain't you," Ernest observed coldly. "What horse did he take?"

The Indian held up six fingers then cupped his arms in a circle. "He take all."

Ernest compressed his lips. "Looks like Dermot was here then," he said. "He come in and killed them all and took the stage changeover team."

"You sure it wasn't these fellas here that did the deed?" asked Alva.

"They got rifles," said Ernest, pointing to the two guns strapped to the ponies. "Inside, it was pistol shots done the work."

"Killed them all?" Alva cried in disgust. "He is a murdering bastard. Why did he do that?"

"He didn't know these two were watching and thought it best to leave no witness. Probably took food, saddles, and maybe weapons as well."

"So now he'll be fully armed and with fresh horses."

"I reckon so." Ernest turned to the sullen Indians. "What color horses?"

The Indian shrugged. "Like night."

"So black, he's gotten six black horses to choose from, and well stocked as well. Damn it all."

Alva shook her head. "So what do we do with these two?"

"Come on," Ernest said to the Indians. "You can fetch some shovels, we have to bury these poor folks in here."

BY EVENING, the work was done, and three graves stood alongside the corral. Ernest let the chestnut run free, allowing it to fend for itself. At first, it did not want to move, thinking the cabin was a place for food and water, but Ernest whipped it up until it ran off along the coach road and headed back towards Solemn Pines.

"Maybe it'll make its way to that JC fella and he'll sell it on to some other poor sucker," observed Ernest ruefully, watching the animal depart.

"It's late now," said Alva. "Shall we stay the night here?"

Ernest nodded affirmation. "May as well, it'll be a roof over our heads."

"What about the Indians?" she asked, looking over at the disconsolate pair.

"We'll run them off too," he said.

The Apaches left relieved that no more was asked of them, and Ernest allowed them to take their ill-gotten gains as he realized they would only be back later for the loot when they had left. Besides, he reasoned, they would leave them alone now, they had what they wanted.

LATER, when the lamps were lit inside the cabin and their evening meal was over, Alva pushed aside the dishes and looked across the hand-built table at a tired Ernest sitting opposite, slumped in the lamp glow.

"You still want to go on?" she asked.

He sat back in his chair and gave her a slight smile. "Why, you having doubts?"

"Just that Dermot could be anywhere by now."

"This is how it goes, Alva. This is only the start. We have to track Mulvenny down wherever he goes."

"So you want to go on?"

"I once tracked a Mexican bandit for eighteen months before I caught up to him. Mulvenny doesn't yet know we are after him, don't worry, he will get bold, full of himself, they always do, and one day he will give himself away."

"So we keep on?"

"He will want to rest soon. He has been running non-stop, so that would be our plan to keep going, but tell me, are you losing hope?"

Alva sighed. "Whenever I doubt myself, I just have to remember what he has done. Murdering Niamh, wounding Irene, and making Aoife's life a misery. He will deserve to pay a price for that."

"Indeed so, Alva, but do not allow it to change you. A thing like this can harden, and I would not have you lose your heart."

She nodded agreement. "I see that, already, he has caused the death of three more people for no good reason except theft, and that saddens me."

"The manner of the creature, I fear. There will be more of it before this is done. We face a callous and hard-hearted killer who does not turn from evil works and will use any means possible to avoid capture."

"So then, where to next?"

"We'll keep going and ask along the way, see if any ugly son-of-a-bitch with a beard and driving six black horses has passed by."

"He will sell them most probably."

"Then we'll have somewhere to start."

Alva reached across the table and took his hand.

"How can you have done this kind of work for so long and not become as bad?"

Ernest pulled a wry face. "I confess, sometimes I'm not so good, you know. I've done things that were questionable at the very least."

She smiled. "I think you are a fine man, Ernest Grant, and I'm glad to know you."

He looked at Alva, her face softened by the lamplight, and, smiling, shook his head in admiration. "Can you sleep in here tonight?" he asked.

She looked around the almost empty cabin, stripped now by the Indians. Even in the dark shadows cast by the lamp, she could see where the dried blood of the murdered family marked the almost bare walls and earth floor. Pages torn from magazines were pinned to the wall and fluttered from the rising lamp heat, a catalogue picture of a woman in a fine dress and flowered hat, a recipe for oatcakes, a childish scribbled portrait of stick figures in crayon, and a printed timetable list for the stagecoach. Each a sorrowful mark of the inhabitants and their innocent interests.

"A sad place indeed, yet you will hold me tight against the ghosts, I think."

"That I shall," he promised.

Despite the gloomy surroundings, they slept well that night.

CHAPTER SEVENTEEN

GLIMMER CITY WAS everything that Dermot could have wished for.

It was big and sprawling, heavy on gambling and loose on law. He sold five of the coach horses within thirty minutes of arriving, so he was gratified to have seven hundred and fifty dollars in his pocket. Dermot stabled the last of the team that he had kept for himself as a saddle horse, then wandered along Main Street surveying the stores and availability of a diner. He was mighty hungry, having escaped across the mountains and then made a hundred and thirty miles driving the team of horses, an occupation he was not used to, but it had meant money in his pocket, and for that he was glad despite all the hassle.

Every other building he passed on his amble along the crowded street was either a saloon, dance hall, or casino. Looking at the lurid painted signs, breathing the scent of liquor and hearing bright sounds from within, Dermot considered there were opportunities to be made in this place.

He was sour over the loss of his brothers, particularly Edmond, who had been a favorite, but Dermot was nothing if not a pragmatic man and quickly considered that he must leave his dead brothers behind him and move on. There was time, he believed. Time to find his feet and then return to Avagar Rhodes and claim retribution for his lost family. He would not forget, and that anger burned deep within him and would not be quenched by time. It was a fire he kept burning low, and it fueled his temper as he assessed the town.

After a successful meal and feeling pleasantly full after his meager fare during the days of struggling across country, he strolled into the nearest saloon. *The Blaine Delight* was run by Kitty Depreece, a strikingly handsome woman not above displaying her wares but also a shrewd lady and known for promiscuity with her many husbands, whom she wed and divorced with regularity.

The saloon was open twenty-four hours a day and supplied food, liquor, Roulette, and Faro. There were tables for Poker, Three Card Monte, and High Dice. The busy place buzzed, the tables were alive with gamblers, and a dance hall at the back thrived where for seventy-five cents a hopeful was able to spin a likely female before being seduced to the bar. Music resounded from a piano where a player performed from a stage at the rear. There was a general fug to the place as tobacco smoke, cheap perfume, and whiskey fumes blended into a comfortably overheated atmosphere.

Dermot felt at home.

He took his place amongst four others at a Faro table and, after explanation of the simple rules, bought himself some ten-dollar checks. He was lucky with his first hand, and the dealer's shoe left him winning double his bet.

The dealer was a loud, jovially spoken huckster in

fancy clothes wearing a long dark jacket, waistcoat, and watch chain and a ruffled shirt with a voluminous purple tie and glittering diamond stickpin. His overly friendly line of patter intended to draw hopeful punters to his table did nothing to encourage Dermot's instant dislike.

Gloomily, Dermot hunched his shoulders, ran fingers through his beard, and watched the man's dealing with suspicion and care. Dermot was naturally that kind of character, suspicious and cautious about everything he touched.

"Gentlemen," came the mellow voice at his elbow, and he looked up to see a vision molded in sequins. She was a full-bodied woman with diamond rings, pearls, and golden rings in her ears and a low neckline that allowed the creamy skin of her momentous bosom free display. "I'm Kitty Depreece, owner of this establishment. Now, are you boys all enjoying yourselves?"

The players grunted approval and nodded that they were. Dermot breathed in the expensive perfume the woman wore as her round form pressed up against his shoulder and left him in no doubt as to her easy availability.

"Now don't you hesitate," Kitty went on. "You need yourself a drink, don't you get up, you just call out, and one of my bartenders will bring you what you need. So don't be coy, fellas, give a good holler." She turned her long-lashed gaze on Dermot. "How about you, mister. You like a drink?"

"I would indeed," answered Dermot. "A glass of fine whiskey will do me. How about if I buy you one as well, me lady?"

"Ain't you the gent." Kitty grinned, running her eye over Dermot's rugged looks. "Why, doggone, I don't usually drink with clients, but in your case, I think I will."

She turned to the bar and, in a foghorn voice that rose above the general hubbub, ordered two glasses.

"Now you must tell me," said Dermot once he had her attention again. "I'm new to this country and to this game, but is that fella dealing supposed to carry two cards out from the stack with one above the other?"

A sudden hush fell over the table, and all eyes turned on the dealer.

"*What*!" the man cried. "No, I never. You watch your mouth, mister. That's a dangerous accusation."

Kitty was looking at him through narrowed eyes. "It is indeed, and I hope this isn't true."

"Kitty, it is not, I swear. God love us, would I—"

Dermot moved swiftly. He reached across the table in a flash and grasped and twisted the dealer's wrist. Two cards fell out from the ruffled cuffs at his sleeve and dropped to the spread of spades already face up on the green baize.

"There, you wee bastard," hissed Dermot. "I thought I seen your sleight of hand."

The dealer snatched his hand back and jumped from his seat, pushing over the chair behind him. His hand was already under his coat, reaching for a cross-draw pistol holstered there when, although still seated, Dermot pulled his own Colt. He fired once before the dealer could bring his piece into play, and Dermot fired upward through the bottom of the table. Fluttering cards and spinning checks flew in the air as the bullet crashed through the tabletop, splintering wood and sending coins flying.

The bullet entered under the dealer's jaw, it flung his head back, and a spout of blood fountained from the top of his head. The perfectly coiffed hair was turned into sticky destruction as the dealer's eyes faded and he slid down to the floor with half his brains flowing over the collar of his fine jacket.

Kitty arched an eyebrow as she coolly waved the gun smoke away with manicured fingers. "Looks like you caught one in the act, my friend. That's a sharp eye you have there, and a fast gun to match."

"I like to keep me wits about me," said Dermot, pushing away the destroyed table and getting to his feet.

"Well then, let's you and me have a word once this mess is cleared away. Rest of you boys share the cash between you, that's only fair, and you can have a free one on the house as well." She turned to Dermot and crooked her finger. "You can come along with me."

THE NOISE, furor, and dead body were cleared away in minutes, a shooting and killing being a fairly normal occurrence in the gambling halls where the simplest comment could set things off.

Dermot trailed after her and approved of her narrow corseted waist and swaying bustle as he did so. Kitty led him up the stairs and into her private rooms above the gambling floor. "Come on in and take a seat. I'll get you that whiskey now."

It was a well-equipped parlor with decorative imported wallpaper and fine padded chairs with windows covered by tasseled drapes. There was carpet on the floor, and the furniture gleamed. Dermot approved as he looked around the richly appointed room.

Kitty came over with two full glasses from the well-stocked sideboard and took a seat opposite.

"So what's your name, stranger?"

"Dermot Mulvenny."

"Then here's health to you, Dermot Mulvenny."

Dermot watched her over the rim of his glass as he sipped the whiskey. "A fine drink, thank you, Mrs." He noticed in the different light that beneath the paint and powder she carried a worn look, there was a softness to her skin that was not quite healthy, and the lines at the corner of her mouth spoke of bitterness. Dermot realized she was somewhat older than she portrayed.

"Call me Kitty. I never favored the other title. You look like you've traveled far, is that so?"

Dermot stroked his beard. "A fair way."

"A man not unused to fending for himself, I would think."

"I know what to do if it comes to it."

"Then look—Dermot, I have place for good men. Men who are not afraid to make their mark, would that appeal?"

He watched her from under half-lidded eyes. "I'll not be much good at waiting table, lady."

She grinned and exposed even white teeth. "No, I did not have that in mind."

"Then what exactly?"

"I have a team of men here that will do as I tell them. Now, if you find you cannot take orders from a woman, then we will leave things here. But if you think you can handle such direction, then maybe we can make some money together."

Dermot swallowed the whiskey and set down his empty glass on a side table with a sharp clack.

He got to his feet and jerked his chin at the door opposite. "Would that be your bedroom?"

She looked up at him curiously. "Yes, it is, but I—"

"Then come, sweetheart. Let's get this settled and not beat around the bush."

"By God! You son-of-a-bitch, you're a randy little devil, aren't you?" Kitty cried angrily.

"There's nothing *little* about me, Kitty dear," Dermot said with a grin. "Come now, step along with me, I'll show you the other side of the rainbow."

"Get out—"

Before she could finish, a grimly determined Dermot lifted her bodily from her chair and forced his lips upon her mouth. Kitty struggled weakly, but then the urge that so often ran through her took control, and she answered Dermot's embraces with a fervor all her own. The pearl necklace at her throat burst apart, and the white beads flew and spattered on the polished floorboards. Dermot's rough hands wrenched the dress apart at the buttons down Kitty's back as he wallowed in her décolletage. It was the kind of feverish demand that Kitty enjoyed, a wildness and danger that spiked her lust.

With a flushed face and panting lips, she pulled him rapidly towards the bedroom door and slammed it open. Taking front stage in the room was a huge four-poster hung with fine net curtains tied by silk ribbons, large white embroidered pillows propped the head, and a softly padded pink coverlet lay across the wide bed. A hand-painted rendering of puffy clouds limping across a pale blue sky covered the walls.

"*Go bhfóire Dia ort!* It's like Little Bo-Peep in here," howled Dermot, surveying the feminine decor with a twist of disdain.

Kitty was roguish in her reply as she led him to the bed. "Just right for an old goat like you, then?"

ALVA AND ERNEST WERE TIRED. It had been two weeks of constant travel and they had found no word of the hunted reprobate Dermot Mulvenny.

They arrived in the small town of Level in want of supplies and some attention to Ernest's horse, which needed new shoes. He took the horses to the blacksmith's whilst Alva went on to the grocery store to buy their needs.

The store was a small dusty place with bare boards and a pot-bellied stove at the center. There were a few shelves stacked with canned goods behind the counter and a range of bolts of material set to one side. Sacks of beans and grain sat on the floor, and the smell of the place was of old vegetables and dry oats. Three men sat around the stove, as it was obviously their regular meeting-place, even though there was no fire alight in the stove. Slovenly-looking men, and Alva noticed that they were dressed in the remains of gray military uniforms.

One held a crutch by his side, and a wooden peg stuck out from his threadbare pants leg. Each of the men stopped their chatter as Alva entered. The fattest and ugliest, facing the door, took a clay pipe from his mouth and openly stared at her with bovine interest. He sat with open legs spread wide and wearing overall pants held up by suspenders over a shirt with the faded remains of a sergeant's stripes on the sleeve.

"My, my," he said with a leer. "Things are looking up in your store, Bob Tanner."

The thin, hook-backed man named Bob Tanner was

dressed in a leather apron and leaning casually on both elbows at the counter. He looked at Alva in a lackluster and bored manner. "Help you, Miss?"

"Hey, girl," called the fat man. "What you doing here in Level?"

"Now you be quiet, Lester Dunwiddy," said the storekeeper sharply. "Leave the young lady alone."

"I'd like these things on the list," said Alva, handing across the paper.

"If I got them, you can have 'em," answered Tanner, taking the scrap and turning to his shelves.

As she waited, Alva turned to the three men gathered around the stove. "Ask you men a question?"

"Shoot," said the Dunwiddy, thrusting the pipe in the corner of his fat lips.

"Any of you fellas seen a bearded man leading a chain of black horses pass by?"

The two other men with Dunwiddy turned their heads and stared silently at Alva from deeply sunken eyes. Both men she noticed wore long scraggy beards on their drawn cheeks. Their clothes showed signs of wear with patched elbows and gray pants that may have been Confederate infantry at one time.

"Why you want to know that?" asked Dunwiddy. "He your pappy and done left you?"

"No," said Alva. "He's a thief and killer. Name of Dermot Mulvenny."

"Irish, huh? You Irish too, girl?"

"That's right, I am."

"Never took to you Paddy people," sneered Dunwiddy. "Did we, boys? Never did."

"The Irish 69th, yeah," agreed one of the men. "Liked to run with pig stickers out, they did. We seen 'em at Gettysburg."

"Yeah," said the one-legged man. "If our damned gunners had got it right, we'd have blown them to ribbons instead of shooting dirt."

"Nope, Daniel," added Dunwiddy. "It was left to us and General Picket to go in and deal with them."

"It was a bloody fight," concurred Daniel bitterly. "Cost me my leg."

"Sure it was, if it hadn't been for that bit of blasted bitty wall and the Irish, we'd have been all over them."

The men rumbled on, sharing their tales of a civil war fought over nine years before, with Dunwiddy complaining the loudest. Alva turned away from them and saw that the storekeeper had arrived and placed a flour and salt sack on the counter.

"Coffee to come," he said. "I got bacon out back, hold on a spell."

"And what do we get?" Dunwiddy complained, directing attention at Alva's back. "Nothing, and now the damned Irish are walking into this place like they own it."

There was a muttering of aggravated agreement from the other two.

"*Hey!* You girl," Dunwiddy shouted. "What do you think on that, you being one of them?"

Alva turned to him calmly. "Before my time, sir. I don't have any thoughts on it."

"Maybe you should," said the blustering man, forcing himself up from his chair, his face red with anger and his fat belly flopping over his pants top. "Should tan your skinny hide for your ignorance."

"Go on," urged his fellow soldier, Daniel, with a low chuckle. "Go to it, Lester, you show her."

"Now, now," said the storeman, coming out with a slab

of bacon in his hands. "You calm down, Lester, there's no need for that." He turned to Alva. "Apologies, Miss, they tend to take it bad. The war ain't over for them."

Alva eyed the fat man hovering before her. "That's no problem," she said. "How much do I owe you?"

"Come here, girl," said Dunwiddy, lunging forward and grasping her arm. "I aim to show you how to respect your betters."

"That's it, Sergeant," called the other veteran in a low, threatening voice. "Do it like we did to country gals back in the day."

Alva stepped back from him, her hand reaching for the grip of the Colt in her waistband. "You stand off, mister. I'll not take kindly to being manhandled."

"You ain't ever been handled by no real man," sneered Dunwiddy, his pudgy hands reaching out for her. "I intend to make that a difference."

"I give you fair warning." Alva pulled out the pistols and cocked the hammer, holding the Colt down by her side. "Stand back, I say."

Dunwiddy loomed in, his face burning, and the urging of his fellows allowing him a wildness that showed in his eyes. "I took many gals younger than you, and I still got it in me, never you fear."

"I'm warning you," cried Alva.

He grabbed her then, both Alva's arms were firmly grasped in his hands, and the fat belly pressed up against her as he pulled her close. Alva could feel his sweaty body heat and smell the unpleasant odor of his tobacco breath.

The Colt went off with a muffled bang.

Dunwiddy opened his mouth in a silent scream as white smoke rose up in a cloud between them. Then he stepped back, tottering on his feet and clutching at his groin.

"Dear God!" cried Daniel, jumping up from his seat. "She shot him, she shot Lester."

The fat man was staring down at the blood pouring from his lower belly, and then his eyes rolled up and he fell heavily back onto the floor.

"Christ!" cried the other veteran. "She shot his balls off."

"Oh, Jesus!" cried Tanner, rushing around from behind the counter. "Damn you all, not here, not in my store."

"Go fetch the sheriff," barked Daniel. "That's bloody murder that is."

His companion shook his head as he stared down at Dunwiddy. "He's done—bleed out in minutes. I seen it before, old Lester is a dead man."

A shaken Alva was standing frozen with the pistol held down by her side. She could say nothing, only stare at the dying man, the mountain of his belly rising over a spreading pool of blood.

When it came to trial, the jury was made up of southern men, many of whom had served in the army and felt the dead man deserved some recognition despite his having agitated the whole affair and being the one who first threatened Alva.

Despite every attempt at leniency, they gave her a manslaughter sentence of three years.

She was to be sent to serve her time at one of the new female reformatory institutions for women and girls that had sprung up in the country. It was a trip back in time for Alva, as the reformatory was called the House of the Good Shepherd and run by a Catholic order of nuns. An imported sisterly order taking the earlier system they had learnt in Ireland, it was in effect a prison outside the previous all-male regime and intended for fallen women and wayward girls whose crimes ranged from larceny to perjury, prostitution, and murder. With the intention that these women should wash away the sins of their past, the introduced idea of the Magdalene Laundries was set up across the United States and run by the Sisters of the Good Shepherd, but there was little in them that was either good or reforming.

Alva was to find herself imprisoned in a gloomy house surrounded by high stone walls topped by broken glass, and within the house were twenty-six adult prisoners who were overseen by seven sisters and a group of trusties called the Solidarity Sisters who did the dirty work.

As Alva was to discover, they were a brutal group of female trusties not above vicious beatings and various tortures. With a rat-filled bread and water room for solitary confinement, restricted conversation of half an hour a day, and rules that changed at the whim of their keepers, it was a grim life of constant punishment.

Once again, Alva was entering a world of separation, obedience, and labor.

Her last view of Ernest had been the sight of his sorry figure standing, hat in hand, as he watched her being escorted to the prison van with chains on her wrists, ready for transport to incarceration. They had no opportunity to speak then, their only words having been shared when Alva occupied the prison cell before departure.

"Hell's Bells, girl!" Ernest had said, sitting opposite

her outside the cell. "This is a sorry state of affairs. I've tried every damned means I can to get the sentence reduced, but these old boys here are a club and each in the other's pocket. They all know that Dunwiddy was a regular asshole, but the stars and bars still rule in this county."

"Don't worry," said Alva, touching his fingers through the bars. "I hear these new prisons are just for women. It will not be so bad, I think, besides, I served time already in the orphanage in Ireland. I can handle it."

"I'll be waiting for you, you can bet your life on that."

"Thanks," she said with a smile. "You know how I love you, Ernest, and that is what will get me through this."

"Wherever you are, look always at the sky and know I will be under it too and thinking of you."

Then they came to take her away.

DERMOT FOUND he had one man who was a problem.

He had wormed his way into Kitty's affections, but she was wily enough to play one man against the other. It gave her leeway and allowed a continuation of her leadership without interruption from any dominating power-hungry man.

Billy Ray Bender was his name, a large, fearsome-looking red-headed man who was fond of carrying a woodman's hand axe in his belt and not averse to using it should the occasion arise. At one time, he too had been Kitty's lover but now had taken a back seat after Dermot's arrival.

The two men circled each other cautiously,

outwardly displaying deference for each other, but underneath, a heated rivalry was brewing.

There were twenty men hired by Kitty, ten of them worked in the saloon as bartenders and waiters. The gamblers who handled the tables were freelancers who paid a percentage to Kitty for use of the saloon. The remaining ten were hard men who collected outstanding debts, policed the saloon, and secretly ran a rustling business against outlying farms and ranches. They raided horses and cattle and drove them down south to trade with Mexicans across the border or find buyers amongst less discerning Quartermasters in the military.

It was of this band that Billy Ray was the nominal leader.

Dermot knew a confrontation would have to come one day and soon. He had found life in The Blaine Delight to his liking, and to own it and all that it promised was the opportunity he saw opening up before him. Once he had taken Billy Ray off the board, all that was left for him to handle would be Kitty, and he recognized that as no problem. Dermot realized he could be king here and lead the kind of life he never thought possible in his homeland. But first, he must rid himself of any likely competitor.

The opportunity arose on a night raid.

"They're moving three thousand head down from the high pastures on the Domus and Partridge Spread," Kitty confided to both men. "It's owned by a company of investors out of St. Louis, so a big enough concern. One dumb hand got loquacious with a dance girl and that's how I heard about the drive. The size is good enough for us to handle, so if you two will get the boys ready, then in two weeks the herd should be on its way down."

They sat in Kitty's parlor, and she moved from one to the other of them, handing out filled whiskey glasses.

"Domus and Partridge are some fifty miles northeast of here, aren't they?" asked the red-headed Billy Ray. His heavyset form sat on the edge of the chair, looking touchy and uncomfortable. He did not like taking second place in Kitty's parlor, he was more used to being top dog. Dermot sipped his whiskey and solemnly watched Billy Ray over the rim of his glass.

"So they are," agreed Kitty. "Far enough away from here to leave us appearing innocent. I looked at the survey map, and I reckon the best place will be at Broadwheel Canyon, they'll have the herd locked up for the night in there. It's narrow, and you can control them on the run out."

"Sounds good," said Billy Ray. "What do you think, Dermot?"

"Wherever is fine with me."

Billy Ray nodded approval and went on, "I reckon we take out the nighthawks first. Real quiet. The rest will be sleeping, and we can run the herd out after that."

Dermot mused a moment. "What about the herders?"

Billy Ray shrugged. "We leave them standing, they'll be asleep anyway."

"Maybe they'll be coming after us?"

"I don't think so."

"Well, I do," said Dermot. "I say we cut them down in their beds."

"What for?" burst out Billy Ray. "They'll be eating dust they come after us."

Kitty could see that the temperature was rising between the two men and she cut in to avoid any friction. "I've sent a message down to Don Alvarado, and he'll be expecting delivery at his hacienda. You'll have to make it in one drive straight down there and across the Rio Grande."

"You see," said Dermot. "We'll have no time for playing games with any herders."

Billy Ray looked sullen. "Or playing at gunplay during the night."

"Now look, Billy Ray, I see what you're saying, but I do think Dermot has a point," said Kitty, playing at moderator. "It would be easier for both of you if you stop any interference at the start of your run rather than all the way down to the river."

"If you say so, Kitty," grumbled the miffed Billy Ray. "But who is it that's running the outfit, me or him?"

Kitty shrugged. "I see no reason why the two of you can't handle it together, you are both capable men."

"It's a matter of experience," said Billy Ray. "I know what I'm doing. Irish here is new to the game."

"I have a name, fellow," Dermot said with a frown. "Best you use it."

"Ach!" spat Billy Ray disgustedly.

"A rose by any other name," said Kitty brightly. "Now, who wants another drink?"

Dermot had seen the crew who would be handling the rustling and thought them a tough bunch with many ex-cavalry and able horsemen, and the rest simple enough to follow orders. He had played the role of silent and foreboding when in their presence, so he was sure they would be careful around him. Any arguments and he would take care of it as it arose. Right now, he was pleased that the night action was acceptable, as it was during the gunplay that he had decided Billy Ray would not be seeing the light of any next dawn.

After Billy Ray had left, Kitty eased up behind him

and placed a hand on his shoulder. "You know," she said, bending close to his ear. "He hates your guts."

"Billy Ray? The poor fool doesn't have the brains, it beats me why you put up with him."

"Well, sure to say he does not have your qualities," she said with a teasing smile. "But he's capable enough in any trouble."

"What, him and his wee axe? Good at chopping firewood, that's all."

She leaned over him, her hands were playing down his chest, and her breath hot on his cheek. "Are you staying tonight?"

"Tell me," said Dermot, swiveling to face her. "Will you tell me how long I have been here now?"

She paused. "Oh, I don't know. Is it three or four months?"

"More like five," he said with a sly smile. "Though truth be told, it does seem barely a week."

Her tongue was in her cheek when she said, "You've certainly fulfilled all expectations as far as I'm concerned."

"Ah! You're the very devil of a woman, Kitty. You'll break the heart of many a man and make ancients of us all."

"Come on then," she said, taking his hand and pulling him to his feet. "Let's not spoil a successful run."

IT WAS full night when they arrived at the overlook for the Broadwheel Canyon.

Dermot and Billy Ray crawled to the rim and looked down at the camp beneath the crag. A mere forty feet below, a cook fire burned, and the cowboys were gathered around. Two nightriders were circling the passive herd that lay stretched across the flat breadth of the canyon.

"I'll send four men down to take care of those two," whispered Billy Ray. "The rest of them will know what to do."

"Make sure they're quiet little fellas taking those guards, we don't want anybody roused."

"Don't worry, they have Indian blood and know what's needed."

"Best we wait until they're all bedded down."

"I know it," said Billy Ray impatiently. "You think to teach me my trade?"

"Not at all, Billy Ray, not at all, speaking my mind aloud, that's all."

"Well, you can take care of the killing, seems that's what you're best at."

"Not a problem." Dermot grinned. "And where will you be?"

"Riding out front to take the herd, of course."

"Fair enough, wouldn't want you to get in the way of a bullet now, would we?"

Billy Ray looked across at him sharply, but Dermot was staring innocently down at the camp below.

"Let's get this over with," growled Billy Ray.

THEY RODE in hollering and whooping to surprise the sleeping cowboys with the sudden shock of their noisy arrival. Dermot rode at the head of his band, firing wildly in every direction but keeping an eye on Billy Ray as he charged ahead.

Cowboys were falling, shot down around the smoldering campfire, and Dermot's crew swirled their horses, picking off the slower drovers one at a time. A few made a break and scattered to find cover amongst the horse herd and around the chuck wagon. They had managed to retrieve their handguns and some of the rifles kept in the wagon and returned fire, blazing away with all the determined instincts of desperate survival.

It was a surprise for Dermot when the horse under him buckled and stumbled before collapsing when a bullet struck it in the chest. The horse tumbled heavily and tossed Dermot over its head, and he landed on the ground in a flurry of dust. Shaken and stunned by the fall, Dermot stared blearily at the raging battle going on around him. Spitting weapons sparked sharply in the dim light, and dust clouded under charging horses as the roar of the firefight filled the night. Dizzily, he searched for his pistol that had dropped from his hand in the fall.

Then the drover loomed out of the mist, his rifle held ready as he ran towards to where Dermot lay sprawled on the ground. With gritted teeth, the hatless cowboy raised the rifle to his shoulder and was about to fire point-blank into Dermot.

The Irishman thought his time had come, and despite his stern nature, Dermot wailed a curse and curled himself into a ball, expecting the hot lead to run through him at any minute. Then out of the darkness burst the tall figure of Billy Ray, bellowing like crazy as he charged his horse forward.

"I got you, Dermot!" he roared, swinging the hand axe overarm and bringing it down hard on the cowboy, striking him between neck and shoulder. The cowboy folded, the rifle flying from his arm as he screamed in pain and fell to the ground.

Dermot watched in amazement as Billy Ray swirled

around and came again, the bloody axe held high. Another swoop over the struggling cowboy, and the man lay still. Billy Ray pulled on the reins and smiled in satisfaction as he reared the horse and looked down at the prone body of Dermot.

"Saved your ass there, old buddy," he called, but Dermot detected the sly undertone of condescension in his voice and was riled by it.

Billy Ray turned to ride away. "Get up, Dermot," he ordered. "We got cattle to run."

Dermot narrowed his eyes and, scrambling to find the Colt in the dust, he found it and raised the pistol. He fired twice into the back of the rider as Billy Ray rode away. Dermot saw puffs of dust pit the back of Billy Ray's shirt as it erupted under the bullet strike, and the big man jerked forward before bending over and dropping over the saddle horn and then falling to the ground.

"Now who's tall in the saddle, ye red-headed son-of-a-bitch?"

Two weeks later, and with their task completed, Dermot led the riders up from the Rio Grande and back into Glimmer City. There, he handed over his horse to one of the men and went directly into The Blaine Delight. A determined-looking Dermot marched stiffly through the gambling hall without sparing a look to either side as he wove between the tables. Kitty was waiting for him in her rooms and she smiled at him, gently lowering her eyelashes in a seductive, welcoming manner as he opened the door.

"How did it go?" she asked.

Dermot threw his hat aside and dropped a jingling

sack onto the table. "Real well," he said, going across to the sideboard and pouring himself a drink. "Don Alvarado paid up without fuss, that's all gold escudos in that bag. Sadly, though, we lost Billy Ray."

"You did?" Kitty frowned.

"Yes, we did." Dermot pulled a wry face. "Took two in the back, poor soul, he's gone, Kitty."

"In the back?" repeated Kitty with a hint of suspicion. "That's too bad."

"So it is." Dermot nodded in agreement. He sipped his whiskey. "You know I've been meaning to say something to you, Kitty dear, and I think this will be a good time."

"Yes?"

"I think times are about to change around here. They say the spinning world revolves and things alter with time." He chuckled, a dry laugh. "Or with the weather, you never know when a hurricane's coming, do you now?"

"What do you mean?" she asked with temerity, nervously half expecting what was coming.

"You're a lost soul, so you are," said Dermot. "This place needs a firm hand at the tiller, so I'll be taking over things from now on."

Kitty gaped a moment in shock, then, frowning, she shook her head. "No—no, you won't!"

Dermot stared hard-eyed at her, his lips bared in a grin that held no humor. "And what do you aim to do about it?"

"Why—I'll—" She froze as she realized, without Billy Ray for deflection, it was now a one-horse race. "I'll get me someone else," she blurted with bitter force and then with a voice full of disdain. "This is *my* setup, always has been. I built it up myself, and nobody takes it away from me, certainly not some peat-digging bog-trotter like you."

"Now that's no way to talk to me," Dermot said with a frown. "Have I not always attended your every need?"

He stepped to one side and set down his glass before swinging around and punching Kitty a savage blow on the side of the face that sent her spinning. Kitty clutched her jaw in both hands and screamed, "*Help!* Help me! Somebody help me!"

Quickly, Dermot was on her, his weight pressing down against her slender form. Almost amused, he realized she wore no corset under her dress, and he could feel the softness of her belly beneath him, and he parted her legs as he had so often done in their bed. But there was no desire in the act, and almost calmly, he bent her over the back of the couch and snaked large hands around her neck. Kitty struggled, gripping his wrists and trying to spit her vitriol at him. Her eyes rolled wildly and she kicked and lashed out with her feet, but the long skirts and bustle hampered her.

"Now there-there, Kitty dear," whispered Dermot, his face so close to hers that she felt his hot breath on her cheek. "Don't make a fuss, will you? We had us a good time, did we not? But it's over now, girl, all over."

Kitty's eyes bulged, and she gagged with the tongue tip protruding from between her lips as Dermot squeezed tighter. Her body thrashed and quivered as, with sudden recognition, she realized that her end was close and life was over for her. Her lungs craved air, and Kitty's eyes pleaded, but no mercy came from the relentless tightness about her throat.

"Bye-bye, Kitty. May the road ahead be kind to you."

CHAPTER EIGHTEEN

ERNEST SAT under the split cane porch that did little to defeat the sun's rays. It was hot, and he waved his hat in front of his face to bring some air to his cheeks and keep the flies away. The stench of dried turds left by stray dogs was strong in his nostrils, and it hung about the place like a miasma in the overheated air. Added to the dense odor coming from the overflowing jakes out back, it made his stay equally unpleasant.

The bar was a poor place, well-used and dirty, with a low, crumbling wall of adobe about the entrance. The Mexican who ran the place cared little for custom and served up weak beer and tortillas with greasy indifference from his dank interior. All expectant visitors gathered here waiting for the release date of their dear ones, and that might come at any time, dependent on the sister-supervisor's whim.

Older mothers and fathers stood there grouped sadly together, and husbands with young playful children who ran about while their lone fathers kept watch. All waited with eyes fixed on the heavy reformatory doors and ears pricked, ready to hear the sound of the release bell from inside the gloomy prison walls. They stood and waited, lounging morosely, silent and tired, with all social conversation now exhausted after days with no sign of any release.

Ernest sat with one booted foot up on the low wall and watched the prison gate as he had for the past fourteen days. When the bell rang and it finally opened, he saw the released inmates stumble out. It was a long walk down the hill to the road, and the shock of release was evident. The way down was a bare and dusty track lined with painted rocks, and the freed women blundered out in a stream, shading their eyes against the harsh sunlight and wincing to see if anybody they knew had arrived to meet them. Not many had come, and those that had lurched themselves up from their post and ambled over to the released prisoners, all of whom seemed completely lost and desolate as they wandered aimlessly down the hillside.

He saw her then, a lone figure outlined against the dark cavity of the gates.

Even at that distance, he could see the difference in her. Alva looked thin and undernourished, her hair was cut short, and she held herself cautiously tense, deep-set eyes flicking around nervously.

"Here you are," he said as they met.

Alva stood a few feet back, and Ernest noted the bleakness in her eyes that seemed to hold the color of stone instead of the vibrant blue he knew. She did not step up and enclose him in her arms, as he had expected, nor did she whisper any words of love about how she had missed him and was glad he was here. It was a cold, hard figure he faced.

"Was expecting you two weeks back," he said,

watching her reaction from under the shadowed brim of his hat. "That was the given release date."

Alva shrugged as if she gave it no mind and sighed. "Thanks for coming."

He leaned forward and gently took both her arms in his hands. "Reckon it's been a hard time for you."

Alva looked away for a moment, watching the other stumbling prisoners, those without friends or relatives, rambling along the road or out into the fields.

"They like to hold back until they can let us all go together," she explained.

"Well, come on, girl. It looks to me like you need a good feed, we'll find us a restaurant. That shithole back there isn't fit for man or beast."

Alva was unresponsive, but she allowed him to lead her down to where he had kept a one-horse buggy stabled behind the Mexican bar.

As he helped her up, she blinked as if some sense of realization had entered her torpid brain.

"How are the girls?"

"They're good," said Ernest, climbing up into the driving seat. "Irene is all healed up, although her arm ain't as good as it used to be. But she's a fighter and insists on still doing stuff around Thora's place."

"And Aoife?"

"Very content, I saw her three weeks ago, and she's making out real fine."

"Good," breathed Alva, as they drove away, but her mind was elsewhere, and she gazed about in a dazed manner as if she saw nothing.

As Ernest geed the horse, he kept stealing sideways glances at Alva and was unsure what troubled her, but guessed that probably her time in the reformatory had not been a pleasant one.

"See you shaved off your mustache," Alva said suddenly.

Ernest rubbed his face. "I did, got tired of shaving around it, so I got rid of the whole damned thing. What do you think, you like it?"

"Not sure," she answered vaguely.

"Thinking of cutting all my hair off too," he added.

It took a moment for that to sink in. "You're thinking of *what*?" Alva asked.

"Yeah, cut it all off. Go bald like nature intended for a man my age."

"I don't understand," she said, shaking her head.

"Sure, maybe you'll like a man with everything on show. You know nothing hidden away, you'd prefer that, wouldn't you?"

"What are you talking about, Ernest?"

"Ah, great! You remembered my name."

"I did, I do—" she said, staring numbly down at her feet. "Yes, Ernest, I'm sorry—it's just all—"

"That's okay," he cut in. "Take it slow, there's time."

"That place, Ernest." She stopped and looked quickly over her shoulder. "I can't believe I'm really free of it."

Ernest was glad to see that some color was coming back into her cheeks and something like life lighting her eyes.

"Yes, girl, you're out."

Although he said it, Ernest realized that something radical had happened to Alva, something that had marked her and would now live in her for some time. It was a sadness to him that a woman so young should have to suffer the sad nature of incarceration and all the tortures that went with it, but he could see by her pallid skin that they were ingrained into her and a part of her character now.

"I got us a hotel room," he said as they approached the outlying houses of the small town. "They got a restaurant too. You hungry?"

"I don't know if I can," said Alva. "I been eating slops for so long it might be hard."

"So a little then."

"Alright, Ernest."

Then she leaned against him with her head on his shoulder, and for the first time, he felt the indication that maybe Alva was coming back to him.

"You're not really going to cut off your hair, are you?"

"Hell, no." He laughed. "Just thought I'd get a rise out of you. No, I was actually thinking more of running bare-assed naked down the center of Main Street here."

He could not see her face, but he could tell that she smiled.

OVER THEIR MEAL, Alva sat picking at her food but eating little.

Ernest kept his eye on her, judging her mood and wondering how he should handle things with the altered Alva. She was twenty years old now, and as he studied her, he felt the old flow of sympathy and care stir in him. She seemed worn and hardened by her experience, and yet he could not deny the desire that still ran through him when he looked at her.

The restaurant was empty. It had been mid-afternoon when they had entered, and Ernest had to use his best persuasion to get them seated and the cook to serve them.

Alva seemed dazed, as if her mind were in two places,

and Ernest guessed that one of them was still back in the prison and under harsh supervision.

He wiped his mouth with his napkin and said, "I know where he is."

For the first time, Alva took a real interest in what he was saying. It was as if he had struck a sudden blow, and she raised her head slowly to look at him directly, and Ernest saw the fire beginning to kindle in the back of her eyes.

"Where?"

"Two days, maybe. Place called Glimmer City. It's a gambler's wet dream of a place. Dermot's changed though, made a name for himself now."

"So have I," Alva said bitterly.

"No, no, not like that. He's big now, runs a saloon and basically the town, and he has a team behind him, maybe twenty men. All of them rustlers and thieves, mostly wanted for some foul deed or other."

"How did he manage to get all that?"

Ernest shrugged. "By killing mostly."

Alva nodded agreement. "That figures."

"What do you want to do?" asked Ernest.

"What do you think?" said Alva with a wry twist to her lips. "I been inside that place back there for three years, and all I had to think about was getting out and dealing with Mr. Dermot Mulvenny."

"You could just leave it alone," he suggested. "That guy is busy now and has what he wanted with all that comes with it in the way of power and money. I doubt if he'll be bothered with you girls any more."

Alva drew a sharp breath and straightened up. "That I doubt, he will not forget his brothers and will want payback for them. It's in his blood, Ernest, and he will only have been waiting for his moment."

"Waiting for what?"

"For me to get out of jail—then he will have all of us together."

"You think he knows about you?"

"That one will know, he can read newspapers."

Ernest saw it then, the bitterness that had come to rule Alva's life. All of it fired and stoked by the brutal treatment inside the so-called reformatory. He read the signs. She was on a mission, and he had to decide whether he wanted to go down that road with her. Yet he could not deny the lingering sense of friendship he shared with this woman, and it was in his mind that he still wanted to participate in her life wherever it might lead.

"I need to go," she said sharply, suddenly getting up from her seat.

"What—why—where you going? Finish your meal."

"No, I'm going," she said. "Leave me be for a moment, Ernest, I just want to walk a while."

With that, she turned on her heel and left the restaurant.

Ernest followed her with his eyes, then shrugged and raised a hand to the waiter.

"Yes, sir?"

"Clear this away, will you. Then bring me a bottle of bonded, be damned if I don't need me a drink."

THAT NIGHT, they made fierce love.

The hunger that ran through them both evolved into rapacious desire, and Ernest was hard put to keep up with Alva's sexual gymnastics. She seemed to crave his body upon, under, and around her as they both ravaged the bed sheets. The night fell away, but there seemed no end to it, and Ernest wondered at the volatile nature of Alva's demands as the sky lightened through the window. He had never known her to be so lustful and energetic, and it reinforced the sensation that something radical had happened to her in the reformatory. There was a crazy wildness to Alva now, symptomatic of some kind of madness, and it seemed to him that this night he had become a vehicle for her liberation.

Her cries were loud and vibrant as she rose to meet him at every climax, but with barely a pause, she called on him again. With skillful encouragement, she raised Ernest to answer the call, and only when they were both totally exhausted did they finally fall away from each other and sleep.

Cockcrow passed, and the sun was high by the time they were able to move and make signs of recovery.

Alva sat up in the bed and pulled the sheets up around her. "I'm hungry now," she said.

Blurrily, Ernest looked up at her. "Hungry for what?" Although he hardly dared to ask.

"Some eggs and bacon," she said impishly. "Why? Did you expect more?"

Ernest buried his face in the pillow. "No, no, I think I have done enough."

Alva slapped his shoulder playfully. "Get up and get me something to eat, I'm starving."

Ernest widened his sticky eyes and stared at her. "Dear God, Alva. What's come over you?"

She looked past him and out of the window. "We have to make a plan."

"Indeed? And what might that be?" He sighed.

"How we can get into this Glimmer City without being seen."

Ernest hooked himself up on his elbows. "You're thinking of that *now*?"

"What better time? Best to begin right away. Don't doubt for a moment that Dermot will not be thinking about it."

Groggily, Ernest rubbed his face and found it felt rubbery and tired and he needed to wash. "Damn that dog, Dermot! I need to wake up and recover myself. Those were some demands you laid on me last night, woman."

"Ah!" she said with a smile. "Don't pout so, you enjoyed it all, didn't you?"

"Hell's Bells, Alva! I'm beginning to wonder if I really know you."

She stroked her chin thoughtfully. "Hmm, well, Ernest, you'd better make up your mind soon, one way or the other."

This was not the woman he remembered, and Ernest could not quite grasp the difference. He felt lost, and there was some part of him that saw only emptiness in their relationship now.

He climbed out of bed and dressed hurriedly. Standing at the door, he said with finality, "You'd better start explaining."

Alva cocked her head to one side, thought for a moment, and said, "How would you like it. You think maybe that last three years were some kind of picnic?" She stared at him across the room, her eyes two hard points of emotionless stone.

"No, I don't think that, not for one minute."

"I saw things in there you would not believe, Ernest. Not just to me but others as well, friends I made, good friends, people that did not deserve that kind of treatment."

"What do you want me to do? I can't change any of it, Alva."

"No, I don't expect you to, but just know, from now, I am what I am. It may not appeal, and in no way am I like the naïve kid you met in New York all those years ago."

Ernest felt a flow of anger pass through him. "So what is it that's so different now?"

She hissed the words through clenched teeth, so low that Ernest could hardly hear them. "I know how to survive."

"Is that it?" he asked, meeting her gaze with one of his own. "So now the rest of us have to suffer what you suffered?"

She looked away from him, her lip twisting ruefully as she gave him no answer.

"Get the hell off it, Alva. I don't reckon this is anything about *survival* we all got that particular cross to bear. I think maybe self-pity plays some part in this."

Alva's pale features suffused with an angry red. "*Get out*!" she shouted. "Get away from me."

"Suits me," said Ernest, walking out of the bedroom and slamming the door behind him.

It was late morning, and Ernest stormed down the stairs of the hotel and crossed the lobby, heading for the restaurant.

"Good morning, Mr. Grant," called the cheerful lobby clerk.

But Ernest ignored him and strode into the restaurant where a late breakfast was being served. There were a few guests at separate tables throughout the sparsely populated room, and Ernest waded through their mumbled greetings and headed straight for the bar.

"You want coffee, mister?" asked the bartender.

"Yes, I do," snapped Ernest. "And something a tad stronger to go with it."

The bartender, a bland-faced man of even disposition, looked him over and gave a slight smile. "Wrong side of bed?" he said.

Ernest looked at him for the first time. "Just give it me and save the pleasantries."

"Coming up," said the barman, unfazed by Ernest's obvious bad mood.

Ernest stood fuming, and as he leaned against the bar, the thoughts raging through his head wondered if he should take his horse directly and get on back to his ranch and the calmer company of his sister-in-law.

The barman set down a black coffee and a balloon glass. "I guess a brandy will hit the mark."

"When that's done, set up another."

"You got it."

Ernest spat venomously and swallowed the brandy in one gulp. The liquor burn did little to assuage the irritation he felt. He sipped the coffee and waited as the bartender hovered, preparing another brandy.

"Another?" asked the bartender.

"Shoot, yeah!"

Looking over his shoulder, the bartender asked, "This what you're looking for?"

Peering over his shoulder, Ernest saw Alva standing, staring at him from across the room. She stood quite still and erect with both hands folded in front, and despite his anger, she appeared quite beautiful to Ernest.

"Hellfire!" he cursed, turning his back and taking the balloon glass in his hand.

"All right." He heard her voice at his shoulder. "Sit down, Ernest, and I'll tell you."

He turned to look at her, took a deep breath, lifted the glass, and swallowed the brandy.

"Come on," Alva urged. "Hear me out."

Begrudgingly, Ernest followed her to a table in a quiet corner, and they both took a seat opposite each other. Ernest raised a finger to the barman and waited until he brought across another brandy.

"How about the lady?" asked the barman. "Would she like something?"

"She stands on her own feet," said Ernest. "You'd best ask her."

Alva declined with a shake of her head.

Ernest was quiet, and distantly he toyed with the glass before him, not meeting Alva's eyes.

"There was a doctor in there," Alva began. "His name was Theophilus Parvis, and he had twenty-five women at first and then one hundred girls under his control. The authorities valued his exploratory participation, they thought he offered a brand new insight into medical practices. I knew the people he treated, they did no wrong. Petty criminals, untutored and maybe a little dumb, but nothing you would consider particularly evil."

Alva was speaking in a flat, even monotone and without any show of emotion.

"There were prostitutes in there, and women who had conceived and given birth out of wedlock, so they were considered dissolute. These were his favorites. He practiced female circumcision, he claimed it was to stop them playing around. Then he removed the ovaries so they would never give birth to any more babies. He was supposedly an authority on gynecology, so nobody stopped him, and the women were forced to accept his inhumane treatment as he parted their legs and did what he wanted to do, whether they wanted it or not."

Ernest slowly raised his eyes to look at her.

"When you first arrived, you were stripped naked and placed in solitary for no good reason, bread and water in a cold, narrow cupboard for as long as they wanted. Could stand, maybe crouch, but never lie down to sleep. If any argument, they had this system they called water dunking, and they held you under until you almost drowned. Then there were regular beatings and cursing, the enforced religion and maintenance of silence all the time, unless a nun clapped her hands. This went on, day after day, Ernest. Until the harshness ate into your soul and you were hard put not to become one of the torturers yourself. I watched young women being crippled and driven crazy on a regular basis."

"You suffered at the hands of this doctor?" Ernest asked, his voice soft and husky.

"I was lucky, but I had to send others to him in my place. You see, I betrayed them so I could survive. Not so good, huh? This is what I have become."

"Dear God! That is abysmal. How is it they get away with it?"

"They are the law, and they have the power, that's how. It made me realize one important thing, and that is that there is no real justice, only the one we dispense ourselves."

"And now Mulvenny will pay that price?"

"Well, nobody else will make him do it."

Ernest bit his lip and considered what she was saying. In a way it fitted in with his own feelings when he had served as a Texas Ranger. An expedient treatment, efficient and final, carried out by any means possible. He and his Ranger troop had not faltered when they caught some thief along the border, whether he stole a broke back mule or a racing thoroughbred, they hung him just the same.

"What are you looking for from me, Alva. You want forgiveness or something, because I ain't no priest, I can't do that."

"No, but I do want you to understand, and I don't want you to lose your feelings for me. I know I've come on strong and maybe not the same as I was, but I will tell you in all sincerity, my heart is the same. Underneath all the excrement heaped on me in that rat hole, my feelings for you were the one thing that kept me going. Give me time, Ernest, it will just take me a while."

There were tears in her eyes, and he felt the strength of her shaky commitment in the words.

He nodded and compressed his lips in agreement before he reached a hand across the table and enclosed hers in his.

"You're a hard woman to shake off," he said. "And I'll be damned if I'll give up that easy."

"That's good to hear," she whispered in response.

"But you are confirmed in your dealings with Mulvenny?"

"More than ever," she said with conviction. "I cannot leave Irene and Aoife at risk. I have lost too much already, and I will not bear more."

"Have to say we two are few in number against him and his twenty-man crew."

She looked at him from under lowered brows. "Then you are with me?"

Ernest met her gaze. "You know I am."

"I have thought about it," Alva went on. "We *are* indeed too few, and it will only work in one way, and that is the same way as the Indians do it. If we cannot get to Dermot directly, then we need to ride in and strike, then run off and come again, eat at them piece by piece."

"Guerrilla tactics?" mused Ernest. "That's how the Confederate skirmishers did it back in the war."

"Exactly so."

"It will need guile and clever disposition."

"Of course, but you can show me how, can't you, Ernest?"

THE NEXT FEW weeks they took easy. Alva was adjusting not only to diet but to a life without the brutality that had enclosed her inside the prison. Ernest left her alone when she wished it, and she would walk the streets of the town with no destination but only to enjoy the new space and freedom. Sometimes she sat and gazed for hours, looking dreamily up at the sky, and all the while he watched over her.

As she slowly came back to him, Ernest felt the old mellowness in her character, and yet it was still undermined by that strain of vengeful determination.

Ernest was beginning to get worried about money now. It was costing him a lot, paying for the rooms, food, and new clothes for Alva. Even so, he bought a new horse and tack for her in preparation for their leaving, but the cost left him with only a few dollars, and Ernest knew they would have to move soon or he would have to make some more money somehow.

It was while Alva was out on her wandering and whilst he was sitting in the lobby checking the local newspaper advertisements for likely work that three men arrived. They caught Ernest's attention as they swaggered up to the desk clerk. There was an air of bravado about them, and with their rough-looking features and dust-laden clothes, they caused Ernest some apprehension.

"Got a question," the lead man said abruptly to the desk clerk.

"How can I help?" asked the affable clerk.

"You got a woman prison up the road, ain't you?"

"We do, yes."

"They say they got all kinds of whores and lowlife bitches in there. When they letting all them freed female inmates out? You know that?"

"Well, that is hard to say," said the clerk. "They tend to do it rather when necessary. There is a bell they ring at the time. Are you expecting a release?"

"We are, young white woman, dark hair, Irish accent," said the man. "So what you're saying is that letting them out could be any time?"

The clerk stole an uneasy glance across at the description but said nothing, and Ernest kept the newspaper raised, hiding his face, but his big ears were all attention. The main man and his companions stood facing the bar, whilst the third member stationed himself behind them and faced the lobby as if giving protection. It did not take Ernest long to decide by this natural defensive stance that these men were professionals and mean parties into the bargain.

"I'm afraid that is the case, there is no set rule. But most people wait at the café nearby, just outside the jail."

"Maybe, maybe," said the man thoughtfully. "Look, we'll be getting us a drink up at the saloon, so you hear anything, like that bell ringing, you come fetch us, okay? Name of Jethro Rant, you got that?"

Rant was the big, red-faced, blustering type of fellow that took the lead. A curled-brim sombrero hung down over his back, and his jaw was unshaven with thick fair curls of hair that grew over the collar of his worn shirt. His hip sported a low-hanging ammunition belt with a strapped-down revolver that he carried slung at wrist-height like a gunslinger.

"We have a bar right here," offered the clerk.

Rant took one look across at the civil-looking restaurant and snorted a laugh, and the other two joined in. "I reckon not," said Rant, grinning slyly. "Wouldn't want to upset your regular customers, fella. We got some drinking in mind and maybe one or two of them comfort gals keeping us company as well. Now it don't look like you got no whores in there, do it?"

"No, certainly not. Perhaps you might prefer The Dice Bucket just along Main Street, I hear that is a fine establishment that will accommodate all your requirements."

"Hah! That's the style. You're a good little fellow. Don't forget, you hear then you come get me, Jethro Rant, right?"

"One thing," interrupted one of the men with him, a tall, slender fellow dressed in a black shirt and purple bandana.

"What you want, Russell?" asked Rant.

"Maybe they already let them out. Could be, you know, before we got here."

"That's right," mused Rant, pouting his lower lip. "What do you say to that?" he asked the clerk.

"Yes," the man said with a nod. "But that was some weeks ago, maybe a month, I'm not sure. Anyway, everybody will have left by now."

"You reckon so, huh?"

"I'd say so, they don't tend to hang around, you understand?"

"Yeah, yeah, well okay, what do you think, Dean?" he asked, turning to the third member of the group, a short, thickset man with an evil-looking scar from eye to jaw.

"If we missed her, then we missed her. Let's go get us a drink."

"You know," said Rant. "Mulvenny might have something to say about that."

"Ach! He can go stick his head in a hole. I need me a drink."

"Besides," added the tall man called Russell. "He ain't here right now, is he?"

"Yeah, come on, you pair of assholes," growled Dean. "I'm going if you ain't."

"Hold on," cried Rant, following both men to the lobby door. "Okay, okay, just one then..."

"Yeah, right," mimicked Dean. "*Just one then.*"

Ernest folded the paper and crossed over to the clerk with a thankful nod. "Mighty grateful," he said. "We'll be checking out real soon, you mind making up our bill?"

Then he ran lightly up the stairs to their room and began to pack.

Halfway through stuffing his saddlebags, Ernest sat down heavily on the bed and took out his poke bag. He counted the few coins in there and considered that he owed the hotel a fair amount now. It left him biting his lip with concern, and that was when Alva returned.

"What's up?" She frowned, seeing him sitting with an open saddlebag and strewn clothing.

"We got trouble," he said and explained the whole situation to her.

"I knew it!" she said, shaking her head and compressing her lips. "I knew he would be waiting to get me when I came out."

"Yes, we need to get away from here," he said, looking across at her, and paused waiting for her reply.

"So let's go."

Ernest spread his hands. "I've run out of money, there's not enough left to pay the hotel bill."

"Oh!" She was surprised, and in her own concern, Alva had just not given any thought to how she was being supported. Now it had come home to her with sudden shock. "We could just run," she suggested.

"We could, but there is an alternative."

Alva nodded for him to go ahead.

"Those three are Mulvenny men out there."

"What about them?"

"They're getting drunk right now, they aim to spend tonight on a bender."

"Yes?" she said slowly.

"They will have money."

"So what are you saying?" asked Alva. "Kill them all?"

"You suggested using guerrilla tactics," answered Ernest, watching her closely. "These are Mulvenny men, well, it starts here."

Ernest watched her muse over the idea and saw her inner self fighting with the callous notion and then over the prospect of the same men arriving at Irene's or Aoife's door with murder on their minds.

"Let's do it," she said abruptly.

Ernest was on his feet and collecting their hardware that he spread out on the bed. There were two Colt pistols and a Winchester rifle, and his Bowie knife. He checked the action and saw that the guns were clean and fully loaded. Then, letting it hang by the grip, he handed one of the Colts over to Alva.

"You want to go now?" she asked.

"No time like the present."

CHAPTER NINETEEN

The Dice Bucket Saloon was a well-used institution, and its warped board front and peeling paintwork demonstrated that. Once it had been a prime drinking house, with a colorful painted board over the swing doors, but now they were a only a faded reminder of earlier days. The Louvre-work on the swing doors was missing in places, and the frame was chipped and stained by greasy hands. Inside was little better, sawdust covered the floor and covered other symptoms of degeneration. Uneven tables were propped on blocks of wood, and the billiard table felt was ripped and repaired with glue and brown paper. Even the bar looked used up with kick marks along its lower border and the signs of long wear with scrapes and scratches all along what would once have been a shiny, polished surface in the heyday.

Not that it bothered Jethro Rant and his compadres. They were all glad to be out from under the stern eye of Dermot Mulvenny, and being given leave to fend for themselves, they inevitably considered this time away from Glimmer City a holiday of sorts. With empty glasses, three beers, and a bottle of whiskey between them, they were fast entering a duller state of inebriation and propped up the bar with some difficulty.

It was approaching evening when Ernest and Alva arrived on the boardwalk outside. A hazy sunset was stretching purple shadows along the dusty Main Street, and abiding citizens were hurrying home whilst storekeepers locked their doors and put up the shutters.

The few who entered the saloon were the dejected and marginal end of the population and scurried more than walked with their scruffy coats held tight to their chests. It was time for them to hold out and sit on a single beer for the night or scrounge some pennies for something a little stronger. Old timers, who weren't about to change the drinking hole they had inhabited for years despite its decline, sat at a table playing cards and sucking on their pipes.

"Are you prepared to front these fellows?" asked Ernest when they stood outside the swing doors.

Alva set her face grimly. "Of course I can."

"Then here's what we'll do. You go in first and call them out real loud. I'll slip in behind you like a regular customer, everybody will be paying attention to you, and I'll circle around and come up on their flank."

"What will I say?"

"Whatever comes to mind, just something to get their attention and keep that Colt hidden down inside the folds of your skirt."

"Then what?"

"They make a play, and you let them have it. Don't falter, Alva, we need to take these boys out, so you'd best be sure of it."

"Right," she said quietly and then cleared her throat. "Yes, whatever you say."

"Be bold, little girl, remember I am behind you."

Drawing a deep breath, Alva stepped up and placed a hand on the doors, then swung them open.

As she moved in, Ernest slipped in behind her and promptly went to her right along the inner wall with the Winchester held down by his side.

"I hear you boys are looking for me," Alva called loudly.

A sudden silence fell over the saloon, only the sound of scraping chairs as people turned to look at the woman in the doorway.

At the bar, the three men were in the process of enjoying a joke together as they recalled an earlier escapade.

"Then he sat on the wall of the godforsaken well and fell right down inside..." Rant was rendering the story, his face red with sweat and a wide grin splitting his face.

"What was that she said?" asked the black shirted Russell, turning to look blurrily at the figure silhouetted by the orange sunset outside.

"I'm talking to you three!" barked Alva.

"What she want?" asked Dean, lowering his gaze and looking at Alva through squinting eyes.

"Who the hell are you?" asked Rant.

"Alva North, you came here for me, didn't you. Sent by that breath of Satan, Dermot Mulvenny."

"By God!" gasped Rant. "It *is* her, this is the one."

All three pushed themselves back from the bar and stood to face her.

"Alva North, huh?" said Rant. "Well, come over here, girl. We want words with you."

"You go to hell," spat Alva. "And take that other scum with you."

"Damn my eyes!" exclaimed Russell in disbelief. "Can you believe the sass on this bitch?"

Dean, the most aggressive of the three, did not pause, and his hand dropped to his revolver. "Dermot wants you alive," he hissed. "But I reckon dead's just as good."

"Come get me then," said Alva boldly.

Her hand flipped out from under her skirt with the Colt ready and fully cocked in her hand.

"Don't think I won't." Dean grinned, and his gnarled hand dived for the pistol at his side.

Both Alva and Ernest fired at the same moment. The rifle bullet took Dean in the head to one side of the scar marking his chin. He fell over sideways with brains and blood spraying over the other two.

As he collided with Russell, it sent the man cannoning into Rant, and both staggered to the side. At the same moment, Alva's .45 bullet went wide, but it struck Russell in his raised gun hand, severing it at the wrist in a bloody cloud. Screaming, Russell tumbled down, the wrecked hand holding his revolver hanging by a few shreds of sinew from his arm.

The bartender, awakening from a bored stupor, reached down to collect his shotgun from under the bar, and as he raised it, Ernest put a Winchester bullet into him. The man catapulted backwards with the double barrel exploding and the blast sent upwards into the ceiling. With a crash, the aged ceiling collapsed, a shower of white plaster and shattered wooden supports from the floor above avalanched down onto the two gunmen.

Those in the saloon had gone crazy at the sudden invasion and were complaining desperately as they scrabbled for cover under upturned tables or secure corners. The noise was deafening as the guns fired and the debris continued to tumble down from the ceiling over the wailing customers. Gun smoke joined the clouds of dust, and it billowed out across the room.

Rant chose his moment in the fog of limited vision to make his bolt for the door and brushed past Alva, who was rubbing particles from her eyes.

"He's getting away!" roared Ernest from the far side of the room. "Get after him."

Blindly, Alva followed after the fleeing gunman, and in the evening light, she saw him bounding down the sidewalk away from her. She raised her gun and fired, and then set off after him at a run. As they both pounded a hasty tattoo of racing feet down the wooden sidewalk, late-going citizens ducked to one side or hid in store doorways and watched the strange sight of a woman in her skirts running after a fleeing man.

Rant looked over his shoulder and shot wildly at Alva, the bullet cracking as it passed close by her head. She saw the grimace distorting Rant's angry face as the orange of the setting sun lit up his features in its glow. There was something manic and demonic in the image as Rant raced on. He stepped out into the roadway, deciding to cross over and head for the livery stables. Alva was panting with the chase, but she pulled up long enough to rest her gun hand against a sidewalk support and take a steady aim.

Rant skipped a beat, and as her bullet struck the seat of his pants, he howled, took another step, and then fell heavily in the road. He was less than a hundred yards away, but Alva set off after him again. Rant, cursing loudly, clambered upright and set off again at a hopping run, one hand clutching his right buttock. Fear and panic were lighting the man, and at an awkward loping and hop-stepping run, he made for the far side of the street.

Standing in the middle of the road, Alva raised the

pistol held steady in both hands and fired. This time, her bullet caught Rant high up in the left shoulder and doubled him over. He fell face down and groveled in the dirt, wailing and moaning with pain.

Alva, breathing heavily, strode over and stood over him, her pistol pointing down at the wounded man.

"Get up!" she snarled.

"I can't, I can't, you shot me in the ass."

"I'll put one in your head you don't get on your feet."

Rant curled around to look up at her. "Who the hell are you?"

"Somebody you should have let be. Now, on your feet."

With much complaint, moaning, and groaning, Rant struggled around and climbed with difficulty to his feet. All the time Alva kept him under the Colt she still held in both hands.

"Back to the saloon," Alva ordered.

With Alva behind him and limping badly, Rant made his way back to The Dice Bucket as the silent residents watched their slow passage from the safety of the sidewalk.

Inside, Ernest was kneeling over the wounded Russell using the gunman's own purple bandana to bandage his torn arm. Behind them, amongst the shattered remains of the ceiling-debris scavenging figures scampered behind the bar, quickly grabbing what bottles of liquor they could and making off like hasty shadows into the street.

"You got him." Ernest grinned, looking up from his task.

"Never mind her," complained Russell loudly. "What you going to do about my hand?"

"That'll need doctoring," advised Ernest.

"He can sew it back on again, right?"

"What are you bitching about?" roared Rant. "I got shot in the ass, look here." He turned to display the bloody hole in his pants. "And that ain't all, I got another one somewhere else as well, I ain't sure 'xactly where."

"In your shoulder," supplied Alva.

"Yeah, see," said Rant. "I got something going on as well as you."

"Both of you," ordered Ernest sternly. "Get over there and sit against the bar."

"I ain't sitting on nothing," complained Rant.

"Well, stand then. Now, shell out your pockets."

"Hey, look, mister, I need a doctor real bad," whined Russell. "I ain't got time for this."

Roughly, Ernest held him back against the bar as he rummaged through his pockets until he found the man's leather pouch and dropped it on the counter with the clink of cash inside.

"Now, you can leave and go get a doctor," said Ernest, pointing at the doorway.

"Where the hell am I going to find one?"

"Look for a shingle," said Ernest, shoving Russell towards the door. As Russell stumbled out, his arm wrapped in the blood-soaked bandana, Ernest turned to Rant. "Now you."

"Is this what this is?" asked Rant in disgust. "A two-bit robbery, is this what you're about?"

"Give me your money, or I come get it," warned Ernest.

Begrudgingly, Rant pulled out a roll of notes and some coins and tossed them on the counter.

"Lousy, cheap, stinking thieves," he cursed.

Ernest backhanded him a slap as he passed him and

knelt down to search through the fallen Dean's clothes for his poke.

"Tell us about Mulvenny?" asked Alva, watching Rant closely.

"What's to tell, nobody don't argue with him, he has the whole town in the palm of his hand, runs every local setup there is going. He's a king out there, the Mr. Big of Glimmer City."

"And he sent you after me specifically?"

"He's got people out all over. He told us all go find three Irish girls."

"How many out looking?"

Rant shrugged and then winced at the pain in his shoulder. "Gangs of three, I think, maybe twelve, something like that."

"He described us?"

"Yeah, a skinny redhead, and one like a nun, and the third is you, I guess."

Ernest stood up and added to their heap of cash on the counter with a purse taken from the dead Dean.

"Robbing the dead," sneered Rant. "That how low you've sunk?"

"Go get yourself some doctoring," said Ernest. "And know this, I see you again and you're a dead man. Stay well away from Mulvenny. You go there and I will nail you, I promise you that."

"Don't worry," sighed Rant. "I had enough of this part of the country."

"And take care of your partner."

"Who?" snorted Rant. "Russell? He won't be able to wipe his own ass from now on. I reckon he lost that hand and I ain't going to take its place."

"Might be you'll need someone to wipe yours as well," added Alva.

Limping for the door, Rant frowned at that thought, one he had not considered until now.

Ernest smiled across at Alva as the saloon doors squeaked shut. "A neat deal, we done well."

Alva nodded agreement. "Indeed, now we can pay the hotel off and get going."

"Three down," said Ernest, poking at the heap of cash on the counter with his finger.

"And nine more out looking, that means Dermot has less men at his beck and call."

"Still, there will be at least eight of them with him, and my guess is they will be the worst of the bunch."

"Best we start early then," advised Alva grimly. "And pray the others don't find Irene and Aoife in the meantime."

BY EARLY MORNING, they were on their way.

At first, it was a silent ride with little said between them. The pale early sun rose over the horizon into a pearly sky that dispelled the chill air and low mist that lay over the ground. The horses puffed, and steam billowed from their nostrils into the dissipating cold air, and the only sound was the clink and creak of their saddles and harness.

After a while, a jolly Ernest asked, "How are you this morning, Alva?"

"I'm well, but you sound cheerful."

"I am," he said. "It's good to be on the move."

"You have a preference for movement, don't you? I wonder how you will take to settling down."

In the lead, Ernest looked back at her over his

shoulder and smiled. "Would you like to tie me down, do you think?"

"No, of course not, but I will not have you restless."

He twisted in the saddle to look at her and placed his hand on the horse's rump. "I shall find no reason to roam, there is no doubt of it."

Alva felt the flutter in her heart at his words and wondered at the wisdom of the task she had urged upon him.

"Perhaps I'm wrong in this, do you think so?"

"To deal with Mulvenny, what, are you doubting that after all there has been?"

"I fear I am abusing your concern, dear Ernest."

He shook his head. "Did not we just get into affray with three of Mulvenny's men? That is proof he will not relent. No, I think you were right all along, if we do not finish with him, he will be on the tail of you and the others until he has had his ounce of flesh."

"I do wonder how Irene and Aoife are faring. I miss them."

"Given half a chance, that redhead would be riding with us now, and the other one, well, she is happy seeing to the poor and needy."

"They are all I have left of the old country now."

"Is that so much to miss?"

Alva snuffed a laugh. "I guess not, it was a miserable existence, sure it was."

"But not improved a whole lot since you've been over here."

"That's true," she said with a laugh. "Lost two friends, fought tooth and nail, and imprisoned, to be sure, I could have done that quite easily back in Ireland."

"But then I would not have met you."

"True, and a dearer heart I could never have known."

They rode on, picking their way between clumps of prickly pear and rolling tumbleweed, the only other occupants of the silent plain. Not even a breeze stirred the air, and the silence weighed heavy on Alva's thoughts.

"Perhaps we are fools to risk this so," Alva mused.

"I don't see it like that," said Ernest. "I keep finding new sides to you, and it gives me pleasure to know it."

"You are a wonder, Ernest."

"Let us just hope that we can settle this matter in Glimmer City and ride home together in one piece."

"Amen to that, dear heart."

OVER THE PAST YEARS, Dermot had changed somewhat.

His beard had grown long and straggly and was peppered with white, and on his head he wore a tired and battered hat. The same clothes had covered his body for a long time, a gray wool shirt under a black waistcoat and watch chain, all worn over dusty pants. At his waist, when he was out in public, he always carried a gun belt with four holstered Colts, their grips pointing out with the blunt metallic confidence that he would never run out of ammunition. He could easily have afforded a fine beaver felt hat from J. B. Stetson in Philadelphia, but he chose to wear instead the shabby hat and clothes that reminded him of past days on the family farm in Ireland when he and his brothers would drive their pigs to market.

The power that his position held had been hard-earned, and he had trodden over many dead men to get there. It plainly showed written in the lines on his face, as nobody can cause that amount of grief without it having some side effect in a physical manifestation. His body too told the same story with his bent shoulders, high on one side and twisted so that it distorted his frame. Worst of all though, was the mental changes that had been inflicted on him.

Ever cautious, he viewed all with suspicion, and even those close never knew when he might change his attitude and reach out with devastating and murderous effect. He liked to sit alone for hours in Kitty's old room and ponder on his wealth and winnings, gloating over it as a miser might with his gold. Sometimes it was the memory of his brothers that still burned in his brain and the deep fire of vengeance that had burned low as he made his way up the ladder of success. But now he more regularly dreamed of Edmond and Séamus in bloody nightmares and tortured himself with the awful and irredeemable fact that their killers were still running free.

Slowly, his sanity was slipping away, although those he kept close did not recognize it yet. They viewed his bizarre and merciless dealings with offenders as if he were a bold and decisive leader. Yet the hangings, whippings, and unique forms of torture he devised only exampled the distorted ugliness that was born in the darker depths of himself and now was beginning to rise to the surface.

There was a terrible hanging tree outside of Glimmer City where bodies hung until they decomposed. Cages were kept, and prisoners held there in dire conditions until their fates decided. Along the road leading into town hung a macabre chain of examples of those who had run afoul of Dermot Mulvenny and his gang.

Until recently, he had kept for himself a string of women prisoners to satisfy his lust, although he found no physical pleasure in this. These slaves paraded before him scantily dressed as paramours, yet their bodies meant little to him, they were only a signature of his success and one recognized as such by his gang of gunmen, and so he maintained this harem out of some warped sense of duty alone. The sad fact was that these poor creatures only assured Dermot of the deep emptiness that occupied his soul.

Things were about to change though.

For now, Dermot had fallen in love.

The girl in question was a fifteen-year-old virgin of Chinese and Indian blood, a tall and slender slant-eyed beauty full of childish innocence with smooth, unblemished ivory colored skin and long, silken black hair that fell to her knees. She had been found amongst the sheds of a railroad mining camp, and his men had stolen her away as a gift for their leader.

Her name was Dylo, and Dermot doted on her. He delighted in treating Dylo as if she were his own daughter and showered her with gifts and spoiled her outrageously. A strange thing for such a cruel man, and yet it is not so surprising that one so evil could also have this touch of gentility in his heart. It allowed the viler nature of the man to exist in the same way that opposites were created in nature, with the darkness of night permitting a brighter sun to shine during the day.

Dermot would watch her and the natural elegance of the creature with bemused admiration. He fawned on her and kept her chaste and happy with his tender concern. In the face of the guileless young girl, he would melt, and the cruelty imprinted on his face would mellow as she smiled at him.

As she opened gift boxes and toyed with the lace-lined silk dresses and bonnets he had imported from

France for her, she asked him, "Uncle Dermot, you are so kind to me. Why is it you do this?"

In her slightly accented little girl voice, there was a subtle cajoling that she knew he approved of, much in the same way that an affectionate pet would curl itself into its owner.

"Because, me darlin', you are my delight and it gives me pleasure."

"But you are not my family."

"No, but I'd like to think of myself as such, wouldn't you like that?"

"Oh, yes, it would be wonderful."

"Then let it be so," Dermot said contentedly, with the normal gloom of his days falling away and lightening his destitute heart. "I can make it so, you know that, don't you?"

"I think you can do anything, Uncle Dermot."

He preened himself under her childlike devotion.

"Bless you, girl. We shall have a celebration to mark the occasion. Tell me now, do you like fire eaters?"

Dylo's eyes went round. "Fire eaters?"

"Yes, indeed, and lions and tigers, great animals, laughing clowns and tumblers that can only make a pretty pass."

"This sounds magical, Uncle Dermot. I have never heard of such things."

"Then we must educate you, dear one. Here in Glimmer City, we shall have the lights and whirligigs of a great Carnival come to town, how does that sound?"

Dylo clapped her hands together. "Oh, yes, yes," she cried delightedly. "I must kiss you, Uncle Dermot." And she did, planting a wet one on his grizzled cheek.

At her touch, the vile bandit and cruel despot Dermot Mulvenny dissolved like cubed ice in warm water.

CHAPTER TWENTY

THEY HEARD the calliope from four miles out.

It was loud, and there was no way of controlling the volume, so the fantastically decorated cart with its organ pipes blasted out a rousing Sousa march that reached far into the night. At the rear, a chimney billowed smoke as a man stoked the fire to keep the boiler heated and steam pumping. A woman in an inner compartment sitting behind blue drapes played the brass keyboard as if at a church meeting, and the driver, dressed in a peaked hat and a flamboyant red uniform, kept the matched white horses pulling the cart at a steady pace around the town. Great golden leaves and curlicues fashioned from wood and painted with gilt decorated the sides, and the cart rolled along with four dainty wheels in yellow and red. A sign above the organ pipes read *The Great Operonicon or Steam Car of the Muses*.

A Midway now existed along the length of Main Street, Glimmer City, and imported sideshows and games bracketed the entire road. At the far end stood a great circus tent in stripes of red and yellow, Union flags hung from the guide ropes, and burning torches marked the entrance. Crowds of people populated the Midway—folks had come from far and wide to witness the spectacle despite the fearful name attached to the town. Curiosity had gotten the better of them, and they arrived in droves.

In the distance could be heard the growl and roar of wild beasts, their fear and anger inflamed by the terrible racket of the crowds and calliope. Outside the tent, painted clowns fooled around, inviting all to enter and explore the exciting wonders of the circus.

Colorful sideshows in tents displayed their wares along the Midway. There was a gorilla and jungle monkey exhibit, a two-headed baby, a Viking giant, and Harlequin acrobats that rolled and tumbled through the crowd, causing amusement and awe. A tall man on stilts and dressed in a Yankee Doodle top hat and tails strolled above the throng, surrounded by four midget Dancing Dolls pirouetting at his feet. A Posing Show with a stage dressed with historical and classical painted scenes, and before them, women posing in static style were clad in a stocking net to give the illusion of nakedness.

And fire eaters who blasted the night with plumes of fire that seemingly came from out of their mouths.

Alva and Ernest arrived on tired horses and angled their way along a deserted and dark alley to witness the scenes along the Main Street.

"What the hell?" breathed Ernest.

"Looks like the devil of a show," said Alva as they both stared from the shadowed alley out into the weaving crowds.

"Suits us," Ernest allowed as he dismounted. "We ain't going to stand out in this crush."

Alva joined at the corner. "What chaos! Can you see Mulvenny?"

"There," said Ernest, and he jerked with his chin in the direction of the head of the street.

At the far end of Main Street, a timber stage that had seen previous use as a scaffold was now a platform with the hanging tree removed. Sitting upon it on a throne-like chair sat Dermot Mulvenny with all the proud arrogance of a lordly potentate as he surveyed the swaying sea of people below him. Beside him on a smaller throne sat the slender form of Dylo, looking suitably dazzled by the whole show. Behind her were positioned Dermot's gunmen, four of them, two flanking the bandit leader on each side. The gunmen stood unmoving and unimpressed, their eyes dispassionately circling the mass of people below on the lookout for any sign of trouble. But the crowds were too busy being occupied with the wonders all around them to think of any unrest.

Snake Oil shows had come to town on previous occasions, but then only rarely, given the harsh regime that Dermot imposed in Glitter City. The locals were duly impressed by this new entertainment arriving, and it left them amazed and without thought of the overlord who sat and viewed it all with little outward show of any pleasure on his grim features.

"Whose that sitting next to him?" breathed Alva. She spoke in a whisper despite the noise all around them.

"I don't know," answered Ernest. "But she's a pretty looking gal. Must be one of Mulvenny's favorite whores, I guess."

"A little young, don't you think?" said Alva, studying

the childlike features but attractive form of the beauty at Mulvenny's elbow.

"I guess age don't bother him none."

"Bit like you then," said Alva, with a mischievous dig in his ribs.

But Ernest's attention was elsewhere. "Look, there's maybe four or so other gunmen about than those up there, and I want to know where. I'll take a wander around and take a look. Can you keep an eye on Mulvenny while I do it?"

"I can, but what do you aim to do about him?"

"I reckon this is a real good opportunity to nail the sucker, but we need to know where the opposition is first."

"Do we keep the horses here?"

"Yes," he nodded. "They're a mite tired for a getaway, but they're all we got at the moment, so keep them close. Meanwhile, keep a close eye and hold your Winchester in your hand."

Alva watched as Ernest pulled his hat low and slipped away to become one with the pressing mob passing by the alleyway. Alva turned to peer back at the stage and studied the young woman with Mulvenny. She was a beauty all right—she thought, but very young for the decrepit older man who sat like royalty on his throne. Mulvenny had aged badly, Alva considered, looking at his glowering face and twisted posture as he leaned forward in his seat like a predatory beast with his gaze wandering vaguely over those below.

Given what he had become, Alva felt that Dermot Mulvenny was truly imbued with an air of malevolence, and she sensed the cold indifference emanating from him like a brutal cloud of enmity. Fear lived in his face, and Alva realized that there would be no way of making peace with such a man. He would hate totally, and his necessity for a gratified act of vengeance was a foregone conclusion.

There was a sudden crack and bang followed by a chain of shattering explosions, and Alva jumped nervously before staring around wildly. For a moment, she feared that Ernest had been exposed and was under attack and involved in a gunfight. Then she saw the young girl on the stage leap to her feet with both hands clutched to her chest as she stared in wonder down the Midway.

Alva turned to see the black night sky above the circus tent alive with the brilliance of bursting fireworks, rockets zoomed skywards and Chinese crackers exploded in chains. By their bursting light, Alva made out the almost classical features of the girl, a smooth blend of high Oriental cheekbones against the delicacy of her lips and large eyes. The long black hair swept around in a whirl as she leapt across to Mulvenny and hugged him with delight at the firework display. Alva was surprised to see him smile in an almost paternal fashion and pat her affectionately on the back. This girl meant more to him than any casual consort he had taken to himself, he was treating her as if she were kin or some kind of beloved.

Ernest was suddenly beside her. "I found one of them," he said. "He won't be bothering us, but this here" —he cranked the lever handle of his Winchester—"is too good an opportunity to miss."

"You're going to take a shot?"

Ernest steadied himself at the corner, poised with the rifle to his shoulder as he drew a bead on Mulvenny. "Amongst all these bangs, they won't know where it came from."

Alva stepped back across the alley, biting her lip in tension as she peered past Ernest in the direction of the stage. The girl on the stage was hopping up and down with childish excitement, and Ernest held himself ready, waiting for her to step aside and leave an opening for him to make his shot. The girl stepped back and Ernest fired. But in an awful final moment and with the swiftness of an agile youth, the girl suddenly flung herself once more at Mulvenny in a show of gratitude.

The bullet struck her in the back, high and between the shoulder blades, the force of impact sending her flying forward and directly into Mulvenny's arms.

"Oh, no!" gasped Ernest, but already, despite the miss, he was swiveling aim towards the bodyguards.

Mulvenny sat in disbelieving shock with the body of Dylo held across him, his hands at her back already stained by the flow of blood. The guards moved forward, drawing their weapons and ready to provide cover for their chief.

Ernest fired again and one of the men buckled and dropped to lie still on the stage floor. The crowd below began screaming and running in terror. They surged to each side of the Midway, colliding with the sideshows and, in their panic, overturning the stands.

Mulvenny staggered to his feet with the sagging body of Dylo held in his arms and he screamed in anguish and rage. His cries bellowed up crazily towards the heavens that still echoed with the bang and blast of rockets.

Kneeling beside Ernest, Alva took aim at the men on the stage, desperate to bring Mulvenny down. The bodyguards were crouching around him, firing wildly into the crowd, not knowing where the assassin's shot had come from. Their crazed shooting only created more panic as innocent bystanders fell under their swathe of firing.

The gunmen kept swaying in front of Mulvenny, and it was difficult for Alva to get a clear shot. She fired in hope but only saw one of the gunmen cry out and turn away as his elbow exploded into a bloody mess.

"Keep firing!" shouted Ernest. "Don't let up."

He continued levering his Winchester and maintaining a steady rain of fire, and the stage splintered and erupted in clouds of sawdust as their bullets struck. One determined gunman lay flat behind the dead bodyguard and returned fire as the wounded man and one other covered Mulvenny's back and hurried him to the steps at the rear and off the stage.

"Blow that one away," ordered a grim-faced Ernest, and both of them sent a hail of bullets at the lone gunman still left on the platform. It was a withering chain of bullets that swept down, and the body of the dead man used as cover exploded under the battering. Blood spouted and clothing was ripped as the corpse was kicked around under the lethal barrage. The gunman took his chance and he was up on one knee, ready to flee, when he was hit. The bullet struck him high in the forehead and took the back of his skull away in a blasting cloud of sprayed head and hair, then he tumbled awkwardly down.

"We go now," ordered Ernest. "We missed our damned chance."

They turned to the horse's intent of making their escape before Mulvenny's men recovered and came after them.

DERMOT, standing behind the stage with Dylo still held in his arms, sobbed bitterly and rocked to and fro on his heels.

"*Get them*!" he blabbered, staring down at the beautiful face already gaunt and pale in death. "Bring them to me, find who it is and I will kill them."

"Come on, boss," said the one remaining unharmed man standing beside him. "Let's get you to safety."

The other wounded bodyguard struggled to keep up as he painfully clutched his destroyed elbow. "Oh, them bastards," he wailed. "They done for me, they surely have."

Mulvenny ignored him. "Find the others, get out there and bring those sons-of-bitches to me."

"Sure thing, boss," said his man. "We'll get them, don't you fear. But Willy here needs some help, he's hurt sore."

Mulvenny knelt down, lowering Dylo gently to the ground. "Willy," he ordered the wounded man. "You stay here with her. Don't you leave her, you hear? I will not have her left alone."

"What about you, boss?" asked the other bodyguard.

"Wainwright? That's your name, is it not?"

"It is."

"Well, you and I will get the others and go find these murdering scum. You hear me? They killed my girl, goddamn them. Shot my beautiful Dylo, now who in the devil's name could do that? What manner of swine could take such a gentle creature like this from me?"

"I guess they was aiming at you, boss," said Wainwright.

"I don't care," screamed Mulvenny, in a mixture of sobs and tears. "She is gone, gone from me."

ALVA AND ERNEST groped for the hanging reins that normally kept the horses standing and waiting, but a fuselage of rifle shots began peppering the alley from opposite across the heads of the panicked horde in the street. Both horses reared up as the firing struck the board walls of the narrow alley, one horse landing on the back of the other before it fell away. Wildly, both animals tried to escape, screaming in fear, stumbling, and crashing against each other as they ran for the exit.

"It's no use stopping them," cried Ernest. "Follow them, the shooters won't see us in the dark."

More haphazard firing followed as they raced up the alley and out into the space beyond. The pair of horses charged away from them and were soon lost in the darkness.

Alva and Ernest burst out into the area beyond Main Street, where, at the back of the houses, were vacant yards and other properties scattered in no particular order. Sheds and outhouses were dark and silent, unlike the noise coming from the street, where a great chorus of sound came in waves through the night. A cacophony of howling followed them as desperate people wailed and screamed in despair, falling over each other as they tried to get away. The firework display continued unknowingly, lighting up the night sky in flashes with detonations joining the continuing gunfire.

Alva and Ernest ran into the darkness, not knowing where they were going as they tried to find a way through the twisting alleyways between the housing. Suddenly, droves of small black shapes began flying through the sky between the roofs, leaping and bounding, swinging perilously close over the heads of the two. Alva ducked as a long-tailed creature swished past her, and it took a moment for her to realize they were the monkeys escaping their broken cages in the sideshow.

Ernest caught her arms and pulled her to a standstill as a great black shape loomed before them. Wide-eyed Alva stared at the huge shape, and she could see its red-rimmed eyes shining in the hairy body. A starburst lit up the sky, and with a terrible sound, the gorilla opened its jaws wide and roared. Alva saw the uneven rows of sharp teeth as the ape bellowed. It stood weaving on thick legs as it blocked their path. The mighty fists began to beat a rhythm of warning on its chest, a hollow sound like the beating of a drum as the creature rose to its full height.

Ernest raised his rifle, but the gorilla paused a moment and then, as if realizing the danger, turned and lumbered off on all fours into the shadows.

"What the devil?" breathed Ernest.

"It's the monkey show," Alva explained. "The stands must have been turned over by the crowd."

"That's an idea," said Ernest. "If we get amongst the mass of those people, they won't find us so easy."

"Let's do it."

Together they turned and headed back towards the thundering sounds coming from Main Street. It was emptying now as the crush forced its way down towards the circus tent, where they were diverted to either side like a stream of water blocked by a rock.

Many bodies lay on Main Street, those who had been crushed and trampled by the fleeing mob. Men, women, and children lay deathly still in bundled heaps or crawled pathetically away on broken limbs.

Alva and Ernest broke out of an alley and turned to begin their run towards the wave of people. As they did, they heard a sudden shout behind them, and there, leading a group of five gunmen, came the bearded figure of Dermot Mulvenny.

"I'll have you!" he roared. "You wheen-baskets, I'll let the Devil cut off your heads and make a day's work of your necks."

Bullets began to crack about them as the gunmen opened fire, and Alva and Ernest skittered from side to side of the empty street as they ducked the blast from behind. Along each side of the road stood the wrecked remnants of the sideshows pulled down and trodden underfoot by the panic-stricken mob, upturned stages with broken timbers and twisted frames dangled across their path. Ripped and torn, gaily painted canvas signs hung like broken wings, and debris from every show was spread across the road.

Scenic versions of Grecian columns afforded Ernest with a moment of cover, and he dropped behind the framed cutout to blast rifle shots at the advancing gunmen. Alva caught sight of a kerosene lamp hanging from an extended arm of a wheel of chance stall, and as she ran past, she struck it with her rifle barrel. The lamp swung away and dropped to the ground, the oil spilling with the lighted wick soon sending out a blast of fire that reached up and quickly ran along the overhanging tented roof.

Stalled by Ernest's return of fire, Dermot and the gunmen were diving to each side of the road looking for cover. It gave both Alva and Ernest time to reach the circus tent that loomed in colorful extravagance above them. The last few slower members of the crowd were making their way around the perimeter to where the caged wagons that held the wilder animals still roared and growled in fear.

Ernest ducked inside the tent opening, and Alva

followed. Quickly, Ernest began loading his Winchester and then checking the pistols. Before them stood the broad circus ring surrounded by folding chairs, and above billowed the high tent roof with a suspended wire and trapeze. A muscled man and an elegant woman dressed in brief spangled tights huddled together on a platform beside the trapeze.

"What's going on out there?" the man called. "We heard shooting."

"Best stay where you are," replied Ernest.

"Are we safe up here?"

"Better than down here."

A clown in a painted face and conical hat was flapping his way across the ring in monstrously large boots. He was bizarrely cursing over each stumbling foot as he went. "Dang these damned things!" he cried in a very unclown-like voice.

"Say, mister!" called Ernest, and the clown looked around with a show of terror on his painted face. Somehow, the contrast between the red nose and wide makeup grin looked incongruous beside his genuinely worried expression.

"What you want?" he replied, holding up both gloved hands. "Don't shoot, I ain't armed."

"How do we get out of here?"

"Don't know about you, but I'm going through there," he said, pointing towards the entrance to the ring where a great swathe of curtains hung tied back by a golden tasseled rope.

"What's out there?" called Ernest.

"That's all the animals, can't you hear them?" Then, muttering angrily, the clown began his clumsy run, heading out through the curtains as fast as he could go.

"Goddamn it!" he complained. "I'm going back to hauling freight, this ain't any fun life for me no more."

"We can wait here," Ernest said to Alva. "Or go on through and take our chance on the outside."

"Out there," said Alva, taking a peek back the way they had come. "They're real close."

The bitter calls of the men following were loud, and the continuing tirade of Dermot led the way as they pounded towards the tent.

Alva and Ernest ran through the curtained gap and on through a wide, empty lobby, making for the dark night they could see through an opening on the far side. Somewhere, an elephant trumpeted mournfully, joining in with the chorus of howling caged animals.

A row of painted wagons awaited them, each one had an open front with sturdy upright bars and was home to feline creatures that prowled up and down inside. A moth-eaten-looking lion with a disheveled mane snarled at their appearance and rushed towards the bars in mock attack before patrolling away in muted coughs. Hyenas chattered and scurried in mad turnabouts, their hungry faces pressed growling against the bars. A pair of cheetahs sloped elegantly around one another in almost dance-like patterns, and in a dark tail-end wagon, a pair of yellow eyes watched them cautiously from the shadows.

"Take cover," said Ernest. "We'll ambush them as they come out."

Ernest ran to the left and took his place down behind some crates whilst Alva held place beside one of the animal cages. She could smell their feral stink heavy with ordure and heat, a rank odor that filled her nostrils as they clumped and battered at the wagon sides. It was a tense moment as she waited for Dermot and his men to make themselves known.

But it was over in minutes.

Three men burst through the opening with Dermot in the lead, and as they came, Alva and Ernest opened fire. Two of the three spun away with cries and their guns firing, one into the ground and the other into the sky. Bright flares of light and the crashing roar of guns as the pair fired and Dermot answered.

Then the unexpected.

Two more gunmen came from out of the darkness around the outer sidewall of the great circus tent. They were behind Ernest and opened fire as they came, catching him in the open with their murderous hail of bullets. Alva cried out as she saw him buckle under the terrible rain of fire. Ernest's tall body curled and bucked as each bullet struck, sending him slamming against the crates until he rolled away and fell to the ground.

Alva was on her feet, throwing aside her rifle and blindly forgetting all about the gunplay, she raced over to Ernest. She knelt beside him and spread her arms in dismay as she saw the pumping wounds.

"Oh God! Dear man, my dear man."

Dermot strode across, his glowering presence full of contented victory as he stood over her.

"You came to my place with your troubles," he said in a low voice. "And now you've damn well found them. God's curse on you."

Alva clasped Ernest, rocking his body in her arms. "My love," she murmured. "Ernest, can you speak?"

Ernest gasped, the words thick on his lips. "Alva"—a slow smile spread—"you're still the sweetest woman I ever saw."

"Not for long," snarled Dermot, catching Alva by the

hair at the nape of her neck and pulling her upright. "Oh, how I will make you pay for my dear Dylo. There are my brothers that seek requite to be sure, but that pure innocent girl was of my heart, and she deserves your heart in exchange, I think."

"What will you do to her, boss?" asked one of the men, already an expectant leer on his face.

Dermot spoke through gritted teeth, his anger written large in the sibilant hiss of his words. "I shall tear the heart from her body with my own hands."

"Will you let us have our way with her first?" asked the other man, the ugly desire rich in his voice. "I've a mind to make her pay for the boys we have lost."

"I think I will do that," growled Dermot. "Strip her down and do your worst, but leave her alive enough for me to have my play." He cupped Alva's chin in his hand and roughly jerked her face close to him. "I want you spoiled, Alva girl, I want you to be ruined body and soul so you will not enter heaven fit in any way to match a pure and sweet child like my Dylo."

He swung back his hand and struck her hard across the face to send Alva staggering back.

"What shall we do with this one?" asked the gunman, jerking his head at Ernest. "He's still breathing."

Dermot barked a laugh. "Let's set him up so he can watch you two whilst you despoil his whore."

With a laugh, the two agreed and took the limp Ernest under each armpit and dragged him up against the wooden crates. With two men, one on each side, they did not see the sorely wounded Ernest reach down and draw the two pistols at his side and cross his arms, pressing each Colt's barrel into either man. There were muffled explosions, and in the shock of the aftermath, the two gunmen dropped Ernest and bowled over, one holding his ribs, the other his stomach.

"Hellfire!" The rib-shot gasped as he fell. "He's done for me."

The other bowed over and dropped into a fetal position on the ground his knees drawn up to his chest as he whimpered out his life.

"What the hell?" flared Dermot as the men fell.

Even as he raised his pistol to shoot at Ernest, Alva stepped forward and swung a booted foot up sharply between Dermot's legs. With a gasp, his mouth opened wide, his tongue erupting from his lips in wordless agony. He bent over and struggled to regain his posture, but Alva stepped forward and snatched the pistol from his trembling grasp. Then she swung it back and brought the two pounds of steel hard against the side of his head. There was a deadly clunk of sound as the metal struck bone, and Dermot swung his head away.

"Finish him," wheezed Ernest. "Don't hesitate."

"Oh, I am ready," growled Alva, twisting the pistol in her hand.

Dizzily, Dermot wove away with one hand held up protectively and the other clutching his aching groin. He fumbled from her until his back came up against the wagon behind. He stood there in a defensive crouch with his back to the wagon and glared at Alva from under lowered brows. "Do your worst, ye godforsaken bitch. A man can only die once."

He did not see the pair of orange eyes glittering in the darkness behind him, but he heard the growl as the Bengal tiger leapt forward. At ten feet long and weighing two hundred and ninety pounds, the massive bulk of the charging beast slammed into the bars behind Dermot. Two great striped paws thrust out between the bars and ensnared Dermot across the chest with ten razor-sharp claws that latched deep into the flesh of his body.

Dermot opened his mouth wide and emitted a moaning groan as the four-inch claws ripped sideways, tearing his chest open like the pages of a book. Before the stunning moment had any further effect on its prey, the tiger pressed between the bars enough for its savage teeth to grasp the top of Dermot's head in its jaws. With a ghastly crunch, the skull was crushed beneath the animal's monstrous bite. Dermot dropped instantly, but the tiger hung onto one arm, growling and coughing as it tugged at the limb, pulling it up to feed.

Alva watched for a moment in shock at the terrible scene, and then, with a shake of the head, she turned away to go to Ernest.

EPILOGUE

Alva looked along the ranch veranda to where Ernest was sitting at the far end in an easy chair with Peter on his lap. She smiled as she saw how her husband and the two-year-old were so engrossed in each other that they barely noticed Alva with her friends standing together in the yard.

"What a fine boy you have," observed Irene.

"He is that all right," agreed Alva. "Both of them are."

"And how are you faring here?"

"Grace is bound away pretty soon, she has found a man who wishes her hand, a good fellow who is with the railroad. So she'll be off with the children, I'll miss them, but the kids are mighty grown now, and anyway, they'll be back to visit."

"So it will be the three of you on the ranch. Can you manage?"

"We'll do just fine."

"And Ernest is well?" asked Aoife, looking more beautiful than a nun had a right to look, dressed as she was in her full white habit now she had taken the vows and joined the sisterhood.

"Not too bad," answered Alva. "They took six bullets out of him, it's a miracle he's here at all. Although, to be honest, some parts do not work as well as they might, but he is alive, and for that I am almighty grateful."

"You did well yourself, so you did, as I'm told by himself," said Irene, red hair glistening in the sun. She had filled out now in the intervening years but was still as wiry in temperament if not so much in body. "Ernest told me all, how you got him up on a wagon, drove to a doctor among the torn and trampled, and then held the poor man at gunpoint until he treated Ernest's wounds."

"By then, I was in no mood for disagreement," said Alva. "Although now I regret being so rough with the man, he was doing his best, to be sure he was."

"Main thing is you got him out safe and alive," said Irene. "And we have no more to fear from the Mulvennys thanks to you both."

"We should also not forget our departed friends," Aoife said in a hushed voice. "Poor Niamh—"

"And Saoirse," added Irene, with a frown of memory. "Dear, sad, Saoirse."

"Aye, they will always be with us," agreed Alva.

The three paused a moment in respectful memory, but the sound of Peter giggling brought them back.

"And how are things now with Thora?" asked Alva.

"Ah!" Irene said with a grin. "We have a houseful, indeed we do, Sister Aoife here keeps us busy, don't you, holy mother?"

Aoife nodded thankfully. "It is seven lost children now they are fostering. It is a good deed indeed, Irene, that you and Thora do."

"It is a houseful of joy with all them little ones

bouncing about the place. Nothing at all like that wretched place we left in Donegal. And am I not Auntie to them all as I am to dear little Peter over there."

"So, y'are," agreed Alva.

"We're not doing too bad, are we?" asked Aoife. "For three waifs and strays out of old Ireland without a penny to our names and only damp and cold left behind us."

"True enough," agreed Alva, glancing across at Ernest, and as she did so, he looked up and smiled at her, took the baby's small hand in his big fingers, and waved them at her. "Not bad at all." She sighed in contentment.

A LOOK AT: ROGUE INDISCRETIONS: WESTERN TALES OF SINS, MISDEEDS, AND GROSS MISCONDUCT ACROSS A WILD FRONTIER

Five gripping tales of betrayal, vengeance, and survival from the dark edges of the American frontier.

From the bustling docks of Manhattan to the blood-soaked badlands of Apacheria, strangers and outlaws collide in moments where courage can mean salvation—or death. In this powerful collection, loners, lawmen, and unlikely allies face treacherous trails, brutal enemies, and the high price of justice.

A young Texas Ranger goes rogue to hunt a ruthless killer through Apache territory. Two friends in a crime-ridden city discover loyalty can be as dangerous as betrayal. A solitary drifter is drawn into a deadly flight across hostile country. An artist's dream turns to nightmare when war and old enemies force him into bloody conflict. A man and his unlikely partner wage a relentless fight against a sheriff's corrupt empire.

Featuring "Bad Men Go to Hell," "Kind Shadows," "Kruger," "A Brush With Blood," and "Wax and Blind Peke,": *Rogue Indescretions* delivers raw, unforgettable stories for fans of gritty frontier fiction and classic Western justice.

AVAILABLE NOW

THANK YOU

Thank you for taking the time to read *The Bad Life*. If you enjoyed it, please consider telling your friends or posting a short review. Word of mouth is an author's best friend and much appreciated.

Thank you.
Tony Masero

ABOUT THE AUTHOR

Tony Masero grew up in a deprived and grey post-war London, where the only relief from bomb craters and food rationing were colorful Western books and movies. The pictures on the screen displayed wide sunlit spaces, glorious forests, breathtaking mountain ranges and, most importantly, adventure and a great sense of freedom. His love of that early thrill has subsequently inspired many of his own books. Living far from the Wild West and any kind of armed culture, he made up for it by practicing longbow archery in the forests of southern England.

At the age of three, Tony's father, a renowned woodcarver, placed a pencil in his hand, an act that resulted in a later career as a Designer and then Illustrator. Working in the international advertising and publishing world, Tony produced a great deal of art for book covers, and through the research involved in their creation is where his interest in writing began.

Research is important in his own books, and many of Tony's tales are based around some historical incident or characters that truly existed. From there, imagination takes flight and, for a person with a visual frame of mind, his books are often imbued with a natural pictorial quality and full of human characteristics that are true to us whatever our origins.

www.ingramcontent.com/pod-product-compliance
Lightning Source LLC
LaVergne TN
LVHW040215110826
845146LV00005B/1292

9798895678190